SCANDAL IN EDEN

SCANDAL

a novel
by
GARET
ROGERS

IN EDEN

THE DIAL PRESS ❧ NEW YORK 1963

DESIGNED BY ALAN M. HEICKLEN
MANUFACTURED IN THE UNITED STATES OF AMERICA
BY THE HADDON CRAFTSMEN, SCRANTON, PA.

For the Boss

Earth gets its price for what Earth gives us;
The beggar is taxed for a corner to die in,
The priest hath his fee who comes and shrives us,
We bargain for the graves we lie in;
At the devil's booth are all things sold,
Each ounce of dross costs its ounce of gold;
For a cap and bells our lives we pay,
Bubbles we buy with a whole soul's tasking:
'Tis heaven alone that is given away,
'Tis only God may be had for the asking. . . .

The Vision of Sir Launfal
JAMES RUSSELL LOWELL

Seen any snakes around here?
—The Feeb

SCANDAL IN EDEN

By Garet Rogers

CHAPTER ONE

The scandalmongers had spent a miserable day. Scurrying about under the October sun they had hustled up and down Hollywood Boulevard, clamored at the gates of movie studios, panted into drugstores to swill down Green Rivers—a pint of soda water which had made a brief encounter with a half of lime, chipped ice, all for the cost of a nickel—and arrived at the end of their day with nothing to show for their efforts. In the autumnal heat the movie folk, from stars to anxious extras, simply hadn't had the energy to sin. Just at the time one spent scandalmonger was buying his ticket to see an old silent comedy starring that exquisitely droll fat man billed as The Feeb, another man in his thirties was driving a black roadster down the Boulevard past the movie house. The hot and harried scandalmonger thought he recognized the man in the black roadster, but then again thought maybe not. At any rate, satisfied that the driver of the roadster was neither great nor near-great, the scandalmonger would have followed his evening activities with a scornful jaded eye. Later that night, though, he would have beheld doings sufficient to keep him peppy and excited for a whole week. As it was, he took his ticket and went to join others of his ilk as they sat screaming with bliss at the mental-defective antics of The Feeb.

The man driving the black roadster presented a profile so jagged it might have been hacked out with a can opener. Full face one saw first the reserve of the mouth, and only later read a rueful gentleness about the dark eyes. He was neither handsome nor homely; suffice it to say that any bum who knew his business would approach this man with perfect confidence for a handout—here was not a face to refuse a reasonable appeal.

The roadster he was driving had been rakish in the Twenties but now, instead of a pretty girl for a passenger, the man transported only a sack of groceries in the rumble seat, which sack swayed exactly like a human being with the motion of the car. Having passed the movie house, the car settled down on the streetcar tracks for the length of its journey past the Hollywood Hotel. Inside this famous hostelry a handful of the illustrious ones were already dining early beneath a ceiling painted with stars. There was Rudolph Valentino's star, though he had not graced the table directly under it for some three years now, for he lay moldering even as Shakespeare, Newton, and Rin Tin Tin did. At the intersection of Hollywood and Vine the roadster nosed left, paused to permit several cowboys, a pair of women in lounging pajamas, and a couple familiar to all Boulevardiers, consisting of a giant in Wild-West garb and a pert little midget in a child's dress and high heels, to cross, and then shifted into second gear to negotiate Vine Street hill. Anyone chancing to notice the driver would have seen that he was wilting from some cause other than the unremitting benignity of the California sun. In truth he was suffering from a chronic hangover resulting from a protracted drinking bout, begun some years ago and with no foreseeable end in sight. He was driving up to his house in the hills with the singlemindedness of one bent on his bottle, which his bootlegger had promised for that evening. This is not to say he lived for the bottle; he himself thought he was living to no end whatsoever, though in his reserved headachy way he was indispensable to a number of hoods, bootleggers, bookies, aspiring gunsels, bewildered deadbeats, and careworn hookers. All of which shady characters plied their various trades on the golden streets of the town their lawyer—for such this man was—still called to himself "Heliopolis," the Sun City. That so many of the citizens of Heliopolis, who dwelt in perpetual summer, were desperately deprived and as a consequence depraved might have been what drove the lawyer to drink.

Vine Street hill behind him, he began to wind upward along a hogback from which arroyos sloped down into the gathering purple shadows of dusk already collecting at their bases. Amid the dry brush called chaparral crowding up to the road were shacks and chateaux, cheek by jowl, just as every-where in this neck of paradise the destitute were treated daily to the sight of splendor and the squanderings of the magical few. Soon the roadster had left the last mansion behind—there was only a Moorish castle on a final curve—and the lawyer was home. Beyond his house the road, no longer paved, took itself off into the brush, wandering all over the place like a drunk coming out of the gloom of a speakeasy into high noon.

Before driving into his garage the lawyer ascertained that his bootlegger had left a parcel at the door. He then drove the roadster into the garage, and in the kitchen located just under the wheels a cupboard door opened with a gasp. The house was built down the hill, with the cellar at the street level, kitchen and dining room below that, and the bedrooms at the very bottom resting only on the attic, wherein the lawyer had allowed an old umbrella, some magazines, and the gold medal he had earned by graduating at the head of his class in law school to collect.

The lawyer, clutching his grocery sack, opened his front door and caught up the parcel. Inside the wrapping was a single quart of Irish whisky, which cost him as much as three pints of Coon Hollow bourbon would have, and almost as much as three pints of Chickencock rye sealed in tins. A scant three feet from the door a flight of stairs led down into the house proper. The lawyer approved of this construction mightily, once having pointed out to his wife that at the begin-ning of a party guests could negotiate the stairs safely, and at the end they had only to make their exits on all fours. "And if they do fall, they'll only bark a chin," he concluded. He had loved his wife out of all keeping because, among other attri-butes, she knew when not to correct him.

This evening the wife was not there; she had not been for years. The lawyer flipped the switch of the chandelier and when it sprang into light below him descended into his house. In the kitchen the cupboard door which had sprung open at the entrance of the roadster above it revealed to him the invit-ing sight of a clean glass. He opened the Irish, capped it with the glass, dug into the grocery sack, pulled out bread, a bag of gumdrops, a handful of marshmallows, a wad of angel-food cake, and emerged, spilling gumdrops as he went, to go down to his bedroom and out its door onto a walled patio. Smiling gravely to himself, he distributed the food about on the still warm flagstones, filled a dishpan with water from the hose, and settled himself down under the eucalyptus tree for his first sampling of the Irish. His manner was that of a contented recluse; he had, in fact, some months ago cut himself off from all human contact outside his work. He was exactly like a phone off its hook—he was busy and would not be bothered. As the twilight deepened, he sat enjoying the aroma from the branches of the eucalyptus over his head, a distinctive scent like nothing on earth except, perhaps, that of a faulty sewer. Inside the house the phone rang quite as if it knew it would not be answered and felt very annoyed at being awakened this way. As the lawyer was no longer one of the legal *haut monde* of Hollywood, it was unlikely that any movie star or other person of international moment would be inviting him to come over and see about a murder. The lawyer closed his eyes as if by doing this he could shut out the sound of the phone. He opened them to silence, to sundown, and to the sight of his first wild skunk waddling through the iron gate of the wall to see what in the way of gumdrops and angel food there was to be had for dinner. On the heels of the skunk came a rambunctious pair of raccoons, and on the stone wall materialized a timorous fox whose dainty tongue lolled at the prospect of marshmallows. The 'possum was not due for hours, as he was of a mystical turn of mind and liked to contemplate the moon dreamily while nibbling dog biscuits. Finishing off his second drink of Irish, the lawyer thought, as he usually did, that here indeed was the true Hollywood wild life, if *Photoplay* magazine but knew it. Once the lawyer had mentioned casually to Chester Dander, the so-correct so-sensitive and so-promising young Negro attorney, "God, I was up half the night. A bunch of 'coons were having a party on my patio, and they kept up the racket until three aye em." Chester's skin, the delicate color of ash woodwork, was capable of a flush almost too revealing to be gazed upon outside a psychiatrist's office. Mastering himself—Chester was always mastering himself over something or other—Chester said quietly, "On *your* patio? What on earth were they doing? Why didn't you call the police?" The lawyer grinned. "Raccoons, Chester," he said gently. *"Raccoons."* Chester had to master himself all over again.

Sometime after nightfall the lawyer rose, made his way with unconcern past the skunk, just avoided stepping on a 'coon's ringtail, and went into his bedroom, where he put the Irish on the cellarette, handy to the bed. He bore the rather flowery name of Mark D'Andor, and as he stretched out on the bed in soggy comfort, a young woman some three miles from him, whose real name was Sally Mae Werksmith, though she would rather have died than admit it, was, in fact, dying, and begging that Mark D'Andor be called to perform certain last legal services for her.

But he was not answering the phone—it was Friday.

Thinking of what a princely fellow his bootlegger was, Mark fell into a doze. After an hour or so he awakened needing a glass of water. He nudged himself off the bed and started up the stair for the kitchen, his body heavy with the languor he thought of as being October fever. As he passed the phone in its hallway niche, it shrilled at him, so that he stood startled and full of guilt as a burglar hearing this summons for the absent owners of the house. Leaning against the wall, he lifted the receiver from its hook. "Yes?" he said curtly. And in the saying he found himself looking up at the crystal chandelier, asking himself yet again what had become of that missing pendant. Or, more to the point, why was it gone in the first place?

"D'Andor," said a voice of quiet authority, "I have a little problem I'd like you to straighten out. This is Seymour Pent—"

"I recognized your voice, Pentlove," Mark said. In his mind's eye he could see the little mogul, elegant as a grandee with his dull-finish chrome hair, his tidy face, and his cheeks as lightly dusted with talcum as a moth's wing.

"You know, of course," Mr. Pentlove said, "where the Lying Inn is located?"

"If you mean that private hospital where all your starlets go to have their abortions—"

"This is no time for levity," Mr. Pentlove chided.

Mark reminded him, "It was you who referred to the place as such."

"Just so you know where to meet me," Mr. Pentlove said, imperturbable. "Be there in twenty minutes, please, D'Andor."

"I wouldn't meet you at the gates of paradise in twenty minutes," Mark said without rancor. "Why can't someone in your legal department handle whatever it is?"

"Because they're paper lawyers," Mr. Pentlove snapped. "And you know as well as I do that drawing up contracts all day doesn't—doesn't——"

"Doesn't equip them to handle whatever filthy mess you have on your hands. A mess that could endanger your wonder works, eh?"

"This is a very bad connection," Mr. Pentlove decided. "It sounded like you said—"

"I did. Wonder works. Your fantasy factory. In brief, what girl is dead, and who got her pregnant in the first place? Was she a starlet, or is the happy father the star?"

Mr. Pentlove breathed.

"And why turn to me?" Mark went on. "Surely not every decent attorney in town has refused you."

Unfortunately Mark had indicated the line of argument Mr. Pentlove might take. "Now look, D'Andor, I'm offering you the perfect opportunity to—ah—pull yourself up by the bootstraps. Get hold of yourself, man. You handle this for me with your former ability and discretion, and I won't forget it. You know that, I don't shirk my obligations."

"Nor I," Mark said. "And since I've invited a number of skunks to dinner, I'd better get back to my guests. Besides, you don't need a shyster, you need a quack to sign a phony death certificate."

"I can't believe I'm talking to Mark D'Andor," Mr. Pentlove said sorrowfully. "Calling your friends skunks, and yourself a s–shyster. I have heard rumors to the effect that you may be seeing a little too much of your bootlegger, but to h–hear you. . . ." Mr. Pentlove had to fall silent from the sheer shock of it all.

He is in a snit, Mark thought; he usually keeps his tongue in chains to prevent that speech impediment from getting loose.

Mr. Pentlove asked with profound interest, "What has happened to the finest young criminal lawyer ever to serve his—ah—"

"Writs?"

"Fellow man," Mr. Pentlove said in stern reproof. "What has—"

"Why," Mark cut in politely, "it's rather a lengthy story, but I'll be happy to tell it to you, Pentlove. As you know, success came to me both early and unexpected. I saved a lovely lady from the gallows who was a ball-peen hammer murderess by avocation. As it happened she went on to become the mistress, temporarily, of a certain gentleman in the movies, or the Industry, I should say, but whose name I will not mention—"

"I'm not at home," Mr. Pentlove said. "My wife is not listening in. Now, D'Andor we are wasting time. Get a grip on yourself and—"

"Pentlove, I graciously decline. Good night."

"Name your fee."

"No fee, however great, could tempt me."

"I have men working for me who could make you a hero overnight. I have men who can manipulate the press to speak of you as the most respected lawyer in town."

"Press notices, adulatory or no, no longer interest me."

"And I have in my possession information involving you which—"

"Shove your information," Mark said in his customary gentle voice. "Or shout it from the rooftops, if you're so inclined."

"I have friends. I have friends with political influence. Within two years at the outside I can have you appointed to the bench."

The offer was so outlandish that Mark was stunned into silence. There is this which must be said about Seymour Pentlove. He never made a promise he was not willing or able to keep. In an industry where deceit was standard operating procedure, he had so shocked the community by keeping his word that Seymour Pentlove was everywhere accused of rank honesty. Fresh out of protests, Mark could only ask, "Pentlove, just whose neck is in the noose?"

"Well, let us hope it doesn't come to anything like that. But it's Archibald Forbes."

"The Feeb?"

Mr. Pentlove sighed. "The Feeb. Meet me at the Lying Inn, D'Andor, and do hurry."

The line went dead.

Mark went to the kitchen and drank deeply straight from the faucet. Thinking with longing of his Irish and his bed, he stood irresolute, and then dutifully gulped down a few marshmallows. Thus fortified with food, he went to keep his appointment with Mr. Pentlove.

He drove down the hill with the finicking care of one uncertain of his sobriety. I am, he thought, looking to the outlines of the distant mountains, the bearer of oil for troubled waters. Or rather, I am to be the intermediary, the referee, and the stake-holder of hush money; I shall officiate as any number of slimy middlemen combined. Phrase it in his mind as he would, he was prepared to participate in the ritual of blackmail. As in all things distasteful, a stylization had been developed through custom to gloss over the details. The bereaved parents, or husband, or (as in one case) the grief-torn cousin of the dead girl always made it known that only money could blot their tears. For if it could be proved that the reluctant father of a child had induced the prospective mother to submit to an abortion, and had supplied money for that event, then he was guilty of a felony. If the girl died, or if she were under eighteen so that the element of statutory rape entered in, the going price of grief shot sky-high. All this, naturally, commensurate with the ability of the man to pay. A B-movie cowboy got off lightly; but a star, and a beloved comedian at that, such as The Feeb, stood fair to lose all but the gold in his cosmetic dentistry. The lawyer's function was to superintend the payoff, and then to inform the bereaved blackmailers that they too had now committed a felony, and would they kindly make themselves scarce. What with all the spurious legal rigmarole of signing waivers and releases (all of which were promptly destroyed), the bereaved seldom tried for a return appearance.

Gaining the Boulevard, Mark thought to himself: I hate the brutish business. It was a fine night and many people were about, the neons heightening the excitement on the faces of the incredibly pretty, incredibly numerous girls going in and out of the movie houses or frankly walking the streets. Driving west, past the squat tower which housed his office, Mark asked himself again: But why me? I am that celebrated sot, that well-known has-been, D'Andor. My practice has dwindled to representing what Pentlove and his kind so endearingly speak of as the "little people." Yet he thrusts a golden ass like The Feeb into my keeping with one hand and dangles a bench before me with the other. *Why me?*

He damned the only thing that had a greater power over him than his Irish—his curiosity.

The black roadster drew abreast of the Red Car as it sped down its tracks. Within its brightly lighted interior a peaked female scandalmonger looked up listlessly from her movie magazine. She had worked late and she was hungry. Instead of the magazine her twenty-five cents could have bought her a banana split heaped with whipped cream and fudge syrup. As it was, she had dined on the cold gruel of gossip items that told her only that the stars were fixed and secure in their firmament. She could have wept. Why couldn't somebody be getting a divorce? Or getting shot? Was no beautiful star ever to be horribly mutilated in a flaming auto accident?

She hungered, and they fed her only tidings of monotonous rapture.

CHAPTER TWO

Only a score of years ago the Lying Inn had been
a spacious farmhouse surrounded by beanfields. Now, like a
gangster hiding out, it sat among its pepper trees effacing itself,
having the air of strictly attending to its knitting. It was a block
south of Sunset Boulevard, yet not one person in ten in the
neighborhood knew it was there. There was a gravel sweep
driveway at the end of which a small sign plucked timidly
at the sleeve of one's attention, to whisper that this was the

SNOWDOM SANITARIUM

Arriving a good ten minutes ahead of time, Mark read
the sign, noted that the Lying Inn had changed hands since
last he heard of it, and then entered. Inside the front hall a
nurse sat behind a high desk and greeted Mark with that
granitic visage calculated to quell anyone who isn't already
completely cowed by the stink of antiseptic, thoughts of
needles, mysterious surgical instruments, clammy bed pans,
and the sound of moaning seeping out from under closed doors.
Unconsciously walking as carefully as if he were on tiptoe,
Mark approached the desk and said, "I'm Mark D'Andor
and—"

"Doctor will talk to you," the nurse said in that nurse's
voice of severe reprimand. Bending to a box she told it that
Mr. Dander had arrived, Doctor Snowdom. The box ordered
her to Show Him In.

Mark found himself in a bleak office with a metal desk
and tubular metal chairs. One wall was decorated with a
clipboard file, while on the other hung a photographic portrait
of a young girl who had quite a bit more than the average
share of hauteur. Across the desk was a gray angular man

who fitted in perfectly with his metallic surroundings. He rose to shake Mark's hand, his own conveying no more warmth and vitality than a rubber glove. "Snowdom," he said with finality and indicated Mark take a tubular chair.

"D'Andor," Mark said, carefully matching his manner to Snowdom's. There was something peculiar about the gray man, and it came to Mark that it lay in the total lack of luster in the pewter eyes. And too, their hue was many shades too light even for Snowdom's pallor.

"I am sorry we were not able to reach you in time, Mr. D'Andor," Dr. Snowdom said.

Not having the faintest idea what to reply to this, Mark nodded.

Snowdom went on, a touch defensively, "I called your numbers myself, both home and office, as soon as she said your name."

"Oh, I see," Mark said. Some explanation seemed to be required of him, so he added, "I was at home. But I was outside and did not manage to get in to the phone in time."

"I doubt if you could have gotten here in time anyway." Snowdom's stiff manner unbent slightly. "She died moments after."

"I understand." Though Mark was wholly attentive, all of him that was not directly engaged in listening or speaking was in such repose that he appeared—even jurors seeing him thus thought so—to be indolent.

"I suppose Miss Pritchard finally reached you."

"Miss Pritchard?"

"The nurse at the reception desk."

"I hadn't realized her name was Pritchard," Mark said. His mystification was maturing into alarm. Someone, a "she," had spoken his name before she died, and the abortionist had tried to summon him. Added to this, there had been as yet no mention either of Pentlove or Archibald Forbes, The Feeb. Mark felt rather like a naturalist following the footprints of a serpent, tracking a paradox as he noted the crushed clumps of turf left by a snake in the grass. To account for his silence Mark took out his flat-fifty tin of Chesterfields and extended it to Snowdom.

Forced by this maneuver to speak, Snowdom said, "No thank you," then reconsidered, as if accepting might put them both more at ease, and took a cigarette and a light from Mark. Exhaling, he said, "Would you mind telling me what your relationship was to Mrs. Tredwell? You see, when she was brought in here Sunday she was in such a state of pain and collapse that she couldn't tell us anything. And the people who brought her in weren't any help at all, either." Snowdom looked apologetic.

"Mrs. Tredwell is the dead woman then?"

"Why—yes."

"And you say she asked for me?"

Snowdom frowned at his cigarette. "Not in those exact terms, no."

"If you recall the exact terms, I would appreciate it if you quoted them."

"Oh. Well . . . I. . . . Actually Miss Pritchard was the one. Who heard what Mrs. Tredwell said. I'll call Miss Pritchard in and she can——"

"I can talk to Miss Pritchard later," Mark said, hastening to avoid being confronted by two incoherent people at the same time. "If you could just give me the general idea, Doctor."

"Certainly. As I recall, what Mrs. Tredwell evidently said was: 'Tell Mark D'Andor to come pick up the pieces.' Miss Pritchard said she didn't clearly understand what your name was, but she was in a hurry to get me, and didn't stop to ask. Then Mrs. Tredwell called after her, 'D'Andor, the lawyer!' " Snowdom again frowned at his cigarette. "Or maybe Mrs. Tredwell said, '. . . my lawyer.' " He looked over at Mark swiftly like one hoping to trap an admission from another.

Thoroughly enjoying Snowdom's attempt at borrowing from a lawyer's bag of tricks, Mark offered him a truth in a disarming tone. "Frankly, Doctor, the name Mrs. Tredwell does not mean anything to me. Naturally, with so many clients over the years. . . ."

"Naturally," Snowdom said leniently.

Mark pressed his advantage. "How did she die?"

Snowdom rather stared; his pewter eyes had the ability,

then, to become intent if never lively. "But I thought Miss Pritchard told. . . . She died of septicemia."

We are inching, Mark thought, toward our objective. Deliberately employing the suave euphemisms of the local abortionists, Mark said, "Septicemia. Ah, yes. Occasioned, no doubt by a bit of necessary surgery? Let us say the removal of a tumor?"

"Let us say," Snowdom said flatly, "by an abortion." He waited, almost with what Mark would have called an air of polite boredom, for Mark's reaction.

Mark was nothing loath. "Septicemia is blood poisoning, isn't it?"

"Oh yes."

"You really must remember hereafter, Doctor, to wash your hands first. We have a legal saying that each side must bring clean hands to court, and here is another instance where—"

"Your humor is appalling, Mr. D'Andor."

"Do you find me funny? I was speaking quite in earnest. When it comes to performing an abortion, your morals are your own concern. Still, I should think that some small regard for technique might enter into it. I know that many of you look on abortion as an act of kindness, relieving a woman of an unwanted pregnancy. But here's an instance where you can easily kill with kindness."

"How refreshing to hear a man of your reputation speak of morals," Snowdom observed. His gray mouth gave promise that with practice it might achieve a smile one day. "But you see, I didn't perform an abortion. Or at least, I did not initiate it. Induce it. When Mrs. Tredwell was brought here she was already hemorrhaging. An examination showed that the fetus had detached itself from the uterine wall. I did a D and C on her, as is mandatory in such cases. That is, I emptied the uterus—or womb—of its contents."

"You keep saying 'brought here.' Did Tredwell bring his wife?"

"No. Two women. Although a man who refused to give his name has been calling here off and on about Mrs. Tredwell's condition. Earlier this evening he called again, and Miss

Pritchard asked him if he knew of a lawyer with a name similar to yours."

Pentlove, Mark thought, has not been idle. The moment he learned I was somehow involved in this, he wanted me on his side. Pentlove is truly touching in his machinations. No detail, no slightest piece of humdrum villainy goes unattended. I should have held him up for a Superior Court bench at the very least. To cover his ruminations Mark asked, "Do you have any alcohol handy, Doctor?"

"What?"

"I want a drink. What do you have in the way of ethyl alcohol?"

Snowdom's mouth was progressing rapidly in schooling itself to a smile. Silently he opened a drawer of his desk and took out a bottle of bourbon. "Water right there," he said, with a nod at a metal carafe flanked by two metal tumblers. He put the bottle before Mark. "Did you really expect I would pilfer my liquor from my lab?"

Mark grinned. "Crude of me. Sorry." He poured himself two fingers of the liquor and passed the bottle back to Snowdom. "Join me?"

"Thank you, no." Without warning Snowdom attacked. "You think I'm a butcher, pure and simple, don't you? Worse, you think I'm a calloused one. That's why you dare to mock me one minute and make demands on my hospitality the next. Well?"

"I think this is damned good hooch, Doctor."

"Hooch," Snowdom echoed with distaste.

"Yep. Derived from a perfectly good Indian word. Or so I've heard." Mark put his glass down and swirled the contents. "You say Mrs. Tredwell was aborting at the very moment she crossed your threshold. I've heard that refrain before, but you sing it more sweetly than the rest of your kind. I suppose it was self-induced? One woman, or so I was told, made the attempt with a knitting needle. Could that have been the case here?"

When Snowdom did at last execute a smile, it was not an effort he should be encouraged to continue. He had what Mark thought of as being various and sundry teeth, in which amalgam fillings were imbedded as plentifully as gunshot. "No, not a knitting needle," Snowdom said softly. "Intercourse. I believe she had been engaged in a fairly strenuous act of intercourse when the abortion began."

Enter, Mark told himself, The Feeb. I was wondering where he fitted in. "About the two women who brought her here. Could you give me their names?"

"No. I can tell you only that one called herself Miss Jones, and the other Miss Smith. They were both very young, and very pretty. Just a pair of flappers. They deposited Mrs. Tredwell and vanished into the night."

"When people start saying things like 'vanished into the night' at me," Mark said, "I take to drink."

"They vanished into the night," Snowdom repeated and pushed the bottle back to Mark.

Mark poured himself another drink and thanked Snowdom with genuine courtesy. "And did the two flappers take care of the financial arrangements for Mrs. Tredwell?"

Snowdom dropped his pewter eyes. "Well, actually, an anonymous donor sent money in the mail. Several days after she was placed here."

"I was wondering," Mark said conversationally, "why you permitted your nurse to spout of Mrs. Tredwell's condition to perfect strangers. And on the phone at that." When Snowdom had no reply to that, Mark said, "I guess I'd better look at the remains." He finished off his second drink. "I have to steel myself," he said in a burst of confidence. "Even photographs in court unnerve me. I have to conceal it from a jury the way I would a case of the shakes."

"I imagine you have them often," Snowdom said, a touch superior.

"All the time. A trembling squeamish lawyer who can't even bear to look at the photographs of his clients' handiwork."

Snowdom was not taken in. "That may be so. But you function, D'Andor, you function. If you came here with blackmail on your mind, you worked hard at it. Only I don't intend to be your victim."

Mark got to his feet. "Don't bother your head about it,

Doctor. If you keep your mouth shut, I think you'll be safely in the clear."

Rising too, Snowdom said, "I'd better be." In the sweetest of voices he repeated, "I'd better be." Walking around the desk, he opened the door for Mark.

Preceding Snowdom through the door Mark glimpsed the upflung head and set mouth of the granitic Miss Pritchard. That worthy woman, Mark saw, had been hard at piecing together the same puzzle on which he himself was working. Miss Pritchard had undoubtedly arrived at the conclusion that since she had not been able to reach Mark, and Snowdom had not, then someone else had. Miss Pritchard was bent on learning the identity of that someone. Just as she tried to gain Snowdom's attention, Mark said loudly, "Doctor, I hope you will forgive certain assumptions I made before talking to you. I wasn't aware when I got here that the Lying—— I wasn't aware that the sanitarium had changed hands. New policy and all that."

"Not your fault, I'm sure," Snowdom said crisply, and quickened his step as one will when speaking with brisk efficiency.

Thus, safely past Miss Pritchard, Mark trotted down a hallway at Snowdom's side. Rounding a bend he suspected that their destination was once the farmhouse kitchen. With his hand on the knob of the door, Snowdom said, "You're not the type who faints, are you, D'Andor?"

"Only once, when I was a boy. At the funeral of an old friend."

"Understandable," Snowdom said.

"Actually he was just a hired hand. A great dumb hulk who worked for my father. He was gentleness itself to animals."

"When you're young the dead are terrifying."

"Especially," Mark said, "when he was hanged."

After a pause Snowdom said, "So that's what goes into the make-up of a criminal lawyer."

"It is not, Doctor, a prerequisite. I'm ready to go in now." Again Mark was obliged to enter first as Snowdom opened the door for him.

The cupboards and sink were those of a kitchen, walls

and woodwork painted in that indefinable green which is the visual counterpart of nausea. In the center of the room lay a sheeted figure, the sight of which filled Mark with stillness. With that classical gesture, so gruesomely graceful, Snowdom lifted the sheet. The face was thinner than Mark had ever seen it, but the wispy bangs cut to lie so artlessly on the forehead were much as they always were. In his own ears Mark could hear himself saying, some years ago, "That's not so much of a bang, baby, as a whimper."

"Well?" Snowdom said.

"I knew her before she married. That's why the name Tredwell meant nothing to me." He arrested Snowdom's hand as it sought to re-cover the face. "Wait. Let me look at Muffin a moment more."

"*Muffin?*"

"She called herself Muffin Naismith," Mark said. "She called herself that in all seriousness. As if it were a name."

"And who is she really?"

Mark shook his head. "In this town that question is either a gross invasion of privacy or an imponderable. Lower the sheet," he commanded quietly. Snowdom obeyed, watchful. "There are bruises all over her body," Mark said, making a question of the observation.

"She had received rough handling before being brought here."

"At whose hands?"

Snowdom replaced the sheet. "That is one of *your* imponderables, D'Andor. Though it might interest you to know that Miss Pritchard is of the opinion she was raped."

"Tell me your opinion."

Snowdom pursed his mouth. "At no time did this woman make any such statement to me. I know only that two girls brought her in after a party and left her."

"And you can't tell me whether or not a patient in your care had been raped?"

Snowdom countered coolly, "Isn't that a legal term, D'Andor?"

"If you're trying to present yourself as an enigma," Mark said, "you're doing just dandy."

"It has come to me—a little late in the game perhaps— but it has just come to me that Miss Pritchard wasn't the one who summoned you. And I didn't either. Why are you here?"

Mark answered the question looking down at the sheeted figure. "I was sent for."

"By whom?"

"Just a girl who always wanted to get into the movies."

Snowdom turned away. "These girls," he said in a voice of disgust, "and their pathological greed for fame. And where do they end up, I ask you, where do they end up?"

"One of them ended up here."

Looking Mark in the eye, Snowdom said with great deliberation, "D'Andor, I call that heartless cynicism."

"Do you?" With a final glance to the sheeted figure, Mark said gently, "I call it surcease." He walked to the door without looking back. "I'm going to arrange for a mortician to come take her out of here."

Snowdom called after him, "You will when I hand over a signed death certificate. And I will hand it over when Tredwell comes for his wife and no sooner."

Mark flung the door open and experienced that sickening leap of the senses that comes with a near-violent collision. Seymour Pentlove, the knob of the door almost within his grasp, danced forward, his feet pedaling desperately against the momentum of his body. He fell against Mark's chest and had to be righted. Behind Mr. Pentlove a large sun-browned man with a face as seamed as a walnut meat laughed in horror at the scene, his smallish eyes begging that no offense be taken at his helpless merriment in such a place. He was dressed in an ill-fitting suit of some dark woolen material, and Mark took him for an undertaker before spying the cowboy boots. The man sobered at once, looking to Mr. Pentlove for orders.

Mr. Pentlove, now steady on his aristocratic feet, spoke with his customary composure. "This is Tredwell."

The big man stepped clumsily up to Mark and recited, "I've come to get my wife, Doctor."

Mr. Pentlove snapped his fingers softly, once and once only, in his exasperation. "Not him," he said to Tredwell. "Him!"

Tredwell swung his seamed face toward Snowdom. "Oh."
He repeated his recitation. "I've come to get my wife, Doctor."

"Identify her," Snowdom said and returned to the sheeted
figure, Tredwell's boots making a gritty noise on the flooring
as he followed after. When Snowdom lifted the sheet Tredwell
swung his head away rapidly as if expecting attack from an
unknown quarter. Snowdom waited, and at last Tredwell said
queasily, "Yeah. That's her." He shook his head as if he could
not puzzle it out. "You know, somehow it's a kind of cryin'
shame."

"Yes," Mr. Pentlove said. He addressed Snowdom, "We
have a mortician's hearse out front. Will you have someone
direct them as to where to go, Doctor?"

Snowdom, his gaze fixed on Tredwell, did not immediately reply. Then, satisfied that the look of dismay on the large
brown face was genuine, he said, "Yes, side door. Take your
wife, Tredwell, and get out of here. The lot of you. Out."

"About the bill," Mr. Pentlove said smoothly. "Might
we take care of that in your office, Doctor?"

Again Snowdom hesitated. Though Mr. Pentlove was
standing with his hands at his side, his meaning could not
have been more clear had he taken out a fat bankroll and
begun counting with a licked thumb and forefinger. Snowdom
said shortly, "My office," and stalked out past them all. Mr.
Pentlove looked after him with a faint smile. To Mark he said
in an amused tone, "He'll be disappointed when he learns I'll
be willing to meet his price without haggling. It always makes
them feel as if they're giving up their honor without a struggle."
Mr. Pentlove set off after Snowdom.

Not speaking, Mark and Tredwell drew up the rear.

The quartette straggled round the bend in the hallway
to bear down on Miss Pritchard at her desk. She watched their
approach, her manner so stiff that Mark knew her to be holding
herself in check. Mark drew near in haste to hear what she
might have to say to Snowdom.

"Miss Pritchard," Snowdom said, "will you direct the
morticians to the—"

"I am afraid that that will not be possible, Doctor." From
rigid control Miss Pritchard went through brief panic and lastly

into a defiance that was altogether splendid. "I called a police ambulance for Mrs. Tredwell."

"You what?" Snowdom shouted. "You called for a police *what?*"

"Ambulance," Mark said.

"Who in hell—why in God's name did you call—— An *ambulance!*"

Mark said as if explaining for the now-frightened Miss Pritchard, "You see, Doctor, if you call for a police ambulance, you get service in a hurry. If, on the other hand, you call the police to come remove a body, you can cool your heels while they take their good time. Isn't that so, Miss Pritchard?"

Finding herself an unsought ally, Miss Pritchard tossed her head. Mark resumed in the same unruffled tone, "But we don't understand why you saw the necessity of calling in the police at all. Would you tell us that, Miss Pritchard?"

"So the coroner can do an autopsy on her," Miss Pritchard replied with a flash of her former defiance.

"I gathered that. But why?"

Miss Pritchard half-rose from her chair. "She was murdered, wasn't she?" she challenged.

"Oh, come now, Miss Pritchard, by whom?"

Miss Pritchard's mouth moved while remaining closed, as if she had bitten off some enormous impolite bite and would have to dispose of it before speaking.

"Did Mrs. Tredwell tell you anything to that effect?" Mark asked conversationally. "Or name names?"

"I'll just save all that for the police, if you don't mind," Miss Pritchard said in an unsteady sneering rasp.

"Don't you think Mr. Tredwell here has a right to know?"

Miss Pritchard sent the gangling Tredwell a single eyebeam of disdain. "The only name I'll name to you, Mr. D'Andor, is your own. She must have been out of her head by then, asking for a—a person like you! But since you're so suddenly interested, I'll tell you that she did. She said to tell you to come pick up the pieces."

"Those were her exact words?"

"Oh, no, those weren't her exact words at all! Oh, no, I'm just lying, making it up out of whole cloth," Miss Pritchard cried in heavy sarcasm. "I just like to fib! Well, I'll tell you this, and it's no lie—she said someone had hurt her. And then she said, 'Don't let the son of a bitch get away with it.' And those are her exact words!" Suddenly tears stood in Miss Pritchard's eyes. "Men! Raping women. Plying them with liquor and then raping them. And then closing ranks and covering up for each other." Miss Pritchard leaped to her feet like an impassioned orator, delivering her finest rhetoric. "And if you men want to know, I consider the whole situation plain mean! Just . . . plain . . . mean!" Miss Pritchard slammed herself down into her chair and wept noisily like a woman who has been needing a good cry for who knows how long.

"Thank you, Miss Pritchard," Mark said, and inclined his head in the perfunctory little bow he accorded any witness, friendly or hostile, at the conclusion of his testimony. He looked to the gaping Tredwell and then to Mr. Pentlove, who was as always buttoned up to the chin in his remarkable poise. "Shall we go, gentlemen?"

And Snowdom, all unnerved, rushed to the door to open it for them. Mr. Pentlove, the last to pass by, said to Snowdom, "Is that woman in there insane?"

"I never thought so before tonight."

"Promise her any amount up to ten thousand dollars to withhold whatever story she is planning to tell the police. We will be in touch with you."

"I'll try," Snowdom said fervently, and closed the door.

The night was cool; a breeze from the ocean ruffled Mr. Pentlove's impeccable coiffure. Ignoring Mark for the moment, he said to Tredwell, "Go home. Say nothing to anyone until D'Andor or I get to talk to you."

Without a word Tredwell departed, his cowboy boots sounding strangely as if he were traversing icy slush. Mr. Pentlove murmured, "He's not really the dead woman's husband."

"I was certain of it. Where've you got your Golden Ass hiding out, Pentlove?"

"My house. Know the way?"

"Once I did," Mark said.

Mr. Pentlove did so love a neat thrust, and he smiled his

appreciation of this one. Without further ado, he went toward his car, his step saved from jauntiness by virtue of his dignity. He was the one mogul of the Industry Mark thought could have carried a rider's quirt or a Prussian officer's baton with the proper aplomb. But, unlike his colleagues, Mr. Pentlove would as soon be caught toting a toilet plunger under one arm.

Above the sound of Mr. Pentlove's motor, Mark heard a police siren. He looked to the farmhouse where Muffin lay dead. All right, he thought wearily, you asked for it, and I'll do it. But in my own way. In my own way I'll pick up the pieces.

CHAPTER THREE

Mr. Pentlove dwelt far from the hurdy-gurdy liveliness of the Boulevard, as was only to be expected, but he eschewed as well the faint taint of *nouveau riche* that dulled the sheen of Beverly Hills. He lived, therefore, on a quiet street just off Los Feliz; and had Mrs. Pentlove taken it into her head to do a bit of neighborhood door-to-door canvassing for her favorite charity she would have called on such homespun titans as C. B. De Mille. Following the taillights of Mr. Pentlove's Rolls, Mark renewed acquaintance with this Tudor house or that French Normandie mansion. Derelict that he now viewed himself as being, he had once had entree to those fortresses of movie aristocracy. Why, in that very hacienda there on the right, he had helped remove from the bed of Somebody's wife the dead body of an up-and-coming sheik. Mr. Somebody had been summoned home to a solicitous coterie of doctor, lawyer, and two awkward policemen, all assuring the lady that the sheik had died of natural causes (and so he had—heart attack) and saying what a shame it was that he had chosen to do so on her living-room sofa, but it was only to be expected when young men became unduly excited while discussing their dawning careers.

Though his mind maundered along on this and similar happenings, it in no way disturbed his thoughts. Like any person who lives alone, Mark had some time since let a part of his mental apparatus take on the function of a chattering companion whose presence kept him company and whose observations were met with affectionate disregard. His disciplined and compartmented thoughts, however, were fixed fully on the guile (or was it gall) of Mr. Pentlove. A dying Muffin

Naismith had spoken Mark's name, and learning of it, Mr. Pentlove had relied on his exquisite cynicism to dictate his next move. If Mark were the one lawyer, drunk or sober, who did not fancy a bench for himself, Mr. Pentlove's acumen was still in the right place. For Mark was faithfully following his taillight, and Mr. Pentlove cared not a fig for motives when he had his results.

The house of Seymour Pentlove was less than hospitable to Mark this night. Entering after him, Mark was greeted by a single light in the foyer and dark rooms to the right and left. Dimly Mark could discern the same gold swags at the windows and the obese pieces of furniture he remembered. But ahead of him was a new floating stairway, up which a balustrade of stainless steel sped like a gleam of moonlight. "You've gone futuristic, Pentlove," Mark said in a normal tone of voice.

Mr. Pentlove effectively shushed him with the barest scowl, so that Mark held his tongue lest the wife or children learn of his presence there and suspect something was amiss.

"This way," Mr. Pentlove said, walking softly. But then, he walked softly through life always, in all probability because he trod daily on the soft faces of those under him, who, in their constant shifting and struggling, afforded an uncertain footing. Under the floating stairway Mr. Pentlove nodded at Mark and opened a leather door. Inside was the taproom; here, Mark gathered, he and his host would converse in secrecy.

There were new mounted heads on the walls, in particular a fine longhorn sheep. But the leather lounges and the bar, the bar Mr. Pentlove had bought from a San Francisco saloon and which had made the journey to California around the Horn, was the same. Mark never saw it but what he thought of his own wretched little cellarette, and gave himself over to unalloyed admiration. And envy. The envy died when Mark discovered at the far end of the bar the hulking decoration that was The Feeb. Mark was one of the unhappy few who could not abide the silliness, the calculated mimicry of the desperately feeble-minded, that was the gift of Feeb Forbes to the world. The face that Forbes lifted to Mark this night, however, was not that of the buffoon but of the perplexed hearty fella. Though he photographed as being younger, he had clearly rounded thirty. He was enormous, but not the slave to his fat one would have thought. He used his body well, he was as trim in his movements as Mark. Aside from the shapeless nose, his features were well proportioned, even to the large blue eyes. So it was only when he was playing The Feeb, Mark surmised, that he distorted his face until the eyes appeared minuscule and alight with an infantile cunning, to contrast with the slack lips turned out in helpless vacuity. Forbes glanced at Mark nonchalantly before bending his attention on Mr. Pentlove. "What's the lowdown? Where does the lawyer fit in?"

Mark did not reply, standing quietly by the bar, unconsciously polishing the wood with the heel of his hand, as he did the jury box.

Mr. Pentlove said in a matter-of-fact voice, "She's dead. In case you were harboring any doubts about it."

"Gee, Mr. Pentlove, that's too bad!" Forbes announced with boyish distress. "Dead. Whadda ya think of that?" This question was addressed to Mark, couched in the insect whine of The Feeb. There was also the hint of a lisp in his enunciation, that or a baby-talk intonation. "It dudden make sense."

"Would you care to know why she died?" Mr. Pentlove asked.

The large blue eyes were steady and without a trace of craft, or compunction for that matter. "Wull, yeah," The Feeb said.

Mr. Pentlove walked past Mark to lean over the bar for a bottle. Pouring himself a neat Scotch in a thimble glass, he drank it off, slammed the thimble glass down on the mahogany, and suffered a brief spasm of revulsion against the taste of the alcohol. He looked to the motionless figure of Mark resting so easily against the bar. "What are you drinking, D'Andor?"

"Nothing," Mark said, and could not believe it was himself speaking.

"Well, I reckon I'd better have me another beer," The Feeb said, and filled his stein, which had been completely hidden by his hand, from the tap.

Mr. Pentlove said to the wall of bottles in front of him,

"She died, or so Snowdom says, of that infection—septicemia."

The Feeb took his shapeless nose out of his stein. "You could blow me over with a feather." He laughed. "How about that? You could blow *me* over witha——"

"The infection set in after he had to abort her," Mr. Pentlove said.

"Sonofagun," The Feeb mourned in the voice of a tot. "Beats all, don't it, them letting guys like that doctor run loose." Into the large eyes had come, unbidden, the glisten of relief.

"But before she died," Mr. Pentlove said to his thimble glass, "she evidently said—or—" he looked to Mark for assistance "—*alleged*——"

"Mrs. Tredwell made the dying declaration that she had been raped," Mark said.

"Tuh!" The Feeb sneered, and an instant later tried to recall the sound.

"Untrue?" Mark asked casually.

The Feeb shrugged his glen-plaid shoulders. "These bimbos, some of 'em, sure have a funny way of putting it. She gets herself fu——"

"Don't say that," Mr. Pentlove said sharply. "She's dead." Suddenly he looked abashed at having succumbed to a charitable impulse.

"—laid," The Feeb amended, banishing a smile from his mouth. "But it was a party, wuddn't it? Where'd she get the rape routine?"

"How long have you known Mrs. Tredwell?" Mark asked, still at ease, still calm.

"Known 'ur?" The Feeb cried, aggrieved. "I din know the broad at all. Hell, I started out with someone else. Then me'n my tootsie run into good ol' Tredwell—me and him did some pissurs together in the ol' days—and he had this worn-out flapper with him. He was callin' her Mrs. Tredwell and stuff, but I kinda had the idea it was some kinda joke among her and him. Where we run into each other was this speak. So we—you know, decided to hang one on. And then I says we should all go on over to the Eden and—"

"The Garden of Eden?" Mark asked.

"I *said,* din I?" The Feeb begged of Mr. Pentlove. "The Eden. (I can allus get a bungalow there ona coupla hours' notice.) So me an my dish—and me oh my, was she table quality!—and ol' Tredwell and the bimbo with him sets out to make a lil whoopee." Launched into his anecdote The Feeb in all his glory appeared. Forbes began to squeeze his eyes and loosen his lips, his large hands growing limp and flapping on his belly as he embellished his story with lewd winks. Yet the eyes, now so determinedly porcine, were watchful. Forbes was aware, Mark noted, that those who did not find him a belly laugh a minute could not stomach him at all.

"What day or night was this?" Mark asked.

"Last Saddiday. So off we goes," The Feeb lisped. "Only in the speak I hadn't tumbled to the fac' that this Tredwell dame was real drunkola. She wuz hot after me, yeah, but you're in pissurs and you run inta that alla time. Dames hot after ya."

Mr. Pentlove felt his temples as if to determine whether he could endure much more of The Feeb.

"Like the guy says about the gun," The Feeb continued, "I didn' know it was loaded. And I just thought this dame with Tredwell was trying to make a lil time with me. Sooo . . . we gets to the Eden, and this and that, and I'm really warmin' up this dish I got—you know how it am—and you know what?" The Feeb paused, mouth ajar in outraged idiocy. There might have been a clock ticking with businesslike efficiency in his head, timing the build-up to his socko punch line. "My ol' pal Tredwell suddenly walks off with my babe, and leaves me holding—the bag! Get it? This broad he was with? He leaves me——" But The Feeb could not continue for laughing at the duplicity of the normal and the trusting stupidity of the mentally deficient. With many an appreciative gasp, and wiping away not a tear of mirth but a trickle from the corner of his mouth, The Feeb sought to control himself.

Mr. Pentlove said pensively, "My father wanted me to be a doctor. And we had every reason to believe that an uncle of mine would have aided me in getting my education. How did it happen that instead I'm here listening to this?"

Archibald Forbes leaned forward so that he was almost

speaking to Mr. Pentlove confidentially. "What's so effing holy about you? Everybody thinks I'm funny but you, Mr. Pentlove. Why is that, huh? Why is that?"

Speaking to the bottles, Mr. Pentlove said, "Two million dollars worth of film in the can. All ready to be released. But this simpleton plays The Feeb when I inform him that a woman he had intercourse with is dead. Two million dollars."

"Now you just hold your horses, Mr. Pentlove," Forbes said, clothed in iron innocence. "In the first place I didn't touch her. All right, I touched her, but—"

"Please," Mark interrupted softly. "I would rather you tell what happened in its proper sequence, Forbes. After Tredwell left, what took place next?"

"What didn't?" Forbes said sullenly. "He took my tootsie and left this drunkola behind. Only some other people had come in by then, so I had to let it ride. The next thing I know the drunkola is dancing all over the furniture—I mean just that too—up one sofa and down the other. And over the table. And waving this swizzle stick or something she had for a baton. Like she was leading a band." Some aspect of this part of his story made Forbes uncomfortable. He spoke with great rapidity. "And that went on for hours. I just ignored her. There were other girls around, and I just—amused myself with them. In the meantime Mrs. Tippy-toes is doing the Black Bottom to the radio and yelling at me to dance with her. Then she treats us to the light fantastic, and she was *fantastic,* you can bet your boots, and then some. Then the next thing Mrs. Drinkola does—"

Mark's weariness left him open to incaution. He said curtly, "The dead woman's name was Naismith. Would you please refer to her as Miss Naismith, Forbes."

"I would appreciate it too," Mr. Pentlove whispered.

Forbes uttered a brief yip of scornful laughter. "Look, I say what I mean, no less. I hit you right in the eye with it. Like pie-throwing, you 'moon' your man right in the kisser, or just don't bother throwing your pie at all. Now if you two can't stand hearing the truth about how that hooker carried on, I'll be taking my pies somewhere else."

"Go on with your story, Forbes," Mark said, under control again.

"All right! So comes the dawn. And *Mrs. Drunkola* doesn't look like she's ever going to run down. Except that she's not so happy-happy any more. I could tell she was going to turn mean drunk next. She follows me out to the kitchen and starts yelling at me what a cupcake she is, and how she knew me when I was nobody."

She was asking him to call her Muffin, Mark thought. And she did know you, briefly.

"I tried to tell her I'd never seen her before that night in my life, but I'd have needed a megaphone to be heard over her hollering at me."

"Tell me," Mark said, "were the others in the bungalow aware of Miss Naismith's conduct?"

"Look, lawyer," Forbes said, "the people in San Fernando Valley probably didn't miss a word. What I should have done was taken a powder right then. Or tossed *Mrs. Drunkola* out on her tokus. Instead, I figured let the other kids polish off the likker. It wasn't their fault this cuckoo was popping in and out of her clock, messing up the party."

"Please cleave to the facts," Mark protested softly.

"The facts are," Forbes said, large eyes limpid with detestation, "that she started pawing at me. I told her to lay off, that I was going to the bedroom for a little shut-eye. And that's—" Forbes looked at Mr. Pentlove sternly "—where I made my mistake. She comes barreling into the bedroom after me. Then she slops her drink all over me. She starts mopping at me, but that's only an excuse to get at my fly——"

"You don't know that for a fact, Forbes," Mark said.

This solemn declaration provoked another scornful yip from Forbes. "Oh yeah? Well, I can tell you this, that when I sat down on the bed I almost squashed her, she was underneath me that fast. And ripping at my clothes, and yelling, and—"

"Yelling?"

"You heard me. And I was trying to pull her off me and keep her from kicking me at the same time. Then right on schedule comes the crying jag, a real rip-snorter, along with—"

Forbes came to such an abrupt halt that Mark had to repress a quickening in his breathing. Forbes's eyes grew as round as cookie cutters, the child's simulation of truthfulness. "I forgot to say, didn't I," he said in a twinkling of inventive detail, "that she had locked the door when she followed me into the bedroom." A flush deepened along his pudgy chops and spread like underground seepage to his ears and hairline. "Yeah, I had forgot to mention that."

"Yeah, you had," Mark drawled.

Mr. Pentlove looked at Mark anxiously. "Go on," Mark said to Forbes.

"And the other kids were banging on the door by this time. So I got shed of that nutsy dame somehow and opened it."

"And then?"

"Lawyer, I did just what you'd have done. I told the dames to sober that cuckoo up and get her the hell out of there. And I left. I'd had it."

"When you were in the bedroom with her, was she in pain?"

Forbes laughed slowly and with rich contempt. "After the load of likker she took on, she wasn't feeling any pain."

Mark said idly, "Snowdom thinks she began to miscarry in that bedroom. While you had intercourse with her. And the nurse says you forced intercourse on her."

"Force—that—crummy—old—hooker?" Forbes echoed in unbelief.

"She was not quite thirty years old," Mark said. "Do you happen to know for a fact that she was a prostitute?"

"Yeah, my Sunday School teacher pointed her out to me," Forbes quipped.

Mr. Pentlove sighed.

"When was the last you saw of Miss Naismith?"

"The last I saw the other girls were dragging her into the swimming pool. To see if soaking her head wouldn't cool her down. God, what a night!" Forbes added parenthetically.

"Did you know she was pregnant?"

With withering disgust Forbes said, "Where I come from pregnant women don't go leaping around like mountain goats. Unless they're unbalanced."

"From your account Miss Naismith was."

Forbes shrugged. "Well, well, our lawyer lad just made himself a point. And, no, I didn't know she was knocked up." With belated indignation Forbes shouted at Mr. Pentlove, "Say, what is this all about anyway?"

"Two million dollars," Mr. Pentlove said, striking straight to the heart of the matter.

"With a dollop of murder tossed in for good measure," Mark said.

Forbes got off his barstool. "Oh, no. Not me. Not Mrs. Forbes' little boy. That's a lot of applesauce, only I'm not having any."

"Forbes, you listen to me. There is a dear little old lady in town who is notorious in legal circles as being a litigation libertine. All her gratifications, physical and emotional, center around filing law suits against famous people. She saves up twenty dollars to have some impecunious lawyer file a complaint, and then she runs around Civic Center telling everyone she meets about her 'legal connections' with people in high places. It is her way of breaking out of the prison of anonymity you celebrities have put her in. Now, the office of the District Attorney just so happens to be full of the same type of libertine. Trial deputies who would give ten years of their lives just to hale someone like you into court. To see their names linked with yours on front pages. And finally to jail you, humble you, and destroy you if possible. Do you begin to understand?"

"I understand," Forbes said sullenly, "that a dumb dame ruined my week end, and you're trying to make something of it."

"The coroner may be trying to make something of it in the morning." Forbes was jarred, but a shrug made light of his momentary perturbation. Mark went on, "If you had intercourse with her in that bedroom and she miscarried as a result of it, you are still in the clear. But if you forced her and she—"

"I did—not—lay—her," Forbes said flatly.

"What did you do to her?"

"Whose flunky are you nowadays?" Forbes asked idly.

He dismissed Mark with a wave of his stein and complained to Mr. Pentlove. "If there's going to be trouble, I'm not sitting here any longer jawing with this has-been. I'll talk to his boss, and if I think he's a big enough lawyer for a star like me, maybe I'll consider it. So who's—"

"Do me the kindness of shutting up," Mr. Pentlove said.

Forbes slammed his stein down in insult. "You can't talk to me that way!"

"My worst suspicions have been confirmed," Mr. Pentlove informed Forbes. "You are a feeb. It's not a gift, it's your true mentality." His voice rose a trifle. "Don't you think I had my reasons for retaining D'Andor? Oh, Forbes, Forbes, I would play fast and loose with your neck with pleasure, but not with two million dollars!"

"He's a drunk," Forbes said, beginning to fidget as if he couldn't settle down in his fat comfortably.

"Yes," Mark said, before Mr. Pentlove could speak again. "I am. Are you ready to get down to business, Forbes, or do I leave?"

Mr. Pentlove stared at Mark curiously, while Forbes made a soft bleating sound like The Feeb, then shook his fat cheeks in a shudder of resignation. Mark said formally, "Do you wish me to represent you in this matter, Forbes?"

"Yes," Mr. Pentlove announced.

Looking at Mr. Pentlove piteously, Forbes said, "I don't get it." When Mr. Pentlove did not answer, preferring to fix his eyes sternly on his thimble glass, Forbes faltered, "Has D'Andor got something on us?"

"I presume so," Mr. Pentlove admitted.

"Oh." Baffled, Forbes asked, "But *what?*"

"I am going to find out why that woman died," Mark said.

"Why!" Forbes cried passionately. "Who cares why? Who wants to know?"

"She did," Mark said. "And I am here because I do."

"And the District Attorney might," Mr. Pentlove put in, in his practical way.

"Shall we get down to business, gentlemen," Mark said.

Forbes maintained steadfastly that he had not molested the dead woman sexually. He had only struggled with a hysterical, drunken woman whose advances annoyed him as much as they appalled him. Yes, he had given the other women money to dispose of the drunken woman at a nearby private hospital; he felt he owed it to the Eden to get her away from there.

"Was it you who called to learn of her condition?" Mark asked.

"I did that," Mr. Pentlove volunteered. "After one of the girls who had been at the Eden with Forbes got in touch with me."

"And who is that girl?"

"A prostie," Forbes retorted smartly.

"Her name," Mr. Pentlove said, taking out a small note-book, "is Olive Jones. And yes, she is a prostitute. She is also a very smart girl. She had sense enough to warn me of Forbes' involvement with a dying woman. I am grateful to her."

"I am sure," Mark said smoothly, "that by now the gratitude is mutual, Pentlove."

"Naturally," Mr. Pentlove replied agreeably.

"And the name of the other woman who took Miss Naismith to the hospital?"

"I dunno," Forbes said. "Just another hooker." He looked from Mr. Pentlove to Mark and burst out savagely, "Jesus, you'd think somebody important had had something happen to them! When actually the only person worth a hill of beans is me!"

"Precisely," Mr. Pentlove said.

"And that in itself should be an indictable offense," Mark commented. "Forbes, write down for me the names of all those you had dealings with on the week end past, and then go home. Talk only to Pentlove or me until further instructions."

When the celebrated lackwit had gone, Mark walked around the bar and selected a bottle of Irish from the lavish liquor display. He drank down two fingers with dispatch, then curled his hand around his second drink as if taking warmth and restorative value from the glass itself.

"Well, D'Andor," Mr. Pentlove said, "what do you think of The Feeb. Do you detest him?"

"I find him detestable, but it's not the same thing."

"Tell me, just how well did you know the dead woman? This Miss Naismith or whoever she was."

"Quite well. Some years ago."

"You slept with her?"

"Frequently."

"And if her death proves to have been a killing, will you still defend The Feeb?"

"Only a jury may say if it was a killing. And I have said I would defend your Golden Ass. It is the only way open to me to interest myself in the matter."

Mr. Pentlove nodded like one in receipt of a threadbare civility. He gave his thimble glass a half-turn, then with studied carelessness stated, "A bench means that much to you lawyers. A black robe and the chance to order other lawyers about."

"And you think that's what lured me out?"

Mr. Pentlove found himself looking foolish in his own eyes. Trying to ignore Mark's grin, he said, "I should be asking myself not what lured you out, but what's keeping you, eh? Now that you've found out I called on you only because I couldn't afford not to. And now that we both know the woman was asking for you before she died. I'm not sure I understand you, D'Andor. Not at all sure."

"Odd. I consider myself an open book. Any fool should be able to read me. The Feeb did."

"But I'm not a fool."

Mark grinned again. "That's the first thing you've said with spirit all evening." Again he took to polishing the bar with his hand.

Mr. Pentlove at once assumed all the pompous dated dignity of a pearl stickpin. "There was a time, D'Andor, when I was willing to take banter from you. But no longer. Not from the man you are now."

"I must remember that," Mark said with mock gravity.

Mr. Pentlove mused, "When did you start going to seed? Was it because of the death of your wife? Or her—ah— conduct before then?"

"No. It had started before that. You've got the wrong

post hoc ergo propter hoc by the tail. And don't continue on with this line of questioning, Pentlove. Even your excellent Irish doesn't entitle you to it."

Offended less at Mark's words than by his superior tone, Mr. Pentlove lapsed into sarcasm and slang, "Well. Excuse me for living!"

Mark looked at him steadily, smiling, deliberately withholding a reply.

"D'Andor!" Mr. Pentlove said in warning, "Don't carry your drunken mockery too—"

"Oh, very well," Mark conceded. "I'll excuse you this time."

Mr. Pentlove drew himself up. "When you have finished your drink, will you please leave here."

"I'll leave here," Mark said, "when you turn over to me Miss Naismith's belongings. Her purse and whatever else that smart girl of a prostitute sold to you." He waited patiently for Mr. Pentlove to see the wisdom of his request. And when that gentleman finally nodded, Mark said, "Get it now, please."

Mr. Pentlove walked behind the bar, and opening a small cupboard with a key attached to his gold watchchain, took out a worn sequined handbag. "This is all."

"Thank you," Mark said. He finished off his Irish and took his leave like one intending only to go into the next room for a moment. It was a peculiarity of his, this offhand leave-taking, and even when he bade someone farewell they would often wait for his return for a full ten minutes or so while he, all unaware, was long gone on his way.

In this manner he had walked away from a girl who called herself Muffin Naismith one rainy afternoon. She waited months for him to come back, but he never did.

Outside the wind had shifted, coming down from the high deserts now. Sand, fine as fog, hung in the night air so that the stars, not quite obscured, appeared to need dusting.

CHAPTER FOUR

Driving home, up into the silence of the hill, Mark saw that for the first time in years he had forgotten to turn on the blue bulb of the wrought-iron lantern that hung from the solarium ceiling. In any other clime and time the solarium would have been properly referred to as sunporch, but the architect had been so taken with the word that Mark and his wife Constance had adopted it for their own. Whenever Mark had had to work at night, or Constance was out late at one of her charity digs, the bulb burned to welcome the other home. The light shone in the black of night like a tiny eerie eye, watchful and menacing as it regarded the roofs of the foothill cottages far below.

No, not in a 'coon's age had he forgotten that blue light, it was the sole sentimentality he allowed himself, and he was damned if he would let self-ridicule cheat him of it. It was the first thing he did upon entering the house—turning on that silly, despairing, and sinister welcome for a dead Constance. From the solarium he went down to his bedroom and emptied the contents of the shabby sequined purse upon the bed.

He learned little. There was a tarnished silver compact he had once given Muffin, or rather, had bought for her when she stood before a jeweler's display window and breathed, in her best boop-boop-a-doop voice, "Oooooow!" at the sight of it. The thing was a small box with three drawers, for lip-rouge, loose powder, and cheek rouge, with a mirrored lid and a carrying chain (now broken and knotted). There was a pocket comb with several teeth missing, and a mad-money coin purse containing two dollars and some loose change.

There was nothing else, nor had he expected more. He had never known Muffin to carry any identification with her when out with a man. As a lone concession to the fact of male contrariness or her own disinclination to meet certain demands, she relied only on her mad money. Mark could remember a five-dollar bill tucked under a lacy red garter, which had lent Muffin an air of dashing jazzy chic, and never more so than when she danced the Charleston, swinging the red-gartered leg and the five-dollar bill for all to see.

She was thus flashily bedecked the first night Mark ever set eyes on her.

Mark had been something less than enthusiastic himself about going to the Halloween party of Lucia Estrella Concepción y Estrados Wilmot. And this despite several factors which must be taken into consideration. It was Mrs. Wilmot's trial which had led him into the full hot sunlight of fame and fortune, her legal fee alone enabling him to finish buying his house in the hills. In the second place a gentleman of flexible moral values where everything except his word of honor was concerned, a certain Seymour Pentlove, had put his imprimatur on Mark by retaining him to defend Mrs. Wilmot. Mrs. Wilmot was a true Castilian beauty, fair of hair and cheek, with long exquisite fingers which she pressed to her quivering lips at least once in every one of her movies, while she struggled to hold back those glycerin tears that the make-up man would soon dab on her classic face. About the only swarthy male star who hadn't got around to raping Lucia Estrella— her professional name—in her films was a Mr. Valentino, and Seymour Pentlove was working hard on that. In this obligatory scene she gazed upon her ravisher with a wide-eyed detachment that approached apathy, as if she fully expected death to overtake her an instant before dishonor did. She was the only actress ever who could seemingly emerge from these imposed sexual encounters as vapid a virgin as ever came within purview of a hot-blooded young rapist. To the camera she presented an everlasting marble purity.

There was a street in town named after her maternal grandfather. It was said that ancestors of hers had been married by a saint—Fra Junipero Serra. But in Hollywood circa 1924 she was known to all as Babe. Her adulteries were so shopworn that only the most indiscriminating of scandal-mongers bothered with them at all. It was a different story, to be sure, though, when she bumped off her nice-chap husband Wilmot with a quart bottle of French perfume.

Called to the scene of the crime, Mark had entered the bedroom, looked down on the crushed skull of Wilmot, and said, "What a stinking mess." His next remark was directed to the chauffeur. "Button your fly before the police get here." Then to the chauffeur's babbled narrative that Wilmot had burst into the bedroom with "blood in his eye," Mark said only, "Get out of this situation and stay out," for his attention was all on the sobbing Babe. Mr. Pentlove sat on the chaise longue, looking on the scene unmoved. Mr. Pentlove took up the phone at his side asking Mark if it were time to call the police. "You mean you haven't yet?" Mark asked, at which Mr. Pentlove raised his plucked eyebrows. (Mr. Pentlove's barber was as fastidious as he, and decreed the plucking.) Mr. Pentlove asked of Mark, "Surely one couldn't be expected to call the police before the attorney had arrived?" And Mark, nodding his acknowledgment of Hollywood protocol in moments of homicide, advanced on Babe. "Self-defense?" he asked, and she barely had time to blubber yes.

So if Mark shrank from attending Babe's Halloween party, his wife Constance adamantly dusted her hands of the matter. At breakfast Constance had rescued the invitation from oblivion on the baroque sideboard and tossed it next Mark's coffee cup. "I am constitutionally unable to be friendly with a woman who signs herself 'Babe'," Constance said, all her highly merited Pasadena hauteur in place, as was the ashy chignon at the base of her neck.

"I wouldn't dream of asking you to become a friend of Babe's," Mark said mildly. "But I do think it might be good form for us to put in an appearance at least."

"You'll be asking me to appear in a line-up next," Constance said, but without anger. "So I can solicit clients for you left and right. Those on my left and right, I mean."

"I know what you mean. But Babe's fee did pay for this house."

"And what you could earn working with my father would pay for it six times over."

"Constance, not this morning. I'm not interested in real estate. And I wouldn't live in Pasadena if you paid me."

"Well," Constance said candidly, "that was more or less Daddy's offer." She looked out the dining-room window. "The only living thing I like in the whole of Hollywood is our eucalyptus tree." Reverting again to the subject of Babe's party, she said, "And besides, what on earth will you wear for a costume?"

"Common courtesy ought to cover it," Mark decided.

Constance laughed. "I asked for that. You know why you're really thinking of going, don't you? Because you're sorry for that trollop. She's just a poor little widow-woman to you. With a lumpy jaw that photographs like an incipient case of the mumps." Before Mark could point out that she was being rather cruel, Constance went on defiantly, "Well, I for one am glad Wilmot did give her her lumps before she did him in. I hate it when you get people like that off scot free. It's not—"

"Nice?" Mark supplied.

Constance availed herself of a surprisingly charming glower. On this subject alone he would not let her get the better of him, and as for any other argument they might have she didn't care. "Mark, you have long since proved to me, or to Daddy, or to yourself, or to whoever it is you're trying to prove it. What was I saying?"

"I'd love to help you out but I don't know."

"Oh, I remember. That you can support me nicely all by your lonesome. And in the manner to which Dad, bless his heart, made me accustomed."

"By all means let us hope God blesses Daddy's heart."

"Dammit!" Constance said softly. "Have the bright lights and the movie stars really gotten to you? Are you impressed? Don't you realize at all that what you're doing is toadying to scum?"

"I think I will remove myself from the premises. I hate hitting a woman." He scraped his chair loudly on the quarry-tile floor.

"Mark," Constance pleaded, "please let's go home. To

Pasadena. People commit crimes in Pasadena too, you know."

"Respectable crimes committed by respectable people who retain only respectable attorneys to defend them. My, that does sound exciting. D'you think I could keep up the pace?"

"At first," Constance said slowly, "you did take every trashy case offered you. And I hated it, but I kept my mouth closed. I knew you had set your heart on buying me everything short of Catalina Island. I know you took that incest case to pay the bills when I had—" her voice grew colorless rather than show emotion "—had my miscarriage. But taking on Babe Wilmot to buy this house was rather more on the order of——." She shook her head and would not finish.

Sitting with his fashionably clumsy baroque chair pushed a good two feet from the table, and looking foolish and not caring, Mark said, "Go ahead. Say it. Daddy's daughter's husband is prostituting his profession."

"I don't care how many loathesome cases you take," Constance cried passionately, "only stop *enjoying* them! Stop wallowing in the notoriety. Stop deteriorating inside."

"You stop," Mark said. "Stop right there, Constance." He had a way of shutting himself away from the world, even Constance. He drew into himself with the finality of a turtle.

"All right," Constance muttered. "You win. Hereafter, though, let's fight over important issues. Not Babe Wilmot. Are you going to finish your breakfast from there, incidentally?"

Sheepish, he drew back to the table. "Know what the famous nut doctor said to his beautiful patient?"

"Don't tell me," Constance begged.

"I will too tell you. He said 'I love you when you're—'." There were tears in Constance's eyes. " '—mad?' " he ended lamely. "Princess, what's the matter?"

"I wish to hell," Constance wept, "I knew," and laid her forehead on the table inches from her plate.

Yet for all her tears and his male notion of how best to assuage a weeping woman, there was a tentative estrangement between them that frightened and angered Mark at the same time. When, that evening, he was ready to leave for

Babe's, he asked, "Sure you won't go with me? Think of all the fun and good times you'll be missing."

"Thanks, no. I'd rather stay home and listen to the radio."

"I won't be long," he promised or wheedled. He himself could not have said which.

As he started up the stair to the front door Constance called out after him, "Have fun bobbing for apples in the bidet." Her laugh—he had always thought of it as rich, assured, and somehow glossy—almost caused his patent-leather shoes to race back down the stair to her.

He was prepared for noisy drunks and rotten liquor; Babe had the discriminating palate of a sot and chose her friends with all the selectivity of a Salvation Army lass exhorting bums to repent. In Wilmot's day—but Wilmot was dead and on the exact spot where he was slain there now stood one of those nameless leftover little beauties one was eternally running into in Hollywood. This one wore dark bangs and was a commendably slavish copy of Olive Thomas. She was wrapped in a pink coat, hugging its thick white-fox collar to her cheeks, and pouting at herself in Babe's pier glass. The girl's mouth was painted almost heart-shaped with cherry lip-rouge, and when she raised her hand palm outward to rest along the side of her face, Mark could see a dot of cherry color on the finger she had used to paint her mouth. He did not think she was yet aware of his presence, but when she spoke she continued to preen before the mirror exactly as she was before, with that dedication to self that he thought women indulged in only when they were alone. "Has anybody come yet?" the girl asked in an impatient strident voice, and took off the coat. In a fringed cherry dress she revealed the chic boyish figure so newly popular; she was spare as a spindle.

Mark stared at the girl in amazement, for there drifted up to this bedroom off the gallery the noise of women shrieking merrily and men booming in laughter as thunderous as the surf. "Why," Mark said, "there must be over fifty people downstairs. Can't you hear them?"

The girl walked to an opened closet, hung up the pink

coat, and took out a leopard jacket. "I meant is *anybody* here, yet?" she said, and donned the jacket. She turned once to the right, once to the left, before the mirror, then made a face. "If you want my opinion, this jacket is plain tacky." The jacket was consigned to its hanger, the girl having decided on a shiny black monkey-fur cape instead. She posed for Mark, one leg bent at the knee and cuddling against the other. "How's about this, huh? More my type, don't you think?"

It came to Mark that she was openly trying on Babe's wardrobe. "You planning on swiping any of this stuff?" he asked conversationally.

The girl shrilled, "Oh, you're a scream. Oh, that's wicked."

"Take it off," Mark said of the monkey-fur cape. "She wore that in court. Besides, the white fox suits you better."

"The fox?" The girl removed the cape at once, suddenly finding it revolting. Reaching for the pink coat with the fox collar, a thought struck her. "You mean when she was in court for her murder trial?"

"Yes."

"Gee. I wonder, you know, where he was killed. She did it with a whole quart of French purr-fume. Can you feature *me* wasting good purr-fume like that?"

Amused, Mark said, "I doubt you would."

"And how!" To the sound of banjo music coming from downstairs the girl executed a few snappy dance steps, making soft spurts of rhythmic noise through a pursed mouth. Abruptly as she had begun she broke off, to stand before Mark wagging two fingers. "Cigarette me, Daddy."

Mark obliged, taking out his tin of flat fifties. The girl narrowed her eyes as she exhaled. The affectation was so effective that Mark smiled. "Thanks loads," she said, a good octave lower than she had so far spoken. "I read Babe's trial in the paper," she said, as if taking up with a topic prematurely abandoned. "Say, did I!"

"Are you a close friend of Babe's?"

"Don't know her from Adam. I mean, I just met her tonight when my date brought me. No, I mean, I read her trial because I think it's very important to keep up with current events. Don't you?"

"Now that you mention it, yes."

The black eyes narrowed, less in affectation than specula-tion this time. "F'instance, there's going to be another war, did you know that?" she challenged.

"No! Really?"

"I read it," the girl said with impressive solemnity. "I read where Pola Negri said we were. She said Poland was act-ing just awful, and you wouldn't believe what she said about France."

"That bad?"

The girl shook her bangs; the gesture was quite appeal-ing. "If you're going to keep up with current events, you can't be afraid to face facts."

"That is so true."

"And that's what I read in this article that Pola Negri said."

Mark frowned in thought. "I must have missed the article."

"Not me. I read every single word in *Motion Picture,* and *Photoplay,* and *Motion Picture Classic.* Of course," she went on in a burst of modesty, "I'd read 'em even if I didn't have this deep interest in current events." After a suitable pause she let Mark have it right between the eyes. "I'm a starlet myself, you know."

He thought, any pretense on my part of being flabber-gasted should earn me a punch in the nose. He pretended to be flabbergasted. "You aren't! Wait a minute, are you Miss— Miss——" He snapped his fingers in exasperation.

"Miss Naismith."

"Of course. And what precedes Naismith?"

"Pre— Oh, you mean the rest of my handle. Well . . . Muffin. It's Muffin."

He thought helplessly: If she tells me her mother read the name in a book, no power on this earth will prevent me from asking, A cookbook, no doubt? He said almost sternly in his effort to control his imaginings, "Muffin Naismith. Very pretty."

She lost a brief struggle not to bridle. As he spoke his own name she showed not a flicker of interest. He touched her thin arm and was mildly astonished at the heat her very skin generated. She was like the hot metal shield housing some silent but devilishly busy motor. He had heard that moviestruck girls lived in a fever of anticipation, but now he found himself wondering if burning ambition could actually raise the body temperature. Not even when he was working himself to exhaustion to earn his way through law school had he known such unquenchable desire as he sensed when touching this moronic, burnished little beauty. An unwelcome pang of pity made him speak to her in a more kindly way than he had so far. "Look, Muffin Naismith, let's go find us some drinks."

He stood aside for her to walk ahead of him, then found himself sweeping the room with a final glance. He turned to find Miss Naismith inspecting him. With a waggish snigger she accused, "You've been in this bedroom before, huh?" To Mark's absent nod, she went on, "I was wondering how come you come up here. I mean, a man isn't like a girl, just wandering around to have a look-see."

"Well, I did have it in mind to try on Babe's sables," he said, but genially.

Miss Naismith said so promptly, "Oh, you're wicked!" that he recognized the phrase as being for her as spontaneous and unconscious as a mannerism. She next made a valiant try for slyness. "Bet you were never in here when Wilmot was alive."

"That's so," Mark said honestly.

"Just when he was—— Wait a minute!"

He waited a minute.

"You're her lawyer! Yeah! I knew I'd seen your picture somewhere. Listen, tell me, which room did she—"

"This one."

Miss Naismith looked with reverent wonder at the canopied bed and the dressing table crowded with crystal *flacons,* thence her eyes moved to the closets crammed with furs and cloth-of-gold hostess pajamas. "Well, he fixed her too," she said with judicial impartiality. "Breaking her jaw like that, he ruined her career on the silver screen."

"I'm afraid the medical attention she got on the prison ward did that," Mark said.

Miss Naismith said quite cheerily, "She can keep all her money. I'll take my career."

"Let's go," Mark said uneasily, and taking Miss Naismith by her feverish arm urged her toward the stair. But halfway down she hung back, looking over the rail at Babe and her rowdies below. "Nobodies," she said bitterly. "Look at them." Obediently he looked while she continued her soft tirade. "Here I read all about Babe and her trial, and Babe and her parties, and Babe and all the important people in the Industry—that means the movies—"

"I know."

"—and all people like that. And I was hoping, just praying I would—" She drifted into silence, looking lost and lonely.

Yes, just preying, he thought, yet no amount of inward scoffing could douse a grudging pity for her. "Just praying you would get discovered?"

"And I haven't met a soul!" Miss Naismith wailed. "And I came with this—*boob*—just to get here, and he mauled me all the way over, let me tell you, and what he's got in mind for going home it won't take a mind-reader to figure out."

"I'd be glad to take you home, Miss Naismith," Mark said helplessly.

"Gee, swell," she growled. "Just between you an' I, I just met this boob a coupla days ago. To hear him tell it he and Tom Mix are just like that." She took a turn for self-disgust. "And I swallowed it hook, line, and sink."

"Yes, that is a shame."

Miss Naismith touched the fringes of her red dress. "You'd think I was a liar if I told you how much I paid for this dress. Why, it's actually a *gown*, that's how much it cost. And nobody to see it." Her black eyes peeked at him from under the bangs strewn so artlessly on her forehead.

No telegram from the county jail asking him to come at once ever contained a greater appeal than this girl's rasping moo of disappointment. Still, clinging to his resolve to return home early, he could only offer to take Miss Naismith with him if she were willing to leave at once.

She debated, looking down on the roistering below. A

man Mark had not seen before was performing for Babe and her guests. Babe herself was perched in the middle of the buffet table, holding her stomach with sobs of glee, watching the performer, a shockingly obese young man, as he went through some obscene pantomime. It took Mark a moment to understand that the fat creature was aping a mental defective in sexual transports.

"That's him," Miss Naismith sniffed. "The fat one I came with. He'll have to get up awfully early in the morning to get anywhere in the flickers, if you ask me."

On this morning, then, Mark thought, he was up with the birds. For Seymour Pentlove, tucked behind the radio speaker in his aloof way, was looking on in actual nausea, though this in no way lessened his apparent interest in the promising clown. "Shall we go?" Mark asked.

"If you insist," said Miss Naismith with a queenly lift of her head.

Passing the living room Mark waved to Babe, cocking his head that she not interrupt her entertainment to bid him good-bye. He took Miss Naismith out into the night. "I hope," he said, "you won't mind missing bobbing for apples in the bidet."

"That kid stuff!" Miss Naismith said scathingly.

Once in the car ("Oh, a Marmon," Miss Naismith said. "I kind of like a Cadillac." "My wife prefers the Cad, too," said Mark), Miss Naismith chattered of all manner of things saving her address, until, driving down the Boulevard, Mark knew that for her the evening had just begun. She was so violently pretty she was absurd, her eyes alight with a fierce possessive joy as she looked to her right down Vine at the Famous Players-Lasky Studios. Faced with the prospect of aimlessly driving all over Hollywood or bluntly demanding to know where he might rid himself of her, Mark vacillated, asking, "Would you like to go somewhere for a drink?"

"I thought you were going to give me the air," she blurted, gasped at the admission, and sought to repair her dignity by adopting a regal manner. "If you insist."

He took her to a speakeasy he disliked, as did Constance, though most girls clamored to be taken there. They sat in the bow windows of what had once been a most recherché harlots' house, fumbling in the near-dark for their drinks, sharing a round table no larger than a Ouija board between them. There was a steel band which Miss Naismith found beneath her notice as competition, while she twanged at him sorrowfully, "If I could just meet someone! One teensy break. If I could get a knock-down to someone important, maybe they'd give me a screen test. And then I'd be on my way!"

"You'll never make it sitting up half the night in a speak, starlet," he said, wishing he had left her to the tender mercy of Mr. Pentlove.

"Starlet," she echoed mournfully. "That's a hot one."

His head started to ache. He thought to himself, if she says "silver screen" once more, I'll groan aloud. Belatedly Miss Naismith remembered that it was her duty to entertain a man, not use him as a wailing wall, and under their Ouija board her thin knees bumped his, while she sparkled at him in the gloom. It came to him that going to bed with her would be like embracing a pinwheel. On the heels of this thought came one of Constance moving like mist under him in the dark, and he said brusquely, "I'm afraid we must go." The lawyer in him demanded point-blank that she inform him of her address, and she complied meekly.

Muffin Naismith lived in a bungalow court not far from Vine. She led him to the first semi-detached cottage to the left of the entrance. A smoke tree in full bloom filtered the light from the street lamp, so that her skin was faint lavender and her mouth purple as the blossoms. She gave the disquieting appearance of having some rich poisoned wine flowing through her veins. Key in the door, she offered her purple lips so conscientiously that it would have been a shocking breach of etiquette on Mark's part not to have kissed her. Genteel as a lady accordion teacher, Miss Naismith surmised that she "expected he would like to come in?" Declining, he very nearly made his graceful escape, but she called him back. "Don't you want my phone number?"

"Oh. Well. You don't want to waste your time on an old married man like me."

For an instant her mouth grew tight with exasperation.

"I'm in the phone book," she said airily, recovering. "Under the name of Sally Mae Werksmith. That was the girl who had this bungalow before me. I thought it was such a coincidence. Her name being Werksmith and mine Naismith. Isn't that a howl?"

"It's dangerously close to being one. Good night."

Again he almost made good that casual leavetaking of his, gaining the curb before she called after him, "You remember, hear? Sally Mae Werksmith. In the *book!*"

Somewhat annoyed and altogether amused, he said too low for her to hear, "If you insist."

Driving up into the hills, Mark reflected on Constance's unjust insinuations. Were he conducting himself like a Hollywood youngblood, he would, this instant, be asserting himself in Miss Muffin Naismith's bed. For if he, in his heart, thought himself to be toadying to scum, then Miss Naismith could rightfully be looked upon as one of the minor compensations. In Hollywood as elsewhere, in Hollywood in particular, fidelity to the marriage vows rarely went hand in hand with infidelity to self.

In truth, he wished he could talk to Constance about the girl. To learn if a member of her own sex would find Miss Naismith somehow pathological, as he did. The town abounded in Muffin Naismiths, and in days to come he might be required to have dealings with them. It seemed to him that, like her counterparts, she suffered as if from a pestilence. Aside from her diversionary tactics—her command of the current vulgate, her winning and shameless entreaties to him to help her further her aims—there was an unhealthiness about her. It came to him that deep within her, like a dark growth, vanity pulsed in a secret and perpetual ecstasy.

What, then, pulsed in Constance? But he shrank from dissecting her, he thought of the wife he had been so set on marrying only in terms usually applied to the unattainable. Last Christmas when he had thought to buy her a comb for her unbobbed hair, his instinct led him past diamante and seed pearls to the calm decorum of jade.

Rounding the first bend off Vine Street hill, he saw that

high above him Constance had neglected to turn on the blue bulb in the solarium.

Letting himself into the house, he knew at once it was empty, though a false welcome burned in the chandelier. The dining room was dark, the tile floor creaking as it cooled in the night air. To his left the art-nouveau lamp in the living room cast its ugly blood-and-bile light on the message pad; though the pad itself bore only the impressions of a shopping list made earlier in the week. He went to the solarium and twisted the blue bulb to life.

He informed himself heartily that she could be any number of places, doing a multitude of things. Constance was a whiz at contract bridge (Mark, darling, no one plays auction any more), and she was a master strategist in that total war known loosely as the Junior League. She was a whippet on the tennis court; and she never never said "*The* Messiah" when referring to Handel's masterpiece, though most of the young matrons of the Lovers of Music Society never never said anything else. In brief, she was correct, proper, yet managed to live in that impromptu whirl that could take her anywhere on a summer's night.

He knew, of course, where she was.

After two in the morning he called Pasadena, and his mother-in-law, that doughty defender of the It Just Isn't Done standard of conduct, answered the phone as promptly as if she had been sitting by it.

"I want to talk to my wife," Mark said.

"Mark, I do hope you're not going to make this any more unpleasant than it need be. Creating scenes will not help matters."

"*What* matters?"

"What matters is that Constance has finally decided on a sensible course of action," his mother-in-law said, twisting meanings with practiced art.

"I'm coming out to get my wife right now."

"That will not be possible. She has separated from you."

He was close to tears. "But she can't. What is this? When I left her earlier this evening—"

"You left her a good deal earlier than this evening, Mark.

You married a decent girl and then expected her to associate with squalid movie people. And when she would not—"

"Those 'squalid movie people,' as you call them, constitute my practice of law!"

"Then may you continue rejoicing in them, for my daughter does not."

The phone went dead.

His pride said jauntily: *So let that be an end to it. It was fun while it lasted.* In rejoinder his hurt whimpered: *Brother, you said a mouthful.* And they shook hands on it.

He was paralyzed. However he prowled the routine of his life, however he brooded, fulminated, and lay awake abject with longing, Mark could not bring himself to make a move in Constance's direction. On the third day of their separation a process-server known to him sidled into his office and with an apologetic simper handed Mark a complaint. Constance, wanting a divorce, had applied to a correct superannuated attorney who had reduced to a paragraph or so the correct superannuated allegations of Mark's marital misbehavior. It would, needless to say, be unthinkable of him to file an answer, to contest the divorce. As for community property, Constance had frostily declared there was none. Mark called the correct attorney and waxed grandiloquent on the subjects of the bank account and the house and even their stock of liquor which was worth hundreds—was priceless, in fact, when one took into consideration the drought of Prohibition and the great American thirst. To all this the very correct attorney replied that Mrs. D'Andor wished nothing of Mr. D'Andor, and that Mrs. D'Andor had been steadfast—nay, adamant—in her refusal to recognize the existence of any community property. Yes, regrettable, Mrs. D'Andor wished nothing of him but her freedom, but still he, the very correct attorney, though in sympathy with Mr. D'Andor's distress, was very very confident that Mr. D'Andor would let Mrs. D'Andor take her decree by default, and permit all concerned to part with sincerest feelings of good will.

Mark drank an appreciable amount of the liquid assets of the community property before nightfall had properly set in. In the murk of dusk he drifted into a high alcoholic content, and in that state denied that Constance had meant to deal him a savage hurt. Her refusal of all that he had sought to provide for her was not indicative of the desire to wound—not in the light of the snug wealth to which she had returned—but at worst an unintentional slight. She was never one to slam a door behind her.

He had finally met a casual leavetaking that surpassed his own and could not recognize it, much less begin to understand. She had even left her perfume lamp behind, and he went down into their bedroom and lit it; then to lie on their bed, breathing jasmine, trying to fix it once and for all in his mind that the woman he had been in a veritable panic to have had dropped in on his life for a spell, then calmly strolled away.

As for any recovery from Constance, his prospects were bleak. In this frame of mind he found himself obtaining the phone number of one Sally Mae Werksmith.

"Is this Miss Werksmith?"

"Miss Werksmith is not here," Muffin Naismith said carefully. "Would you like to leave a message?"

"Thank you, but that won't be necessary. I just wanted to take her to dinner tonight."

"Oh." Muffin cleared her throat. "Mind if I ask who is this?"

"High time you did."

There was a pause during which he envisioned the girl clearly, her black eyes hard on the mouthpiece of the phone as if she could force it to give up the secret of his identity. Reluctant to take the smallest chance with her silver-screen career, she could not decide whether to welcome him or deal with him severely as a masher. "You said you are who?" she parried.

I should say John Barrymore, he thought. Or D. W. Griffith. He disgusted himself, the temptation for the hurt to be heartless offered itself over and over to him these days. "Just Mark D'Andor," he said. "Will you tell Miss Werksmith how sorry I am not to find her in? And that I'll call again some—"

Muffin interrupted with all the determination of a zealot

seizing the floor at a town meeting. "Oh, cut it out! You're
wicked. You know good and well I told you this girl who had
this phone before I did was named Werk—"

"I'll be at your door in fifteen minutes."

"What's the matter, couldn't you scare up any movie
star for tonight?"

"I thought I made it clear to you. My name is D'Andor,
not De Mille."

"What's more, you've got your nerve calling me at nine
o'clock for a date."

"Nine? My God, so it is. You probably had your dinner
hours ago." He was unabashedly contrite.

Her silence was inscrutable. Somehow he could not
attribute it to mere pique. "Muffin?" he said in the command-
ing tone he would have used on a shilly-shallying witness.

With great delicacy she said, "Well, ordinarily I eat
dinner—" she seemed to be searching for just the right words
"—I eat dinner . . . very fewly."

Dammit, he thought, and tried to imagine how Constance
would look had she to make the admission that she went
around hungry half the time. The dogged misery in the girl's
voice had him chattering briskly, "Really, I didn't know it
was so late. Won't you reconsider and—" She'd collapse
from hunger, he was telling himself, while spending her last
nickel on a call to Central Casting. "—an exception this
time?" And swallow your pride, he advised her soundlessly;
since it's not nourishment it will leave plenty of room for a
steak.

"If you insist," Muffin said, both grudging and gracious.

Her door was open, she was sitting on a pull-down bed
that occupied most of the room. Other than the bed there
was an easy chair, and a tile-inset table bearing a neatly
stacked pile of movie magazines. She was framed by a kitch-
enette consisting of a sink and hotplate; all that met his eyes
was defiantly immaculate. She was sewing a label into the
neck of a red jacket, and greeted him between snappings
at the thread with her small glittering teeth. "Absquatulate!"
she ordered him briskly, and when he rather hovered just
within the door, not certain he had heard her aright, she trans-

lated, "Siddown! I got to finish getting this label sewn in."
He took the chair, then had to lean forward to admire the
label she was exhibiting to him with an air of triumph. "I.
Magnin," she said, plying her needle. "I got three now. Course
I have to go to a different dry-cleaner's every time."

"Oh?" Mark murmured blankly.

"Cert! You bring 'um in a gawment, and when you come
back for it, you yell your head off that they snitched your
I. Magnin label. Maybe they didn't exactly snitch yours, but
you can bet your boots they did someone's. They sell good
labels up to a buck. Fifty cents, I. Magnin. They got 'em, all
right," she snorted sagely. "And since they don't remember
which one had which, you got 'em over a barrel if you yell
loud enough." She nipped at the thread, and held up for his
admiration the label attached to her shabby jacket with expert
stitching. Jumping to her feet, she nevertheless took time to
smooth the worn coverlet where her fragile flanks had
depressed it. She was wearing her red "gown," and he was
actually intrigued to discover that the worn jacket matched
the shrill hue of the gown exactly. The hours she must have
spent to achieve this perfect mating—while eating fewly—
caused him to view her for the first time with something
approaching respect. Helping her into the jacket, not letting
his glance quite move to the bed, he found himself staring at
her for the second time, while she patiently repeated what
she had just said. "Look, could you lend me a quarter?"

He gave her the coin without comment. She popped it
into an envelope, already addressed, and licked the flap.
"Thanks, kid." She tapped the envelope to make certain that
the coin was securely trapped within. "Armand Beauty
Cream," Muffin said. "Fill out the coupon and enclose twenty-
five cents in coin or stamps, and you get the Beauty Cream
and the Armand Genuine Cold Cream Powder, that soft dry
wonderfully ad-heering powder made with a base of cold
cream. Say, speaking of stamps, d'you happen to have one
on you?"

Mark's love of wild animals was plumped out with pleasure watching Muffin eat. He tried not to smile on her openly,

when, her own plate cleaned, her black eyes darted covertly to his roll, his potatoes, and most of his steak. He began to tell her of a former client who excused his shooting someone with the explanation: "I wasn't aiming at him, honest. I was just firing into the air, and he came out and bumped into the bullets," and during the telling quietly substituted his plate for hers. When at last she was replete, leaning back in her chair, over which the jacket was draped with the I. Magnin label prominently displayed, he caught her wrist to satisfy himself on a certain point. He was right in his surmise, her wrist was no larger in circumference than a monocle. She began to confide in him, her pallor gone and a rosy eupepsia in its place. She was working as a stenographer—temporarily. And though she was not one to raise her voice in her own behalf, her acquaintances and co-workers felt themselves under no such restraint, spending a good part of their working day informing Muffin how pretty she was, and declaring themselves at a loss to understand how anyone, having seen Muffin Naismith, could ever look on Jeanne Eagels with anything but pity. In brief, the consensus was that Muffin Naismith was the nerts.

She was not, however, and contrary to her articulate co-workers, the nerts in bed. Under the single bulb over the pull-down bed, and divested of her red-fringed gown, she was as bloodless and as enthusiastic as a mushroom. She lay under Mark as crumpled as if he had felled her with a blow to the head, and he, having proceeded too far to retreat, could only hasten with all dispatch to a sketchy climax; feeling with his jerking movements and flickers of erotic satiation as the male lead must in one of those crude spasmotic movies shown for stags.

Relieved of his weight, Muffin eased up on her elbows and sparkled anxiously at him, wanting to be rewarded like any good little animal who had tried very hard to turn her tricks. Mark closed his eyes and patted her. There was no way, to be sure, he could ask her how she expected to advance herself by the granting of her favors, when she was totally unlettered in the disciplines of love.

"Now tell me," she wheedled, "who all you know." She bounced about like a restless brat.

Not opening his eyes he said, "Why—let's see. I know a goodly number of attorneys, and a badly number of boot-leggers. And I——"

"Stop razzing me! You know what I mean. *Connections.*"

He made a mental survey of the list of connections he knew, or for whom he had performed demeaning legal serv-ices ("Aha!" his mind commented slyly, "demeaning?"), and he visualized their playful cruelty were he to elect one of them to immortalize this thin prattling creature on her sacred silver screen.

"Well?" she pouted.

As a means of gaining time he sat up to reach for his flask, but found his attention caught by numerous bruises on her flanks and inner thighs. "What the hell?" he asked plaintively. "Did I do that?"

She hugged her knees. "If you must know, yes."

"Well, I'm a fine one. Believe me, I am very sorry. Why didn't you tell me I was battering you black and——"

With softspoken pride she cut through his self-reproaches. "Oh, you couldn't help it. I've got the Devil's Pinch, you know."

"The what?"

"Devil's Pinch. That's what they call it when tender people like me bruise so easy. A breath, I mean it, a breath of wind can do it." She touched a bruise as fondly as if it were an accomplishment.

"Surely some doctor——"

"Oh, no," Muffin contradicted him, offended. "I've got it real severe. I'm the despair of doctors. No kiddin', the *despair.*"

He knew better, he told himself, than to try belittling (by suggesting it is curable) a woman's pet infirmity. "I'm sorry to hear that," he mumbled inanely.

Muffin grinned and bestowed an accolade on him. "You're the first guy in I don't know how long to take on about it, though."

She was being game about it. No man who could help her

in the slightest was ever going to leave her bed feeling himself anything less than one hell of a fellow. There were some, he supposed, who took delight in the bruising, thinking it proved them manly.

Muffin read his thoughts. "Yeah, some of them think they're real he-men, all right. I don't tell 'em different."

He pulled her down and held her lightly, thinking that her prettiness was a calamity. No harelip, no withered limb could warp the life of the average moviegoing girl like the congenital defect of beauty.

Muffin snuggled, asking with mindless amiability, "How's the wife?"

"She's divorcing me."

"Gee whiz, that's too bad."

He harbored no doubts of her sincerity. "Never mind."

"Yeah, but do you mind?"

"Yes."

Muffin rested her chin on his shoulder. "Nice guy like you, she'll come back. And then everything will be jake. Meantime, want Muffin to come take care of you, Daddy? You know, cook for you?"

He thought her transparency disarming. "That's nice of you, but we have a housekeeper of sorts to do that. Swat dust around and throw a casserole together, when the mood strikes her."

"Did you say *we*? You mean you had a housekeeper even with her there? Your wife must be haywire to walk out on a set-up like that. Where'd she go?"

"Home to Pasadena."

Muffin was scornful. "Oh, one of those rich Pasadena stuffed-shirt types. I met a real classy guy from Pasadena once." She laughed without rancor. "He thought he was too good for me. I just laughed it off when he never showed up again."

"That is the wisest possible course to follow."

Her arm crept around his chest. "Let's talk about important people. Big producers and movie stars and all. Now, who *do* you know?"

CHAPTER FIVE

If Hollywood stayed up at night to play, it never-theless rose at an early hour, submitting without complaint to the Spartan demands of fame. Wise to the habits of the industry, Mark put in a cautious call to Mr. Pentlove on the stroke of seven. The producer was alert and, for him, perky, his orange juice and coffee an hour in his past.

"Any developments in re the Golden Ass?" Mark asked noncommitally.

"None that I know of," Mr. Pentlove replied, sounding so at ease now that everything was in Mark's hands that Mark nearly succumbed to an old half-forgotten surge of self-esteem. To have Pentlove entrust Mark with two million dollars was indeed to honor his past performances and legal services.

Mark said, "I trust, then, that our mutual friend remained undisturbed."

"He sounded fit and calm when I spoke to him a few moments ago." A note of disapproval seeped into Mr. Pent-love's voice. "Though he was still in bed."

"Let the dog lie. I think I'll begin by asking a few ques-tions of your cowboy of last night. You gave me his address, but what is his first name?"

Mr. Pentlove chuckled. "He is none other than the cele-brated T-Bone Tredwell. Mr. T-Bone Tredwell, the stunt man."

Mark smiled ironically, as if for Mr. Pentlove's benefit, applauding that gentleman's cheeriness. Mark rang off and devoted himself to his coffee. He would not have said he was hung over, but rather that his body, his very flesh felt glum. His tongue was oddly unacquainted with his teeth, his dental arch seemed subtly to have rearranged itself during his sleep. Though his hands were steady, they were not as hands properly should be—weightless tools which performed conscientiously and well. He was aware that the hands of a drunk gave away more secrets than those of the most loquacious deaf-mute.

But for time's being of the essence Mark would have walked to the first destination of his day, in order to ventilate his mildewed mind. Below the crest which his house topped there ambled a street like a downhill gully, known as the Gulch. Here was the Hollywood ghetto whose denizens were cowboys, extras, stunt men, and aging he-vamps. At nightfall Mary Pickfords well in their middle years emerged, their hair in long yellow curls thick as mailing tubes, and their feet, clad in ankle sox, thrust into spike-heeled pumps. The Gulchers were the hewers of wood and carriers of water peculiar to the monolithic enterprises of Hollywood, to which they clung as doggedly as if they had been indentured. The southern stretch of the Gulch took unto itself another name—Poverty Row; here were clustered the barnlike structures where cheapie movies were ground out as fast as the cameramen could crank with their overdeveloped right arms.

One of the seasoned citizens of the Gulch was Mr. T-Bone Tredwell, who dwelt in a shack located in the back yard of a bungalow. At seven-fifteen that morning Mark's car disrupted the quiet as he searched for T-Bone's number. The narrow lane of the Gulch was lined with flivvers and an occasional roadster, all parked heading downhill; on working days, the Gulchers coasted out of gear down to Poverty Row, and used the engines only at the close of day to chug home. Mark spied the bungalow behind which T-Bone resided, almost hidden by a sorrowful Packard on blocks.

Shaded by pepper trees, the hut had a screened porch overgrown with wild roses which were being mined by an agreeable lazy work shift of honeybees. Looking through a sizable hole in the screen, Mark beheld T-Bone himself lolling on an old car seat, a former furnishing, Mark decided, of the Packard put to pasture at the curb. Mr. Tredwell's boots rested on a low table that was a slice cut from a redwood tree and propped up on bricks and several Sears, Roebuck catalogues. Next his boots was a cracked plate smeared with streaks of egg, to the consternation of two bees who were mucking about in the mess and not knowing what to make of it. T-Bone was enjoying a mug of coffee, and this he waved at Mark, saying, "Walk right in." His walnut-meat face was incurious; at a glance one knew him to be a man who took what life offered without comment.

T-Bone extended a hand without rising and, the handshake over, waved his coffee mug at the table. Mark lowered himself gingerly to the slice of redwood.

"Don't let them bees bother you," T-Bone said, "they come around regular." In recognition of Mark's precarious perch on the table's edge, he pushed the plate aside with one booted foot, so that Mark might make himself more comfortable. "I guessed you'd be wanting to ask me some questions," he volunteered. He rubbed one of his boots along the front exactly as if it itched. After a brief consultation with himself he offered almost shyly, "Want some coffee?"

Mark promptly accepted, experience having taught him that one who is playing host will usually impart information more readily than the person who sits rigid (and therefore suspicious) like a stranger. There was chicory in the coffee, and Mark savored it, never having outgrown a boyhood penchant for the homey weed. To add to the festivities, Mark placed his opened tin of flat fifties on the table, and T-Bone with a grunt of appreciation tucked one cigarette behind his battered ear and lighted another. "I was always all thumbs with makin's," he confessed.

"Help yourself," Mark said. "Now, Mr. Tredwell, as a lawyer I find there are certain personal questions I must ask you. About Miss Naismith. Would you tell me why she was called Mrs. Tredwell?"

"I told you last night she wasn't my wife."

"Mr. Pentlove and I appreciate that fact."

T-Bone received this with wonderment. "You do? Horsefeathers, it wasn't as if I stayed single as a favor to Mr. P, or anything."

Ahem, Mark's mind said, please to continue, Counsel. "Then how did she come to be identified as your wife?"

"Well, that was just ribbing. But when Mr. P asked me to help him go get poor Muffin, I went along with the gag."

"To accommodate Mr. Pentlove? To do him a favor?" Mark corrected himself.

"Well, I figured he wouldn't kick me off the lot if we met up again, and that's for goldarn," T-Bone admitted candidly. "Only I kind of liked Muffin. I was really sorry to hear she—" T-Bone hesitated, then said reverently "—you know, departed. I figure Mr. P had it in mind to fix her up a real nice grave and all. Muffin would of liked that—this big cheese taking care of the—remains. He might not of known she was alive, but he sure knew she was dead." His smile was melancholy. "Poor Muffin, she finally snagged the big cheese's attention. She told me once she would of died for the chance. And she did."

"You sound as if you and Miss Naismith were quite friendly."

"She wasn't my sweetheart or anything like that. Just a nice woman. Her and I met on the lot. I was one of the stunt men on The Feeb's last picture. And she was in some crowd scene in something else. So we tied on the feedbag a couple of times. But she was picky, get me?"

"You are saying that Miss Naismith was selective in her choice of friends?"

"Horsefeathers, not her! That was her big trouble. Go out with guys I wouldn't trust a good-lookin' sheep with. No, I mean *picky*. We'd be eating somewhere and she'd be all over me about 'Hold your fork like this.' Or 'Take your spoon outa your cup, that's a booby trap.' Pickin' on people. *Picky*."

Mark nodded, remembering her habit of fault-finding when her inner discontent became insupportable.

"So," T-Bone continued, "I started to calling her Ma. Only she didn't cotton to that, her being a good deal younger than me. So then I'd just say, 'Yes, ma'am, Mrs. Tredwell, no, ma'am.' Like she was a nagging wife. It was just a joke." Again T-Bone rubbed the front of his boot thoughtfully. "Funny thing, when they took her to the hospital, that they would say she was my wife."

"She had no identification on her person," Mark said.

"And the other women undoubtedly took her for your wife when you called her Mrs. Tredwell."

"Would I of left my wife at the Eden?" T-Bone demanded indignantly.

"Tell me about that last evening you saw her," Mark said, wishing to hew to the topic.

"Nothing much to tell. We started out for a bite and maybe a drink or some such, and—"

"Excuse me. Would you give me her address?"

"Now that," T-Bone declaimed, "*is* funny. I didn't know. She moved to this new place after I met her. She was living in some fleabag hotel before that, and before that she told me she was living with some old guy who had a castle and all the money in the world and was crazy about her and she had to run away from him in the middle of the night or he would have set the dogs after her. Muffin could sure spin a yarn, I'll hand her that."

So she could, Mark agreed privately, but that one, in substance, was true.

"I'll always remember how mad she got when I called her Big Ben one time. Like a clock, is what I meant. Tick-talk, tick-talk. Blew her stack."

"About that last time you saw her," Mark prompted patiently.

"Yeh. Well, she and me set off right from work. She wanted to drink some first, and then we'd eat. She'd get a snootful if you didn't watch her; not to be speakin' evil of the dead, but she would. So that night, Saturday, we was in this speak, and I was figuring it was time to get her to put on the feedbag when she sees The Feeb coming in. And if she hadn't," T-Bone put in as an aside, "she'd be alive today. Or if I hadn't let her talk me into taking her to that speak near the Eden. I like to hang around my own water hole, but she always wanted to go where the big-timers were. And The Feeb was the one came in that night." With sudden heat T-Bone demanded, "Wouldn't it have to be him? Any other star and Muffin would be okay. That's what she liked about being with me," T-Bone explained with a mixture of modesty and quiet assertion, "everybody knows me and always says hello."

"And The Feeb said hello?"

"Sure he did. And Muffin was all one big glad eye. She put on this English-accenty act, and started tryin' to tell The Feeb she knew him when, and gets him and this dollie with him to sit down with us."

"What was the girl's name?"

"Dunno," T-Bone said, and paid strict attention to rubbing his boot. He was a laughable liar. "Anyway, she should of been home with her school books. He likes peepies."

"Peepies?"

"Little chickens."

"I merely wanted to make sure," Mark murmured.

"And he treats 'em sickening. He's the whole time putting his fat hands where he shouldn't, under the table, y'know, and this kid with him just sits there looking scared and misseribill."

There was a pause and Mark spoke into it to preserve the flow of revelations. "Then what?"

"Why, Muffin says we should all make a night of it, and The Feeb takes her up on it and says let's all go to his bungalow at the Eden. And we do."

"Just the four of you?"

T-Bone drank some of his cold coffee, the protruding spoon handle scratching against his Saturday-morning beard. "If you want the truth, I wouldn't of gone with The Feeb on Muffin's say-so. But the peepie give me a look saying 'Help.' " T-Bone fell to ruminating. "And I don't feel sorry for what I did. I feel sorry for Muffin, but not what I did."

"What did you do?"

"Well, after we got to the Eden, Muffin really showed what a bottle-baby she could be. She kept her nose in a glass mosta the time. And The Feeb was trying to get this little dollie to go into the bedroom with him. Only she wouldn't. She kept getting closer and closer to me, I thought she'd climb in my shirt next. So about the time some pimp and a couple floozies come in—"

"What were their names?"

"Names?" T-Bone looked at Mark as if humoring a precocious child. "People like that don't have any," he said flatly. "You just yell 'Hey, Toots,' or something, and whistle. And they come."

"Go on then, please."

"So I said to The Feeb's dollie that I'd take her home, this was her chance to break clean. Only . . ." T-Bone suddenly presented an expression of chagrin, remorse, and confoundment. "Only Muffin wasn't having any. She wanted to stay on with The Feeb and the floozies. I mean, Muffin was *fast,* yeah, but to—— She told me to go on with the kid, and not come back. She was going to make whoopee with Feeb. So I and the dollie left."

"What time was this?"

"Ohhhh . . . around midnight."

"And where did you deposit the dollie?"

"At her home," T-Bone said, his tone adding, "and let that be an end to it."

"The address?"

T-Bone shook his head.

"Are you trying to protect the girl because you're interested in her?" Mark asked, all understanding.

"The girl? Horsefeathers!" T-Bone exploded. "She's seventeen years old!"

"Oh?"

T-Bone grinned. "I did kinda take a shine to her mother, though. She's a widow, and we got to recollecting, and sure enough her husband and I was both in *Birth of a Nation!* Small world, you sometimes wonder if it's bigger'n a baby's fist."

"Did you go back at all to the Eden?"

T-Bone was shamed. "That's where I done wrong, I admit it. But the widow was so glad I'd drug her kid away from The Feeb, you see. She said she hoped I hadn't ruined my evening." T-Bone grinned feebly. "Anyway, she had this way all figured out to make it up to me."

"You never saw nor heard from Miss Naismith again?"

"I should be tarred and feathered for admittin' it. But— no."

"Did you know she was pregnant?"

T-Bone shifted uncomfortably. "Some of the women at

the studio were talking of it. But I never put any stock in women's gabble." He looked at Mark with an open countenance. "Mr. P said that's how come she died, so I guess it was true. Only I can tell you, it wasn't mine."

"Whose, then?"

T-Bone took to rubbing his other boot. "Search me."

"I'm sorry, but it will be necessary for me to know the name and address of the young girl you took home," Mark said.

T-Bone complied reluctantly, then burst out, "Whyn't you people just let poor Muffin do like the Ben-Hur slaves? And that goes for the coroner feller too."

"I don't understand."

"Like Ben-Hur," T-Bone repeated as if Mark were proving himself backward. "The wop extras that was the slaves and soldiers on the galley. All in chains and armor. When the director said for them to jump into the sea—remember?—they did."

"Yes?"

"They sunk from sight," T-Bone said. "What else?"

CHAPTER SIX

Seymour Pentlove thought himself suddenly stricken by doubts, and was relieved to find it was only a touch of hyperacidity. The making of movies starring The Feeb and ridiculing the torments of a low-grade moron left his sensibilities intact. What the public was fool enough (and cruel enough) to enjoy concerned Mr. Pentlove only insofar as it could be turned to the making of money. But to find himself involved, even if at one remove, in the smut surrounding the death of a harlot, and having as a consequence to depend on a has-been and a drunk like D'Andor he found unsettling. If, in times past, D'Andor never brought less than his best to a case, the present might prove otherwise. Yet Mr. Pentlove knew better than to request that the lawyer share the burden with some more highly respected colleague. Still, if some remnant of pride had inspired D'Andor to answer Mr. Pentlove's summons for help, then it might very well resurrect the ingrained tenacity of the dedicated defense attorney. Once the matter was safely disposed of, D'Andor could slink back into deepest obscurity, for all Mr. Pentlove cared.

Viewing the calm of the Saturday morning from his bedroom balcony, he could not but congratulate himself, doubts about D'Andor aside. For all those who could link The Feeb with the dead woman were under Mr. Pentlove's thumb, or within easy crushing reach. Let that hysterical woman at the Snowdom Sanitarium babble as she would of "Mrs. Tredwell's" dying declarations, the trail would end at the office of the sottish Mark D'Andor. And lawyers, Mr. Pentlove had heard, could always claim some sort of "privilege"—he was hazy as to the exact technical ramifications—that legally permitted them to keep their mouths firmly shut.

Years ago Mr. Pentlove had dallied briefly with a young woman who spoke of D'Andor in highest terms of praise. She had committed a heinous crime. It was a matter of homicide, but to Mr. Pentlove's mind falling afoul of the law while unknown and penniless was the ultimate felony in the first degree. Fortunately, Fate and the tip of another lady jailbird had brought D'Andor—himself unknown, but determined to remedy that—to save the silly woman and place her feet on the path of righteousness. Which path had crossed that of Mr. Pentlove's, then continued on to a husband and home in Santa Barbara.

Thus it was that when Babe Wilmot phoned Mr. Pentlove to give him the gladsome news that she had bumped off her husband, the name of Mark D'Andor sprang to his mind.

"He was a seaworthy one in those days," Mr. Pentlove said to himself sagely. "Watertight when it came to sentimentality and crackpot ethics. No bilge in his hold." These nautical musings stemmed from Mr. Pentlove's horror of ever finding himself all at sea.

Indeed, for the rest of his days he would never forget the way D'Andor had strolled into Babe's bedroom, wrinkled his nose at the fumes of perfume, murmured a few words to Mr. Pentlove, dismissed the chauffeur, asked one question of Babe, and then, without warning, neatly broke her jaw. "I hope," D'Andor had next said to the stunned Babe, "I didn't damage any of your teeth. But you see, your self-defense story had to be spruced up a bit. Also, this way you won't be able to talk to the police."

"Admirable," Mr. Pentlove had breathed.

"Will you call her doctor, please?" D'Andor said to Mr. Pentlove. Then returning to the slobbering, grunting Babe, he lifted her back onto the bed, soothing her, "The doctor will ease the pain. That's it, don't try to talk. . . . Soon the doctor will take away the pain. . . ."

On the witness stand Babe's testimony consisted of moans, nods, and mouthings, owing to the fact that her teeth were wired together. A pity that some intern on the prison ward had been permitted to fool around with that lovely jaw. The swelling on the right side became permanent. Ah well, the talkies would have overtaken her, and Babe always did sound like chronic tonsillitis.

Continuing to muse in metaphors (Mr. Pentlove had trained himself to do so—after all, that's all movies were), he wondered what it was that had sunk the seaworthy D'Andor and all hands lost. His wife had died under circumstances pointing to suicide. But that, surely, cast only an interesting sidelight on the man's nature.

But there, this Feeb Forbes mess might be the very case the man had been needing to rehabilitate himself. Get all shipshape again. The Industry could never suffer from a surfeit of good lawyers so long as the lads and lasses of filmdom committed everything from bigamy to mayhem with a polo mallet, and all in the sweet name of frolic.

Mr. Pentlove leaned over his bedroom balcony to favor his pate with the sun. From this position he was able to see a Ford, self-important with polish, turn into his drive. Mr. Pentlove's spirits lifted, for this visitor he recognized as being Ted Savant, a studio cop and therefore one of those stalwarts who acted as game wardens to the wild life of Hollywood. Not infrequently the Ted Savants of the town beggared the efforts of the metropolitan police, especially when it came to investigation, stilling wagging tongues, and concealment. Mr. Pentlove approved mightily of Ted; here indeed was a man who was not only seaworthy but seagoing, carrying as he was valuable cargo for Mr. Pentlove. A young girl was Ted's sole passenger, and Mr. Pentlove lingered on his balcony to watch Ted unload her. Savant exited the car, his hair polished and glowing no less than the Ford or his Sam Browne belt. He walked around the car and started for the side portico, while the girl sat on in queenly languor waiting for someone (a footman, perhaps? Mr. Pentlove asked of himself, highly diverted by this scene) to come open her door for her. Without stopping Savant looked over his shoulder and snapped, "You a cripple er somethin? Get movin." With a toss of her head—blondined tufts flying, all but the spit-curls glued to her cheeks with mucilage—she opened her door and thrust out a finely turned leg. Mr. Pentlove saw again a cosmetic practice so abhorrent he would almost rather have seen his daughters amputees than practice it. Winding up the Achilles tendon of the girl's bare leg was a tattoo simulating the lace clockwork of a fancy stocking.

With a soft noise of disgust, Mr. Pentlove turned and hastened toward his hideaway office over the portico. In the hallway he encountered any number of daughters (God had not seen fit to bless him with male issue) and shooed them to another part of the house. In a voice quaking with fervor, Mr. Pentlove had once assembled his women to lay down the law: "No, I will *not* invite John Barrymore to dinner. I wish never to see paint upon your faces. I intend to be able to say to the men you will marry that you are pure and unsullied virgins. And the day I will no longer be able to hold up my head in this community is the day one of you will be seen chewing gum! Is that clear?" [Solemn chorus: "Yes, Papa."]

In the center of his hideaway office Savant stood at attention, holding the girl's arm as sternly as if she were a miscreant. Mr. Pentlove entered and seated himself behind the desk. The girl watched him, not quite daring to be sullen.

"Flirt Smith," Savant barked by way of introduction.

Mr. Pentlove took a turn for the hospitable. "And won't you be seated, Miss Smith?"

The girl plunked herself into a chair, crossing her bare decorated legs.

Mr. Pentlove began spurting little civilities like a valet flinging cologne into the air of a musty room. "So good of you to give me your time, Miss Smith. Miss *Flirt* Smith? Nice. Concise. Memorable. Would go well on a marquee."

Miss Smith took out a cigarette and tapped it nervously on a thumbnail. Tapped it and tapped it. She squared her jaw. "I don't know anything," she said, at once positive and argumentative. "So tell your bully-boy to take me home."

Savant remained motionless at his post, blocking the door.

"About what? Anything about what?" Mr. Pentlove cooed.

"What happened to that nutsy dame at the Eden."

"But you do know, don't you, that Mr. Forbes did not harm her in any way?"

"And how'm I to know that?" Miss Flirt Smith challenged, tapping ever harder with the cigarette.

"Because you know that at no time was he alone with—ah—Mrs. Tredwell. Don't you."

Miss Smith looked down the length of her cigarette as if sighting some object to Mr. Pentlove's left. "I do?"

Mr. Pentlove purred, "We are not trying to be headstrong, are we?" When Miss Smith did not find it in her to reply to this, Mr. Pentlove moved on to another subject. "Lovely weather for the beach. How would you like to take a little vacation in a cottage I own just above Malibu? I won't be using it this year."

"Tough titty for you," Miss Smith observed.

Behind her Savant either cleared his throat or growled.

Mr. Pentlove smiled quite as if this were the most charming remark he'd heard in he didn't know when. "The other young lady," he said bracingly, "who was at the Eden has gone on an extended trip."

"She took it on the lam, you mean," Miss Smith said, growing snarly. "She was just a drifter, anyway. But I happen to like it here."

"In that case. . . ." Mr. Pentlove spread his hands.

"The Feeb was locked in the bedroom with that nut and I pounded and pounded on the door to let me in," Miss Flirt Smith said dreamily.

"I see." Mr. Pentlove nodded. "You are a prostitute, are you not? Isn't that—ah—means of livelihood against the law in this—"

Miss Smith laughed with pure unsullied merriment. "Are you kiddin'? This burg is so wide open it's—drafty!"

With his most fatherly manner Mr. Pentlove asked, "Who is your pimp, Miss Smith? It may be that he's the one to talk some sense into your head. Savant, will you find the man, whoever he is, and have him brought here so that I—"

"You want him to bloody my nose for me?" Miss Smith screeched.

"Just for a starter," Mr. Pentlove said.

Miss Smith bent on him an eye green and steady as a go

signal. "The Tredwell dame busted into the bedroom after The Feeb," she said. "He didn't ask her in, I know that."

"Are you an honest person?" Mr. Pentlove asked curiously.

Miss Smith had obviously never consulted herself on the topic, one way or the other. "Why," she said with alarm, "I guess I am!"

Mr. Pentlove beamed. "Good. Good. Because that means that you wouldn't want to see an innocent man punished for something he didn't do. Isn't that right?"

"Well, hell's bells," Miss Smith said, "who would?" She looked at her cigarette to discover she had fractured it with her incessant tapping. Dropping it to the floor, she said, "Are you trying to tell me that The Feeb is in trouble over that dame?"

"Not yet," Mr. Pentlove said cautiously.

Miss Smith leaned forward earnestly. "I was sorry for that Tredwell nut, in a way. But the truth never hurt anyone, and it can't hurt The Feeb. I saw what I saw."

Her version of the hysterical playfulness of Muffin Naismith coincided with that of The Feeb. It dovetailed, with the exception of a few minor incidents. And on those incidents Mr. Pentlove refreshed her memory so that Miss Smith took his instructions for her own truth, and by the light in her green eye gave warning that she intended to hold it fast. Should the need arise, she would do nicely under oath, Mr. Pentlove decided.

When the little interview had drawn to an end, Mr. Pentlove slithered gracefully around his desk to shake the hand of Miss Flirt Smith. His hand came back with money still in it. "Oh, come, Miss Smith!" he protested, genuinely distressed. "Let it be my pleasure."

She dimpled, and he found himself seriously questioning that she could be a day over twenty-two. "Golly," Miss Smith giggled. "I could use it, all righty. I won't lie about that."

"You're not the type to lie about anything," Mr. Pentlove assured her, and tucked the bills into the neckline of her dress. Her flesh was moist. He withdrew his hand at once. His mind barely breathed a sigh: *Alas.*

With Savant gone, the spunky Miss Smith in tow, Mr. Pentlove lit a cigarillo and added to his mental store a new and most delicious way of skinning a cat. By appealing to Miss Flirt Smith's better nature he had obtained what he wanted—Mr. Pentlove's tidy teeth gleamed in a smile of unalloyed derision—and had showed himself the soul of generosity to boot by giving her something under half of what he had been prepared to pay her. Moreover, she had taken to his coaching nicely, absorbing each detail with the trustfulness of a dutiful child. Her pimp, whoever he was, trained his women well.

As for his coaching, Mr. Pentlove decided he would pit Miss Smith against D'Andor as soon as possible. If she held up under his questioning then she could be relied upon.

Like too many laymen, Mr. Pentlove thought a lawyer was only someone on whom to test your best lies. But then, when the legal gentlemen got to nitpicking, it took a clear-sighted layman to see the dog for the fleas.

He thought of Miss Smith's penultimate remark of their session, after learning that the woman she called Mrs. Tredwell was dead. "Aw!" Miss Smith intoned. "The poor nut. I ask you, Mr. Pentlove, isn't that a crappy way to go!"

Where, he asked, are the jazz babies of yesteryear? Miss Smith, for all her tattooed ankles, was of a new breed. He supposed the Depression could account for part of it. There was a shockingly maudlin sympathy for failures and the weak and whining in the air. Only The Feeb and his fellow playmates seemed unaware that one by one the carrousels had broken down, the calliopes had died on a final sorrowful whistle, and the paint on the little wooden steeds was bleeding in the rain.

He lifted his phone and had the operator ring D'Andor's office. The secretary D'Andor shared with another attorney came on with that voice so crisp and decisive that it invariably brought to mind the picture of someone crunching his way through a head of lettuce. But when that good lady, however, learned with whom she had the honor of speaking, an actual lilt accompanied her promise to find Mr. D'Andor as soon as she could. Things, that lilt said, are looking up around here, if the august Seymour Pentlove has deigned to ask for our services again.

CHAPTER SEVEN

In 1919, when Mark D'Andor was admitted to the bar, he was twenty-two years old—though record and repute said he was a couple of years older. He had taken the first written examination ever required by law for admission to the bar, and had presented proof of having studied law—as opposed to "reading" law in somebody or other's law offices —in an accredited institution. Among the legal lights of this world the fledgling lawyer and bridegroom had sworn to uphold were several militant hen attorneys, one woman on the municipal bench, a Judge Natalie Fickett, who (the scandalmongers said) had received her appointment as recompense for sleeping with the Governor (skeptical scandalmongers asked, "What Governor? Frémont?"), and one woman capper known to all as Chico.

Capping was not considered a profession, but its practitioners unswervingly maintained that they were in the "legal business." Of necessity a capper labored at his business behind bars, for it was his job to approach newly arrested alleged felons and suggest that they retain Attorney X or Attorney Y to defend them, should they have no one particular in mind. In turn, and especially when the case proved lucrative, Attorney X or Y then caused to be delivered to the capper a little cash token of appreciation. The trick, of course, was to be in the right spot at the right time when something big was in the offing, or when the capper felt a sudden need of money. Chico, a fortyish woman of Mexican descent, had her heart set on buying an expensive lace mantilla for her niece's wedding. Chico went down the list of her recent misdemeanors; she was tired of throwing bricks through windows, and it offended her dignity to be drunk and disorderly. She consulted her brother, the father of the bride-to-be. To this good man's mind, as well as Chico's, "Hell, going to jail is no crime!" Chico's brother was of the opinion that she was still a handsome woman. How about soliciting? With misgivings, for she was singularly free of feminine vanity, Chico set out, and to her astonishment was approached and then arrested by the first plainclothes man she encountered. So far so good. But that morning Judge Natalie Fickett suffered from a sour stomach, and when Chico tried to plead guilty, Her Honor would not hear of it, ordering Chico to post bail and go find herself an attorney. Chico wailed and cursed in Spanish. And went. It would be unthinkable, certainly, to enlist the aid of any of the attorneys for whom she capped, and other lawyers, knowing her by reputation, would be leery of—— Chico brightened. Was this not the day the new ones were to be admitted to the bar? She sped on her way. She arrived just as the ceremonies were over.

The one who caught her eye was a thin, eager youth who was so in love with the snooty blonde on his arm that he struck Chico as being more than a little loco. Chico strode over to him and clapped her strong swarthy hand on his shoulder.

"Counsel," Chico boomed, "I have great need of an attorney. I am," she added hastily, "a poor woman with many mouths to feed." Drawing her new attorney to one side, she confided, "I tried to earn bread in the only way a woman knows. But I was arrested."

His ears still ringing with the appellation *Counsel*, Mark D'Andor, for it was he, nodded vigorously. In his fervor he forgot to ask a fee. And also, in his fervor, he won an acquittal for Chico on the grounds that the police officer had approached Chico first and thereby afforded her the defense of entrapment. Chico found herself out on the street, a free woman.

Chico and her brother drank tequila and laughed uproariously; then, all business again, Chico found herself a brick and sallied forth. This time, to his pain and chagrin, Mark could not save her. Chico referred four cases to him. She had a wager with her brother—one lace mantilla—that Mark would not catch on until she had sent him an even dozen. By then, Mark was up to his ears in criminal law.

Chico in her lace mantilla at the wedding looked every inch as if a street in town were named after her grandfather, and her ancestors had been married by a saint.

So it was to Chico that Mark applied to find out quietly what might be doing in the Coroner's Office. She reported that a post-mortem had been performed on the woman tagged as Muffin Naismith. There would be a coroner's inquest at two that afternoon, at the end of which some abortionist was very likely to find himself in great demand.

Mark drove that roadster of his, so like an aging flapper, straight to the car park in back of the Eden.

The Eden consisted of a main hostelry, pink stucco with red tile roof, and a number of bungalows, pink stucco with tile roofs, congregated around a swimming pool, pink tile with red trim. When Mark arrived, sometime after ten in the morning, a party was already in progress—or still in progress. Bungalow Nine would seem to be the situs of the celebration, its door wide open in welcome to any passer-by. Two girls emerged wearing identical swim suits with white tops cut low under the armpits and wide canvas belts cinching the black shorts. Each girl carried a glass of orange juice, and Mark would have said without hesitation the juice was spiked with gin. After the girls came a burly man wearing only the trunks of his suit and the kittenish leer of the tourist having his first fling with "starlets." Mark paused to let the trio pass; it was drawn up in the rear by a woman who pricked Mark's interest. She was showing weariness and wear; close on thirty, she no longer had the resilience to go without sleep. She bore her hangover like a weight, blinking wretchedly in the sunlight. Like her companions she had a glass of orange juice, but Mark would have said without hesitation that hers was not spiked with gin.

A week ago, Mark thought, following the woman's sagging shoulders, Muffin Naismith must have looked like that. A good decade older than her sisters of the party, the strange woman oddly suggested a tired child. She sat herself at the edge of the pool, wincing when her ankles sank into the cool water, and brooded over her orange juice.

Mark continued on toward Bungalow Ten, but a whisper of bare feet caused him to look back. One of the young girls accidentally on purpose was stumbling into the woman, dumping her in the pool. The woman surfaced, hair straight, countenance woebegone. To the laughter of the others she contributed no response, either of good-natured squealings or sputterings of anger. She swam on her side to the edge, carefully holding her glass aloft. Mark turned back and extended her a hand. She accepted it solemnly, at the same instant her gaze warning him. Promptly Mark sat down so that the girl who had slipped up behind him pushed with all her strength at an obstacle which was no longer there and herself flipped into the water. Amidst the catcalling and glee Mark completed his rescue. "Thanks," the woman said briefly, and simply stood and dripped.

Not unkindly, Mark said, "Why don't you go home?" It was as if he were addressing Muffin Naismith. "You can't keep up with those—whoopee wantons—much less outclass them. Why don't you go home?"

"Why don't you," the woman queried, "mind your own business?"

"I am on business."

"And I'm home." She turned her head to Bungalow Nine. "For almost two weeks this has been home sweet home. That fun-loving bachelor in the swimming pool seems to have forgotten the fact that he's my husband."

Mark's manner was that of polite interest. "Here on movie business?"

"He writes." The woman amended her statement, "Or did."

"He'll get back to it. The climate does that to people when they first get out here."

"He hasn't written a decent line since we got off the train," the woman said, banging herself on the side of the head to expel water from her ear. "Not that he ever did. Indecency is his forte. He thinks he's found the mother lode with your—whoopee wantons?—out here."

"I imagine it is somewhat trying for you." Mark's tone was a model of impersonal sympathy. "And I probably don't know the half of it."

The woman grinned knowingly. "No, but you seem pretty damn interested in finding out. Well, thanks again for the helping hand."

"Not at all," Mark said, and waited for all the world like a bellboy silently demanding a tip.

"You want a cup of coffee?" the woman asked, again with her knowing grin.

"I do indeed. How about having it on the side patio? Away from the danger of getting dunked again. I'll meet you there, Mrs. . . ."

"Tobino."

"Mrs. Tobino," Mark repeated with the lawyer's scrupulous attention to names.

"You're a cop, aren't you?"

"Why do you think that?"

"There was one around here earlier. Uniform, Sam Browne belt, and all. Not a plain-clothes man like you," she said with deliberation. "See you in the patio in a few minutes."

Mark entered the main building of the Eden, his tension lessening in the gloom that hinted of moisture and mold, both so precious to those who dwell in a hot dry clime. He shut himself into a phone booth, twisting so that he might see Mrs. Tobino when she entered the patio. There were only a few Edenites enjoying late breakfasts under the trees, each group seated, by mutual accord, as far as possible from the others. When Mr. Pentlove came on the line, Mark asked,

"You know of a writer named Tobino?"

"Not yet," Mr. Pentlove said. "Savant obtained a list of Eden residents this morning. Mostly writers. And knowing the cattle writers are, they'll be tractable. Savant's checking on Tobino now."

"Well, before you inform him of his sacred loyalties to the Industry, I'll have a chat with him," Mark said, as he was not in ignorance of Mr. Pentlove's propensities toward shutting people up or coaching them, thus adding to his lawyer's problems. He hung up and went out to the patio.

Mrs. Tobino joined him, dressed as if for a round of golf, even to the brown-and-white sport shoes and the white gloves (woven tops, leather palms). Her short still-damp hair was sleek as a boy's and she looked as ridiculously out of place as only an Eastern matron could, and remained as serenely unaware of it as only an Eastern matron would. Looking about her at the other women, clad in wide-legged pajamas and sunglasses, her expression said clearly, "I will never get used to seeing people dressed like that in public." Then, noting with approval that Mark had already ordered the coffee, she settled herself to play hostess. Pouring for them, she announced, "At least this is halfway civilized. This patio is the only place in Hollywood so far I've found that makes sense, sugar. I mean, of course, *sugar*?"

"No thank you."

She plopped two cubes into his cup, and he made a mental notation that she was a person who did not pay strict attention to what she heard. She rattled on. "God, what a hangover. For a while this morning I felt absolutely maimed. Now then, I imagine you want to ask me about last week end. What part of my information should I enlarge upon?"

Mark smiled in a way meant to convey self-consciousness. "I would appreciate it if we could go over the whole thing together. Just once more. If you please, Mrs. Tobino."

"Well, there's nothing much to tell. Except that there was prostitution and drinking going on in Number Ten. Incidentally, I do hope you vice-detail boys will scoop up those two tramps cavorting with my husband. They claim they're starlets. Back home we would say that that's really calling a spade a demitasse spoon. Frank, I needn't tell you, isn't fooled either." Mrs. Tobino smiled with womanly scorn. "My husband—Frank—discovered sex at an early age, around twenty-eight. He put down on paper what odds and ends he knew, and lo and behold he was a great writer! So now that he's really an expert on the subject he knows that all prostitutes have either hearts of gold or tattooed ankles."

"Tattooed?"

"Oh, yes. That trull who came to borrow some ice from us last week end had hers done. So she could go barelegged and look as if she were wearing expensive whore's silk stockings. Frank was all agog. He'd been itching all night to have a look-see to find out what an enormously fat man like The Feeb did for fun."

"Did he find out?"

Mrs. Tobino laughed this question to oblivion. "All he saw was The Feeb snoring in a chair, and some lounge-lizard drinking with the sane tramps, and a third one on a jabbering jag."

"Did you say *sane?*"

"Compared to the jabbering one they were pictures of propriety. Odd thing about that woman, though. She didn't strike me as being a professional like the other two. Naturally you people on the vice detail would know more about that than I."

"Tell me how she did strike you, Mrs. Tobino."

Mrs. Tobino drew closer to the table, all cozy and confidential with this personable man who put such a high value on her opinions. "For one thing she was older than the others. I think once she must have been astonishingly pretty, but she was too disheveled really to tell."

Only once had Mark ever seen Muffin Naismith anything but pin-neat, and then even, under the circumstances, she could not have been called a slattern by the remotest stretch. "Explain to me," he said.

"Well—her hair was mussy. And her make-up was atrocious. There were ladders in her stockings. Of course we must take into account her drunken state."

"You have keen powers of observation."

Mrs. Tobino savored that for a moment. "And when I last saw her she. . . ."

"Please go on," Mark prompted.

"It's—revolting," she warned, putting her hand on the coffee pot and then forgetting to pour.

"It is necessary for me to know," Mark encouraged her.

"After a sleepless night, let me tell you," Mrs. Tobino said portentously, "the racket took on a new note. There was less radio and laughter and more howling."

"Howl—"

"I mean it. This woman, whose voice I got to know quite intimately, if you take my meaning; I'd listened to it for hours, she shouted like a deaf person—you know how loudly they sometimes talk? But come morning she gets on a crying jag. You listen to that a while and your nerves begin to feel like shredded wheat. The next thing I hear is a lot of pounding and yelling. This was later in the morning. So I went over and looked in the door. The two young prostitutes and some man were all banging at the bedroom door. And the other woman was inside screaming. So I went around to the side—I'd discovered by accident, you see, that I could look into the bedroom window of Number Ten if I stood in just the right spot. And this woman was on the bed fighting and clawing like a wildcat. And The Feeb was trying to calm her. Finally he took some ice and—" Mrs. Tobino came to a dead halt, widened her eyes, and looked about her like one emerging from a spell. Then came her brittle comment: "You seem far and away too interested in that one woman. You're not a cop."

"I did not tell you I was," Mark reminded her.

"You her husband? Checking up on her?"

"No, Mrs. Tobino, my wife is dead."

"Sorry," she said briskly. "You're a private detective employed by her husband," she deduced.

"I'm an attorney. And I would be happy to tell you why I need this information—you've been so cooperative and sensible—but I'd be violating a client's confidence if I did. I'm certain you understand."

Mrs. Tobino had evidently been on very short rations of flattery for a length of time, for she warmed again to Mark at once. "Fair enough," she said. "To continue, the next thing I saw was the howling woman being dragged into the pool by the girls. They walked her back and forth in the shallow end, and gradually she quieted down. The last of her was when the girls were bundling her off toward the car park. If my opinion had been asked I'd have said to deposit her on the doorstep of the nearest booby hatch."

"Are you saying that she was actually maniacal? Not just hysterical?"

Mrs. Tobino patted her cheek, deep in thought. "Borderline," she concluded.

"I'm not sure I understood exactly where the ice came into it."

"Oh." Mrs. Tobino looked about her, then lowered her voice. "That was when Forbes was trying to calm her in the bedroom. Over her yelling I heard him call her a bastard. And then he put some ice where an old wives' tale says it will do the most good. The word *hysteria,* you know, comes from the Greek word for the womb."

Mark gaped at her deliberately, the befogged male.

"He inserted the ice in her," Mrs. Tobino said with careful enunciation.

"And did it calm her?"

Mrs. Tobino said in a withering tone, "Would it you?"

"And he called her a bastard?"

"Yes, it's peculiar, isn't it? It's like calling a woman a son of a bitch. Right pew, wrong church, as the old joke goes. Actually, I didn't know what this Feeb person was doing to her until he popped the ice back in a glass. I saw the flash and then heard a tinkle."

"Over all the noise?"

"The glass was on a bedstand, so I was able to connect the faint sound with what I saw."

"And then?"

"Then I went back in my own bungalow." Mrs. Tobino rested her chin on a hand. "Tit for tat. Now you tell me. What happened to that woman anyway?"

Mark took a calculated risk. "She died."

"She *what?*"

"Miscarriage," Mark said briefly.

"I'm sorry to hear that." She drank a sip of cold coffee. "Well, I must be getting back to our bungalow. I've got Frank on a fairly loose rein out here, but I don't want any of your local maidens to get the idea she can muscle in. I've nursed his work along for ten years, and now that the payoff has arrived I'm wifey-bye and wifey-bye I intend to remain." She pulled on a glove, then settled down for an instant more. "You going to sue someone?"

"Sue? Oh, no, no. I'm afraid I used the term *miscarriage* interchangeably with *abortion*. I didn't mean to mislead you."

Mrs. Tobino looked him in the eye, her own clear and glinting. "Well, well, go to the head of the class, bright boy. Pret-ty slippery, aren't you?" She opened her purse and took out pad and pencil. "Since I was too thickheaded to ask for your name before, I'll just have it now, if you please."

Mark spelled it out for her carefully and courteously. He then handed her his card for good measure.

Somewhat put off by his sudden turn for the candid, Mrs. Tobino needed a moment to rally. "Impersonating a policeman," she said, her manner revealing that she knew full well he had not. Then, completely recovered, she said spitefully, "I'm not one of your dumb movie stars, you know. I've got your number, shyster. Some abortionist kills a woman, and hires you to come nosing around to find people who will swear she took some kind of a physical mauling beforehand. Thirty-six-hour binge, and all that. So your quack can say he only finished what someone else started."

Mark offered for her consideration, "But might not that have been the case? The ice and the—"

"You listen to me, Buster Brown. I'm not covering up for any filthy abortionist."

"In all fairness, Mrs. Tobino," Mark interjected quietly. "You admit that you yourself saw the ice—"

"What ice?" she asked flatly.

"Why the ice you saw inserted—"

"Not me." She drew on her other glove. "No ice, and no dice. More coffee?"

"No, thank you."

She filled his cup to the brim, then rose and left, the cleats on her golfing brogues striking the stones of the patio loudly.

Mark poured the cold coffee from his cup into hers, and then got out his flask and poured himself a drink. Mrs. Tobino and her ilk were the bane of a trial lawyer's existence. She could prove treacherous; the oath was meaningless to her except as it afforded her the opportunity to commingle fact and fantasy according to the dictates of her prejudices. Were Archibald Forbes to be arrested, she might turn as quickly on him as she had on Mark. But her husband was only a hireling on probation, and the great movers and shakers of the Industry could shortly make clear to him where his and his wife's duties lay.

He wondered idly what Mrs. Tobino had told the man in the Sam Browne belt, who was not a policeman as she had thought, but the obnoxiously efficient Ted Savant.

There were couples around him now ordering lunch, and fortified by his Irish, Mark left the patio.

The pool was quiet, deserted except for a fleshy woman lying along the edge. From the open door of Bungalow Nine came the sound of a typewriter. Frank Tobino, Mark surmised, wanting to get some new discovery about sex down on paper while it was steaming hot. A radio was playing in another bungalow, and most of them had their doors open to invite a draft. Starting to pass the fleshy woman, he heard a slight snore. He bent to touch her and his fingers made white pits in her pink skin. He woke her. "You were asleep," he said. The woman felt of her shoulder, muttered something about God, and tottered off for shade. He deduced that it would be useless to question her. Had she been at the Eden for as long as a week she would either have gained a protective tan or been hospitalized by now.

Alone, he gazed at the pool, the shallow end marked off by a rope strung on cork floats. Back and forth past the rope, six days ago, under the baleful noon sun, Muffin had been led—or dragged. Ice had been applied to her by an aggravated Feeb Forbes. And all the night before she had been noisy and madcap, dancing and leaping over the furniture. That was in keeping with what he knew of Muffin Naismith. Noisy, yes, her strident voice had enviable carrying powers, but one never received the impression that she was shouting in the way—as Mrs. Tobino said—a deaf person will. Disheveled? Not even on Snowdom's slab had she been that. Septicemia notwithstanding, Muffin would have called for comb and lip-rouge when it came time for dying. Her devotion to grooming was as much a part of her as the hectic mannerisms and the drawn yet fiery aspect of a consumptive.

Walking slowly now, he reviewed the possible implications of the ice. It seemed to him that he did have a vague recollection of having heard of its efficacy when inserted into hysterical women. Contrariwise, he could summon up no fragment of half-heard woman-talk that would point to such a heroic measure bringing on a miscarriage. Were this result so much as a five-per-cent expectancy, he felt certain that the ice treatment would have gained currency as a popular means of self-induced abortion.

Added to that, if Mrs. Tobino could hear the tinkle of ice over Muffin's voice in full volume, then that lady was doomed to come straggling in late on Judgement Day, having been distracted by the thunderous boom of a raindrop.

Per Muffin's request, he was meticulously picking up the pieces, but in opposition to what he deemed might have been her secret wishes, he was holding himself in check. She could command pity as no other creature he had ever known, and of all forms of subjugation it was the most tyrannical and meaningless.

He passed Bungalow Ten on his way to the car park, moving between it and Number Eleven toward the back. The kitchen door of Ten was open, and appeared to be vacant. He walked into a cheerful kitchen, the shelving decorated with dadoes, and goose-stepping little Dutch girls in decals on every available cupboard door. The lid to the icebox was raised for airing. Looking out of the kitchen Mark saw a shaft of light, dancing with motes, pouring in through the front door and down the hallway. Opposite him was the bedroom. Entering it he remarked upon the spanking-clean appearance of the taut green counterpane, the spotless dresser top, and the polished mirror over it. For the first time he was able to visualize Muffin Naismith enduring the last days of her life. This austerity and cleanliness would have won from her a glance of approval. The mirror stared with hard uncompromise at the bed, and looking in it Mark saw that there was no bedstand anywhere. At once he went to the opened window facing Number Nine. A frail net curtain hung between him and the view, but he could readily discern Frank Tobino seated at the window opposite, frowning over a typescript, and drinking Mexican bottled beer.

Mrs. Tobino's voice sounded out. "Frank? Phone! Hurry up, it sounds important."

Mr. Pentlove, then, had not been idle this morning either.

Turning again, Mark examined the room with great care. He saw not so much as a pinpoint of blood anywhere. Yet Snowdom said Muffin had been hemorrhaging at the time she was admitted to the Sanitarium. He could not feature her (she was always begging people to "feature *her*" doing something or other) writhing on that neat bed, pawing at The Feeb, and howling in drunken grief.

A venerable judge had once said to Mark, "Show me a man who laughs in a high register, and I'll show you a man who is petty and mean." And Mark, contributing his own morsel of wisdom, had said, "Show me a woman who wails loudly when she weeps, and I'll show you a woman who still harbors high hopes of getting what she wants."

Mark opened each drawer of the dresser, to find them empty. He went back out to the hall and opened the next door he came to. He entered and was as startled by a tiny shriek as the maid was by his unexpected appearance. She was sitting on the rim of the tub enjoying a cigarette. "Didn't mean to frighten you," Mark said.

"You got a light walk on you for a man," the maid said, voice still shaky. "You part cat?"

He grinned; she had a saucy way about her he liked on the instant, and there was an irrepressible touch of impudence in the grin she sent him back, giving as good as she got. She drew on her cigarette, sucking in her plump caramel cheeks.

"You always clean this bungalow?" Mark asked casually.

"*Now* what's Mr. Forbes said I took?" the maid asked, with no particular show of indignation.

"Nothing, nothing at all." Mark said reassuringly. "He just thought he might have left his cough medicine in the cabinet."

"Cough medicine, huh. And here I thought all along it was for snakebite."

Mark opened the cabinet to inspect its pristine interior.

"You certainly keep things neat," he said in open admiration.

"I do my work."

"I should imagine that after some of the parties around here, you have that work cut out for you."

"Hoo hoo! That'll bear repeating!" She drew deeply on her cigarette.

"Hooch spilled all over everything," Mark went on conversationally.

"Sticky as all get-out," she agreed.

"Rings on every available piece of furniture."

"Underneath even!" the maid hooted. "Some you just can't polish out. Have to have the whole piece refinished."

"Like the bedstand," Mark said, closing the cabinet and pretending to straighten his tie before the mirror.

"We didn't know he was going to be with us last week end. Mr. Forbes, I mean. Or I'd have put another in for him. I tell you, that cough medicine of his—the real cough medicine —eats right through the finish like lye or something."

"And stains like blood too," Mark murmured. "But he swears by it."

"And I swear at it."

"Any time he gets it on his own sheets the laundry tells him to take his business elsewhere."

The maid flipped her cigarette past Mark, a slight watery plop rewarding her practiced aim. "Bet they don't do no such thing," she said stoutly. "His friends can get messy, but Mr. Forbes makes it up to the help. He acts like a fool in his movies, but in real life no kinder man walks this earth. And that's a fact."

"Oh, that reminds me. He couldn't remember whether he'd left you a little something extra for the mess last week end. I said I'd ask if I saw you."

The maid made an unsuccessful try for slyness. "I thought that's what the bottle of likker was for. I just naturally lugged it home."

Then his leavetaking, Mark thought, was somewhat in the nature of a decampment. "Well, he had to leave in a hurry. Some business came up. That's why he wondered if you'd been taken care of."

The maid lit another cigarette. "That's what I just said. That's why I took the bottle. The note said I was to have it."

"Oh, he did leave a note? He couldn't remember if he had or not."

"You tell him next time to hold his left arm high over his head." The maid demonstrated, arm extended upward as if she were clinging to a streetcar handstrap. "His *left* arm, mind you. And keep it there."

"I'll be sure to tell him," Mark promised.

"Only surefire way to stop a nosebleed," the maid affirmed. "Lying down just makes it worse. Why that big sweet man just curled up on his bed and bled all over kingdom come. You tell him what I said, now!"

"I certainly will." Mark took five dollars from his pocket and gave the money to her. "This is for the medical advice. And a bargain at the price."

The maid laughed with unabashed glee. "Hoo! This must be my windfall week!"

"Oh? How's that?"

"Well, first of the week I found me this beautiful lavalière. Biggest I ever saw. You'd swear it was a diamond wasn't it so huge. And now I can buy me a gold chain to wear it on. Yes, sir, I sashay out in it and I'm going to knock my girl friends dead."

"There are worse ways of dying."

"And that'll bear repeating," she chortled. "You're not as funny as Mr. Forbes—nobody is—but you got a right cute way of saying things. Real gentle too. I bet you, I bet you got a way with horses and women."

"I'll cover that bet—when it comes to horses."

She cocked her head. "I bet you'd even be good with mules. And a higher compliment I can't hand no man."

"A better one might come to you one of these days." Then he hastened to add gravely, "But I thank you. I thank you very much."

He made that casual departure of his as if he were merely going to stroll into the next room, instead of away from the Eden and environs forever.

He went round the other side of Number Ten this time,

and looked into the bedroom window. He could see quite clearly a corner of the dresser, the bed, and a closet door. After that he took himself to the car park. Seated in the roadster, its leather redolent of the stockyards under the insufferable impact of the sun, he laid his arms over the steering wheel and rested his forehead on them. He thought: Blood on the sheets, blood on the sheets. . . . And then: What princeling or aspiring potentate of this golden realm casually planted his seed in Muffin? And then: Does it matter?

I haven't the heart or the stamina for it any more, he told himself. But my trouble is that I've told myself so many times that every man is entitled to a defense that now, when it's give up or drink myself to death, I've come to believe it. I cannot even exclude The Feeb. Of all the beliefs for a man like myself to hold. . . . God, I'll be dunning Pentlove for that bench yet. Won't I be the cat's meow in my black gown, and my head full of highfalutin claptrap!

Near him a car came to park. There were high heels clicking over to him in a trot. "Mark?" a girl's voice said. "Is that you, Mark?"

He raised his head and the sunlight struck his eyes like a blow. His temples thronged with busy spurts of pain and random aches. He managed a smile. "Pep! God, Pep, you— You look stupendous."

Pep bent over so that her double ropes of pearls clacked against the car door. "Mark, are you all right? The sun hasn't got you?"

"I'm fine. I was just resting my eyes for a moment."

"You could rest the body a little too, from the looks of you," Pep said with asperity. "Come on in and have lunch with us."

"I can't. I've some errands to run." Mark looked past her to the impatient portly gentleman waiting for Pep. "Besides, yon Sugar Daddy is beginning to do a slow burn."

"You'll do a fast one if you sit in this sun any longer." He noticed that Pep had just found enough room between her freckles to eke in a faint wrinkle across her forehead. "Someday I'm simply going to have to marry you," she scolded.

"Just to knock some sense into you. You're thick as a slat everywhere but in your head. Now get out of this sun!"

"I'm going, I'm going. I'm leaving this moment. And I'll get the marriage license right away."

"You do that," Pep said. "And call a girl in a blue moon, why don't you?" She touched his face. "Bye-bye, Bagel."

He smiled at her retreating back. Her stride, her lion-colored hair, her resourceful body filled him with a momentary bliss. He had never declared himself in love with Pep, yet he would rather lark around town with her than eat.

As his bliss faded he grew ashamed of himself. In his mind's eye he could see Pep deepening the trace of a wrinkle in her forehead, pretending to study her menu and instead fretting over him because he had let her catch him looking down on his luck and down in the mouth about it.

Yet were he to tell her of Muffin's death, and his involvement with The Feeb, and the wherefores thereof, he was positive Pep would say: "Mark, nuttin' you do or don't do will hurt that poor Muffin one bit. But if you can get to be a judge by defending The Feeb, then hop to it. Why, as a judge you could disperse justice all over the place!"

"Dispense," Mark would say.

"Well, hell yes, that too! Goes without saying!"

CHAPTER EIGHT

Pep Baines did not so much defy description as weather it. People were forever bringing to her attention her sundry attributes or faults. "My, you're tall!" or "Are those your real teeth?" To the latter Pep usually replied, "Is there any one in perticular you have in mind?" She was forever on the go, though getting somewhere in life was not one of her objectives. Her hair was the exact color of the big pyramid (the one behind the dromedary) on a package of Camel cigarettes. If she had a philosophy for living, the sole subject on which she was reticent, it was that too many of us are inclined to recognize the few glorious days granted us only in retrospect. This determination to savor to the fullest whatever came her way endowed her with an exciting air of expectation.

Mark D'Andor, a man with a heavy criminal-case load, saddled with a mistress he did not want, and burdened with a nagging longing for a wife who did not want him, first laid eyes on Pep Baines at the most popular social event to come along in years.

He met her on the grounds of Mongrel Studio, an epithet the studio had earned by virtue of having more sons-of-bitches at its helm than any similar business venture in town. The biggest mongrel, Top Dog as he was affectionately known behind his back, had accommodatingly dropped dead at the suggestion of a director with whom he was having a slight difference of opinion. Shrewdly estimating the vast number who might wish to bid Top Dog farewell, and bearing in mind the seating capacity in the temple, Mongrel officials arranged for a ceremony called the Eulogistics to be held on Set Stage 29 for those not invited to temple. A Sunday was chosen for these funereal doings to prevent claims for time off from work.

Mark, along with any number of other lesser local luminaries, had received an engraved card summoning him to Set Stage 29. Not one to miss the opportunity of harkening to Eulogistics, and hoping also to buttonhole someone—anyone at all he hadn't pestered before on the subject of the career of Muffin Naismith—Mark planned to attend. The added message at the bottom of the card, *B.I.O.* (it took seven phone calls to unlock its meaning—By Invitation Only), strengthened his resolve. Muffin had been tiresome the night he had received his card and he had gone home early, then to sit up half the night amusing himself composing formal acceptances:

> Mr. Mark D'Andor
> freely confesses himself
> ravished
> at the very idea of attend—

But he did not send any of them because he was uncertain as to whom this conveyance of his delight should be addressed.

Arriving a touch late, Mark was seated far back from a dais swagged in black velvet and strewn with paper flowers from the prop department. The laudations had not quite begun and he entertained himself by appraising those so uncomfortably seated on folding chairs in front of him. For an instant he thought he spied an up-and-coming star in a polka-dot dress, but when the girl turned her head he knew himself mistaken. He occupied himself by liking her hat, a breezy affair consisting of a black lace doily topped by a rose the delicate color of a slice of ham. Someone mounted the dais and started to speak, but though Mark did his honorable best to be attentive, he found himself looking at the girl in the polka-dot dress. Her coiffure and apparel were admittedly slapdash, but her unconcealed enjoyment at what was at best deplorably dull singled her out from all the other pretty girls sitting so stolidly, listening and hearing not a word that was said. The girl had verve, she strained to hear every word over the incessant coughing, and Mark concluded that she was one of those rare women who could forget herself for minutes at a time, goggling at life as if it were a series of supercolossal happenings. Mark bent but half an ear to the speaker, satisfied with knowing only what phrase, what encomium gave rise to her eager response. She listened with parted lips to a natty male, still in the process of being groomed for stardom, reciting Kipling's "If." The turn of little Darleen Bunny, who came next to lisp that she had always called the deceased Daddydiddums and would miss Daddydiddums so fiercely that it would blight her whole child-hood—Mark was paraphrasing for himself—brought to the polka-dot girl's mouth a smile of triumph. "I never did believe that little Darleen was *really* a thirty-year-old midget," Mark fancied she was telling herself.

All in all the Eulogistics moved along at a sprightly pace, a handsome profile replacing a choked-up flapper with butter-flies painted on her knees, ending with a smasheroo finale of all Eulogisticians crowding onstage to hold hands and sing "Danny Boy" to the accompaniment of a xylophone swathed in black crêpe paper. Mark reminded himself severely that the deceased had been named Daniel, and that there was no cause, no earthly excuse whatsoever for wildly desiring to guffaw. Only the rapt appreciation of the polka-dot girl took his mind off his low impulses.

Black curtains swung across the dais, and the audience (as Mark thought of it) turned to a man to its neighbor and started chattering. Chairs were shoved about in quick order so that intimate gossip circles were formed. Some few, though, were walking to the exit, the girl among them, her rose riding high. As she passed Mark he noted that she was not merely tall but possessed of an unfashionably robust body, sprinkled here and there (her arms and temples, for instance) with a galaxy of freckles. She was clutching a patent-leather bag to match her spike-heeled sandals, those heels giving the world to know that she was no more ashamed of her height than she was of her full bust, and would no more think of shambling around in flat shoes than she would of pressing her full breasts flat with surgical tape (the current rage).

Mark fell into the tail of the line which led him out under the June sun. The limousines, motors running, drivers standing at attention by the running boards, were awaiting their passengers to take them to the cemetery. Mark wandered up and down like one pacing the length of a long train, past Cascade Falls and Amberhurst and Perryville, looking for his own Pullman car. Finding his limousine as numbered on his invitation, Mark debated showing the card in case the driver wished to punch it. The issue unresolved, he found himself upsy-daisied and plumped on a jump seat facing two portly gentlemen taking up the entire back seat and completely unaware of his presence. Outside there were tootlings of horns and squeals of clarinets as the two marching bands took formation, one at the head of the cavalcade, and another two cars ahead of Mark. The drivers leaped behind their steering wheels; there was something reminiscent of the cavalry in their split-timed precision. The polka-dot girl came running alongside, digging into her patent purse, and calling the number of a car to each driver she passed. Mark swung the door open and extended his hand. "All aboard!" The strength of her grasp pleased him—it bespoke her ability to give as good as she got in other physical exertions.

"Whoosh," she said as Mark moved over a jump seat for her, and raised her hand to ascertain if her rose were awry. "Thanks." A whistle blew and her blue eyes grew black with exhilaration. "Hey, we're moving!" She stuck her head out the window to see the band two cars ahead. Returning to the occupants of the car she cried, "I love the drum majorettes! All in black with those black plumes. Just like the funeral horses when I was a kid. Remember them?"

The two gentlemen opposite her received this remark much like horses themselves, with bland equine indifference. She flushed and looked down at her purse. Mark had barely time to think, She's not as insensitive as her ebullience might lead one to believe, before she raised her head and smiled full on him.

". . . said to her," one of the portly gentlemen took up as if there had been no interruption, ". . . . I don't care what kind of a woman she was, she didn't wear a toga slit all the way up the leg like that. And what's more she didn't fart around in no bolero doesn't reach much lower than her collar bones. And she had the insubordination to say——"

Mark said, "I'm Mark—" and got no further because of a blasting from the band.

"I'm Pep," the girl called back. "Say, I hope I'm in the right phaeton."

"For my money you are," Mark assured her.

She dug into her purse. "I was sure my ducat said number—"

"Too late now," Mark said, curiously lifted in spirits.

Opposite them the gentleman shouted vis-à-vis to his colleague, "I said so it isn't a toga. It's seven veils. And you're playing the biggest vamp in the——"

Pep discovered her skirt had risen to reveal the rolled tops of her stockings. Tugging, she said in the bright voice of one offering a distraction, "Swell day!"

Mark looked out at the cloudless skies of June and the tiny flags whipping on the fenders of their limousine. "Swell," he agreed, thinking: *What is so rare as a day in June? Then, if ever come perfect—*

"Too bad it's going to rain."

"Rain? In the summertime?"

"It did once before, I remember it distinctively. Besides, I can feel rain in my bones," she prophesied. She craned her neck. "Oh, lookee, we're going to go right smack down the Boulevard. Isn't this—" Recalling the solemnity of the occasion, she lowered her voice. "I mean, it's a real proper tribute."

"Fitting indeed," Mark said, trying not to grin from ear to ear.

" . . . a canapé tray," the gentleman opposite was saying, his ire increasing with every word. "I ask you, a sterling silver canapé tray she's got under her arm. I ask her, I ask, 'So what're you going to do, put a apple in his mouth, and be done with it?' And she—"

"All those people lining the street," Pep said, awed. "And all gathered for one sad reason."

"Something certainly snagged their attention," Mark said, himself craning around to see the drum majorettes tossing their plumes and stepping high.

"I'm so grateful to this girl for letting me have her ducat," Pep said. "I'm not in the Industry, and she works at Mongrel. So naturally she got an invitation and I didn't."

"That's no excuse for careless omissions," Mark said.

"Oh? You mean like I was fated to be here? And someone almost pulled a blunder?"

"If you're here, you're fated," Mark said with conviction.

Her expression grew merry. "And all because my girl
friend thought Ee-yule-oh-gistics meant they'd be reading his
will. And she figured he probably hadn't left her anything. And
if he had then some lawyer would come tell her."

"What does your friend do at the studio?"

"Her? Oh, she's in the mail room." Pep turned away for
a moment to wave majestically at the crowd on the curb. Then,
leaning past Mark to wave to those on the other side of the
street, her face inches from his, he was presented with his first
view of pure uncomplicated bliss. "I'll be leaving the cortege at
the cemetery gate," he said. "It's just a jog downhill from where
I live, so I just trotted down and took the Red Car to the studio.
I left my car in the garage, you see." Reviewing what he had
said in his anxiety to have her leave the cortege with him, he
felt foolish.

"Oh, I see," she murmured vaguely. She peered round to
the front. "They're stopping up ahead, we must be there."

"Yes, well I wanted to explain why I don't have a car
with me. However, there are always taxis."

Pep thought this over carefully before nodding in accord.
As if moving on to something else she said experimentally, "I'll
bet you something. I'll bet you—a drink!"

"All right."

"Bet you can't give me Rudolph Valentino's full name."

"I owe you a drink."

With a chuckle she rattled off, "Rudolpho Alfonzo Raffaeli Pierre Filibert di Valentina d'Antonguolla!"

" . . . you call that a *head?*" the irate gentleman opposite
yelled to his companion, looking markedly liverish at this
juncture. "A head of what, I asked her, *lettuce?*"

Mark seized Pep's hand. "Let's go get that drink."

She held back, momentarily troubled. "If you think it
won't be rude to leave now. I'd hate to, you know, weep and
run."

"Believe me, no one would think of it in that way. Absolutely no one."

"Well . . ." She recaptured her breezy bliss. "Now's the time. Since it is going to rain."

He opened the door and helped her to the running board.

" . . . and I said," the liverish gentleman bellowed to his sympathetic colleague, ". . . I asked her, 'What did you have to drop the head back down in the pit for? *Butterfingers!*' "

Lying on Pep's studio bed, Mark drew a long sigh of release and rolled on his side to let his hand rest on Pep's naked breast. "It's a gift," he said, adding when Pep grinned over at him, "how do you do it?"

"Forecast rain?"

"What else?"

For answer she kissed him, drawing him over her as she would a light sheet on a cool afternoon. "I'm hungry."

"You say that with a certain regularity. You said it just before lunch, as I recall."

"I've got this short memory," Pep explained. "So could you tell me if we ever had lunch?"

They grabbed each other and rocked about laughing. Past her shoulder he could see the unseasonable rain streaming down the window, and the afternoon took on all the lost enchantment of a rainy day spent exploring the attic. He had not let eagerness or urgency drive him to the snatching and clutching that came with haste. There was the leisurely removal of the rain-spattered polka-dot dress, and the graciousness with which Pep presented herself clad only in green teddies, and lastly the sensuous chuckle as she fell onto the studio couch in his arms (and he in hers) and said, "Gee, Mark, ain't we got fun?" He had answered, "In a manner of speaking."

Now as their laughter died he felt that drowsiness composed equally of release and melancholy. "What is so rare as a day in June?" he murmured.

"February the thirty-first?" Pep hazarded. "Bagel, what are you talking about?"

"A poem. A long one I once committed to memory."

"Say it," she commanded.

"Pep, it's pages. And I've forgotten long passages. Come to think of it, I never recite it unless I'm drunk. Don't you have something like that, that you dredge up when you're drunk or out of sorts?"

"Don't be out of sorts, Bagel. Just tell me what it says about June."

"What is so rare as a day in June?" he repeated and sank his face to her breast. "Then, if ever, come perfect days. . . . Perfect. . . ."

When he awoke he was astonished to see by the Big Ben alarm clock forever dancing nimbly on its three legs on her chiffonier that he had slept for several hours by her side. "It's a gift," he said again.

Being rare, but not so much so as a day in June, Pep left him no doubts as to her state of hunger. Contemplating the rain, he wished some clever girl would once and for all do away with the "getting a bite to eat" ruse of getting a man on his feet. Perhaps, though, it fell to the province of the man to think of some positive way of showing his appreciation other than taking the girl to dinner, and short of crudely placing money under the legs of the Big Ben, and then buttoning up his fly and looking around for his tie.

"Dammit," he groaned, "why did I leave my car at home?"

"You gave me a detailed explanation in the limousine," Pep said. "Why did you?"

"How was I to know it was going to rain? Not having a crystal ball—"

"Mark, not one man in a thousand—"

"Shut up. Where'll we go for dinner?"

She kissed him with a hint of sadness. "You're married, aren't you?"

"No. Not any more."

"But there's somebody you're feeling guilty about."

He extinguished the thought of Muffin like a lone candle gleaming through the wet dusk from a window. Or perhaps she was more like that blue bulb in the solarium he could not prevent himself from turning on each night for Constance. Thinking of that empty house he said, "At home there's only a curdled creature with the name of Mrs. Sauer. On my oath, that's her name. She comes in to dust around and cook when the mood suits her. Which is about once a week. If that."

He thought of the days before Constance had so casually left him. He never knew whether she would be home or not. Of a night when he had to stay downtown waiting for a jury to wind up its deliberations he would try to call Constance.

"Who?" Mrs. Sauer would shout into the phone. "Mr. D'Anders? He's not here."

"No, Mrs. Sauer, this *is* Mr. D'Andor—"

"She's out too," Mrs. Sauer would reply in her perpetual state of anger and crash the receiver onto its hook.

By the time he would arrive home, there was only the burning chandelier and silence to greet him; those two and a scribbled note for him in the icebox. Mrs. Sauer always impaled her communications on toothpicks thrust into a cold roast or the Crab Louis. *Mr. D: Here's your supper.* When he awoke and dressed he sometimes heard Constance's Peke snoring away with her in the guest bedroom.

"No," he said to Pep, "we're no longer married."

"Why?"

"I don't know. Unlike Mrs. Sauer," he said absently, "she neglected to leave me a message stuck in the leg of lamb."

"Oh, yeah," Pep said, "I see what you mean. In a pig's eye. Say, how's about my rustling up something for us right here? I got all the fixin's and all the mixin's, and a guy up on the second floor I know will sell us a bottle of gin. Just knock on the door, tell him Pep sent you, and hand him four bucks."

During the brief interval of his hesitation she reached across him to pull down the shade and turn on a lamp. She stood up; taking a fringed Spanish shawl from the tambour table, she wrapped it about her and padded barefoot to the bath. From the door she said, "And I got a parcheesi board too."

He thought of his house, dark and damp, and the phone ringing and ringing, its antiseptic mouthpiece wiped with Listerine by the germ-fearing Mrs. Sauer. In his mind's eye he saw himself standing in his dark kitchen, hands over his ears, while Muffin raged at him to answer, answer, ANSWER her ringing of his phone.

The bathroom door opened and Pep stuck her head out. "Besides, there's all those mussels I got to do something about."

Mark sat upright. "What is to be done about muscles? How do you mean?"

"Not to mention the lobsters and a halibut the size of a barn door," Pep said. "And the halibut and the barracuda have got to be cleaned." She closed the bathroom door again.

Mark would not have admitted to being drunk, but he was, however, rapturously tipsy. He and Pep had eaten the lobsters and emptied her larder with the rapacity that only people planning to vacate the premises can. "I don't mind moving my clothes," Pep said, "such as I got. But I hate moving food. All those boxes of stuff, and when you do get in your new apartment, what've you got?" She answered for herself, "You got salt and pepper, and some wormy cereal, and a box of Arm and Hammer soda."

"And a pretty kettle of fish," Mark said, looking into the icebox. Wedged in with a small cake of ice were two enormous fish and a pile of mussels. He sipped at his gin. "Do people eat mussels?"

"They do," Pep said darkly. "Only I forget which months." Hand on her shawl-covered hip, she changed the subject, and looked at him from the corner of her eye. "You wouldn't be needing a secretary, would you, Mark? The thing is, I've decided to get myself a job." As he shut the lid of the icebox, she said in an altered tone, "On the other hand, you might want to keep me."

"I thought you were done with being a kept woman."

"Only by guys who bunch me up in a tiny dump like this, and expect me to live on fish. What that boy friend—that ex-boy friend—of mine needs isn't a woman. He needs a cat."

"We're going to have to clean and cook that fish, you know," Mark said in a practical tone. "Or give it to the landlord or someone."

Pep slammed the gin bottle down on the kitchen table. "Him! You know what he and darling Fisherman stuck their heads together and thought up? That Fisherboy would pay half the rent and the landlord could take the rest out in trade.

And yesterday," she snarled, "he turns up for his share in his undershirt. He knew my boy friend would be at the beach all day trying to halve the population in the ocean." She tossed her head and grinned. "Boy, do I talk fancy when I get mad. I meant he'd be trying to catch all those fish and—"

"Stewed," Mark put in thoughtfully.

"You're not sober yourself by a long shot," Pep reminded him.

"No, I wasn't having reference to our happy state of intox—— Some kind of a fish stew I had in San Francisco once."

"Oh, that's *cioppino*. And with a ten-pound barracuda and a thirteen-pound halibut I'd have to make it in the tub!"

"Certainly," Mark agreed. "Go turn the water on and I'll start carrying in the ingredients."

Sitting on the edge of the tub, Pep said to Mark, as he made his sixth trip from the kitchen, "Did you bring the pepper?" She lifted a strand of seaweed from the mop handle with which she was stirring.

"No," Mark said. "But I remembered to get the lobster shells." He tossed them into the tub along with the fish and mussels. "I would say a soupçon more Arm and Hammer soda," he suggested. Adding the soda, he sat beside her and took over the stirring. "Good cook like you, you should get married. You're young, and you're certainly gorgeous, and—"

"And I'm a whiz-bang in bed," Pep finished. "Thanks."

"Incidentally," Mark said diffidently, "what did you do about the landlord yesterday?"

"Paid him his rent money and threw him out on his can." Pep grew wistful. "Being kept sure isn't what it's cracked up to be. Don't you think a dash of Tabasco would help?" She emptied a bottle onto the floating halibut. "Maybe if I'd found me a nice old millionaire and gotten off on the right foot, I would see it differently. Say, somebody like those old boys in the limousine with us, Mark."

"That pair of complaining old curmudgeons?"

Unhesitantly Pep said, "They were sweet. When men talk about business instead of giving the glad eye to every girl they see, you can tell they're good providers. To tell you the truth," she went on, pouring more gin into his glass for him, "I was hoping mebbe one of them would look at me and really see *me*. Or d'you think looking so much like Carole Lombard cramps my style?"

"Carole Lombard looks like you," Mark corrected her gallantly.

Pep threw back her head to laugh and Mark peered critically at her molars. "I'll keep you," he said, coming to a swift decision. "I just didn't want to commit myself until I'd seen your teeth. Old horsetrader's trick."

Pep poured the last of the gin into Mark's glass and then added the bottle to the cioppino in the tub. "No you won't, Mark. You're not old enough, or rich enough, or—free enough. I'll get me a job and bide my time."

"You think you'll find a sugar daddy who is single?"

"Nope. Just one who doesn't already have a mistress."

"Here, you stir a while," Mark said, handing Pep the mop. "And for your information, I don't have a mistress."

Pep applied herself to the mop handle. "Mark, if you don't have a woman on your conscience, then you'd better see your doctor. Any man looks like you do, he's either got a nagging woman or a nagging backache. I just wouldn't have the heart to add to his problems. I wonder what month people *do* eat mussels?"

"And I'm wondering what message we ought to leave in the gin bottle." Mark fished it out, then produced a pocket notepad and his fountain pen.

A solemn Pep wrung out the mop and stood it upright. Then, taking the pad and fountain pen, she absently licked the point of the pen. "You do it," she said, thrusting the pad at him.

Mark wrote busily, rolled his message into a tube, and placed it in the bottle. He set it afloat amid some seaweed.

"What did you write?" Pep said. "What did you write, Mark? Mark, what——"

"Oh, just something about how you look right now."

Pep fussed with her shawl. "Don't I look all right? Tell me, how do I look?"

"That's one compliment you're going to have to fish for."

Pep chased him out of the bathroom with the mop. Cornering him, she dropped her weapon and asked softly, "Wanna go back to bed, sweetie?" She yawned.

"Rain check, Chef," Mark said. "You need your rest."

"Rain check," Pep giggled as he led her to her studio couch. "What is so rare as a rain check? When it's pouring buckets outside."

But when Mark stepped out of his taxi, the stars were out. Dimly he could hear a phone ringing. It stopped when he was halfway down the entrance stair. He sat in the dining-room window, smoking, listening to the last of the raindrops fall from the eucalyptus tree. He thought of his quoting from a poem of James Russell Lowell for Pep. That poem, "The Vision of Sir Launfal," was his secret joke against the world, though in truth he kept it more or less of a secret from himself that he admired the thing, for all its glib grandeur and toplofty nonsense. Once, in his cups, he had recited the entire work, line by line, for Constance. She had alternately hooted or interrupted him to say, "But, seriously, Mark, it is a little like you," then to lapse into helpless laughter again.

This thinking of Constance while looking at the tree reminded him of her adamant refusal to have it topped, despite its dangerous canopy of brittle branches far overhead. "The only living thing in Hollywood I like," she used to say. Mark's thoughts were not conducive to sleep, he warned himself. He would be recalling next how he literally hounded her into marrying him, giving her no peace until she consented, and triumphing over her because she had never wanted for anything in her life, and did not know how to withstand the assaultive force of wanting in another. "Princess" was the only sobriquet he had ever given her. As simply as that he placed her above all other women; she was the unattainable attained. When he was courting her he used to be terrified lest he stank of the grease from the plates he washed to support himself and pay his law-school tuition. And when they were first married he had believed her to be happy; though not as he was, exultant with a lovely wife and a career that promised excitement and fame.

He forced himself to think of Pep Baines instead.

Inwardly he grinned, picturing her asleep scant feet away from the halibut and barracuda floating serenely in their makeshift *cioppino*. He hoped Pep would not take offense at the money and a second hasty note he had slipped into the bottle.

His phone began to ring as if weary of the whole damn thing—yowling and yowling through the night with no one to answer it. Mark took a last look at the outlines of the surrounding hills illuminated by starshine.

"Yes?" he said, answering the phone.

"Mr. D'Andor? I'm a neighbor of Muffin's. Now she's all right. I found her in plenty of time. The doctor says she'll be all *right!*"

"What—"

"She's asleep now. The doctor said she'd upchucked most of the pills she took anyway. We can all thank the good Lord I found the poor little thing in time. When I walked in and saw her in that tub full of blood—well, I just can't tell you!"

"*Tub* full of—"

"She could of drowned, you know. The doctor said actually that was the worst danger. Not her wrists. Anyway, it's a good thing I heard her snoring. You don't hear someone snoring in their *bathroom* every day of the week, now do you? And since our baths are adjoining—well, thank the Lord is all I can say."

"She tried to—"

"I'm staying right here at her side. The doctor says it'll be soon enough if you come 'round in the morning."

True to the tradition Muffin had left an accusatory note to Mark. It read in part: . . . *don't expect you take me where your fancy movie friends are. But don't forget, they had to start somewhere, same as me. Just because I'm younger and haven't gotten my big break yet, doesn't mean you can treat me like I'm beyond the pail or something.*

Her note was a classic in its way. It spoke of Mark's present treatment of her, and how she firmly expected him to mend his ways in the future. But nowhere was there a mention, a hint, of approaching death.

Mark tore up the note. He gazed down at Muffin in her neat pull-down bed, with her neatly bandaged wrists crossed over her stylishly miniature breasts. "Baby," Mark said, "wouldn't you have been surprised if you'd waked up dead."

Muffin closed her eyes. "You know that casting director you told about me?"

"At Mongrel? What about him?"

"I phoned him up. And his office said I should come there Saturday. To the CD's office. At eleven. So I did, I was there on the stroke of eleven. Only there were all these other people there, and I had to sit with 'em like I was just a nobody too. On long benches, that's what we sat on. There was this ugly old secretary who kept coming to the window—you know, the square window they have in his office so they can see just who's out here—and she kept calling all those other people up to the window and talking to them. I sat all day. I was the last one. And this girl who was just ahead of me, she wasn't even *pretty*——" Muffin began to sob. "They had her in to talk, in to talk to the CD himself. Then when she came out, I went up to the square window and. . . ."

"And?"

"The secretary said they'd filled the part. And s-slammed the window in my . . . face."

"I'm terribly sorry, Muffin. I'll talk to him again about you. Maybe he mislaid your name. I'll—"

"And then all day yesterday I tried to reach you. Because it was so t-terribly important. Only I couldn't."

"I'm sorry about that too." He was. "Tell you what, I'll—"

Muffin opened her eyes and repeated slowly and distinctly, "They picked that other girl who wasn't even pretty, and they slammed the window *right in my face*." She closed her eyes.

He sat on, in the single chair in the room, while she slept. It was beyond his powers of understanding how this girl could fill him with a dismal pity while at the same time leaving him inexplicably unmoved.

Pep Baines called him at his office. "Listen, Bagel, you left half your bankroll at my place the other night."

"Please, Pep, consider it a loan."

"You're damn tootin' I'll consider it a loan. Oh, and my

ex-boy friend paid me a visit. We had a real Donnybrook, and he gave me a black eye."

"He—You come to my office and I'll sue him for—"

"Naw. I had it coming to me," she said cheerfully. "The way I see it, it settled accounts. But what I really wanted to tell you is—I got a job."

"That is good news."

"Sure, manicurist. Anyway, lemme give you my new address and phone."

As he wrote them down he shook his head ruefully.

"Oh you bet," Pep said with weighty irony. "I can sure pick 'em when it comes to finding me new diggin's. Everybody on the block's been gabbing about that Naismith kid who tried to pull an el foldo. And how her handsome lawyer sweetie raced to her bedside. Of all the streets in town to choose from. . . . I ask you, can I or can I not pick 'em?"

"It's a gift," Mark said. "Anyway, where you are—are you comfortable?"

"A hell of a lot more'n you are right now, pal," Pep said. "If li'l Muffin ever springs you—that's a legal word, isn't it?— if you ever get sprung, then give a girl a ring, huh?"

CHAPTER NINE

Sitting in his car in the parking lot of the Eden, it seemed to Mark that just the sight of Pep had given him heart. Her ready fund of stoicism, her wry acceptance of things as they are, gave him to feel that he had let his old hounding pity for Muffin degenerate into mawkish regrets over her death. There had been times aplenty that if he had known of the ice treatment for hysterical women he would have availed himself of it with her. He had befriended Muffin as he might a stray kitten, to find an imperious cat on his hands, demanding, sleek, and capricious. But he had unwittingly assumed responsibility for her, and now it would be a disservice to her to let her death become the target of smut because of her brief association with Archibald Forbes.

Knowing, through the good offices of Chico, that a coroner's inquest was to be held concerning Muffin that afternoon, Mark consulted his watch to determine how much time was available to him to have the matter hushed up once and for all. As was the routine, a deputy would shortly be scouring the streets around the Hall of Justice in search of a coroner's jury for the afternoon session. The drunks and the stoolies, the Civic Center wisenheimers would have made themselves scarce. Of necessity the deputy could not be selective; any human being who could shamble, stumble, or stagger into the hearing room under his own power, suited the deputy right down to the ground. The deputy had his work cut out for him; no courtroom habitué having once fallen into his net cared again to be shunted into a dank basement room with a corpse and called upon to determine whether the remains had met with a natural death or no. Consequently, an attorney who wished to tamper with the verdict wisely supplied the deputy with a jury of his own. Refuges for the poor and rescue missions were always a ready source of supply for jurors.

Reviewing the missions in his mind, Mark selected one he had not called upon heretofore, but of which he had heard much from a colleague. His decision made, he got out his flask and drank off the rest of his Irish. Then, his inner wants attended to, he drove to the Land of Milk and Honey Mission, located a few blocks from the Hall of Justice.

As he had expected, the Land of Milk and Honey Mission was busy, and from the bleatings issuing from its store-front windows it would seem that the Pastor, the Reverend Parker Kingdom, was leading his sheep in song. Mark entered and was caught up by a female voice rising above the others as rich and sweet and exotic as that rare treat of his boyhood— tobacco-flower honey. Surrounded by his flock stood the Reverend Parker Kingdom, a big black man who, by the very force of his spirit, made one think of him as a giant, though he was only an inch or so over six feet. Still in his middle thirties, he was fortunately prematurely gray so that he brought to mind a prophet, full of the wisdom of years but yet blessed with the indefatigable strength of youth. He was the father of eight children, all by the same wife, and his private life was spotless. A lusty man, he practiced what he preached, and if God did not love his servant, the Reverend Parker Kingdom, then one can only contend that the Christian religion took a wrong turning in the road somewhere back.

Made aware of Mark's presence, the Reverend Kingdom brought the song to a close and strode to his guest to shake his hand. "Welcome, welcome," the Reverend said, as if he meant it.

"Thank you. I'm Mark D'Andor—"

"The attorney?" the Reverend Kingdom burst out eagerly, as if the town abounded in D'Andors but had but one lonely lawyer to do its legal business.

"Why, yes, I am—"

"My brother-in-law," the Reverend Kingdom said, "speaks of you constantly, Counsel."

Mark smiled. "Yes, Chester is a good friend, and a very fine young attorney."

"In*deed*!" the Reverend Kingdom exclaimed, unable altogether to refrain from eyeing his flock to make certain they were listening to this exchange. "And to what do I owe this singular honor, Counsel?"

Falling into cadence Mark said with sincere regret, "Much as I would like to say that it was the music which brought me in, I must admit that a legal matter is the culprit."

"Oh, culprit! Counsel!" the Reverend Kingdom chided in high good humor. "What can I do for you, sir?"

Mark lowered his voice. "I'm in urgent need of a—ah— little jury. Eight men. In the press of cases, I wasn't able to ____"

"Eight men right now?"

"I'm afraid so. If it isn't too much of an imposition."

The Reverend Kingdom turned to his attentive flock. "You," he said pointing, "and you and you and you and you and you and you. Oh, and you. That makes eight?"

"Excellent," Mark said.

The Reverend Kingdom adjured those chosen. "You're to go with Mr. D'Andor here and do whatever he tells you."

There was another handshake, mutual expressions of good will, and Mark was out on the street with his eight men. They grouped about him quietly, passive. "You're to be jurors," Mark said. "I'm afraid the pay isn't much. The deputy will take care of that. But we won't require much more than an hour of your time. All you need do is bring in a verdict of 'Natural causes.' That's all. The first case presented to you will be a woman named Naismith. *Naismith*. And you're to agree on 'Natural causes.' All right?"

He led them toward the Hall of Justice, advising them to scatter somewhat when they arrived. He did not wish them to appear the handpicked flock they were. Crossing Spring Street he sighted the deputy accosting witnesses and litigants, and finding no one without a valid excuse to escape his clutches. "Naismith," Mark said once more. And then, "Natural causes. All right?"

"Not me," one of the men blurted and stopped in his

tracks. Mark looked at him in mild dismay. "Something you don't understand?" Mark asked.

"Something I didn't until now," the recalcitrant one said. "We're supposed to let that deputy over there take us down to the corpse room. I heard of it. Sitting in a room with corpses and—"

"*Corpses!*" a second juror quavered. "We're going to be put in a room with dead—"

"Now, now," Mark said. "All you'll see will be a white sheet. And there'll be the deputy and someone from the District Attorney's office, and a clerk and—"

"Dead bodies," another juror finished for him, and set off back for the Mission at a trot.

Mark watched them go. He told himself: At the rate they're going they'll arrive at the Mission in a clump, at a dead heat.

Slowly he walked back to his car. Muffin Naismith's last chance to be declared dead of natural causes and buried without attendant scandal was gone. Though she had cried through the small hours of more than one night for notice, he doubted she would have relished the attention she would receive now.

Again on the Boulevard, driving west toward Vine, he looked to the squat octagonal tower that rose above a bank and housed his octagonal office. Time was when to sit at his desk in that stubby spire and look to the Boulevardiers five stories below was to think of himself on top of the heap. And so he was, he told himself, King of the Dunghill, that lofty eminence up which he had struggled by paying lip service to the law, but nevertheless serving his clients ardently and faithfully, according to his own garish lights. It had taken a decade for the malaise to set in, for the belated symptoms of corruption to make their appearance. Constance may not have detected (or cared about) the odor of grease on his hands when he was a student, but the first whiff of rot had sent her scurrying home to placid stuffy Pasadena for safety.

Hollywood and Vine was a pleasant sight with its clusters of the handsomest youngsters the nation had to offer. Trotting in and out of the stores, with their movie magazines clutched to their breasts and their teeth flashing in the sun, were the hopeful beauties and their beaux with machine-turned rugged jaws and black-satin hair. But not one of them that Mark saw this hot joyous afternoon could hold a candle for looks to the girl Muffin Naismith had once been.

Turning up Vine toward his house, he thought: The only thing that stood between Muffin and happiness was the absence of a harelip. But this sort of thinking was far and away too close to the cultivated cynicism of a Seymour Pentlove, so that he knew he needed a drink, some rest, and, if he got around to it, something to eat.

The thermometer stood at 103, but in his bedroom, two stories under the cellar with only the attic underneath, Mark found coolness and sleep. Later he awakened to darkness and took food out to his animals and freshened their water. He sat in a low lawn chair of redwood, a bag of cookies on one arm, and his tin of flat fifties open on the other. The crusty bull 'coon climbed onto his lap and finished the cookies there. Next, sampling a cigarette and finding it to his taste, he finished them off too.

Mark awoke to full daylight, and since it was seven in the morning of a clear hot Sunday, Mr. Pentlove was calling him on the phone.

"Yes, Pentlove?" Mark said by way of greeting, before that gentleman could announce himself.

"Ah, D'Andor, you sound like your old self," Mr. Pentlove said bracingly. "There is a Frank Tobino who has a few items of interest for you. Mrs. Tobino, I understand, was not exactly charmed by you. But I think they're both under control now. Shall I have Savant bring Tobino up to your place?"

"Why, hell no," Mark said. "You think I want every rag, tag, and bobtail writer and movie serf in general knowing my home address?"

"I see your point," Mr. Pentlove said readily. "Where shall I have Savant deliver him?"

"Charlie's speak," Mark decided.

"As you wish, Counselor."

"Oh, it's 'Counselor' is it, these days, Pentlove? What've I done to get back so rapidly in your good graces?"

"Oh, just because I'm happy to hear you sounding in fighting trim."

"It just might come in handy," Mark said mildly.

"Oh? Anything—bad turn up?"

"No. A bit upsetting at the most. As of now. I tried to nip the whole thing in the bud, but didn't have enough time to choose my cast of characters. Look, Pentlove, send Tobino to the speak. More anon."

"As you say, Counselor," Mr. Pentlove agreed. Had he started to whistle some lighthearted tune, Mark would not have been too astounded.

Charlie's speakeasy was a disreputable establishment frequented by touts, cameramen from Poverty Row, an occasional lawyer, and those few fortunate enough to know that Charlie served a steak breakfast on Sundays, more or less in propitiation for his rotgut dispensed to revelers the night before. When Mark arrived the door was unlocked, its peepholes—set rediculously low, almost at child's-eye level—unmanned. Inside, the windows, which were draped with black velvet at night, were open to the morning and the thick odor of French-fried potatoes hung on the air. Several customers of the night before, very much the worse for wear, sat girding themselves for the ordeal of raw eggs in tomato juice before attempting a steak. Seated in a captain's chair near the piano, Dionicio the blind musician slumbered, his copper eyes wide open. He answered to Dion, though a special few, Mark among them, were privileged to call him Genius, for the not unlikely reason that such he was. Dion's unconscious copper gaze was not a pretty sight, and those still under the weather avoided it, including Frank Tobino, who sat in burly displeasure with his surroundings.

"I'm D'Andor," Mark said, joining Tobino.

"Yeah," Tobino said, receiving the information with no show of enthusiasm. He looked about him. "What a crummy joint. Who's the blind greaser in the corner?"

"An untutored piano player," Mark said, "who knows all thirty-two of the Beethoven variations."

Tobino brightened. "You don't say! Say, let's wake the Mex up and have him recite 'em for us. Has he done all thirty-two himself?"

"Repeatedly."

Tobino looked to the sleeping Dion with respect. "It's the very thing I'm trying to tell my public," he informed Mark piously. "That all sex is good. Even a disgusting blind greaser has a right to it. *Thirty*-two! I'll be a son of a bitch."

Mark asked him silently: Why put off 'til tomorrow what you can do today? He looked past the glowing Tobino to Charlie and nodded his order for breakfast.

"Nobody writes honestly about sex," Tobino was saying. "Present company excepted, of course. I was," he said impressively, "banned in Boston, you know."

"You do come to Hollywood highly recommended, don't you?"

Tobino took this as a compliment rightly deserved, but for modesty's sake did not reply, busying himself lighting a cigar instead.

"About the events of last week end at the Eden," Mark said. "The party in Bungalow Ten. What can you tell me about it?"

Tobino rolled his cigar between his lips, taking deep enjoyment in the doing of it. Slowly withdrawing the cigar he said, "God! That frigid loud-mouthed piece of tail."

"Frigid?"

"Sure. The noisy one. Frigidity's the worst sort of neurosis, you know. But I guess I don't have to tell you that. We're talking about the Naismith broad, aren't we? That was her name, I finally learned."

"Tell me about her frigidity. Do you know this of your own knowledge?"

Tobino said with the single narrowed eye of great cunning, "All I had to do was get a load of her to know I wouldn't touch her type with a ten-foot pole. The which," he went on in a bass giggle, "I can't truthfully claim to—"

"Were you in Bungalow Ten at any time that week end?"

"Yeah, I moseyed over Sunday morning with some ice."

"What did you see?"

Tobino waited until after Charlie had placed Mark's food before him. "Well, there were two of the best-looking babes I ever laid eyes on. Only young. What's that word you got out here for girls who are under age? San Quentin quail?" Tobino wagged his head in worldly scorn of the native customs of California. "A completely mid-Victorian way of looking at sex. If a kid's old enough to want it, then she should be old enough to have it. Any other system is prudery. But, hell, I don't have to tell a lawyer that. It's attitudes like that that try to make sex ugly." Tobino leaned over Mark's plate in his perfervid delivery of his philosophy. "When it's—well, hell—beautiful! And that includes all thirty-two variations! Wouldn't you say?"

"I'm not as schooled in the subject as you seem to be."

Tobino's eyes glistened with pleasure. "Well, hell, man, it's my life work. To educate the poor puny neurotic frigid ——"

"Oh, yes, speaking of frigidity, you say that that was your opinion of the Naismith woman. Why?"

"Why? Because when I walked in she was all over The Feeb. Teasing him up and hollering about how she had this moshun pitcher career too, and feeling him up while she was doing it. Oh, she was a sight for churchgoers on Sunday morning, let me tell you."

"What was The Feeb's reaction?"

"What would yours be?"

Mark was unable to answer, occupied as he seemed to be with cutting his steak.

"He was trying to get out of it in a nice way," Tobino said, replying to his own question. "You know, kind of shoving her away, but good-naturedly. But I'm not telling you anything about him you don't know. He's the greatest tragedian of our times, if the stupes only knew it. He's the tragedy of impotency, he's the symbol of the mass fathead prude who's become impotent because of his straitlaced fears of sex."

"That is a most interesting analysis of his screen personality, but—"

"Oh, D'Andor!" Tobino said sadly. "You think it's an act with him? Why I saw the way the two cuties and the other guy were looking at The Feeb and this neurotic dame. Pitying. Just pitying. You find me a better word for it."

"What were the others doing?"

"Just sitting around drinking their breakfasts. And waiting for The Feeb to ante up what he owed them. The two girls and their pimp, as if I have to tell you who they were."

"What, if anything, happened after that?"

"Oh, I dumped off the ice and The Feeb used it as an excuse to go out to the kitchen with it. The set-up was that he wanted the others to stick around, you see, and not leave him alone with the frigid dame."

"Why do you say with such conviction that she was frigid?"

"Because I heard 'em in the bedroom a little while later. And the crackbrain was jabberty-jabberty-jab at him, the way a fridge does when she has to put up or shut up and won't do either. You've run into dames like that; I'm wasting my time telling my grandmother how to suck eggs."

"Did you hear other sounds from the bedroom?"

"Not me. I was back in our Bungalow Nine by then, so I just moved to the solarium to get away from the racket. And they call *that* sex!"

"There are several popular euphemisms for it, as well."

"I'll tell you something," Tobino said, wearing the furtive smirk of one giving a confidence, "I've seen some of the best stuff I ever saw in my life in this town. And that includes Paris. After I graduated from Princeton I went to Paris, you see, to get away from the stifling atmosphere we have in this country. But deliver me from the freaks you got here in Hollywood. Their likes I've never seen before. Where do they all come from?"

"Their home towns," Mark said.

"They think they'll get in the movies, is that it?"

"They stake their lives on it," Mark said levelly. "Tell me, Tobino, later Sunday morning, didn't your wife perhaps mention to you that she'd seen what was going on in the bedroom?"

Tobino drew on his cigar, the picture of a man in full possession of himself. "She saw nothing but the crackpot dame trying to get The Feeb to give her what he hadn't got to give. And the woman was in a crying jag by that time too." Tobino uttered a bass chuckle. "Adele sometimes forgets I'm the writer in the family. So I just told her that the day some studio is willing to pay her seven-fifty a week—" Tobino paused to let the stunningly high emolument sink in "—the day they pay her seven hundred and fifty smackeroos a week to make up stories, then's the day to start spinning her yarns."

Though Tobino took Mark's smile for a tribute to his talent, Mark was actually amused that Tobino would brag of what was to him a munificent sum and to the elite writers of the Industry an insulting pittance.

"You through with your breakfast?" Tobino said. And when Mark nodded, he ground out his cigar on Mark's plate. "The way to handle a woman," he intoned, dropping a lid at Mark, "is to give her all she can handle in bed. And tell her the rest of the time to button her lip. But hell, I don't have to tell you that."

"On the contrary, you've told me quite a lot, Tobino," Mark said.

Tobino guffawed in appreciation. Noting that Mark was through with his questioning, he suggested, "Say, how's about waking the greaser and asking him about those thirty-two tricks?"

"This is his day off," Mark told him. "Thanks very much, Tobino. I may be in touch with you again."

After Tobino had sat on at the table for a good ten minutes, he went out blinking into the sun where Ted Savant sat in his sparkling Ford awaiting him. "Where went the mouthpiece?" Tobino said.

"Mr. D'Andor? He drove off ten-fifteen minutes ago."

"Well, I'll be a son. . . . The way the bastard got up and leff the table I thought he was just going to the men's room."

CHAPTER TEN

The day, still at the morn, was already so hot and dry that there was an excitement to it. Mark didn't yet want to start drinking, nor did he wish to be either at his house or his office. Both contained phones as insistent and incessant as the pangs of conscience, and all lawyers early learn to resent the machines, second only to doctors hoping for a night's sound sleep. He thought of his friends, before remembering that as of the past year he had none. He had cut himself adrift, and after their hallooings from the shore had grown dimmer and dimmer they had let him go.

He went into a movie house and settled himself to watch Joan Crawford, but found himself instead reminded of Pep and her neat way of scraping up an acquaintance or cadging a drink by rattling off the multitudinous names of Valentino. "Now there was a funeral," she once said, referring to Valentino's. "But it didn't have the zip of Top Dog's."

After Muffin's wrists were healed, he saw Pep now and again, but she was with someone else and he, as always, seemed doomed to serve a life sentence with Muffin. Later, when Constance died, he took to keeping late hours in his office, overpreparing the simplest case to engage his thoughts. He had not yet turned to drink, though he glanced often in its direction.

On one such late session in his office, the elevator door opened to reveal Pep. She was wearing her manicurist's black silk dress with the white collar and cuffs, and carrying the familiar patent purse. Her hair was in its usual casual disarray, and her stride as she entered his office so spoke of excellent health and its attendant high spirits that she seemed to be the walking testimonial for some rare elixir. From the black patent purse she drew out an envelope, put it on Mark's desk, and perched beside it. "The moola, Mark," she said. "How've you been?"

"What moola?"

"The money you left in a bottle. For a shipwrecked shady lady. Thanks for the loan." She looked about his office in admiration. "Nice dump. Where does the lucky secretary have her desk?"

"Downstairs." He pointed to an iron circular staircase. "Pep, take your envelope back. You're making me feel like a fool."

"Take it," she said, a note of hardness entering her voice. "Don't make me feel like a tramp." She rose and paced the octagonal room. "Always wondered what was up here in this funny little tower. And I never once tumbled to the fact that it was your office. Why, I've passed here a million times. Sit down, will you, Mark, I'll warn you if the Pope or somebody like that gets off the elevator." He resumed his chair and she came to stand behind him, looking down on the Boulevard. "Lots of times I'm on a date I've looked up when the lights were on. Late at night, too. You must have more people to handle than Central Casting."

"I've been doing a lot of reading," he said carefully. "For a while I wasn't keeping up with the new decisions."

Pep looked to the walls covered with the usual state reports. "Looks like hot stuff, all right." She put her hands on his shoulders. "I've moved to a new dump. Say, I'll bet you—"

"Filibert."

Pep laid her cheek on the top of his head to laugh. "Oh, Mark, you're the eel's heels!"

"It happens to be one of Valentino's better names," he said defensively. "And I've got a bottle right in my desk drawer. Want a drink?"

She rubbed her face against his head. "No, I want you to c'mon out and play."

"You know how much I'd like to, but there's some work——"

"Sure." She raised her head. "Sweetie. . . . About your wife. I'm sorry. I read it in the paper. Her picture—she was really beautiful. It's no fair when the old el foldo gets them that young and beautiful, huh, Mark."

"No," Mark said and stared down at his desk blotter. Pep's strong hands dug into his shoulders, seeking to massage the tension-taut muscles.

"And those other items," Pep said carefully. "Those snide little cracks about her in the columns, before she died, I mean. I never did believe that anybody who'd *ever* been a wife of yours would be caught dead with some movie bum. I don't mean caught— I mean—"

"It's all right," Mark said. "People use the expression every day."

"I'm sure she never gave him a tumble. Look, loosen up, will you. You're taut as a bowstring. And you're about as fat as one too."

"I'm in the pink of condition," he said politely.

"Sure. And in a blue funk to go with it. Say, should I blow, or stick around until you toss me out on my ear? I mean, I got a date which I just might cancel if you get on your knees and beg me."

He reached back and covered her hands with his. "Believe me, Pep, any other time I'd— Pep, I'm just poor company."

"I hadn't realized you were still bound hand and foot to little Cream Puff. She your cross-eyed bear these days?" Pep rushed on before he could say anything. "If you ask me, you're just letting her take you for an easy Mark. A pun, and I'm proud of it. It's none of my business, only if you are still tied up with her, I'd like to know. I got this notion she was only a kind of temporary permanent fixture in your life; you catch?"

"I'd love to see you on the witness stand some day. You'd tie a cross-examiner in knots."

"Well, knots to you. I guess I'd better ankle on out and keep my date. He's a big director."

"Have yourself a good time, Pep."

She was airy. "Oh, I'll manage. Fritzie may be old as the hills, but he's got young ideas."

"Fritzie? You are moving up in the world."

"This office was as high as I wanted to go tonight," Pep said brashly. "Maybe I should put on the little lost kitten act like Muffin does. Well, hell, she is a swell looker, I'll hand her that."

"She'd be pleased to hear you say that," Mark murmured.

"Only I'd rather give her the back o' my hand," Pep said, and came round the desk. Bending over to look Mark in the eye, she continued, "Look, Filibert, I don't care whether you shake little Goody-Two-Shoes or not, because I don't think that's what's riding you. But I sure hope to hell you shake whatever *is* riding you, and do it soon."

"God, I like you, Pep!" Mark burst out.

She smiled and kissed him. "Oh, before I forget, my new phone number is in that envelope too."

"Thank you."

"About your wife . . ." Pep began. She contemplated him for a long moment. "That's what it's about, all right," she said with resignation. "Be good to yourself, you hear, Bagel?"

She was gone.

When next he saw Pep she strode into his office at midday. She was hatted and furred and hung with pearls that could have passed for candy-coated balls of chewing gum. She held her sheared beaver coat closed by using her hand as a clasp at the hip, the fingers of that hand slipped through the back strap of a lizard purse. Her feet were shod in lizard pumps with spike heels, and with her height and girth made monstrous by the teddy-bear coat, she was passing impressive.

"Why, Pep," Mark gasped, "if you aren't the biggest thing in my life these days! You look great!"

"Great is right," she agreed, shaking the floor with her walk. "Great with child. Mark, I'm in clover." When he leaped around his desk to seat her and hold her hand, she waggled a hideously huge cabochon ring under his nose. "Like it? It's pseudo-real."

"Oh, I could tell that at once," Mark said enthusiastically. "Now you tell me, whom am I to congratulate?"

He was reseating himself as Pep said, "Hold your horses. I want to start me one of those posterity lawsuits." She shifted on the chair in which he had seated her. "You sure this thing will hold my weight?"

"Yes," Mark said, and added automatically, "and you mean a paternity suit."

"All on a friendly basis, of course," Pep said, and extracted a cigarette holder from her lizard purse. "You probably know, Fritzie and 'Melia never had any kids of their own, so the sweet old goat is practically walking on air. And just to give you the whole—"

"Fritzie and 'Melia!" Mark shouted. "Do you mean—"

"Who else? Like I was about to say, the whole story is that 'Melia is happy for the old boy too. It's Fritzie's kid, all righty. I played fair and square, and they know it. Oh phooey, why am I waving this cigarette holder? My doctor won't let me smoke any more anyway. You know Fritzie and 'Melia, don't you?"

Overcome, Mark muttered, "Met 'em at Pentlove's. Which of the pair do I sue for paternity?"

"You're a three-alarm riot," Pep assured him. "I guess I didn't really mean sue him. Fritzie said he wanted me to see his old fuddy-duddy attorney about setting up the trust fund. But I said I always used you."

"Only once."

Pep narrowed her eyes. "That had all the earmarks of a nasty crack. You've changed, my friend."

"Not as much as you," Mark said pointedly. "You're going to have to spell it out for me, Pep. Are they to sign a bill of sale for this baby, or what?"

Pep put her holder back in her purse, snapped it shut, and slipped her fingers through the strap in back. "I guess this is a matter for Fritzie's fuddy-duddy lawyer after all. See you around, Bagel."

"Be that as it may, Pep, I'd advise you to consult me before committing yourself to anything."

"I told you," Pep said impatiently, "I'm in clover. I'm having Fritzie a son—the doctor thinks it's a boy, something to do with the heartbeat—and Fritzie's absolutely having fits and starts he's so proud. He's seventy-six, Mark. That's why he wants to set up this trust fund for me and my baby."

"Is he or is he not going to admit paternity?" Mark asked bluntly.

"Admit? He'll probably have little boys down on the Boulevard passing out handbills." She stood up and Mark came to escort her to the elevator.

"Whose idea was this anyway, yours or Fritzie's?"

"Well, he hadn't been keeping me more'n a few weeks before I figured he was trying to give himself heirs," Pep chortled. "So I nosed around and found out in the last ten years he's kept an even dozen girls. But I hit the jackpot. Course, I always suspected having babies would be one of my long suits. I like to watch my health, you know, so I'm fit as a fettle."

Mark confessed himself to be staggered. "Tell Fritzie for me I admire his— No, just forget that. Uhhh. . . . But what do you intend doing with yourself, in general, that is?"

"Oh," Pep said, "after the baby's old enough, Fritzie'll likely put me in his movies."

"In that case, I'll be seeing you then."

"Consider yourself invited to my first premiere," she said breezily. She lumbered into the elevator and stood with her finger on the button. In a voice that suddenly sounded oddly lonesome, Pep remarked, "We ought to be better friends. That day we met I thought we were going to be; *real* friends, I mean, not just shimmy partners in bed. So why aren't we?"

"I've wondered too. I think of you constantly, Pep. Yet I never do anything about it. Look, Pep, tell you what. The next good funeral either of us gets invited to, let's take the other along."

"Oh, that's a nifty!" Pep cried. "It's a date." She gave him a glancing kiss. "Not wishing anybody bad luck, but see you soon, Raffaeli."

"Another one of Valentino's names?" When Pep nodded, Mark cautioned, "You're using them up pretty fast on me."

"Phooey," Pep snorted, "there're enough left to last us a lifetime."

When Pep triumphantly gave birth to a nine-pound boy, Muffin seethed. "Of all the common, cheap—— A big strapping girl like that making goo-goo eyes at that silly little old man. She may think she's the Queen of Sheba, but I can tell you she's the laughingstock of Hollywood. And then having the gall to name her illegitimate brat after Fritzie. Some girls sure want to get in the movies bad is all I have to say."

"I'm gratified and grateful to hear it," Mark said.

"What do you mean?"

"As you covered the subject both succinctly and briefly, I'm edified to learn you have no more to say."

Muffin disrupted her precise stacks of movie magazines in her rage. "Don't tell me that that old fool thinks it's his kid!"

"To my best knowledge he does just that."

Muffin, miffed, envious, and scarlet with contempt, opened her jar of avocado cold cream and began to smear her face with it, quite unaware of what she was doing. "I certainly can't feature myself pulling such a cruddy trick," she raged, the pale green cream making a very pleasing and Christmasy contrast to her red skin.

Mark said with all the forbearance at his command, "Muffin, do me one favor. Stop saying *feature*. You sound like coming attractions. Wait until you are one."

"Rub it in," she whimpered, doing just that with her hands. "Rub it in."

"Sorry," he said, begging himself: In God's Name, get up and walk out of here. Forever.

Abruptly Muffin's mood changed. She began pacing the cramped room, deep in thought. She stepped over Mark's feet as he sat on the edge of the bed, went to the window, then retraced her steps, avoiding his feet again. "Mark, you've met this Pep Baines, haven't you? Sure, you have!" She snapped her fingers ineffectually, coated as they were with the cream. "Suppose you were to throw a little cocktail party? And invite some of your clients. And Pep and Fritzie. That way I could meet him right—a really classy knockdown." Her imagination was almost too far ahead of her tongue. She rattled on, "I'd make this good impression on him. And I could become palsy with Pep too. That'd cinch it! Because that way I'd naturally see Fritzie a lot, and when he wanted to find a fresh new star for one of his vehicles I'd be Johnny on the spot!" She sank to her

knees before him, buttocks resting on her heels, and raised
her glistening green face to him. "I can just feature it, can't
you? That's exactly how we'll work it. They all say you have
to make your own breaks. But that doesn't say you have to do
it the crummy way like Pep Baines. We'll have this swank
select little cocktail party. It'll be the nerts! We'll—"

"We will do no such thing," Mark said, as gently as he
was able. "I'm sorry, Muffin. It would never work."

Still in obeisance before him, she placed her hands on his
knees and wept into them. On one thin arm was a black sullen
bruise. Her weeping rose and fell as he listened bleakly, thinking that the greatest injustice of all existence was that the
stupid and the shallow and the selfish had as infinite a capacity
for suffering as any saint. Were there only their stale sexual
dialogue between them to hold him he could abandon her, but
her greed had become an actual need, and her anguish therefore real. She held him fast, as in the legal concept of adverse
possession. She exercised squatter's rights on his pity.

CHAPTER ELEVEN

On Monday morning Mark's sun city, his Heliopolis, was atingle with the excitement of the still, dry heat. The studio up the Boulevard from his office had sent out a call for extras, and all the young pretty people were thronging thither, expectant as children looking through the fence of a private playground and seeing one vacant swing seat ready for occupancy. The lobby of his office building was as yet empty, for banking hours had not begun. He boarded the elevator and pressed the unnumbered button which would lift him straight to the summit of the squat spire and his office.

As he stepped out he heard his phone ringing (as it always was), while back and forth across the frayed carpet a young colored man paced, looking anxiously at the instrument, obviously debating answering.

"Hello, Chester," Mark said warmly. "Take a seat. Guess we've beat the secretary on the job this morning," he explained, and perching on the desk's edge picked up the phone.

"Tobino all in order?" Mr. Pentlove asked without preamble.

"Buttoned up," Mark assured him.

"I'll be bringing a most trustworthy young lady in to see you this morning."

"Can't she make it under her own steam? You ought to have her letter-perfect in her lines by now."

"Really, D'Andor, when you start straining on gnats—"

"Later," Mark said with much meaning.

"Oh." Mr. Pentlove rang off.

Still perched on his desk, Mark took out his tin of cigarettes and extended it to Chester. "Coffin nail?"

"Gave them up last Lent," Chester said with the air of superiority that accompanies this sort of declaration, "and found out I could do without them entirely." He crossed his hands behind his back, palms out. Even when pacing in agitation, Mark noticed, amused, Chester's walk was reminiscent of his staid strut when addressing a jury.

"Didn't know you were Catholic," Mark said.

"Episcopal," Chester corrected him with courtly condescension.

"Will you light!" Mark commanded. "It's too damn hot to watch you tramp off the last of my threadbare rug."

Chester promptly sat down, elegantly crossing his legs. Despite the heat and his state of agitation, his sartorial crispness was unwilted. Mark was suddenly made aware of looking seedy, hollow-cheeked, and vaguely hung over. Reaching behind him to open a desk drawer, he asked, "Did you give up hooch for Lent too?" and displayed his tin of Irish.

"Don't let me stop you, Mark," Chester said by way of refusal.

In the act of pouring into a metal tumbler, Mark paused to smile at his guest, his expression exhibiting neither offense nor amusement, but only an impersonal mildness. "You wouldn't, Chester, don't worry." Still, he had not poured, and put the tin away, its contents untouched. He was a mite ashamed of himself for causing Chester to flush. All unbeknownst to the so quaintly correct, the so uncommonly courteous Chester, most of his colleagues at one time or another simply could not resist the temptation to fluster him. The man blushed as painfully as a schoolgirl, his close-shaven beige cheeks taking on the dark luster of ripe plums.

"What's up?" Mark asked, looking behind him as he closed the desk drawer, thus giving Chester time to master himself.

"They've picked up Doctor Snowdom for murder," Chester said. "I talked to him in jail yesterday. In fact, I've already been to Civic Center this morning."

"You going to represent Snowdom?"

Chester plucked at the crease in a pantleg, righting it so that it stood up neat as a blade edge. "He's Negro, you know,"

Chester said. "Or I guess you don't know. He's been passing for years."

"I'm not that well acquainted with the good doctor," Mark said in an off-hand manner. "So he's booked, eh?"

"Oh, yes. They'll go after a second-degree murder rap. Abortion murder. Of a girl named Muffin Naismith."

Mark shook his head, confounded by the vagaries of those who should, at all times, be keeping their wits about them. "He must be lacking a few marbles to have retained you," he said so matter-of-factly that Chester nodded in solemn agreement. "If a jury thinks Snowdom is a white man, then they'll wonder why no man of his own race would take his case. And if he blurts out that he's Negro, they'll send him to the rock pile just for daring to perform surgery on a white woman. Whatever the medical justification. Are you going in as attorney of record?"

"I thought," Chester said slowly, "I might prevail upon you to associate in."

"Wouldn't it be simpler all around to cop a manslaughter plea?"

"That was my first thought. Until I came up against the unavoidable fact that the man is innocent. Besides, the D.A.'s office won't lower the charge to manslaughter and go to trial on it. They know I could waive a jury, have a court trial, and knock prejudice clean out of the box that way. When," Chester cried passionately, "are we going to get those illogical rules changed so that we can waive a jury on all felony charges, if we so desire?"

Mark thrust his hands in his pockets and grinned at his friend. "I dunno," he confessed. Chester looked uncomfortable; a man with less dignity would have appeared sheepish. "Let's you level with me, huh, Chester? Your sense of humor didn't bring you all the way out to Hollywood on a scorcher of a day like this."

"Sense of humor?"

"Two fool names like ours. D'Andor and Dander. Sounds like a soft-shoe, songs, and patter routine. I'll see if I can get us booked at the Pantages."

The slow appraisal Chester bent on Mark had Mark

wishing he had taken that drink after all. "What's happened to you, Mark?"

"Now, dammit, that's the second time in less than a week someone has asked me the same idiot—"

For once Chester had the keen pleasure of watching someone else flush and struggle to master himself. "Old friends," he said softly, "take advantage when it comes to speaking out of turn. No offense, Mark."

"I'll be damned offending and offended if you don't tell me what you really want me to do for you. Now, spit it out!"

But Chester took a maddening turn for the dreamy. "Did I ever tell you that I sat through one of your first trials? Remember the Mexican boy in Pasadena?"

"Sure. One of Chico's nine million relatives. You were there?"

"I was. I went to school with that boy. I thought him a punk, but I was sizzling over the way the cops were always mauling the Mexicans and the Negroes, trying to get us to confess to anything lying around loose on the blotter."

"God!" Mark said, grinning foolishly. "It mortifies me even to think of it. Oh what a tricky little fire-eater I thought I was!" (And oh, he thought with a spasm of pain, how angry his father-in-law had been when he took the case.)

"You were a fire-eater," Chester said quietly. "The day you got that boy off was the day I signed up for my correspondence-school course in law. Up to then I wasn't quite sure. You decided me."

"No kidding?"

Chester jerked his head gravely, hastily retreating into his customary manner, half shy, half standoffish.

"Well," Mark said, "since I seem to have led you astray, tell me what I can do in mitigation?"

"You can tell me if you're acting in behalf of Archibald Forbes."

"Ah," Mark said, and added at once in perfect candor, "yes."

He walked past Chester and leaned over the rail of the spiral stair leading down to the office below. He saw a type-writer with its cover on, a basket containing some blue backs, and a lone camellia in a bud vase on the desk. Coming back to Chester, he said, "And?"

"Speaking of fire-eaters, I had my ears scorched off yesterday. By a Miss Pritchard."

"So. Enter the villainess of the piece."

Again Chester bent on him a steady regard before speaking. "What puzzles me—confounds me, if you must know—is that you knew the dead Naismith woman. The relationship must have been one of friendship, or at least trust, for her to have asked for you just before she died."

"You haven't begun to cover the ground, Chester," Mark said evenly.

"But you're covering for the man who raped her and then dumped her bleeding into the nearest private hospital!"

"Miss Pritchard's accusations are based on conclusions," Mark said sharply. "Will she swear on the stand that Muffin Naismith said, 'I was raped'? Will she?"

"No."

"For the simple reason that she won't lie, she's too self-righteous for that. And in spite of the fact that she'd like to punish some man, any man, for the existence of sex. She's hipped on the subject."

"The coroner isn't." Abruptly Chester laughed. "Mark, I never in my life before saw you prick up your ears. You usually try to look half-asleep when something triggers you."

"Let's have the coroner's ideas on the matter," Mark requested calmly.

"The mucous membranes of the birth canal were highly inflamed."

"Yes, she died of septicemia."

"And the vagina appears to have been punctured as well."

"*Punctured*?"

"That's the term that was used."

"Couldn't Snowdom be responsible for that?"

"He says no."

"Chester, I understand your willingness to believe your own client, but this is stretching it a—"

"I am not," Chester put in coldly, "going to stand by and let Snowdom be crucified. Just to preserve the good name of a man who makes his living by mocking the miseries of the feeble-minded."

Very deliberately Mark seated himself behind his desk, got out his Irish, and poured himself a stout drink. "Here's mud in your eye," he said blandly, and drank it down. "There's a bit more than a man's good name at stake. Money, you know. Filthy lucre. So, what's your proposition, Chester?"

"I have none. But I had to see for myself if all the things I've been hearing about you are really true. I don't mean your drinking. I learned early in life to respect the—troubled and the unhappy. People who don't have sorrows don't feel the need to drown them. And I've never seen you in court unprepared, no matter how hung over you were. It's the other things. I want to know if you're as unscrupulous as they say. And I'm not referring to that vicious story that went the rounds about your having broken that actress' jaw to get her off. I never believed a word of it."

"When you grow up," Mark said, "you will."

Chester opened his mouth to speak, then very slowly closed it. The two lawyers inspected one another openly; Chester gravely, Mark wryly. At last Chester continued on, "On my way out here I reminded myself of the time when Rookie Castle was disbarred. He was braving it out, stalking around Civic Center, looking like—like an open wound. And you came along and said, 'Hello, Rookie, got time for a snort?' That was long before," Chester went on carefully, "you fell into disrepute. And many's the time we've lunched together. You may have been a bit on the flashy side for some people's taste, Mark, but there was no one, in or kicked out of the profession, you didn't treat like a white man. But now you've turned up in a position to stand between my client and justice. And with all the talk—"

"Use your head," Mark said, "and take it for the gospel truth."

Chester pounded his fist on his knee, heedless of his pants crease. "Mark, what did they offer you? The ones who are protecting Forbes? What *could* they offer you? Your wife back?"

Mark clasped his hand around his glass.

"I deserve an answer," Chester said. "I ask as a friend."

Mark shook his head like one trying to swallow a mouthful of bitter medicine. "They offered me *me* back."

"They can't deliver." Chester got to his feet. "You know, of course, that I'm going to drag Forbes in this thing up to his ears."

"We'll play rough, Chester. You may find me somewhat lacking in the regard-for-the-niceties department."

"Yes, I've already had a sample of that. When you walked in on that ass of a brother-in-law of mine, and traded on our friendship. Trying to pack a coroner's jury with a bunch of benighted—"

"Had I been successful, Snowdom wouldn't be on the hook," Mark pointed out.

"Mark, I don't obstruct justice, I fight for it. And conning a blabbermouthed bible-whacking demagogue—" Chester's voice shook "—like my brother-in-law does not come under the heading—"

Angry himself, Mark said, "For your information, Chester, the Reverend Parker Kingdom happens to be a damn fine parson!"

Chester smiled grimly. "He just doesn't shape up too good as a person." And having bested Mark by seizing on his slip of the tongue, Chester took his indignant yet saddened self elsewhere.

Mark next could rejoice in guests when the elevator door opened to reveal Mr. Pentlove tenderly handing out a most striking girl, her charming face held as in a vise by two thick iron-willed spit curls. Standing up in welcome, Mark took her measure with a knowing eye. Her jaw was set, yet her step was hesitant. Almost imperceptible to Mark was Mr. Pentlove's tightening of his grip on the young lady's arm. Mark was all chairs and how-do-you-do's and won't-you-sit-down's, light's-not-in-your-eyes-is-it? affability. Miss Flirt Smith cozily settled, and Mr. Pentlove decorating another worn chair, Mark resumed his place behind his desk. All this said and done, Miss Smith crossed her bare legs and swung a tattooed ankle.

Ducal as all get-out, Mr. Pentlove took it into his head to

play chairman and said, "If we're all comfortable, shall we begin?"

With an ingrained suspicion of lawyers and other individuals she thought to be in quasi-official positions, Miss Smith was trying to look everywhere but at Mark. Experimentally Mark said, "Warm for May, isn't it, Miss Smith?"

"Oh, yes!" she agreed vehemently and smiled with great friendliness at his left ear.

Mr. Pentlove closed his eyes and tapped a talcumed chop.

Mark laughed easily. "Now, Miss Smith—may I call you Flirt?—you're not here to agree with me. Or Mr. Pentlove, for that matter. If I say it's May, and you know damn well it's October, then speak up. Right?"

"She is the soul of honesty," Mr. Pentlove said to Flirt in a somewhat ominous tone.

"Then by all means let's have Flirt tell me what she knows about Miss Naismith in her own words. Ready, Flirt?"

Miss Flirt Smith took a deep breath. "Well . . . I was attending a quiet little get-together Mr. Forbes was throw— uh—having at the Eden. And Mrs. Tredwell, only her name's Miss Naismith, I guess, and Mr. Forbes, and Mr. Sligh, and I, and Miss Jones was there. And I. And T-Bone Tredwell and some other kid, but they left very early. And I. At the Eden, it was."

"Oh, yes," Mark said as if he had just recalled this fact. "How was the party?"

Flirt wrinkled her nose. "Kind of— Well, Miss Naismith was in a extremely hysterical mood. All night. If she did the Black Bottom once she did it a hundred times. And loud! I hate to speak bad of the dead, but she was a real wet smack. She was after Mr. Forbes the whole time, and I and he could hardly . . ." Miss Flirt Smith looked at Mr. Pentlove for assistance.

"We're all adults here," Mark put in smoothly, though he had his doubts about young Flirt; "we'll understand."

"Well, Mr. Forbes and I could hardly be alone together. After all, that's what I. . . . So, when me and Mr. Forbes came back into the living room Miss Naismith was still making a specter of herself."

"She was in constant motion, all night?"

"Except when she had to go to the—John." Mark suppressed a smile, suspecting that capitalizing the word in her mind removed it from the realm of vulgarity so far as Flirt was concerned. Like a girl of illustrious background and breeding, Miss Flirt Smith said primly, "When she went to the John was the only time I knew her to sit down and act like a lady."

Mr. Pentlove decided to read each and every word of Mark's law degree hanging on the wall.

"Now you say Miss Naismith was loud," Mark said. "Tell me a little more about that."

Flirt swung her ankle in thought. "She—she talked like everybody was deaf or something. And she'd turn the radio up, and then talk even louder," Flirt said, her slight frown indicating puzzlement.

Mark also thought the information important, but in what way he could not fathom. "Why not let's move along a bit, here. Tell me about what happened when Mr. Forbes and Miss Naismith went into the bedroom."

"He *went,*" Flirt said with powerful conviction, "and she *come* after him. He was trying to get away from her. But she locked the door. Because I heard Mr. Forbes yelling at her to give the key to him. Then she started on a crying jag, and then she started hollering. So me and the other girl went and banged on the door to let us in."

"What about the ice?" Mark asked idly.

"Ice?" Flirt looked to Mr. Pentlove for confirmation of her hearing.

"Yes, the ice. Didn't Miss Naismith take a drink with her into the bedroom?"

"Oh, that." Flirt shrugged. "There wasn't a stick of ice in that glass, not one. The man next door lent us some earlier, but it was all used up."

A stick of ice, Mark commented mentally.

"When Miss Naismith started to scream—'holler' I believe you said—weren't you alarmed enough to look through the keyhole?"

"With a key in it?" Flirt countered witheringly.

Mr. Pentlove was suddenly done with his reading of

Mark's degree, and took to reading Mark's expression instead.

Mark asked lazily, "Miss Smith, how would you like to be arrested for resorting?"

"For what?"

"Resorting. Prostitution. Something like that."

She gasped at the very idea. "Why—Mr. Sligh wouldn't let 'em."

"Your Mr. Sligh," Mark said, "would let you rot. He's got other girls to keep him set up in business. I happen to be acquainted with Mr. Sligh. So, to continue: If the police were to pick you up for questioning and you told them the story you just recited for me now, they would see to it that you were given all the time you needed to think it over. And they would keep you under wraps until you came up with something more pleasant to their ears."

"Now, see here, D'Andor," Mr Pentlove said suavely, "they can't arrest people for telling the truth. And Miss Smith is—"

"Yes, the soul of truth," Mark finished for him. He returned his attention to the frightened Flirt. "Did or did you not hear Mr. Forbes ask Miss Naismith for the key to the bedroom when they were both in there?"

"Yes!" Flirt insisted.

"Yet you were unable to peek through the keyhole because the key was in it."

"I looked," Flirt said faintly. "Only just as I did, he came up and jabbed the key in the lock."

"Did he unlock the door?"

"No. I tried it right after. It wouldn't open. So we went on banging. Then later he opened it."

"When you were admitted to the bedroom did you see any blood?"

Flirt looked at Mark straight on. "Not me," she said, and he knew she meant it.

"Would you say Miss Naismith was drunk when you entered the bedroom?"

"And how!" Flirt said in disgust.

"And Forbes?"

"He—— Well, he was more like a guy who'd had just about all the ballyhoo he could take."

"He'd just gone through a rather sobering experience," Mr. Pentlove murmured. "Trying to quell a noisily deranged woman."

"You said a mouthful," Flirt assured Mr. Pentlove, both awed and envious of his prowess in rhetoric.

The phone rang, and excusing himself, Mark answered it.

In measured tones Chester Dander said, "Mark, I have just left the D.A.'s office. Miss Pritchard was there too. And I'll tell you something, Mark, they think she's a real spellbinder. They hung on every word."

"And?" Mark asked tersely.

"Why, they're going to pick up Forbes. This is your last chance to rid yourself of a very nasty mess. Get out of it while—"

"You're in it."

"But I," Chester said, "will be in full control of my case. Whereas that crew you're mixed up with will be tampering with witnesses behind your back and—"

"You're telling me," Mark said, with a steely eye for Mr. Pentlove. "But I thank you for the tip. Hell, I appreciate it, and you know it. Whatever little differences we may have had——"

"I have always," Chester interrupted in a formal voice, "felt obligated to you. But we're even now. Good-bye, Mark." The phone went dead.

Mark smiled at Mr. Pentlove sweetly. "It has just hit the fan," he told that very nearly imperturbable gentleman. Mr. Pentlove sat quietly serving himself to large helpings of umbrage at that smile. "Shall we get to some facts now?" Mark suggested, and bent his attention on Miss Flirt Smith, permitting Mr. Pentlove to keep his anger idling like a motorcar if he so desired.

The afternoon wore on, and Flirt cried that she was wore out. Yet she repeated with mulish insistence, "No ice in the glass she took into the bedroom. No *ice!*"

"Did it sound to you as if rape or intercourse were taking place in there?"

"Inter— The Feeb?" Flirt was growing shrill with weariness. "He can't."

"You know that of your own knowledge?"

She looked to Mr. Pentlove, who shrugged.

"Yeh," she muttered. Rallying, she said, "Ask any girl in town. They'll tell you."

On one other point was she adamant. She did not know the identity of the other girl in Bungalow Ten. Flirt knew only that she was not one of her Mr. Sligh's regulars.

"All right, thank you," Mark said. "We'll go over this again. I have to get down to the jail."

"A moment with you, Counselor," Mr. Pentlove said, flicking Flirt toward the elevator like a speck of dirt. In a lowered voice he asked, "Did you say jail?"

"That's where our boy is, Pentlove." When Mr. Pentlove had no comment, Mark said, "They picked him up for questioning. I figured he could give a good account of himself. He may not have recited the *Critique of Pure Reason,* but I doubt if he incriminated himself in any important detail. If he is impotent, as Flirt says, then the causal element of the death, insofar as he is concerned, is eliminated. The very fact that he didn't instantly demand I be called makes him look good—cooperative. More important, Pentlove, is that Ted Savant dig up the other prostitute. And fast."

Mr. Pentlove now showed what he could accomplish in the way of a sweet smile. "Ah, D'Andor, easier said than done. The young lady, it would seem, has long since shaken the dust of Hollywood from her little round heels."

"She was the one who sold you Muffin Naismith's purse."

"Yes, yes, she did that," Mr. Pentlove recalled fondly. "She had the itch to travel, she told me. We'll never see her again, I'm certain of it."

"If there's one thing I'm leery of," Mark said, "it's certainty. Incidentally, have Ted send up Benny Sligh to talk to me."

"Good as done," Mr. Pentlove vowed.

"And give me five bucks."

"Give— Did you—"

"I said that you owe me five bucks. I gave that amount to a maid at the Eden."

"My dear D'Andor," Mr. Pentlove said in reproof, "why haven't you reminded me of your retainer before." He extracted his checkbook.

"I want," Mark repeated, "just five bucks. If other expenses crop up, I'll hit you for the money. There was no mention of a fee in our original bargain. Only your promise of my appointment to a bench."

"But this is preposterous!"

"I'm so glad you think so," Mark said.

"D'Andor," Mr. Pentlove snapped, "like anyone else in this world, you have a price. I know what it is, because in times past I've paid it. What's your angle?"

"I have none," Mark said. "Though once in a while I can't resist throwing you a curve. Look, Pentlove, I really had better get downtown and see what the Golden Ass is up to."

CHAPTER TWELVE

The Feeb was in top form, and his repertoire unlimited. From the time the squad car had come for him, through dinner (sandwiches furnished by grateful cops), and way past nightfall his performance had continued. Hampered as he was by the nice-nellyism of films, he embraced any opportunity to display his finest talents, which lay in the direction of the obscene. The obese mental defective struggling to master the complexities of sex was The Feeb's *pièce de résistance*. Only an occasional and unremarked glint in the eye revealed the man Forbes, expertly manipulating the gross body as if it were a puppet, or perhaps a gorilla suit. When one of the police entered the room where The Feeb was holding forth and announced, "There's a mouthpiece out there asking for you," The Feeb capped his act with a drollery, a play on words, accompanied by sucking his thumb with thick rindlike lips. From the doorway Mark was in time to see the curtain-ringer.

Mark had had a gruelling afternoon with the soul of honesty, Miss Flirt Smith; he had been drinking all day, had smoked too much, and, as he did too frequently, had forgotten to eat. His very bones were weary, and his empty stomach threatened at any moment to set up the paralyzing spasms of dry retching, the only sincere tribute to The Feeb of which he was capable. But for appearance's sake, Mark added his laughter to that of the others. The uproar died gradually, one of The Feeb's audience clasping himself about the middle and weeping copiously. Mark observed to himself: That cop will sleep the sleep of the just. A good belly laugh is the best known palliative for life's general run of woes. Mark accorded himself the privilege of ceasing to laugh first, as it would seem nicely in keeping with his position as an attorney. When the police gentlemen had somewhat regained their composure, Mark said, "You about through with my boy here?" To which a detective who had held himself aloof in the corner replied dryly, "I am. Why aren't you, D'Andor?"

Mark pretended not to hear. He spoke to the group at large. "My boy's got to get his sleep. Otherwise he's liable to get thin and haggard."

The Feeb rolled his eyes, sucked his thumb, and whimpered. Several of those present must slap his back and thank him for the evening's entertainment before they could bear to part with him. Above the hubbub the antagonistic detective asked Mark, "Aren't you even going to ask if we booked him, Counselor?"

"Booked him?" Mark echoed blankly. "For what?"

"For making me laugh I almost split my gut," a jovial cop said.

Mark led his client out, The Feeb crying noisily for an ice-cream cone.

The night outside was cool; there was the bracing hint of fog in the air. The Feeb straightened his shoulders and stepped along smartly at Mark's side. He was Forbes once more, an enormous man who handled his great bulk without a trace of clumsiness. When he climbed into Mark's roadster there was none of the cramming and grunting of the obese trying to get comfortable. After they were in motion, Forbes opined, "What a crummy buggy. You must have hit the skids if this is all you can afford. I got four cars, myself. I got a Deusenberg with a klaxon that goes Shave-and-a-haircut, two bits." He sang out the last of the sentence.

"Unostentatiousness," Mark said, "must be the coming thing. Incidentally, Forbes, you seem to be on the defensive. What did you let slip to the cops?"

Forbes leaned an arm on the door and gazed idly at lighted store-display windows. "Nothing to let slip," he said.

Reaching the end of Vine they began to drive up into the silent hills. As they climbed higher and higher, Forbes began to peer about him excitedly. The fog had not risen to the hills and the road lay before them under moonlight, smooth and pale as cream poured from a jug. "Say," Forbes said, "say, if we're where I think we are— Sure we are. Yeah!"

Forbes sat laughing to himself, thinking of another comedian who was once considered to be the funniest man in the world.

Before the advent of the Twenties, in the halcyon days of the silents, the then-funniest man in the world had owned this entire hill and the high arroyo which separated it from the next. There were no houses in those days, only chaparral and Scotch broom and cactus, and flowering Spanish bayonets looking as if they took substance not from the sun but the moon. The Funniest Man in the World owned this Eden, complete even unto a snake—or, actually a whole slither of them. *Crotulus crotulus,* Forbes remembered, was the scientific and revoltingly apt name for the sluggish lethal rattlesnakes—the only animal that somehow he did not find it fun to kill. The Funniest Man in the World had had a close call with one of his snakes in residence, and he bent his mind to freeing his Eden of them. He struck on the solution of importing a special race of wild boars, which loved nothing so much as the delicacy of snake meat. The boars were taken off a ship at San Pedro harbor, and hauled by truck up into the hills—this one along which Forbes was now riding—and freed.

God, they were efficient, Forbes thought. "Any rattlesnakes up here?" he asked Mark.

"No."

Forbes smiled in the darkness. As a very young man his solid girth had made him valuable as a general handyman around the studios. He had strength, he could lift great weights, and those tasks which required large hands and power behind them fell to young Forbes. Of all the movie folk Forbes liked to watch, The Funniest Man in the World crowned his list. There was from first meeting an unexpressed kinship between the two. A pair of jolly fatties was the way the world saw them, but the Funniest Man read in Forbes' glance the secret detestation of the slender weaklings who surrounded them. Forbes was invited to several very unusual parties given by the Funniest Man.

While this friendship grew, the boars in the hills prospered. The remaining snakes, on the other hand, packed up and moved, never to return. On an inspection trip up to his holdings an interesting aspect of the wild acres was uncovered, though it was Forbes who concocted the scheme upon which the Funniest Man seized with squeals of vicious laughter.

There were, among the Funniest Man's acquaintance, a number of handsome slender princes and potentates of the movie empire. It was the joy of these petal-pale beings, jointly and severally, to boast of their manliness when it came to roughing it on hunting trips. A select group of these fearless white hunters was invited by the Funniest Man to a wild-boar hunt and barbecue in the hills.

All foregathered at the northern end of Vine Street, dressed like pukka sahibs in sun helmets, with cartridge belts girdling their slim waists. One exquisite chap, a director, was accompanied by a little colored boy bearing a spear, that director then conveying to the other guests in a cultivated series of curt monosyllables that it was correct to administer the *coup de grace* to a boar with a spear. In the open cars the guns gleamed in the sun, and when the safari was on the move the wire spokes of the wheels glittered, though gradually the churned dust of the road dulled their luster. One car had a coughing spell and could not continue, its passengers doubling up with those in a foreign model with smart wicker-basket seats. Forbes had arrived in a heavy truck rented for himself and his host. Up into the hills they climbed, the truck drawing up the rear. A boar was sighted and the intrepid hunters greeted its appearance with manly cries and several wild potshots. "No hunting the boar from the auto," one of the gentlemen cried out in horror. "Not sporting!" His companions dropped their heads in mortification. Then, having gained the crest, another boar was sighted and the lead auto came to a halt, its radiator knocking against its ribs in the dry exhaustive heat. Out poured the hunters, guns at the ready, dancing about in the dust and peering into the brush.

A boar, a black brute with a grunt like a tuba, appeared directly on the road above them. The lad with the spear, still sitting in the back of an auto, whistled in awe and clutched his weapon. Before anyone could draw a bead, the boar charged. All hunters scrambled for safety, and by the time they were back in their autos three more boars were making their presence known. As in a planned charge the shockingly ferocious brutes began attacking the autos. There was a great deal of dust, manly shrieks of terror, and wild gunfire. More boars came charging out of the brush. Someone screamed, "Steer the son of a bitch!" as one of the crowded autos was rammed dangerously near the rim of a sharp drop. Past the big truck in which Forbes and the Funniest Man sat, another auto raced backward in a slide, its wheels discing the loose dust. The lad with the spear had been displaced onto the rear of his auto, and he lay spreadeagled on the burning metal surface, still gamely clutching his spear and trying to keep from being flung off as the auto spun around under attack.

When Forbes at last had to wipe away his tears and catch his breath there were only the furied boars and the dust. Far down the hill were the sounds of the safari's motors as they sped for Vine Street. The boars set siege to the truck, and Forbes and the Funniest Man slaughtered them with rifles until the very dust began to stink. Filled with the highest of spirits they dismounted and began counting the kill.

A shaft of light caught Forbes' eye. "Son of a bitch!" he yelled. "Looka that!" Even as he was watching the boar died, the spear extending upright from its heart, and the dust settling on him pungent as powdered mustard.

"That's the one," the Funniest Man said, licking his lips, "we're gunna eat!"

He was a sweet guy, the Funniest Man in the World. The Feeb was born one night when both fatties were deep in their cups. The Funniest Man encouraged Forbes, advising him on how best to bring out The Feeb's most salient traits. He introduced Forbes to a number of prominent people, and though they laughed fit to kill at The Feeb, they were doubtful that moviegoers were ready for the sexual sufferings that were the very heart of The Feeb's act. When the Funniest Man died of a heart attack at twenty-seven, The Feeb very nearly died with him. Forbes was invited around to parties to play The Feeb, but no one cared, or dared, to risk good film on him. Until

Seymour Pentlove, with his impeccable taste for the genuinely vulgar, saw in The Feeb a folk figure all America would love.

Shaking off his remembrances of things past, Forbes said, "Any boars around here?"

"Bores?" Mark echoed. "What bores?"

"Let it go," Forbes said.

Inside Mark's house, Forbes looked about in appreciation. "Quiet old dump. Got the place to yourself, all right. Bet you could fling some wild 'uns up here. Give me a drink, Counsel."

Mark complied, coming to join Forbes in the living room. Forbes squinted his eyes. "Say, you mind turning off that blue light in your solarium? It bothers me."

"I do mind. Here, sit with your back to it."

There was a time of silence, Mark aware that Forbes was measuring him. He found himself listening intently to the tinkle of ice in Forbes' glass. Finally Mark asked with no great show of interest, "What did the police say they wanted with you?"

"Same old hootenanny. What happened to Naismith at the Eden. They've charged the doctor, I guess you know, with murder."

"I know. What did you tell them?"

"Same as I told you."

"Did you mention the ice? You neglected to speak to me of it."

Forbes was absolutely still, his arm arrested in the motion of bringing his drink to his mouth. "Ice?"

"The ice a witness saw you insert into Miss Naismith. When you two were—isolated—in the bedroom."

"Inserted where?" Forbes asked stupidly; too stupidly for Mark's liking, there was a trace of calculation there.

Mark told him, adding, "You were heard to make the remark that it would cool her off."

Forbes sniggered. "Too bad I didn't think of it. That would have been one hell of a good idea."

"There is someone who says you did think of it."

"Except for one thing, Counsel, we'd run out of ice."

"The man from Bungalow Nine says he lent you some earlier that morning."

"Yeah, he comes barging in with a napkin of ice, and his eyes bugging out on stalks. What a hick. Thinking he could sample one of the bimbos for free, with me footing the bill." Forbes sniggered again. "I should have handed Naismith over to him. Only I was getting ready to strike the set and clear out. Pay off the babes and go home, you understand."

"The coroner's report," Mark said randomly, "states that Miss Naismith suffered a puncture in the wall of the vagina."

Forbes's gaze was steady. "That doctor really must be a butcher. To have carved her up like that."

"How do you account for the blood on the sheets?" Mark asked, deliberately switching around in his questioning.

"Nosebleed." Forbes laughed heartily at his own expense. "She busted me one. Naismith did."

"Then why did you find it necessary to hide them?"

"Well, there was this thing about the door having been locked. That made it look fishy."

"Especially as you had gained possession of the key and put it in the door. Why didn't you open the door then?"

"Am I on trial or what?" Forbes demanded indignantly. But when Mark did not reply, he shrugged and went on, "All right, I had tried to lay her. She kept teasing me about it." Forbes lit a cigarette and went on smilingly, "She kept taunting me that I couldn't. And she was right. I couldn't. You know what old Bill Shakespeare said about likker: 'It puts a man on, and it takes him off.' "

To his annoyance, Mark revealed his surprise. Forbes grinned in mockery. "What's The Feeb doing quoting the Bard? Is that your next question?"

"No, I still want to know why you didn't unlock the door."

"I told you! I'd taken about enough from her, so I decided to shut her big mouth once and for all. If laying her was the only way I could subdue her, then O.K. Only . . ." he raised his brows in resignation. "Only I couldn't."

"Did you manage to achieve penetration?"

"Naw, I was as impotent as an oyster by that time." Forbes winked at Mark. "So that's when she ups and busts me one in the snoot."

"Is that when you called her a bastard?"

"I did?" Forbes laughed in disbelief. "Boy, she musta had me spittin' mad by then. I called a woman a bastard? Whooee!"

"I have the sworn statement of another woman," Mark said in experiment, "to the effect that you are impotent at all times, drunk or sober."

Forbes let himself down slowly into a cold black rage like one descending into a swimming pool on a chilly night. It did not seem possible that those eyes so distended with outrage could ever be squeezed into the piglet slits of The Feeb. He was so pallid that Mark half-expected the great bulk to sink down onto itself in a faint. "If I ever get my hands on the bimbo that said that," Forbes whispered, "I'll ram. . . ."

"Ram what?" Mark prompted mildly. "Ice?"

Forbes recovered on the instant. "Jesus," he said and took a drink. He was now merely rueful. "Everybody automatically assumes a fat man can't make the grade. And a lot of it is my fault. I should remember that. As The Feeb, impotency is my stock in trade. Well, hell, it sure makes a merry tinkle at the box-office."

Tinkle, Mark thought. Increasingly the word was plaguing him. "I'm still not clear on why you simply didn't announce you'd had a nose-bleed and left the sheets on the bed."

"Because that insane woman began yelling she was hurt. Hell, I hadn't touched her except to try prying her off me, but if those girls had come in and seen her thrashing around on bloody sheets—My God, the place would have been crawling with cops in no time!"

"It may be soon," Mark promised him.

"I didn't lay her," Forbes said factually. "And I didn't insert ice up her. Now will there be anything else?"

"Did you pay the other women to take her to the Lying Inn?"

"I did. When they drug her out of the pool I saw she'd started to bleed. Christ, that really scared me. Bloody sheets in the closet looking like I'd butchered me a boar on the bed—"

"Your choice of words . . ." Mark began, but did not finish it.

"God, was I relieved to find out she was just having herself a miscarriage," Forbes said prayerfully. "What a worthless hunk of meat that bimbo was. Knocked up, and drunk, and crazy. A complete stranger and she kept yammering how well she knew me, and then when she's kicking the bucket she decides I was the one who did it. I raped her. Good God, she—" He could not go on, powerless to express his disgust. "If she had lived wouldn't she have been a millstone about my neck! I'd never have gotten her off me short of—"

"You would have," Mark assured him. "She knew how to impose involuntary servitude on a man, but she did it by playing on his pity." He took polite notice that Forbes had finished his drink. "Another drink?" When Forbes refused, Mark said, "I'll call you a taxi. This is enough for tonight."

Mark came back from the phone to find Forbes musing, a sneer on his round face. "Lemme tell you something, D'Andor," Forbes said. "You're wondering why I'm not the least bit sorry that that bimbo died. You are, only you're too busy with your bottle to let it amount to much. You're sorry for her. Christ, you're probably even sorry for me!"

"I would not relish going through life playing The Feeb," Mark said evenly.

"See! That's what I mean! But let me set you straight about me. So we'll have a perfect understanding about the type person I am. When I was a kid I never cried. You get that? I *never* cried. My mother even took her little fat boy to the doctor about it once. She thought I was nuts because I didn't blubber every five minutes the way the other brats did. But for as long as I can remember I always knew that bawling is a waste of time. That's for dumb women like the Naismith dame. So if slopping all over yourself about your own troubles isn't worth the effort, then that goes double for doing it over anyone else. And especially over Naismith. She's about as great a loss to the world as when the wind dies. There's always a fresh breeze to come along. I don't feel anything about her, and certainly not—pity."

Mark studied his client with the deceptive ease he had developed to conceal his deepest concentration. At last he said lightly. "Good."

Forbes was caught off guard. "Good? Why do you say that?"

"Why," Mark said easily, "I thought for a moment you were going to say you felt no remorse over Miss Naismith's death."

"Remorse? Oh. If I'd said that then you would think I was guilty in some way."

"No, it would mean you thought you were guilty in some way. There's a difference. Defending a client who considers himself guilty is hell. I feel I ought to sit him in the box with the rest of the jurors. I'm fighting to save his life and he's beside me looking through coffin catalogues, checking off the models he likes best. I don't give a damn if he *is* guilty, I just don't want him feeling that way. Usurpation of the jury's prerogatives, you see, deciding your own case for them."

Forbes absorbed this for some time. "You mean you wouldn't care if here and now I confessed I killed Naismith with a twenty-five pound block of ice? You'd still handle my case?"

"Of course I'd still handle your case," Mark snapped. "The guilty are the ones most in need of legal counsel, for God's sake!"

Forbes set up a helpless tittering, managing to say only, "Counsel, you scare hell out of me. There's nothing worse than some professional wreck still clinging to his one last ideal."

"You're no fool, Forbes."

"Yeah, Counsel, but keep it under your hat. A thing like that get out it could ruin my career. Sounds like my taxi outside." Forbes walked under the chandelier in the hall, causing it to chime, and went out into the night.

CHAPTER THIRTEEN

The saints preserve us fumbling criminal lawyers, Mark thought, from the callously innocent. With great care, like one leading a drunk along a precipitous trail, he took himself downstairs to bed. There to lie mulling the sorry wherefores of Muffin's death. It occurred to him that his role was less lawyer than that of an investigator following strewn wreckage back to the point of impact.

Muffin had always had a penchant for catastrophe; it was uncanny the way it camped on her doorstep. All too often lamentations were her chit-chat. Her silk stockings forever sprang ladders, her new "perm" was too kinky, she found no solace in the company of other girls—they were all deplorably common, and invariably jealous of her as well. Even in repose she was shrill. What joys she knew were mere caprices, sops at best, carelessly tossed at her by a fate that maliciously withheld the only thing she really wanted. As a consequence she was subject to sudden overwhelming desires. One time her sample of Princess Pat face powder had not arrived in the mail when she had set her heart on its doing so, there were only bills in her box; these she thrust at Mark and he accepted them, if not with grace, then with resignation. He had bought her, that evening, the silly silver compact with the little drawers—though he knew that within her heart of hearts it could not begin to assuage her for the cruel failure of her Princess Pat sample to arrive.

Another time, a party was given to introduce a new star—a German shepherd dog—and she was not invited, though there was no earthly reason why she should have been. As a result of that agonizing oversight her darting eye fell, with lustful wanting, on a Siamese kitten. Forlorn in a pet-shop window, it was a raucous wail issuing from toothpick bones wrapped in fur. Muffin viewed the kitten as an exotic trinket, cuddling it while the proprietor of the shop explained to Mark that he was letting it go for a song (five dollars worth of music) because it was flawed with a white hind foot. Mark's money bought him a memorable evening, for Muffin was of good cheer, announcing, "Let's us all go home and I'll throw us a real feed together," and was as good as her word, and better in her pull-down bed than he had thought possible. Muffin did grow a trifle impatient, of course, when the kitten slunk under her bathtub, trembling and refusing cream. Muffin dragged it out and began to bully it, thrusting its nose into the cream to make it drink, until Mark took the little creature from her, and dipping his fingers, let the animal nurse from them until it fell asleep on his chest; Muffin occupied herself thinking up names. Since the kitten was an adjunct to her private vision of herself, the name would have to be clever, jazzy. None of Mark's suggestions was within shouting distance of being worthy.

In the weeks to follow, when his laggard footsteps took him from a courtroom to her door, faithful to his servitude and in need of the release-cum-irritant of loveless lovemaking, he was forced to endure as well any number of monologues on Muffin's part, all beginning with "Us. . ." Snuggling the kitten she would complain poutily, "Us didn't eat our din-din. Us is a bad putty tat. A bad wittle tattums, us is." Then holding the animal aloft for inspection, she demanded of Mark, "Isn't us toot?"

"Us is the apotheosis of tootness," he agreed, coming closer to disliking an animal than ever he had in his life. And because Muffin would not dress to go out for dinner, nor cook for him, nor open her legs, dawdling and posing instead with the cat, he added tartly, "Tarry on," and she giggled at what she thought was baby-talk on his part. Still, it served to render her agreeable if not downright jolly, and he received in part what he came for.

It was sometime after the advent of the kitten that Mark was inspired to have his secretary discover the whereabouts of Manny Amen and invite that gentleman over to the office.

Manny, once the servitor and bootlegger to local *bons vivants,* knew Everyone, and Mark would have thought of him sooner had not Manny inexplicably dropped from sight. Some neuralgic trouble or other was said to be at the bottom of it. But Manny Amen was a man of parts, and were anyone to know of some obscure citizen of Poverty Row in need of a strikingly pretty ingénue with a voice like a dentist's drill and an accommodating nature to match, Manny would be he.

Manny arrived one morning on the stroke of nine, slapping his feet strangely as he left the elevator. He advanced toward Mark wearing a brave hopeful grin, his knees rigid, his shoes smacking the floor like planks insecurely strapped to his ankles. "So hi ya, Counsel," Manny said with the perfervid cheeriness of the down-and-outer, and fell unceremoniously into the first chair he encountered.

"Fine. And you, Manny?"

"Can't complain," Manny asserted vigorously out of a wide grin, sweat oozing from his nose, his eyes like a cur's seeking a home.

"How're the legs?" Mark asked.

"Funny," Manny said. "It's really funny. I got something brand new. Real exclusive." He was full of glee, all but his dismal gaze. "Jake leg!" he declared triumphantly.

"Good God, what's that?"

Manney winked. "You never was one for my jake, was you? Irish is your tipple. Only client for Irish I ever had." He spread his hands, inviting Mark to share a delicious joke. "I should of laid off my own merchandise. Would you believe it? The docs finally figured it was the Jamaica ginger. Yeah. The Jamaica goddam ginger. That's why I always called my gin jake, because I flavored it with the ginger. Did give it a nice gin taste, you have to admit that. Why, I could give you one testigoddammonial after another from clients who were crazy about my jake. And that rotten ginger was what played hell with the old nerves." He paused for effect, then said intensely, "I'm writ up in a doctor's magazine. Wouldn't that slay you? They got a fancy name like locogoddammotor-a-taxi or something near that for it. It isn't," he went on with pride, "curable, you see. When they're not using the fancy name the docs just call it jake leg. Boy, wouldn't that tickle your funnybone!

'Course, it's what people always say about Manny Amen— if it's new, then old Manny's the first in town to have it." Modesty required that Manny not pursue the point further.

Torn between congratulating Manny and commiserating with him, Mark cleared his throat. "Manny, what's this I hear about your setting yourself up as an actor's agent?"

Manny was all sly winks and grins. "Counsel, it's the coming thing, let me tell you. Always the first with the most, that's Manny. Strictly legit, too. What can I do for you?"

"Help a pretty girl. I'll give you the money to have a screen test made of her. You must know someone who'll be willing to shoot a little film after hours, when no one's looking. Then I want you to show it around. Get her any break you can. I'll put you on a retainer until she's able to pay you herself. And, Manny—she's not to know I had anything to do with it. Can you help me on this?"

"Can do," Manny said, sweating more than ever. But ancient loyalties struggled within him and won. "Look, Counsel, you like this girl? Then do yourself a favor. *Take* her to the movies, don't get her in 'em."

"It's what she wants most, Manny."

"Yeah," Manny protested, "but you've done me lotsa good turns, Counsel. I'm just wanting to make sure I'll be doing you one."

"You will be," Mark said ardently.

"One thing I did for you," Manny decided suddenly, "was sell you my Irish and drink my jake myself." He laughed uproariously, sweating and hitting his damaged legs in his hilarity.

When Manny sobered, Mark said, "Will you do this for me, Manny? See if one of your old clients can give this girl a break?"

"When did I say I wouldn't?" Manny said indignantly.

"She really is very pretty."

"And that's your fault?" Manny demanded. He grew morose just thinking of women. "Dames! Before I got my jake leg I had me a real looker. And she was as cold as a china chamber pot on a January morning. Or is that your trouble too, Counsel?"

"Near enough," Mark evaded. "I'll give you her name and

address. Pretend you saw her on the street and was struck with her movie potentialities."

Manny sighed. "In other words, she's like all the rest—a total sap?"

"I'm sorry to say that that is a fair estimate of her mental powers."

"Okay, you're on," Manny said. "Only I'll need a century note to get operating."

Manny sweated and glowed while Mark wrote him a check.

Muffin was at once arch and imperious, holding the little cat to her cheek and peeping at Mark. "Us haddums twite a day," her said. "Someone very very important," she continued on, dropping the cat to the floor, "has discovered me." She adopted an air of mystery, not so much to provoke Mark as because she was uncertain just how to go on.

"Oh?" Mark said, and contained his surge of hope, quietly smoking. "That does sound like good news."

With a change of mood Muffin began to pout. "Only thing is," she said, "us is in season." She stared coldly at the half-grown cat.

"What!"

"That damn cat is in heat!" Muffin said sharply. "And I can't sleep with all her yowling." Reverting to her coyness, she climbed on Mark's lap. "And Mr. Amen says I've got to have lots and lots of sleep all the time. I've got this dewy freshness to preserve. Mr. Amen's a stickler for good health, you see, because he got gassed and ruined his."

"You don't say?" Mark inquired. "Your Mr. Amen sounds mighty frank-spoken."

"Oh, yes. He got gassed in the World War," Muffin said, impressed. "He told me." Remembering her objective she lapsed into baby-talk. "So the fing for Us to do is move up to your house."

"Now, hold it, Muffin. I thought it was long understood between us that I could not have anyone living with me. Many nights I bring work home with me, and I have to be alone. Besides," he pointed out, "what if Mr. Amen gets you a part?

You don't drive, and you wouldn't be able to get down the hill—"

"I didn't say us, I said *Us*!" Muffin snapped. "That stupid cat. I guess I didn't tell you, I've been so busy with my career and all—but I named her Us. And you got to take Us up to your place." She jumped to her feet, glaring down at Mark. "Oh, I know I'm not welcome in that precious house you built for Constance," she said in the vicious voice of resentment. "Now that she's dead I'm surprised you'd haven't made a national shrine of that house. But I'm not—"

"Shut up, Muffin."

Her voice rose. "But I'm not without pride, I'll have you know! You've always treated me like a nobody. You come around like you're giving charity. Well, you're going to learn plenty about me one of these days. When I'm a big star you'll have another think coming. There are other people who know, even if you don't, that I'm not just an ordinary-type girl. You're going to find out I'm pretty few and far between!"

"I'm sure of that, Muffin. But I can't take Us. A cat wandering around alone all day. It would be cruel."

Muffin smiled gaily, astonishingly pretty in that moment. "Then I guess I'll just have to call the pound. You know what I heard? They put all these animals in this cage and then they back up a car to it. The exhaust is what kills them. Did you ever hear that?"

At Mark's feet the cat sat as if comprehending every word. With a wail it leaped into his lap and began washing its one white foot. "Let's go home, Us," Mark said, and this time did not so much as say good night before taking his casual leave.

Released in his house, Us, driven by the deep-seated demands of nature, promptly disappeared. Mark did not see how she could have gotten out, but late that night he listened to a pack of coyotes making a kill and lay clammy, sure that the little half-grown city cat was furnishing the pack a skimpy meal.

It was on the second night that he sat up in bed, the moonlight streaming past the patio wall and through the window on to his coverlet, and heard in the bowels of the house Us' mournful caterwaul. He searched everywhere, Us' voice sounding loud in each room he visited. He hollered down the heating vents and received silence in reply. He returned to bed and was at once surrounded by Us' cries for rescue. He called Muffin, explained his trouble, and said he would be down for her. Perhaps she might coax Us from her hiding place.

"Are you cuckoo?" Muffin said in sleepy outrage. "Mr. Amen said I got to be dewy at all times. I'm meeting this very very important person tomorrow, and no silly cat is going to have me looking like a groan. Mr. Amen is going to introduce me to the producer who's making *Jazz Me, Baby*."

After Us had been imprisoned in the walls of the house for three days. Mark got a hammer and chisel and went to work. He pried out registers and he tapped the walls, calling and calling. And finally, hearing faint cries of hunger and thirst just underfoot, he lifted some of the flooring in the living room. Discovering nothing, he stood in the hallway under the chandelier, listening intently. Out of the corner of his eye he saw Us seated in the kitchen in front of the icebox, expectant that someone would come open it any moment.

He fed the cat and called Muffin to tell her the good news. Muffin said, "Listen, I *gotta* get my beauty sleep! You and that dumbinski cat—"

"Aren't you being a little tart?" Mark suggested mildly.

"What! How dare you call me a—"

"You misunderstood me. I merely meant that you sounded—"

"Mark," Muffin pleaded, "don't you understand? I'm having a screen test tomorrow. This is my big big break. And if I look like a hag and ruin it, I'll—I swear I'll kill—"

"You won't look like a hag. You'll look beautiful."

"I will if I get some sleep," she grumbled. "And that's another thing. Mr. Amen says I got to start living practically like a nun or somebody. I owe it to my career to keep this fresh look I got."

"I quite understand," Mark said, concealing as best he was able a surging sense of relief. "Only— Muffin?"

"Oh, now what!"

"I just wanted to wish you luck. I hope you wow 'em."

He picked Us up and took her to bed with him, thinking that he had simply exchanged one pretty little demanding beast for another. At dawn Us sat at the window squalling to be let out. "All right," Mark said. As he opened the window for her, he added, "Good Luck, Us. Be careful. And above all— I hope you wow 'em."

For a time Us slept in at night and wanted her two squares a day. She and Mark were polite, each preoccupied and given to long stretches of silence. He was at peace, having no woman and wanting none. A time or two he thought of looking up Pep Baines, wondering if she could spare him an evening from the demands of motherhood. Then he did not bother to make the effort.

Gradually Us went wild, making rare appearances for a handout or a dry place during the rains. She grew scarred, rangy, and powerful, arrogance and insolence personified. She had met the fierce world of fang and claw and had found it no great shakes. It was gruelling work being a predator, but for Us it was a living. Over the years Mark forgot about her for months at a time, until, of a hot still night he would hear again her battle cry ringing out among the stars.

CHAPTER FOURTEEN

Dr. Snowdom's preliminary hearing was of scant interest to the press, and beneath the notice of scandalmongers. Like the ancient Greeks, the scandalmongers were of the opinion that tragedy befell only kings or persons in high places. There was a lone cub reporter with a face as shiny as a pie tin who, with his infallible nose for news and unerring judgment of men, marched straight up to Dr. Snowdom and asked him in confidence what his prissy-looking Negro client had been charged with. Snowdom forbore to answer, looking quickly to Chester Dander to see if he had heard, and was relieved to see that he had not. With commendable restraint Dr. Snowdom then said only "Go peddle your papers, Sonny," and the offended cub might have gone and done just that but for spying a gentleman whose face he thought he knew, hiding behind a book in the spectator's section. The cub took himself to a seat affording him such view of Mark D'Andor as the book permitted, and from that coign of vantage he stared unceasingly at Mark, while visions of scoops and by-lines danced in his globular head.

Snowdom, first on the docket, entered the bar to take his place next Chester. The judge appeared, was enthroned, and sat glooming, looking ever and again to the trickle of sunlight which leaked dispirited as fine rain down the air shaft beyond the window. Chester, meanwhile, was practicing his self-mastering exercises. Behind his book Mark grinned, knowing Chester was as emotional as a diva though he fondly felt he presented to the world the impassivity of a haddock. And when the deputy district attorney glanced idly at Snowdom, Snowdom promptly began looking guilty as hell, as if protocol demanded it of him.

The deputy attorney, with a trial technique all his own, did not launch the hearing so much as sidle into it. A coroner's assistant mounted the stand to recite with antiseptic boredom what the autopsy of Muffin Naismith had revealed. Death due to septicemia resulting from an abortion, the witness droned and stifled a yawn. The body bore bruises. There was a lesion of the vaginal wall. The witness struggled to overcome the soporific content of his testimony.

Softspoken Chester rose to his feet to cross-examine. To his first question the witness said, "What? Talk louder, I can't hear a word you're saying."

Chester betimes was contending with his first blush of the day. "I am referring to the vaginal lesion. Could that lesion have been caused by means other than surgery?"

The witness shrugged. "Like what means?"

"Why," Chester said, "intercourse."

"Intercourse?" the witness echoed, looking at Snowdom with a new respect.

"Yes," Chester said.

Again the witness shrugged. "What with all the inflammation present, it would be hard to say."

"Could that lesion have been caused by a forcible act of intercourse?"

"If you're talking about rape," the witness said, apathetic as ever, "there's no end of injuries we've seen. And others show no signs of internal injuries at all."

"Then could this lesion," Chester began, "have been caused by—"

"I don't know," the witness said. But just as Chester drew a deep breath, the witness added, "Only I personally don't think so."

A policeman mounted the stand to tell of his summons to the Snowdom Sanitarium and the events thereafter. On cross-examination Chester meticulously elicited from the policeman who was where, when, and every statement made. Lowering his book, Mark quite approved of Chester's determination to eke out every last bit of information and at the same time box up the witness so that he could not come forth with new and damaging testimony at some future trial.

"Were there any statements made you have not repeated here?" Chester asked.

"Objection," the deputy attorney said in a rather haphazard manner.

"No," the witness said.

"*Will* you stop speaking!" the deputy attorney snapped.

"All right," the witness said. "Only I don't have any more to tell anyway."

The deputy attorney let his hand drop loudly to the counsel table in disgust.

A detective took the stand to say that Dr. Snowdom had admitted to performing a dilatation and curettage on the deceased. But to Chester's inquiry he replied that Dr. Snowdom had stated that the surgery was imperative as the abortive process was under way at the time she was brought under Snowdom's care.

Chester sat down. The deputy attorney requested that Dr. Snowdom be bound over for trial on the homicide charge. Slowly Chester got to his feet. "I wish to present a witness, Your Honor."

"Counselor, you know it is not customary," the judge said.

"No, Your Honor; however there is sound precedent for my producing a witness at my own discretion."

"Proceed," the judge said, glooming again at the window.

Chester addressed the bailiff. "There is a Miss Pritchard in the corridor. Would you please bring her in?"

"Pritchard!" the deputy attorney yelped. "But she's a witness for the people."

And that, Mark reminded himself, is one of the things I came here to learn.

"I have Miss Pritchard under subpoena," Chester said.

The deputy D.A. sank into his chair. "Have it your way, Counselor," he said airily. "Only remember— She's your witness and I have no intention of sitting here and letting you cross-examine her."

"Excuse me, Counselor," Chester said, flushes and blushes

all in order and under control, "but I assure you I intend no misconduct."

Chester looked to the bailiff, and Miss Pritchard was brought in. She was wearing a pleated cloche hat that closely resembled a lampshade even to the ribbon through it, under which her tight mouth and pinched nose boded ill for just about anyone Mark would have cared to name.

On the stand Miss Pritchard proved fractious as a bronco, and the deputy district attorney brightened to the point of perking up considerably. And this in spite of the fact that Miss Pritchard announced that if she knew one thing in this world it was that Miss Naismith had been tampered with before entering the Snowdom Sanitarium.

"Tampered with?" Chester repeated meaningfully.

"That's what she said," Miss Pritchard vowed, then threw back her head so that she might peer up at the judge from under her pleated hat. "Whatever she meant by that," Miss Pritchard told the judge.

"Whatever is right," the opposing attorney said to no one at all.

"Would you give us the deceased's exact words?" Chester requested.

"Certainly not," Miss Pritchard said.

"I should think not," the deputy district attorney said in approval. He appealed to the judge. "Your Honor, I have been as patient as possible. But counsel has produced nothing but hearsay, conjecture, and irrelevancies."

"The testimony is offered as an exception to the hearsay rule," Chester said. "A dying declaration—"

"I will overrule the objection," the Court decided.

The district attorney was exceeding unhappy. "But, Your Honor, the witness herself has told us that the deceased was running a temperature at the very moment these—"

"Everybody runs a temperature," Miss Pritchard informed one and all loudly. "We'd be stone-cold otherwise."

"That," the judge said, "will be enough of your volunteered information, ma'am."

Embattled, Chester had begun to glow like a particularly splendid sunset. "Miss Pritchard, will you tell us exactly what Miss Naismith said as she was dying?"

"She asked for a lawyer."

"Yes, yes, of course. But what else, if anything, did Miss——"

"Why, she said a man had hurt her and for me to see he did not get away with it."

"How had he hurt her?"

"Well, for heaven's sake, he raped her, didn't he? Just what does someone have to do to a woman before you men will consider her to be——"

A split-second before the judge could growl, Chester asked of Miss Pritchard, "Did Miss Naismith tell you she had been raped?"

"No."

Chester swayed slightly, and an unidentifiable sound escaped the other attorney. Gentle as always, Chester plodded on. "Would you please tell the Court what Miss Naismith said, in her exact words?"

Miss Pritchard sat up straight. "She said, 'He hurt me. He hurt me inside. Don't let the son of a bitch get away with it.' "

"Thank you," Chester said, almost with a sob of relief. "And did Miss Naismith mention any names?"

"Certainly. She intimated Feeb Forbes had done it."

"*Done what?*" the judge shouted.

Miss Pritchard flung up her head so violently that the pleated-lampshade hat nearly fell off. "Raped her, what else!"

"Did she use that word?" the judge demanded.

"Son of a bitch? That was the least of the words that poor dying little thing——"

"Did she use the word *rape!*" the judge insisted.

"And what's wrong with that, I'd like to know!" Miss Pritchard countered.

"Miss Pritchard," Chester begged softly, "did Miss Naismith say she had been raped by Feeb Forbes?"

"I've told you six times that she did," Miss Pritchard said. "Why don't you listen?"

Chester fell into his chair. "And when did Miss Naismith say this assault had taken place?"

"Just before she was brought into the Sanitarium. When d'you think? A year before?"

The judge leaned over to Miss Pritchard. "Madam, this is a court of—" He sighed and plainly showed defeat. To Chester he said, "Any more questions of this witness?"

"No, Your Honor."

"Cross-examine?" the judge said unhappily to the deputy district attorney.

"Not me," that attorney said with great conviction.

Miss Pritchard glowered on one and all, showing no favoritism.

Mark had unobstrusively walked down the aisle and into the row of seats just behind Chester. With a respectful nod to the court, Mark bent toward Chester as if he had a piece of vital information for him. With a rather dazed look on his face, Chester turned around to Mark. "Nice going, Chester," Mark whispered. "I didn't doubt for a moment you could do it."

As calmly as he had come into court Mark left it. He went to a public phone and called Mr. Pentlove. "Where's Forbes?"

"Here on the lot."

"By noon he'll be under arrest, if not earlier. With no intention of punning, I'm telling you that the fat is now in the fire."

"I see. The man who was at the Eden fracas," Mr. Pentlove said evenly, "is cooling his heels in your office, waiting to talk to you. Any instructions for Forbes?"

"Yes. Tell him this time he's not to play The Feeb for the boys downtown. Tell him to keep his mouth shut, opening it only long enough to ask I be called. There's no chance he'll try to run, is there? Take it on the lam?"

"I should imagine it would depend on whether he's guilty or not," Mr. Pentlove decided. "But as I don't intend to talk to him of this until I receive word that the police have come on the lot, I doubt if he'll have much choice. What happened at Snowdom's hearing, anyway?"

"That," Mark said, "is the question everyone in that courtroom is asking himself."

"But what about Snowdom? I thought they were all set to pin it on him."

"You're half correct. The D.A.'s boys have rather been playing pin the donkey, but all along the objective has been your Golden Ass. They had Miss Pritchard under wraps, and since her testimony could be only favorable as regards Snowdom, it had to be they had her in mind for other purposes. This morning's preliminary hearing was just a way of putting the fear of God in Snowdom. Now that he's a free man, he's probably this minute licking the hands of the nice deputy attorneys. Begging them to tell him how he can help them convict Forbes."

"*Tsk!*" Mr. Pentlove said irritably. "I was in such hopes, D'Andor, that you could push the whole blame off on Snowdom. What a nuisance this thing is turning out to be!"

"I can quite understand your disappointment," Mark sympathized. "Having had your heart set on a real miscarriage of justice."

"D'Andor!" Mr. Pentlove began on a rising note of outrage.

"Save it," Mark said. "You can reach me at my office."

II

In his office Mark repaired at once to the desk drawer in which reposed his tin of Irish. Sensible that Archibald Forbes would soon be singing for him, he put the Irish away as soon as he reached a state of quasi-wellbeing. When the secretary below rang him, he thought the summons had come, but she wished only to announce that a Mr. Benny Sligh was at Mark's service and had been for some time. Mr. Sligh was therefore granted audience.

Mr. Benny Sligh sauntered from the elevator, cigarette on his lip, smoke drifting up his nostrils, that ultimate expression of virile disdain. Aside from the cultivated manipulations of his cigarette, Mr. Sligh did not lack other charms. His walk and method of seating himself was that of a churl on his day off playing the aristocrat. Hair and eyes shared the same thick black glister, and his fragile nostrils were a lesson themselves in the art of appearing supercilious. He was all dolled up in natty pin-striped navy, with a navy shirt and a terra-cotta tie. He was handsome the way a stiletto is, limited but very much to the point. In manner and dress Mr. Sligh left no smallest detail to chance, lest one not recognize immediately that he trafficked in trollops. Mr. Sligh said, "Shake, Counsel," not bothering to extend his hand, and crossed his legs so that he might feast with unalloyed delight on the sight of his narrow foot encased in terra-cotta suede. Without removing his cigarette, Mr. Sligh asked with negligent grace, "What can I do you for? Mr. Pentlove hinted I might be of some small service."

"Yes, thank you. You pimp for Flirt Smith, don't you?"

Mr. Sligh was pained. "I sure wish the jerks what writ the penal code would of knew what they was talking about. Counsel, I *pander*."

"You have a point, Benny," Mark conceded. "You do, though, perform the services of panderer for Flirt?"

Mr. Sligh became alert. "Say, you haven't heard any complaints about her, have you? She get out of line with somebody?" To show he was in earnest Mr. Sligh removed the cigarette from his mouth. "One thing I won't put up with is one of my bimbos giving anybody her big lip."

"No, Miss Flirt Smith is the soul of honesty," Mark assured Mr. Sligh, who lounged back in his chair but was not entirely mollified. "I am wondering, though," Mark went on, "about Olive Jones. Where is she?"

Mr. Sligh fingered his terra-cotta tie. "You can search me. Never heard of her."

"She was one of the girls you brought to The Feeb's bungalow at the Eden week end before last."

"Oh, that one," Mr. Sligh said with elaborate disgust. "Some free-lancer I picked up at the last minute. I had a call from Mr. Forbes, and Flirt was the only one at liberty. So I saw this other bimbo working the lobby of the Eden and just took her on for the night. I just picked her up for a spare."

"Your business arrangements are your own affair," Mark said; "what I want to know is where she can be reached."

Mr. Sligh shrugged with wintry disdain. "She could of long since blew out for parts unknown. Just a drifter, like I say."

"Benny," Mark said quietly, "I got me a whole drawer here full of fresh new John Doe subpoenas. One of them will surely fit you to a *t*." Mark put his hand on the drawer that was virgin of all but his tin of Irish. "You've not been in court for so long, Benny, that you must have forgotten what it can be like."

Mr. Sligh took a turn for the sullen. "I'm all paid up and you know it. There isn't a cop in miles who would touch a hair of my head."

"Ah, but you see," Mark explained in a friendly manner, "if I were to subpoena you, and put you on the witness stand—that would be different. We'd have a long detailed discussion of just how you make your living—among other things. And at the conclusion of your testimony the judge himself, I've no doubt, would order the transcript of your testimony to be sent forthwith to the office of the District Attorney. You haven't—" Mark went on in a jocular tone "—been laying protection money on Superior Court judges, have you, Benny?"

Mr. Sligh twisted his compact head from side to side, irresolution personified. ". . . done to you, Counsel, jazzing me this way?" was all Mark heard of his mumble. "What're you trying to mix me up in?"

Hand still on the drawer, Mark said, "I want to know the whereabouts of that second girl, Olive Jones. And I'm not trying to mix you into anything. You are already in it up to your horns. And if the D.A.'s office finds that girl before I do, believe me, Benny, you will wish you'd gone the way of Manny Amen, *insane asylum* and all, before I'm done with you." Mark opened the drawer an inch. "You're giving me no choice, Benny!"

"Jesus H. God!" Benny exploded miserably. "Hold your horses. My God. Son of a bitch!" On a wail of profound anguish he ended, "Gee whiz!"

"You must tell me, Benny," Mark said in a more kindly tone. "I thought Mr. Pentlove had made it clear that you were to cooperate with me in—"

"Mr. Pentlove!" Benny nearly sobbed. "Counsel, it was Mr. *Pent*love that . . . ."

"Oh."

Benny looked to his terra-cotta suede shoe, but took no joy from it.

"So it was you who shipped Olive Jones out of town. Where to?"

"St. Louis," Benny muttered.

"And you gave her a going-away present just to make certain she didn't try to ripen her new friendship with that nice Mr. Pentlove?"

"Well—sure," Benny admitted, feeling himself on firmer ground.

"Did you use a knife?"

Benny looked at Mark abjectly. "No. Cross my heart." He added in a low whimper, "I just kind of let her teethe on my knuckles a bit." With the passion of one unjustly put upon, Benny hurled at Mark, "And Mr. Pentlove didn't give me so much as a hint that this was what you wanted to talk to me about!"

"No? What did he say we would discuss—the new finger waves?"

Benny giggled sorrowfully. "No, nothing like that." He sought to pull himself together. "Just—about how that Naismith dame was after The Feeb the whole time I was there."

"How long were you at the Eden?"

"Oh. . . . Midnight on. I left right after The Feeb did."

"When the girls took Miss Naismith out of the pool?"

Mr. Sligh took hold of himself. "Yeah. And it become apparent to us all that she'd gone off her trolley."

"Is it your custom to deliver girls and then sit around chaperoning them all night?"

"When," Mr. Sligh said crisply, "I'm not sure one of them is out to give satisfaction, yeah. Flirt, she knows her business. But the other one, you see, was not a regular of mine. I hung around to make sure she behaved herself."

"And did Olive behave herself?"

Mr. Sligh shrugged judiciously. "The Feeb had no complaints."

"Then what was it that Olive Jones saw that convinced her she could shake down Pentlove? Hmmm, Benny?"

"Saw?" Benny quavered. "Saw where? Saw when? What was there to see? I ask you, what was there to see? *When*? I mean, you know?"

"She might have seen the ice in Miss Naismith's glass when Miss Naismith went alone into the bedroom with Forbes."

"Ice!" Benny bawled. "*What* ice?"

Mark closed his eyes. "Benny, tell me this, then. What is The Feeb's pleasure?" His eyes came open to meet the suave smirk of the worldly Mr. Sligh. "Is he capable of having intercourse with a woman?"

"Well. . . ." Mr. Sligh murmured indulgently, "some you know, does a bit better than others. Every guy has to do the best with what he's got, eh, Counsel? Some just—" Mr. Sligh gave his nails a quick buffing on his lapel "—struggle along, and are thankful they get that much. Flirt's very good at helping," he threw in with professional pride.

"Has Flirt ever told you that The Feeb was rough with her? Tried to hurt her in some way?"

"I'll break her neck!" Mr. Sligh promised. "If she ever does!"

"Benny, I will ask you again, what did Olive Jones have on The Feeb?"

"Ask me until the cows come home," Mr. Sligh said flippantly. "And I'll still tell you—nothing. Unless it was that the Naismith dame—" he sniggered "—come out at the last minute about her being in a state of motherhood. A fine thing!" Mr. Sligh could not contain his repugnance. "You may not know, Counsel, but I'd seen this Naismith around town before. Well, you know the kind. She's just a piece of flopsum. Like something that washes up on the beach. And goes out with the next tide." He said all this in a condescending manner, as if Mark were somewhat thick-witted, at the same time taking out a silver cigarette case with a lighter mounted on its top. "But . . ." Mr. Sligh continued, declining to take a charitable view of Muffin Naismith, ". . . it takes all kinds to make a world." Over the flame of the lighter Mr. Sligh made what he was certain would be his nearest thrust in many a moon. "How much's the Naismith dumbbell dame trying to get from The Feeb?"

"What makes you think she is trying to shake down The Feeb?"

Mr. Sligh, affronted, said icily, "Counsel, I wasn't born last Tuesday at nine in the morning. Flirt's holed up somewhere, *I* don't even know where, and Savant hightailed all over town 'til he caught up with Olive, and Mr. Pentlove has me do the honors of seeing her off on the train. Next thing I know, I'm to come talk to you and say how Naismith wasn't no society girl makin' her debut when *I* took in her little act—and you ask me how I know she's breathing down The Feeb's neck."

"She's not breathing," Mark said.

"What's that agin?" Mr. Sligh asked, with good reason.

"I said: She is not breathing."

The cigarette rolled from Benny Sligh's sagging lower lip. He caught it awkwardly. "She's dead?" When Mark's expression alone confirmed this, Benny blurted, "Why, that's a filthy shame! The hell you say! How did it happen?"

"Don't you know?"

"Well, Jesus H. Bible! How would *I* know?" Benny Sligh was awash in dismay.

"She had a miscarriage after she left the Eden."

After a few seconds had elapsed Benny nodded. "I'll tell you something, Counsel," he said solemnly. "I'd seen her around, like I say. I got the feeling here was a dame gone to the bow-wows. All the way. But she wasn't like the others, the pros. You could tell she used to be a real looker. I figured any other town but this, she might of showed some class. Hell, she might even of been some guy's wife."

"Finer eulogistics I never heard, Benny," Mark said in all seriousness. "And from a man who is an expert on women."

"Any time," Benny mumbled modestly. "You—uh—defending the doc or whoever it was killed her?"

"No, I'm defending the man who didn't kill her."

"The Feeb?" Benny gasped.

"Yes. Benny, what did he do to Naismith in that bedroom?"

"Nothing," Benny said positively. "The bottles was all in the living room. I swear it!"

CHAPTER FIFTEEN

If Seymour Pentlove seemed bent on proving himself an adept at skullduggery, Mark was not without resources of his own. But when Mr. Pentlove sought to dabble in good deeds, Mark was past his patience and put out about it. This was the case when T-Bone Tredwell stomped off the elevator soon after it had lowered the dapper Mr. Sligh to earth. Entering Mark's office, T-Bone threw an amount of cash on Mark's desk, flung himself into a chair uninvited, and began his ever-lasting stroking of his boot tops. "Old lady Werksmith'll wanna bury her own dead once she hears about where the money come from," T-Bone said angrily.

"Dammit," Mark said, "where did you get all that money?"

"Mr. Pentlove feed the kitty right after you done," said T-Bone as if he could see no distinction, fine or otherwise, between Mark's contribution to the disposal of the remains of Muffin Naismith, nee Sally Mae Werksmith, and that of Mr. Pentlove. "So when I get more money in the mail, I figure that between the two of you, you're trying to bury Muffin like a cat covering up a mess with dirt."

"I sent you my money," Mark said furiously, "because I thought that as a friend of Miss Naismith's you would take care of her with discretion and dignity. I am less the judge of people than I thought, Tredwell, for it never entered my head that you would think of writing an old woman a letter causing her to refuse—"

"So I ain't wrote it yet," T-Bone said sulkily. "But that's what anybody would say if they knew the truth. If the lawyer who's going to defend her killer—"

"And who might that be?"

"Well . . . " T-Bone shifted from petting his right boot to his left, "that's gotta be you, don't it?"

"Which, the killer or the lawyer?"

"Oh, the killer's The Feeb," T-Bone asserted energetically, as if wanting to make certain Mark was clear on that point. "He just got nabbed on the lot. And *you're* the lawyer. So what I'm going to do is take up a collection."

"To take up a—— For what purpose? To pay my fee?" Mark asked, sounding childishly sarcastic in his own ears.

This suggestion so baffled T-Bone that he abandoned his boot and sat in startled contemplation of Mark. "Well. . . . horsefeathers!" he declared. "To bury li'l Muffin, of course. Not to pay—"

"Take the money I sent you and spend it exactly as I instructed you in my letter," Mark snapped. "I'll throw Pentlove's back in his teeth, if that will please you. And whatever you do, don't upset some old woman in Kansas more than you need by writing her that her daughter's murderers are trying to—"

"Iowa," T-Bone corrected Mark fastidiously. "Muffin was from Iowa. Only her mother can't read, anyhow. The preacher from her home town, he can. Her daddy, you know, he was a English lord."

"A Scottish laird," Mark said, and could cheerfully have chucked T-Bone out the window when the seamed walnut-meat face uttered, "Oh, that so? Thought it was this English—"

"And her other gentlemen friends probably thought Muffin was the Kaiser Wilhelm," Mark said. "Now, Tredwell, will you be so kind as to do what I asked you, and get out of here?" He took from the pile of money on his desk the amount he had originally sent T-Bone and shoved it at that perplexed creature. "Do as I tell you!"

"All right, all right. Horsefeathers," T-Bone muttered, and pocketed the money. "She thought you hung out the moon, though."

Drawn up short, Mark said, "What?"

"She thought you hung out the moon," T-Bone repeated.

"The way she talked about you I could tell she thought you was the fellar who hung out the—"

"Muffin Naismith spoke to you of me?"

With a final pat for his right boot, T-Bone got to his feet. Looking down at Mark, he said contemptuously, "She wasn't scum, you know. Maybe her daddy was just a Ioway farmer and not no English—"

"Scottish!" Mark shouted.

"—Scottish lord, like she said, but that don't give you leave to knock her up and not even pay her rent so she has to light out of a fleabag hotel in the middle of the night and go who knows where and all the time tryin' to hold her head up and be beholden to no one, even if her daddy wadn't no *Scotch*——"

"Are you crazy?" Mark asked in all seriousness.

Equally taken by this question, T-Bone countered, "Are you? Doing what you're doing now after doing what you did?" With an air of loathing and pity combined, T-Bone stomped out to thumb the elevator button viciously, then to yank the door open and yell down the shaft, "Get that horsefeather up here!"

CHAPTER SIXTEEN

In a town where such substantial folk as Benny Sligh flourished, and Manny Amen failed only because his poor brain had been poisoned by his own jake, it is surprising that Rookie Castle fell on evil times. He was born William Castle, but everyone called him by his sobriquet long before he was disbarred from the practice of law for rooking his clients. Some said he got his nickname from his unconventional and premature use of the rook in chess, but the facts, lost in antiquity, were of no import once Rookie succumbed to temptation and consequent exposure and public shame. What bore a rill of laughter through the hot, dusty courtrooms thereafter was Rookie's maniacal clasping to his bosom of The Practice of The Law. If he could not represent clients before the bar, he was assured—by law—the privilege of representing himself, as any citizen fool enough to may plead his own cause. By way of ensuring that he never lacked for wrongs entitled to legal relief, Rookie went about buying up bad debts and having similar hopeless cases assigned to him. Thus his handsome hungry face was as familiar to the courtroom habitués as the ravaged visage of the sot Mark D'Andor.

But no lawyer in the county carried himself in court as Rookie did. No one could touch him for courtliness, though D'Andor occasionally gave him notable competition, with Chester Dander a close blush behind. No one could raise an objection or cross-examine in a voice so freighted with frock-coated solemnity. And no one had ever been as snippy a scalawag as Rookie before he was so ceremoniously booted from the bar on his twitching behind. Had Seymour Pentlove known Rookie in his golden days he would have enshrined him; as it was, it fell to Mark to employ him as a sometime investigator and to look on him as an old and trusted friend.

Now, wily when it came to interrogating future prosecution witnesses for fear of accusations of intimidation or coaching, Mark nevertheless felt that the truth belonged to both sides. Or, as he realistically thought of it, the chunk of meat belongs to the dog who snatches it first. Needful of information, Mark had put in calls to every likely Municipal Court, and had finally run Rookie to earth in Small Claims, where he was politely flattening a deadbeat. "Hi," Mark said, "I need your help." Rookie replied, "Be out there in an hour," and hung up the clerk's phone.

First and foremost Mark wanted Rookie to locate the last address of Muffin Naismith. This Rookie had not, so far, been able to do. For a wonder, Central Casting knew not of her whereabouts for two full months before her death, though her skipping out on a hotel bill might have accounted for that.

Then, as soon as Archibald Forbes was placed under arrest, Mark sent Rookie to have a chat with a Miss Pritchard. Above all else, he was to determine if the dying Muffin Naismith had mentioned rape, bottles, or ice.

Miss Pritchard had had a rather upsetting session with her numerologist. Her horoscope was at once obscure and foreboding. After her still strangely anxious employer had been freed, she listlessly took to seeking what comfort she could find in a daily resorting to bibliomancy. The trouble— as all who have tried it can attest—with attempting to tell one's fortune by opening the Bible at random is the frequently silly advice gained thereby. On this day, Miss Pritchard, cheating a little, knowing exactly where the begats were (and not wishing to fuss with *them* again), opened her Bible to what would have to be the New Testament. She was deservedly rewarded by ending up in the Concordance.

> *Bulrush* [she read]: Heb, Gk, *bot n.* "the reed shaken with the wind" Mat. 11:7.

At odds with herself, alone in the living quarters of the Sanitarium, from which all patients had been removed at the time of Dr. Snowdom's arrest, she washed her hair, had a good cry, and brooded again with a thrilling fascination on the dying remarks of the little Naismith. She had so wanted, though she could not have said why, for the man who arrived to "pick up the pieces" to be the very glass of male beauty— Ronald Coleman would have been nice. Instead Miss Pritchard found D'Andor hawk-faced and observant as no drunk had a right to be, and remote as no lover certainly had ought— though Miss Pritchard had decided at the very sight of him that he was not Naismith's lover—and with no feature worthy of a moment's fantasy, unless it were his remarkable oxblood eyes. And they, Miss Pritchard had decided, were all too too knowing and gentle at the same time for comfort.

In the empty Sanitarium that was once a farmhouse the shrilling of the doorbell was unpleasantly loud. "Now who can that be?" Miss Pritchard cried aloud, and snatched up her cap, preparatory to dealing with the police, or having some process-server shove who knows what at her. "I'll give you your walking papers," she said, "whoever you are."

Through the net curtains fastened at top and bottom of the glass door Miss Pritchard looked out at the handsomest young man she had seen outside the confines of her virginal fantasies. Snatching open the door to deal with him with the same heartless dispatch with which handsome young men had once dismissed her, Miss Pritchard found herself the recipient of a courtly inclination of the head that was by no means a bow but carried all the respectful connotations of one.

"Miss Pritchard?"

"The same," Miss Pritchard confessed in confusion.

"My name is William Castle. I hope I haven't disturbed you at your duties?"

"Disturbed?" Miss Pritchard echoed. "Duties?" she sniffed. "You?" she cried with a high laugh. "Me?" she ended with a snort. Having thoroughly dissected his sentence, she waited for him to present her another. Somehow she found that he had taken her distrait attitude for an invitation to enter, and was now standing in the entrance hall waiting for her to show him where to go. Miss Pritchard led the way to the staff parlor, remembering sufficient of her manners to inquire if Mr. Castle was not finding the weather oppressively warm.

To her pleased confusion he answered her question fully and at length, comparing the heat of this October to that of others, interrupting himself to ascertain whether she wished to comment or make corrections in his recital. In this way they were able to enter the parlor and be seated, all without fuss, so that Miss Pritchard found herself the object of the ardent attention of a young man whose fine narrow head and aristocratic hands cast an actual shadow across her heart, coming between her and the sunlight admitted by the Venetian blinds.

Mr. Castle volunteered forthrightly that he was investigating the Naismith death, adding to this that Miss Pritchard was under no obligation to answer any of his questions and would be perfectly within her rights to show him the door—which act he would view in a kindly light, though he would be disappointed as well. All in all, this William Castle was like an emollient for Miss Pritchard's troubled spirits, and she spoke freely.

On one point only did she refuse to yield to him. She was firm in her interpretation that the dying woman Naismith meant rape when she spoke of the injury which had been dealt her. "I am convinced to my toes," Miss Pritchard said, "that that Feeb person hurt her sexually. That I have sworn to, and will again."

"Have you been asked to swear to it again?" Rookie ventured delicately.

Miss Pritchard grew arch. "Isn't that what you're here for?"

Young Mr. Castle took alarm. "To *coach* you?" he cried, aghast. "Miss Pritchard, I had not talked to you five minutes before I knew that you are not the type of person to say one thing one day and another the next."

Miss Pritchard blinked. Somehow he seemed to have gotten ahead of her in the conversation.

"Some witnesses do that, you know," Mr. Castle was saying parenthetically. "They vacillate so that what they speak as gospel truth on Sunday becomes a flagrant lie on Monday."

Gospel, Miss Pritchard thought, the word diverting her mind back to her bibliomacy; that's where I'll look for my fortune. It took this young man to tell me that.

Rookie was pressing on. "But I know that what you say

to me, and what you will say in any court in the land are one and the same. That Muffin Naismith did not say she had been raped. She did not use that word."

"No," Miss Pritchard agreed at once, "she did not. And wild horses can't make me say she did."

"In spite of the bruises," Mr. Castle said ringingly. "Did Miss Naismith say anything about having had a headache and having had ice applied—"

"Oh, headache, tush! The poor little woman was *aborting,* Mr. Castle. She had other pains to complain of. And as far as the bruises went, I made a few of them myself trying to calm her."

"It must have been terrible," Mr. Castle said rather breathlessly.

In a gossipy outburst Miss Pritchard chattered, "Oh, but a nurse sees everything in her time. Oh, yes. Miss Naismith, for example. She had the most extraordinary case of capillary fragility. I never saw the like. If I had been she, I would have had myself a pair of leeches. Only sensible thing."

"Leeches?" queried a flatteringly intent Mr. Castle.

"You heard me. Leeches. She was probably always going around with discolorations. Black and blue marks. But leeches, you see, could have drained off the discolorations. Especially when she got disfiguring ones on the face."

"But this is completely new to me!" blurted Rookie. "I had no idea some people were more susceptible to bruising than others. Is that so!" he marveled.

"Oh, there's things and things you laymen don't know," Miss Pritchard said with creamy satisfaction. "Naturally," she went on to confide in Mr. Castle, "she would have wanted to keep her leeches free of contamination. Never lend out your leeches. They can transmit venereal diseases, you know."

"*No!*"

"Yes indeedy. My father was a barber, and he kept them. So I know all about them."

"At least, then," Rookie said, settling down for a long chat, "someone of your vast experience wouldn't go casting about for wild explanations as to the cause of the bruises.

Such as deciding Miss Naismith was hurt with a bottle, when it was readily apparent that she bruised eas—"

"Who said anything about bottles?" Miss Pritchard snorted. "I never heard the like. Why, I told you—I myself left great big black marks on her trying to subdue her."

"Her legs thrashing about and all," Rookie murmured daintily. "I guess?"

Miss Pritchard had taken kindly to Mr. Castle, and there was much she wished to impart to him. "You have no idea," she said, "how the dying can toss around. Wait till I tell you. . . ."

When Rookie had at last to leave, Miss Pritchard held him a quarter-hour more through serving him tea and sandwiches little thicker than a pair of playing cards. Then, no sooner had the door closed on his back than she hastened to her room to peek at random into the Gospels, at last to know her fortune for the day.

Her forefinger pointed to a passage in Mark: *For from within, out of the heart of men, proceed evil thoughts, adulteries, fornications, murders.*

Miss Pritchard closed the Book and her heart to young Mr. Castle as well. To the empty farmhouse she said, "The fat man did it. He fornicated with her and murdered her. My way has been made clear."

While she was washing the tea things Dr. Snowdom came in. His face was nearly the same dull pewter pallor as his gaze. "I've been with the District Attorney all afternoon," he said by way of explanation of his low spirits. "They've arrested Archibald Forbes for the felonious murder of Naismith."

"*Aha!*" Miss Pritchard said.

"You'll be hearing from the District Attorney's office too, naturally."

"Naturally," Miss Pritchard said in triumph. "I am the one, after all, who knows what that Forbes man did to her."

Dr. Snowdom slumped down on the single stool which furnished the diet kitchen. "At least," he said in a dispirited way, "I'm no longer implicated."

"And never should have been," Miss Pritchard declared. "You did only what any doctor would have done to help that poor little woman." Her stout championing of her employer was not cheering him in the slightest. "Would you like some tea, Doctor? You seem . . . tired."

As if he had not heard her, Dr. Snowdom said, "And D'Andor will be defending Forbes. He was evidently downtown to see Forbes in jail this afternoon."

"That man drinks," Miss Pritchard said with conviction.

"Yes. And he knows something I wish he didn't."

"Why, Doctor!" Miss Pritchard said. "We both know you haven't done any— Haven't helped any girl out of a situation since you bought the San. The great Mr. D'Andor will have to find another way to frighten us, let me tell you. I know what I know," Miss Pritchard concluded in a voice full of malice and menace, "and so does he!"

CHAPTER SEVENTEEN

All over Hollywood the scandalmongers were making whoopee. Heads together over their Green River sodas in drugstores or their jake in speaks, they jabbered of the arrest of The Feeb, eyes sparkling and dimples adorning many a happy cheek. Banished were cares, old frustrations and woes shed, the scandalmongers reveled in their ancient rites celebrating Rape and A Movie Star and Death. Muffin Naismith was canonized a starlet in headlines, and a silent movie in which she had appeared in one reel—*Jazz Me, Baby*—reopened on the Boulevard.

Mark D'Andor, as attorney of record, found himself again the darling of reporters, the prodigal returned. Flanked by the talcumed Mr. Pentlove (in his agitation that poor gentleman had used slightly too heavy a hand as he dusted himself with his after-shave powder, so that he looked as prettied-up, as "lifelike," as a corpse), Mark arrived for the Archibald Forbes preliminary hearing. There was a faint sloshing sound every time Mark made a sudden movement, though the full pint flask in his breast pocket scarcely made a bulge. A ruckus among the reporters at the doors of the courtroom (one broken camera and one dented nose) signaled the arrival of The Feeb. Extra bailiffs sent to maintain law and order plunged into the fray to rescue The Feeb. And down the aisle they escorted him, wearing the lost grief-stricken expression of a child, standing at an open grave. He had never appeared quite so *fat*, so helpless. To use the word *virile* in connection with him here would be as out of place as uttering it in a nursery.

When such quiet as was obtainable was obtained, Mark

calmly addressed the court, stating that the defense waived a preliminary hearing. The deputy D.A. was very unhappy at this turn of events, but no more so than Mr. Pentlove. In a trice The Feeb was whisked out the door leading to the judge's chambers and thence to the County Jail. The reporters did not get Mark's drift, but then neither did Mr. Pentlove. The deputy D.A. thought he was beginning to see the light. Sitting directly behind the deputy Dr. Snowdom sighed, greatly depressed and anxious, while Miss Pritchard did nothing to conceal her sense of letdown.

"D'Andor," Mr. Pentlove said in a shaking voice, "are you drunk?"

And Mark answered cryptically, as if he had not understood, "Not now, Pentlove. Later."

"But what are you trying to do?" Mr. Pentlove begged.

"I'm trying to get out of here. I've got things to attend to." Mark saw Rookie Castle bending over Miss Pritchard, all ears about something, and Mark stalked past him as if he had never in his life seen or heard of Rookie before. With Mr. Pentlove trailing him, he gained the corridor where the reporters awaited him. To them Mark gave the standard interview: "Now, gentlemen, you know I'm not going to reveal my line of defense at this point. But I will say that my client is innocent of any and all accusations brought against him."

To Mr. Pentlove he said, "Go to your office. Or go home. Just go somewhere. I'll get in touch with you later."

"Indeed you will!" Mr. Pentlove assured him. "I expect you at my house tonight, D'Andor. For dinner!" he added in a threatening tone.

Mark drove back to his office, there to pace the threadbare rug as Chester had done, awaiting Rookie. But when Rookie arrived, he was a dry well with not a droplet of information. "I must find where she was living at the time of her death," Mark said.

Rookie shrugged. "Pritchard swears the only address their records show is the Eden. And just for the hell of it, I checked there. She was not in residence. I gave the clerk at the hotel a ten-spot, and he still maintains that she skipped with her possessions. The cops had been there but got no further than I did."

Mark gave Rookie ten dollars, then made a notation to have Mr. Pentlove reimburse him that night. Then he had the secretary send up Miss Flirt Smith and Mr. Benny Sligh. Mark spent the day harassing, tricking, and trapping the pair, giving them a taste of what they would face on the witness stand during cross-examination.

Mr. Pentlove, it would seem, had been moved by the dangerous turn of events to favor Mark with a private premiere of The Feeb's unreleased films. But first there was dinner served English-breakfast style from a sideboard, with a single male servant in attendance. The Misses and Mrs. Pentlove might have been on a little jaunt to Siberia for all Mark saw of them. Dusk came in the long narrow windows, turning the napery blue until the candles were lit. And looking at the flames through his wine, Mark said with rue, "One trouble with pickling yourself with hard stuff is that you lose your appreciation of wine."

"The Irish, please," Mr. Pentlove said to the servant. And when the man had left the room, he looked at Mark imploringly, struggling within himself not to bring up business while at table.

"All right, all right, Pentlove," Mark said, grinning. "Here it is. I dared not risk a preliminary hearing. The judge, if he so chose, could have held Forbes to answer the charge of manslaughter. Manslaughter alone. In spite of the fact that the D.A.'s office want to try him for murder in the first degree."

"Yes?" Mr. Pentlove said quietly.

"Let us suppose that that had happened. Forbes is then tried for manslaughter. It makes for too easy an out for the jury. The facts won't support felonious murder—at least, not in my opinion. But the jury could think: 'Well, *something* went on in that bedroom. So we'll just convict him of manslaughter. That way he won't be punished too severely, and he won't get off scot-free, either!' But I don't want a compromise. I want that jury to think only in terms of acquittal or the gallows."

Mr. Pentlove smiled fondly on Mark. "Excellent! Good straight thinking, D'Andor. A stretch in prison would ruin The Feeb."

"So would stretching his neck," Mark reminded Mr. Pentlove.

Mr. Pentlove tittered merrily at Mark's little drollery. Recovering, he said, "Shall we go on into the taproom?"

Seeing Mark and Mr. Pentlove enter, the lone male servant placed the Irish and a glass on a table beside a leather lounge against the wall. Mark promptly sat down by his drink, and Mr. Pentlove joined him, his customary thimble glass of brandy and cigarillo to hand. With a look of great import, Mr. Pentlove pressed a button behind him. Across the room a panel, mounted guns and all, slid silently into the ceiling. The servant stood to one side manning the projector. On the screen which the panel had concealed there appeared the title of a movie starring The Feeb.

Mark watched what he could only take as a deliberate effrontery. The Feeb's listing waddle, giggles, and obscene antics provoked no response whatsoever from host or guest. When at last it was done, Mark sat looking at the blank screen, half-waiting for the operator's message to flash on, as in the old days when the film broke: *One moment please*. Mr. Pentlove pressed his button and the panel slid down. The manservant left the taproom.

"Well?" murmured Mr. Pentlove.

"I was most impressed with the sound," Mark said. "A high technical achievement, believe me."

"Thank you."

"Will people with empty dinner pails really pay money to see that thing?" Mark wondered in a hushed voice.

"By the millions. *If. . . .*"

"Do not belabor the point."

"I'm not completely at ease in my mind about you," Mr. Pentlove said, taking a turn for the confessional.

"I've been aware of that, Pentlove."

Having broached the subject, Mr. Pentlove veered away from it erratically. "Do you realize you are the only person I permit to call me by my last name alone?"

"I am?" Mark was somewhat startled by the wealth of meaning which Mr. Pentlove invested in this simple statement. "Then I'll be happy to oblige you and call you *Mister—*"

"No, no," Mr. Pentlove protested. "The part of you that speaks to me as an equal I like."

"Your power doesn't cow me," Mark explained. "Tell me what it is about me that disturbs you."

Mr. Pentlove looked straight ahead. "Your willingness to defend Forbes. Your . . . bland. . . ." He waved a hand in the air like a baby saying bye-bye.

". . . detachment?" Mark supplied

"Yes."

"Muffin Naismith is dead. Oh, I imagine if I were a member of the District Attorney's staff, I would prosecute Forbes to the hilt. If I were ambitious. Careers have been built on far shakier foundations than that of being one of the central figures in a *cause célèbre*. Which, incidentally, is a thought foremost in the mind of some deputy D.A. at this very moment. Only, I'm not ambitious. And I'm incorrigibly defense-minded as well. I repeat, Muffin Naismith is dead. Vengeance and retribution will fertilize no flowers on her grave."

"You *are* a cynic," Mr. Pentlove said, with envy.

"Hardly. That's entirely too difficult a posture to maintain. Let's just say I am mindful of the many innocent people, studio workers, who are dependent on The Feeb for their livelihoods. Or is that too spurious, too sugary for you?"

After a moment's meditation Mr. Pentlove made his selection. "Too spurious, D'Andor."

"I think I know what is troubling you. The physical details of this case are such that you wonder how I can speak of them in connection with a woman I knew . . . intimately."

"How can you?" Mr. Pentlove asked curiously.

"Let me give you Tom Powell's definition of the legal mind—he's quite a legal writer, by the way. Powell said that if you can think of something that is inextricably attached to something else, and still not think of that something else— then you have a legal mind. The ability to separate the inseparable, if I make my meaning clear. And added to that, you're wondering about something else. You've undoubtedly heard that while the prosecution tries the defendant, the defense prosecutes the victim. Right?"

"So I have heard," Mr. Pentlove admitted.

"It won't apply in this particular instance. It would conflict with my reasons for taking the case," Mark said, but pointedly did not elaborate.

"Oh," Mr. Pentlove said. After a pause he said, "Oh?"

Mark poured himself more Irish and reached a decision. "I'm going to tell you something, Pentlove. And because you adhere faithfully to your own unscrupulous code, I think you'll understand."

"At least I have a code," Mr. Pentlove put in modestly.

"Exactly. You see, Pentlove, when I was a boy I saw the last public hanging to take place in my state."

"Really! Where was that?"

"Nowhere in particular."

Mr. Pentlove lowered his eyes in apology. It was not courteous at all for one Hollywoodian to ask another his place of origin. "Ahem," Mr. Pentlove murmured.

"The last public hanging," Mark resumed. "And in the town square. The man had been tried and convicted of rape."

"You don't say. A Negro, of course?"

Mr. Pentlove had the grace to blush before Mark's broad grin. Mark said, "Was that a social commentary on your own part? Or were you just trying to get a geographical fix on the locale?"

Mr. Pentlove contented himself with clearing his throat.

"No, he was white, as a matter of fact," Mark continued on. "And he was hanged of a fine Saturday morning in June. . . . 'What is so rare as a day in June?' to quote the poet."

"Tennyson?" Mr. Pentlove wanted to know—pleased, as Mark had noted in other people, to have verse spouted at him.

"No," Mark said. "I attended the hanging, as you may have guessed. Along with every male who was able to walk or even get driven or carried there, and a goodly number of females. There were also any number of toddlers and tots seated astride Daddy's neck to get an unobstructed view of the show."

"My God!"

"There was a lot of eating going on while we awaited the arrival of the hangman and the condemned. Ice-cream vendors, hot-dog wagons, that sort of thing, all over the place."

"To let you go to a hanging . . ." Mr. Pentlove pondered. "What on earth could your mother have been thinking of?"

A mere shadow of a spasm passed along Mark's lower lip. "Oh . . . I suppose she was thinking that the parlor curtains weren't the precise shade of ecru she wanted. She'd tinted them in tea in preparation for a—visit—from the preacher."

"But——" Mr. Pentlove said, then let it drop.

"All the boys in my grade at school were there. I was nine at the time. All week we had followed the erection of the scaffold with great interest. To cut a story short—the hangman arrived, and then the convicted man."

"Was he wearing a mask—the hangman?" Mr. Pentlove breathed, his natural instinct for the dramatic gaining control.

"No. He was not a local man. They had circuit riders for that sort of thing. The hangman mounted the scaffold, followed by the victim."

"The *victim*!"

"I always thought of the condemned man as being a victim, too."

"I understand," Mr. Pentlove lied.

"But as far as that goes, the victim herself was there too."

"She was *alive*?"

"Very much so. And in the pink of condition. In attendance she had her son—a lout if ever there was one—her husband, and most of her near and distant relatives. She was a blowsy slattern all dolled up in a flowery flimsy dress for the—Hmmm?" Mark broke off to inquire.

Mr. Pentlove was looking down his nose at Mark. "Is this your idea of a joke?"

"Are you accusing me of gallows-humor?" When Mr. Pentlove refused to reply, Mark went on in the same even tone, "I am shocking your sense of propriety. If you don't want me to, I won't continue."

Mr. Pentlove unbent slightly. "I appreciate your confidence," he said stiffly. Yet his attitude remained watchful, as if he feared Mark were going to tell him something he would rather not know.

"As I say, the woman was there. She was about the same age as her rapist, and good-looking, I reckon, in a hot florid way."

Mr. Pentlove pricked up his ears at the word *reckon,* but did not interrupt.

"She crowded up right to the foot of the scaffold. And the condemned man—he'd refused a hood—could look directly down on her. He stood there in the sunlight staring at all of us. People he'd known all his life. Yes, all his . . . life. And we stared back, slobbering on our ice-cream cones and sucking on pop bottles and gnawing hunks out of our hot dogs—"

"Jesus Christ!"

"And then the woman, the so-called *victim,* began to berate the condemned man. At first she was mostly righteous, shouting that he was getting what he deserved and so forth. But suddenly the ecstasy of it seized her—"

"The what, oh my God?" Mr. Pentlove whispered.

"Ecstasy," Mark repeated evenly. "Everybody there knowing that the hulking man up there had taken her by force and was going to hang for it. He was always thought to be so harmless before that. Gentle with animals. But he had chosen her to take by force. And in the throes of her orgiastic excitement the woman started cursing the man, damning him and calling him by name. Then as they lowered the noose over his head she burst into shrill, shrill obscenities. The crowd egged her on, and she hollered higher and higher, stretching up on tiptoe to look into his eyes. He looked down at her like—like——" Mark spread his hands. "He was in mortal terror, I mean that literally, he was congealed, but she was breaking through to him. And he yelled back at her, exchanging four-letter word for word with her. The tears actually *popped* from his eyes. She was stretching up to him and he was trying to lean forward, like—lovers being parted. An instant later they sprung the trap. The hangman knew his onions, you could almost hear the knot snap the neck. The condemned man jerked once, and was still. Then the woman fainted."

Mr. Pentlove released a long-pent breath. "I consider

that a most improper thing for a boy of nine to have wit-nessed," he said helplessly.

Mark smiled and disagreed. "Not if you want to give him a concise and unforgettable demonstration of the difference between justice and retaliation."

"But he had raped the woman," Mr. Pentlove said.

"Oh, yes, he did it."

"Was he feebleminded?"

"No."

"Who—" Mr. Pentlove began, then decided he most definitely was not going to ask *that*.

"He was just a local handyman," Mark answered him anyway. "Do you understand what I'm trying to say? There were only two places to be that morning. Up on the scaffold with the condemned, or down among the ice-cream-eaters with the victim."

"Or you could have been at home where you belonged," Mr. Pentlove snapped defensively, as if Mark were attacking him.

"No, that man would still have been hanged. And we would still have been responsible. It takes three to complete a crime. The perpetrator, the victim, and—the ice-cream-eaters."

"You believe such a piece of . . . hogwash?" Mr. Pentlove protested.

"I always have," Mark said with containment. Then, as Mr. Pentlove looked at him in open scorn and dismay mingled, Mark added, "But this is the first time I've ever put it into practice. The other times, the other cases, were for money. Or glory. Or whatever it was I was wallowing in." To Mr. Pentlove's widening silent sneer he said, "Whatever you think, don't think that I'm trying to paint myself as some sort of fool visionary. I'm merely trying to—"

"I know what you're trying to!" Mr. Pentlove said hotly. "But you won't place me among the ice-cream-eaters, D'Andor. And you won't hold me responsible for Forbes. I didn't create that swine; I'm not God. I didn't turn him loose on the world."

"Didn't you?"

Mr. Pentlove was suddenly beside himself. "I'm a businessman, pure and simple! What Forbes does off the lot——I'm a businessman, nothing more!"

"Sorry if I sounded as if I were singling you out," Mark said. "It's the way you and your kind have turned this town into a—a devil's booth, that's what I'm speaking of. To quote my favorite poet again, 'At the devil's booth are all things sold, each ounce of dross costs its ounce of gold; for a cap and bells our lives we pay. . . .' Except in this case someone else paid with her life, and you're perfectly willing to hide the fact in order to preserve The Feeb's cap and bells."

Mr. Pentlove opened his mouth and Mark nearly jumped down it. "Pentlove, didn't you even for the duration of a second give Forbes the benefit of the doubt? When you learned that a woman was dead, didn't you instantly assume that he was guilty of it? Didn't you have Benny Sligh work over that 'smart' prostitute and ship her out of town? Must I remind you that Forbes has to subject women to indignities for his pleasure, or hasn't that been the fear in the back of your mind the whole time? Pentlove, it is your firm and unshakable opinion that he is impotent; it is because you capitalize on it. That's the *leitmotif* of every film you'd made of him. So since you seem to know how Forbes did manage to injure Muffin Naismith, would you be so kind as to let me in on the secret? Before the District Attorney springs it on me in court, *ice-cream-eater*!"

Mr. Pentlove half-rose from the leather lounge in fury, then sank back. "You are i-impertinent, D'Andor! I-impertinent and a hypocritical h-has-been, and a drunk to boo-boo-*boot*!"

"Dear me," Mark drawled.

"Nor will I take any more of your h-hoity-t-toity . . . ness." Mr. Pentlove struggled on, not allowing the appearance of his impediment to impair his rhetoric. "Why, I've picked men up out of the gutter who hadn't f-fallen as low as you, and with a lot more cause. You had some private sorrows, yes; of them I won't speak, but you used them as an excuse to turn into a sot. Why, ruthlessness was always your m-middle name, so don't come quoting Shakespeare to me—"

"I never," Mark denied.

"I want just one thing from you—no sass!"

"No sass," Mark repeated, as if making mental notes.

"Just get Forbes off. And save your poetry and hypocrisy for the bench. I can put you on one," Mr. Pentlove ranted, "and don't think I would hesitate!"

Mark smiled lazily, "All right, all right, Pentlove. Only don't take on about it so." He finished his drink and rose. "Oh, before I go—you owe me ten bucks."

Deep into the night Mr. Pentlove fumed and prowled his house, upstairs and down, his dressing gown a whisper as it brushed the stainless-steel balustrade of which he was so proud. What had happened, he asked himself, to the forthright shyster D'Andor had given every promise of becoming? Had he been outnumbered? *Hah!* What if D'Andor had had to fight the competition he, Seymour Pentlove, bested every day of his life! The fool, he didn't know expedience from corruption; he tossed the baby out with the bathwater.

A son Seymour Pentlove would have liked, like D'Andor —once.

And now look. Quoting some poet nobody gave a second thought to (Mr. Pentlove had researched at length in his library), from some asinine poem about a simpleton named Sir Launfal in search of the Holy Grail. The Holy Grail, Mr. Pentlove thought, holy cow!

There was no accounting for the change in D'Andor; the man's very nature had altered to the grain. Mr. Pentlove could not fathom it. He told himself heatedly: When D'Andor's drunk he acts bored, and when sober like some s-supercilious s-saint. He'll be telling me he t-thinks The Feeb is innocent n-next!

CHAPTER EIGHTEEN

On the eve of the trial of Archibald Forbes, Mark worked late in his office snug in its squat spire; worked until the lights in the movie houses along the Boulevard went out and the Red Cars rattled by below, shuttling what was known as the Boulevard of Broken Dreams. There was a hot wind frisking after bits of newspaper and chewing-gum wrappers, and far down the darkened street appeared a fierce yellow eye, bent with uncompromising diligence at the gutter down which revolving brooms swept all manner of waste. Above the brooms were spigots, spraying water on the dusty street. Then, the street-cleaner gone on its ponderous way, tame monster of the lonely night, the pavement dried at once, and the Boulevard seemed swept bare of sound and life as well as trash.

For the main, Mark occupied himself with the dossiers of tomorrow's veniremen, supplied him by Rookie Castle. Using a printed list issued by the Court, Rookie had laboriously sought out each person, hoping to learn of his likes and dis-likes, and—most important—of his prejudices. If one of the veniremen had already served on a jury, Rookie had been at great pains to learn whether he had voted for prosecution or defense, and why.

Studying Rookie's reports, Mark checked those names which would be totally unacceptable to him, weighing their number against his twenty precious peremptory challenges. Contrariwise, there was a woman upon whom he spent loving thought for the reason that, on the morrow, the deputy D.A. would probably become positively beamish about her. She was a lady in her late fifties, a pillar of her church, the grand-mother of three male children, and (according to Rookie) self-righteous. She was a woman whose prudery could force her to regard the death of Muffin Naismith as the judgment of the Lord, and to whom Mr. Forbes would then become that nice clown who afforded her grandsons such innocent plea-sure and who, sad to relate, must have fallen in with evil companions. Still, the vindictiveness of the rectitudinous had to be given a target, and in this instance there was only Muffin at Mark's diposal. Once again he was faced, as in almost every criminal trial of his career, with attacking and prosecuting the victim, while the deputy D.A. prosecuted the defendant. This trial promised to be no different, but now, sternly defense-minded as he considered himself to be, he shrank from his duty.

Nor was there any comfort to be had in contemplation of his opponent. Though several gentlemen had been rumored at various times to be preparing the case, Mark could not say with certitude which of them would receive the honor of mauling The Feeb in court. In the office of the District Attorney there raged a constant bickering, backbiting scrap, not unlike the contention of curs for a bone. The trial attorneys had won through to their present eminence over years of grubbing in Complaints or dabbling in preliminary hearings. It was there-fore not unnatural that the deputy D.A.s felt a jealousy toward a defense lawyer like Mark D'Andor, who had gained a county-wide repute in his first year of practice.

In Mark's estimation, the deputy district attorneys rather popped in and out of the woodwork for years until at last they were deemed properly seasoned. And by that time they were humorless, sour, and puritanical. Worse, they were sober.

The unappealing prospect sent Mark out into the night for company.

The grille on the door to Charlie's Speak was manned this night by a gentleman who, not without dignity, bent over to be treated to a view of Mark's vest button as he inquired who it was that sought entrance. Admitted, Mark said, "Tell me, was that peekhole a mail slot or something once? You're asking for lumbago constantly bending over that way."

"Asking for!" the keeper of the door retorted bitterly and caressed his sacroiliac.

In the stench and gloom, Dion of the sightless copper eyes sat at his piano glowering at the music rack with unblinking hatred. Ordering rum for himself and Dion, Mark went to lean his arm on the lid of the small studio piano, no higher, or not very much more so, than the rail of a jury box. Dion asked acutely, "That you, Counsel?"

"Yes. How did you know?"

"You polish things with the heel of your hand when you're thinking. You're doing it now."

"Dammit, I thought I'd broken that habit!"

Dion laughed. "Before you're done with The Feeb's trial, everything in the courtroom is going to look like a new coat of varnish."

"Here's our rum, Dion," Mark said. He placed the two glasses on the ringed lid. "Dion, do something for me. Tonight do me the original thirty-two."

Glowering unceasingly at the rack, Dion said, "You going to get the fat boy off, Counsel?"

"I am. Dion—the original thirty-two, how's about it?"

"Like fun I will," Dion said, softening his refusal with a laugh. "Want me to lose my job? Lemme do you—'Honey-suckle Rose.' Mama don't 'low no Beethoven in here." He drank off half his rum, closing his lips down over his copper glare to greet the liquor. "Put me out," he gasped. "I'm on fire! Counsel, Charlie just served you up his private stock. Boy and howdy, a drink like that I got to do it justice." He twisted on his piano stool, "Hope that isn't a touchy word with you tonight, Counsel."

"It never is," Mark said mildly. "Unless it's used as an excuse for a necktie party. I don't hold with hanging people."

"With you, everybody's innocent," Dion said with a chuckle.

"No. With me, everybody's guilty. It takes a whole slew of people to commit the simplest crime. So I can't go along with the idea of hanging the first man who's handy."

Dion placed his hands on the keys. "Counsel, this tune is for you," he said, and his fingers stated quietly the theme

of what he would refashion into the thirty-two variations of
Beethoven:

> Show me the way to go home,
> I'm tired and I want to go to bed.
> I had a little drink about an hour ago,
> And it went right to my head. . . .

"I had a little drink about three years ago," Mark said,
"and I haven't reached the bottom of the glass yet."

Dion said nothing until he reached a legato passage.
"That little dead lady used to come in here off and on. Miss
Muffet, I'm speaking of. Manny Amen brought her in. That
was when his jake had already ruined his legs, but still hadn't
reached his brain. I always knew whenever she was here. Had
a voice like a popcorn whistle."

Dion laughed in the pessimistic way in which he vented
all amusement. "She was always talking about the silver screen.
But in my mind I got to thinking of her as the 'silver scream.' "

Mark bent to the unwavering glare. "Tell me . . . Even
though she had a—carrying voice—did it ever strike you that
she was slightly deaf?"

"Oh, you mean talking up the way deaf people do?" Dion
shook his head. "No, I never thought of her that way." He
reached past Mark with a yellow hand to strike a black key.
"Did The Feeb have anything to do with her death?"

"No, I don't think so. But I did."

"How do you arrive at that?"

"I haven't yet. The thought just came to me. That's what
I'll have to find out—how I did it."

"Cut from the same cloth, you and me," Dion mused in
time to the music. "I had a gift for music, and you had one
for people. Except I treated my gift like it was a curse, because
I was blind, and I didn't want God to go thinking that just
because I could play anything I heard just once, He'd made
it up to me. And you act like you stole yours from somebody
and are trying to ditch it before you get caught red-handed.
That's why you get drunk and go around saying things you
don't mean."

"I'm no drunker than usual, and maybe I do mean it."

Dion toyed with a trill. "Damn your eyes, Counsel. I may be a blind man, but don't say I haven't got vision!"

Smiling faintly and absently polishing the lid of the piano, Mark nodded. He strongly suspected, and Dion's perceptiveness confirmed it, that to Dion a person's silence had all the range and nuances of the spoken word. "I'd better get some shuteye," was all he said.

He made his way past the reveling scandalmongers, head down and unnoticed, then past the gentleman at the door, bending over to peer through the mail slot and into the night.

His mind sang in a bleary weary melancholy voice: Show me the way to go home. . . . Constance had once set out for home, but had not made it. . . .

After not hearing from Constance for almost eight months after she had left him, Mark came home to find her sitting on their entrance stair with a drink in one hand. The door was ajar and she must have heard his hurried, puzzled footsteps and then the final footfall when he saw her and halted, yet she acknowledged his presence only by a slight tilt of her head and the swirling of the liquor in her glass. Looking down at the top of her head, Mark could not recall ever having seen her from this angle before, and noting that either the late afternoon sun glancing off the chandelier or the faint marcel wave made her hair appear to flow continuously into the pale chignon at her nape. Not looking up at him, Constance said, "Mark, why ever did we buy that crystal chandelier? Don't those gobs and gobs of pendants look exactly like the jewelry of some fat old duchess?" He had forgotten how Pasadena her voice was, a certain brittle infelicity of inflection, her unintentional assertion of superiority.

"I can't remember last when I poked around in the jewelry of a fat old duchess," Mark said, gathering himself to approach her, to meet her eyes, as clear and deeply gray as rainbarrels. "In fact, I haven't even poked a duchess in I don't know how long." He had reached the step above her. "Won't you come in and set a spell? Or is this as far as you care to go?"

"I've often sat here, Mark. Didn't you know that? The house looks so empty and untenanted."

"Well, it feels empty and—" he began, but decided against enlarging on that aspect of his life. He sat beside her gingerly. "How've you been?"

"Well, thank you. And you?"

"Oh, I keep busy. My bootleggers give me no little trouble. Beating a federal rap isn't easy."

Constance swirled the contents of her glass. "I should imagine. I for one find this rum indefensible. You don't drink it, you subject yourself to it."

"It does rather manhandle one, I have to admit." He was unable to look at her; he feared at any moment he might start trembling. "But it's Charlie's best. Uh . . . You don't have to drink that stuff, you know. There's plenty of Irish."

"I saw it. Only I spied this rum and decided to give it a try."

"Experience is sometimes a costly school." He had made the remark idly, and was unprepared for the long level look she bent on him.

But Constance said only "Hmmm."

After a silence Mark complained candidly: "I don't know what to do with my hands."

She laughed when he held them up, and caught his hands in hers. "I'm thinking of getting married," she said, adding with a diffidence foreign to her, ". . . again."

"Oh? How very nice." In his excess of politeness he sounded to himself like the most stilted of fools. "To—uh—whom?"

"You."

Either he must stammer his delight or take refuge in lawyerisms. He began to lecture earnestly, "Well, you must understand that 'getting married again' isn't the proper terminology."

"Oh, it isn't?"

"Not a bit of it. We're still married insofar as the law is concerned. Yes. Therefore all that would be required of us would be for us to resume our conjugal relationship. Cohabitation and all that sort of thing. A marriage is not dissolved until a final decree is entered, and you're four months short of that. So any resumption of the—"

"I fear," Constance said, "that I need you."

"That is nice to know. You see, the point is that inasmuch as we are still married, we have merely to—"

"Cohabitate."

"That among other things, yes. However, like many laymen, you understand the word to mean— What it *does* mean is to live together as man and wife. Whereas most people think that it means—— Constance, my God I've missed you! And you left your perfume lamp behind, anyway," he reminded her brightly, gripping her hands in his.

"Shall we go light it?"

"Splendid! If there's anything I like it's— Princess, quit swilling that rum and kiss me!"

Again she laughed. "Oh, Mark, I love you when you babble!"

He carried her down the rest of the stairs to their bedroom. The sun had gone down behind the opposite hills, and opening the curtains to admit the dusk seeping up from the canyon, he turned and thought for one heartbeat that she was only his longing raised to the degree of hallucination. He lit her perfume lamp as if the remembered scent of jasmine, which was one in his mind with their lovemaking, would lend her substantiality.

With a grave smile Constance came to him, arms extended, palms up, as in times past. She was the only woman he knew whose sleeves were buttoned from wrist to elbow with tiny material-covered knobs secured with maddeningly delicate loops of silk. Those buttons always captivated him; they were a part of her elegance, like her long hair, colorless as the dawn, which she refused to have bobbed or permed.

Last of all, Constance lay naked on the bed and pulled the pins from her chignon, shaking the strands free. Mark pressed himself on her, burying his hands in that hair and closing his eyes so that when she began to rock gently in his embrace he felt, as he always had, that she was like a scent drifting under and over and all around him.

The alteration from her soft receptivity was abrupt, accompanied by a snarl in her throat. Her hands actually tore at him; he was helpless, taken by surprise, locked in combat in a gruelling contest for the prize of ecstasy, her hands frighteningly adept in indignities.

Finally, spent and lying at her side, he waited until his panting subsided. Then, in his most controlled voice Mark said, "Who taught you to do that?"

"I've forgotten his name. But I could give you a most accurate description of him. Didn't you like it? It seemed to excite you."

"Let us put it this way, it doesn't become *you*."

"Would it if you had taught it to me?"

"If I had asked it of you out of love, yes."

"And all along," Constance said, "I was thinking of it as being a new specialty of the house."

"Constance, I believe we have already exhausted the subject." He was staring at the ceiling, as he knew she was. Her voice had never sounded so light, brittle, and proud.

"Mark?"

"Yes."

"I know what you're thinking. You know how some people beggar description? You think I beggar revulsion."

He thought: I fear you are losing or have lost your mind. But before he could express this in some manner calculated not to alarm her, Constance said—as if he had spoken aloud, "No, I haven't. I thought too, when I first met him, that I was demented. And I haven't forgotten his name, and I never will. But there was only one way to know. That's why I—"

"Dropped in? For a spot of rum and a roll in the hay?"

Constance took the rebuke without comment. After a pause she said, "On the way home to Mother, I met a man. You could almost put it that way. He's a would-be actor. He likes the entree I afford him to the Tennis Club. In case you're interested, he doesn't give a hot buttered biscuit for me."

"Since I love you, I do admit to a mild concern."

Constance turned her head, and in obedience to her unspoken request Mark looked at her. Her expression was as stiff and artful as that of a shepherdess painted on porcelain. "You never loved me, Mark. You *prized* me."

"You bet I prized you. But I loved you too. Do now." In a very brief time he had come to hate the faint smile on her mouth; he could imagine her looking exactly that way while some doctor told her she had a painful fatal disease.

"This man I met," Constance said softly, "is almost tired of me. The fact that I'm—*humbly*—in love with him only amuses him. Just to be with him in public while he licks his lips over other women is debasing. You see, he's a blackguard."

Mark wrenched his gaze from her smile, again staring stonily at the ceiling. "Oh, is that how that word is pronounced. *Blackguard*. I never knew." He discovered he was smiling too. "Constance. When he does tire of you. . . . Will you come back to me?"

"No. After him, no man in this world can cut the mustard for me. I know. I've tried."

"Just the same—the latchkey is always out. And I'll keep the blue bulb burning." Mark said to the ceiling, smiling, "Will you excuse me, Constance? I'm going upstairs and get drunk."

He was sitting in the dining-room window looking out at the tree when Constance appeared in the doorway. She said pleasantly, "Would you do me a favor, Mark? Get one of your hoodlum clients to rub me out. Then everybody would feel better all around." She turned to leave, but had one parting thought, "And to think I left you because I thought *you* were turning into trash."

Later, when he emerged from the dining room, there was only the glass with a finger of rum in it left on the entrance stair to show that Constance had been there at all.

Around four in the morning his father-in-law was on the phone, weeping and incoherent. It took Mark several minutes to extract the information that Constance had leaped or been pushed from the Pasadena bridge.

On a Friday the scandalmongers began to arrive at the Hall of Justice around seven in the morning, breakfasting as they stood in line on cold greasy pieces of fried chicken, traditional staff of life of the courtroom habitué. The day gave promise of great heat and attendant thirst, and in the growing line alliances were being formed, one scandalmonger holding the place of another while he went from water fountain to rest room, clutching his paper bag of chicken wings and a small thermos of coffee—also greasy. The pensioners, the earliest of birds, bore the pain of varicose veins and the long stand with fortitude, and on empty stomachs. They would sell their places some three hours hence to the highest bidder, then totter out to a soda fountain or speak, to gorge and argue the merits of a case about which they knew nothing then and would know even less after reading the first accounts in the paper. For the rest of the spectators, once in the courtroom two trials would commence—that of The Feeb for first-degree murder and the trial of endurance, the ironical suffering brought on by a parched mouth and a distended bladder. Once one of the less hardy of scandalmongers could no longer withstand the clamors of nature and abandoned his seat, another was ushered in to claim it, and the loser, his comfort attended to, joined the foot of the long line in the corridor and was downcast all day.

Himself arriving two minutes before the courtroom doors were flung open, Mark was presented an unexpected pleasure. It was his great honor to see Seymour Pentlove, tinted pink under his talcum, demanding admittance of a huge deputy sheriff guarding the doors. Those in line greeted each of Mr. Pentlove's threats, arguments, and entreaties with catcalls or encouragement. To Mark fell the exquisite experience of sailing up to rehabilitate Mr. Pentlove by explaining "Oh, he's with me," and watching the mouth of the Man of Power tighten with exasperation when the doors opened to this off-hand sesame. Yet it was rather a pity to see Mr. Pentlove publicly humiliated, and Mark said as they moved down the aisle, "You mustn't forget, Pentlove, you're off your own reservation down here. This is my happy hunting ground."

"Do you know," Mr. Pentlove retorted bitterly, "that I really believe that that big moron of a sheriff out there didn't know Who I Was?"

"Come, come," Mark said. "Our sheriffs are fine boys all. I hold it as a firm conviction that some of them are even educable."

Mr. Pentlove was dubious of such optimism, and in silence took the seat Mark indicated in the row directly behind the defense-counsel table. Mr. Pentlove bent on his neighbor, Rookie Castle, a glacial stare. "Pentlove meet Castle," Mark said. "You two gentlemen have more in common than you'll ever know." Then Mark strode past the bar to the defense table, Rookie looking at his back wistfully, Mr. Pentlove with an unreasoning resentment. After all, could not he, Seymour Pentlove, place the drunken D'Andor up on the very bench itself? Mark was undoing the straps of his brief case to get out his dossiers; Mr. Pentlove clearly saw the flask of Irish therein, and his dour mood lifted somewhat. Put to the question, he could not have said for the life of him why D'Andor's easy assurance irked him so, or why he treasured that defensive contempt he held for the man to whom he was trusting two million dollars.

Mark was otherwise occupied, for he had drawn as opponent an old rival, T. Amos Slake. And T. Amos, had he but known it, was in appearance Mark's *beau idéal* of the proper District Attorney. Mr. Slake wore his black hair parted precisely in the middle so that, with head bent, he bore a startling resemblance to a macadam road with a white traffic line down its center. He was perpetually as red as the Jonathan apples in the fruit stalls around town, for his stiff Herbert Hoover collars had a virtual stranglehold on him. Most compelling of all was the absolute symmetry of Amos Slake's face. Each half was the mirror image of the other. No lowering of one lid or faint flare of a nostril marred the integrality of the hemispheres of his head. All in all, he looked so wholesome that you immediately felt somehow he was good for you. Everybody knew, of course, that Amos considered himself gubernatorial timber.

His dossiers turned face-down, Mark nodded to Amos and gave him a temperate smile. Amos' smile in return was tempered. No exchange took place between these unlikely gladiators, for, like a battle charge in a De Mille movie, the spectators roared into the courtroom, crunching dropped bags of chicken underfoot, and the ladies, bless them, snatching at sleeves or belts or trailing scarves to remove impediments from their onslaught. A gentleman fell on the field of valor and promptly had his hand mashed, and a matron requested to vacate those seats reserved for Mr. Slake's witnesses had many compliments for Chester Dander and his crestfallen ewe lamb, Dr. Snowdom, before relinquishing the precious piece of earth for which she had fought so valiantly.

Then, all was still but for rattlings, shiftings, coughings, hawkings, giggles, hissings, and a female voice which began clearly, "*Get* your. . . ." but died away. The air of the courtroom was tangy with the strong odor of human exertion.

Mark looked bored.

Amos Slake had papers and papers to shuffle and considerable rummaging about in the back of his high Herbert Hoover collar with a long forefinger to be got past, and after that he still had to fidget with the ring clasp of his gold-plated mechanical pencil, all of which activities proved him a very busy Deputy District Attorney indeed.

Mark, arms folded across his chest, casually looked in Chester's direction, thinking: Chester had better have a fresh supply of angry flushes and indignant purplings ready when I take on his shrinking violet. As if startled by a klaxon, Chester flinched and found himself looking wide-eyed at Mark. Mark tilted his head and winked. Chester got to his feet, entered the bar, and sat beside Mark, all in readiness to be friendly or reserved as the occasion might demand. Amos Slake forgot to toy with his gold mechanical pencil for staring; yet his expression clearly said that not for the world would he interfere with one attorney conversing with another, and also that not for the world would he want the lawyer of his own witness coming within a mile of that devious D'Andor.

"Greetings, Chester," Mark said. "We're making Amos nervous."

"I'm not sure this is quite proper," Chester said. "What can I do for you?"

"Take heed," Mark said pleasantly. "First thing, I'll be asking the court to kick your ewe lamb out of here until Amos calls him to the stand."

"Oh, I've prepared him for that," Chester said understandingly.

"And secondly," Mark said with the same level voice of one uttering trivial pleasantries, "when Snowdom does get on that stand I'm going to feed him to the mincemeat machine, digit by digit. Arms, legs, and all. I am going to impeach him, if I have to 'color' his testimony to do it. You understand what I am saying, don't you, Chester?"

"Perfectly," Chester said.

"What you told me in confidence is the weapon I'm going to turn on your client."

"Any weapon to hand," Chester said, holding himself in check, "when you're defending a man from the rope. I'd do the same in your place."

"You'd never!" Mark's scoffing laughter earned him a nice magenta hue decorating Chester's temples. "Chester, don't even think of aping my tactics. You'd trip all over your golden spurs."

"Are you quoting from that damn-fool poem again?" Chester challenged.

"Sorry. But I did want to warn you."

"In other words, you're going from the unorthodox to the unethical?"

"I'd love to split hairs with you, Chester, but I doubt if we—if you—have the time."

Chester set his jaw. "Mark, believe you me, I have the time. You can kick Snowdom out of the courtroom, but try kicking me. I aim to fill him in every night on what I learn here during the day."

"Chester, you are shaping up. Yessir, you are shaping up," Mark said thoughtfully.

"And furthermore," Chester said, "I'm not warning Snowdom of your mincemeat machine until it's too late for him to stampede. When Amos wants him on that witness stand, that's where Snowdom is going to be. Savvy?"

"Regrettably, yes," Mark said with a grin.

But Chester showed him what could be accomplished in the way of dental magniloquence, and then, in that unbending walk of his, repaired to his seat.

At nine-twenty the spectators had their first glimpse of The Feeb as he was ushered into the barred anteroom to the left rear of the bench, known as the bullpen. He was not a happy Feeb, though he lifted a hand, white and fleshy as a leg of lamb, in response to the applause that greeted him, and smiled in sorrow to show he was that touched. When The Feeb was then led into the courtroom to take his place at Mark's side, a paper flower from a woman's hat landed on the counsel table and he caught it up to bury his face in it and shudder his great shoulders. Above the uproar T. Amos Slake could barely make himself heard as he denounced the demonstrators and commanded the bailiffs to restore order, finding time in the midst of his fulminations to point a finger at Mark, thereby lumping him with the noisy rabble. Mark quite enjoyed the spectacle of Amos' agonizings, confident that The Feeb would end the applause the moment his sense of timing told him to.

"Are you done slobbering over your flower?" Mark asked Forbes with polite interest.

A muffled "not yet" came in reply.

Then, at the precise instant dictated by The Feeb's instinct, Forbes lifted his head and with an unbearably moving tenderness fitted the shabby posy into his lapel. "What is that weed, anyway, a rose?" Mark asked.

"Whatever you call it, it smells as sweet," Forbes said, his expression denying his note of bravado. He was frightened, and Mark wanted him that way. A cocky Feeb would be disastrous.

"Now turn and smile bravely at the orderly people," Mark said.

The Feeb complied at once, saying out of the corner of his mouth, "Don't tell me my business, Counsel. To my fans you're just another straight man."

"Your fans," Mark said pointedly, "will not be impaneled as your jury, I'm sorry to say." The clerk emerged from chambers, and at a signal from him the bailiff began rapping for order. *Sotto voce* Mark continued, "However, I do advise you to wear that flower every single day you are in this court. And make certain the reporters play it up."

"You *must* think I'm feebleminded," Forbes said, in the act of rising, "to overlook a trick like that."

When all were standing and silent, Judge Natalie Fickett

saw fit to grace the courtroom with her presence. Experiencing the same little contretemps with robe and step she always did, Her Honor rather hopped up, narrowly missing that pesky staff of the flag, and flung herself into her highback chair, still all in one piece. Both T. Amos Slake and Mark let out breath neither had been conscious of holding. A whisper of a snicker from Forbes had Mark longing to stamp Forbes with his footprint for all time, in a spot known only to Forbes' intimates. Perched safely on her eminence, Judge Fickett peeked past her set of Codes at those assembled, reminding Mark, as she had before, of a child who needs a Webster's Unabridged on her chair to bring her to the proper height at table. To Her Honor's chirpy inquiry, Amos shot to his feet to declare—or declaim, as Mark thought of it—that the People were Ready. With his understated dancing-master's grace, Mark rose to say so was the defense.

The clerk proceeded to draw from a box the names of twelve persons. There was a hush among the spectators not unlike that which prevailed on Tuesday nights at the movies when the lights came on and the squirrel cage wheeled in front of the screen, those in their seats blinking at their ticket stubs and holding their collective breath, waiting to learn who would be the lucky recipient of a set of lumpish crockery. The panel now so drawn stepped with every indication of abysmal stage fright into the jury box, next to stare defensively at just about everybody in sight but Archibald Forbes. Out of the corner of his eye Mark was gratified to note that Forbes bent upon the twelve a flabby countenance of bewildered blamelessness; there was no hoodlum or bootmaker among Mark's clients but gave a token smirk of innocence at this juncture and would not have profited from seeing The Feeb, the master, at work.

Judge Fickett raised herself high enough to survey the twelve over her Codes. There was always about her the air of busyness of a sparrow, never more so than when conducting a *voir dire*. In rapid fire she asked collectively of the nine men and three women in the box if any of them were stone deaf, given to falling fits, hateful of the forces of law and order, or felt in the mood for having a heart attack in the near future. These questions so occupied the prospective jury that it mulled them for several moments with scholarly concentration. "Are any of you impelled to speak up?" Judge Fickett prompted. When no one was, she bethought herself to add emergency surgery and childbirth to the list of misfortunes that were mankind's common lot; but no, not one in the box was so inclined in those directions either. Her duties done, Her Honor was cheery as a cricket, bouncing her eyes in her head until they settled in pleased discovery on Mark. "Counselor, you wish to question on *voir dire?*"

It was always a bit of a chore for Mark not to let the peppy old hag suspect how much he liked her, so with a stern aspect not customary with him he said, "If the Court please."

Mark asked of the first man in the box if he had formed any opinion of the case. No, he had not, that person said indignantly, widening his eyes and looking at Archibald Forbes for the first time. Mark nodded negligently. He had no quarrel with this man; according to the dossier, he would vote for an acquittal out of sheer confusion. Mark's questions were brief, almost desultory, aware as he was that T. Amos liked to hone his fangs on the panel, thus unconsciously ruffling their vanities and implanting in their stalwart breasts a faint resentment which none of Amos' later emotive catch-phrases and outraged invective (directed against the defendant) would quite erase.

Amos was in keeping with Mark's expectations, and lacerated this same first man in the box with questions couched in a tone of voice that would have incensed an escaped convict who was lying in his teeth in order to save the life of a pervert who had left the convict's wife and puppy dog to burn to death while he saved the mother-in-law. This accomplished, Amos sent Her Honor a winning smile and modestly announced that the State was satisfied with juror number one. Number One folded his arms across his chest and fumed. Before going to the next member of the panel, Mark gave him the faintest of smiles.

There were two people among the talesmen in whom Mark had a crucial interest. One was the grandmother of boys who were of the Feeb-fan age; the other, a woman also, was a divorcee and the mother of a girl-child of around seven. As Mark continued on with his *voir dire,* moving swiftly from person to person, there gradually fell over him his courtroom attitude, a shade more dynamic then a phlegmatic calm and not so artfully polished as to be a suspect suavity. What it cost him—considering his inward seethe of tension and anxiety—only his great thirst at the end of a day could truly attest. He began to sense, as he did with most of his clients, Forbes' first unrest—wanting, as all seemed to, the hot-shot display of a T. Amos in his behalf.

But, turning away from a talesman, Mark glimpsed Mr. Pentlove and read on that precisely displayed collection of choice features an expression of respect and content. Intent again on the panel, he listened less to answers than to inflections, speech patterns, and waited most of all for that note as imperative as the command of a gong—the assurance in a voice that its owner would not be bullied by anyone. That single golden note that betokened the holdout, the juror who would hang a jury higher than Haman rather than hang his head before his own conscience. To his surprise, Mark found his man in the person of a retired minister—a sobersides with all the stuffy aplomb that went with his cloth. Thinking he must surely be wrong, be losing his grip (I'm too damn sober to know what I'm doing, Mark's mind said), he asked of the minister, "Sir, in your opinion, were you to hear of conduct on the defendant's part that you found morally distasteful, would that influence your opinion as to his guilt or innocence of the act with which he is charged?"

Taking his good time, the minister said, "I'm not one to judge." His voice was so quiet that Amos might have missed his reply.

Mark rushed to the next question, any question. "Have you formed an opinion of Hollywood actors, Sir?"

"I have not."

"Or Hollywood actresses?"

"I have not."

A swift glance showed Amos, upright and noble, readiness itself as concerned accepting the retired minister. He, Amos, certainly had no questions.

It was by then time for lunch.

The Feeb was called for by his deputy custodians, one of whom put a possessive hand on The Feeb's arm and led him away, the door of the bullpen slamming shut just as the first photographer burst into the courtroom. There were only Mark and Amos, and the spectators rummaging about among their half-gnawed chicken wings and drumsticks for a spot of lunch, for the hapless gentlemen of the press. Behind Mark Mr. Pentlove said fretfully. "D'Andor, I do hope you know of a place that is both *cool* and serves decent food. Which I won't be able to eat anyway, if I smell much more chicken."

"Sorry," Mark said, "but I'll just be grabbing a sandwich from the stand in the lobby. Try the Obispo Hotel. You might like the dining room there."

"I never have," Mr. Pentlove said unhappily. "And I own the Obispo." So saying he took his departure, looking every inch the grandee and attracting more than one munching scandalmonger's practiced eye.

Mark repaired to the Men's where he snapped down two capsful of Irish from his flask, took note of himself in the mirror looking rumpled and dogged in the best Clarence Darrow tradition, and returned to the courtroom. Rookie Castle was now seated at the counsel table, trying to devour a ham sandwich as limp and dispirited as a pancake and studying the dope sheets on the veniremen. "Had yourself the hair o' the dog?" Rookie said.

"So give me a chihuahua for my birthday," Mark replied agreeably. "Rookie, how about this divorcee? Does she still think men are the berries, or is she down on them in general?"

"From what I could find out, nobody slides on her cellar door, no more no more."

"Ah."

A glint of a grin on Rookie's face had Mark chattering, "Rookie! You didn't! My God, you didn't try to date her up!"

Sanguine crook that he was, Rookie said thoughtfully, "I did toy with the idea."

As thoughtless as Rookie was thoughtful, Mark blurted, "You trying to get me disbarred or something?"

Rookie found that a capital idea, laughing openly at Mark. "Could be I'm lonesome. You know what the great Coke said."

"I'm afraid it has slipped my mind."

"He said, 'Once forsworn, and ever forlorn.' "

"I swan if that doesn't sound just like him."

"And he said, 'One ought not to have so delicate a nose, that he cannot bear the smell of swine.' "

"Hogs," Mark corrected him triumphantly.

And Rookie, who prided himself on his ragbag of tattered old saws, was utterly put out. "Stealing my thunder," he muttered, and shuffled the dossiers busily. "By the bye, what was the machine-gun-fire *voir dire* of the preacher all about?"

"He said something I hoped T. Amos hadn't caught. So I didn't linger."

"Are you crazy, taking chances with an opinionated old prig like that? Watching you play it by ear," Rookie complained, "makes me so nervous I could scream. And all the while Sir Seymour sits and purrs as if you knew exactly what you were doing."

"I may not," Mark said, "but Seymour Pentlove does."

Court reconvened, Mark was again conducting a *voir dire* should he wish to challenge for cause. The divorcee, the bone of contention between himself and the faithful Rookie, was to all appearances prime material for a juror. Yet Mark would have as soon welcomed T. Amos Slake into the box. She was as fetching and crisp as new folding money, but she wanted very very much to become a member of the jury. Knowing that not one person in ten thousand who greatly desires to serve and sit in judgment does so out of a wish to help the defendant, Mark used up a precious peremptory challenge and said, "Your Honor, I ask this lady be excused."

"She is," Her Honor chirped.

Amos was crestfallen; he had had his heart set on her. And he was, as a consequence, almost desultory in his acceptance of Jurors Seven, Eight and Nine.

A few more questions, and then a lengthy *voir dire* of a man whose mother's uncle's cousin's husband had once been on the police force, and Mark, having accepted that gentleman as well, was done. "Your honor, as of now the panel is satisfactory to the defense."

Judge Fickett, not a whit wilted in the heat of the late October afternoon, asked of Mr. Slake if he could finish off by the end of the day's session. Amos writhed within the punching confines of his collar. Like any good prosecutor, next to nitpicking he loved jury-picking; certain it is that he did not subscribe to a statement once made by Mark, "The only vital question I want to ask of a juror I am not permitted to. I'd like to ask, 'How's your sex life?' and if he tells me it's fine, then I know that here is an individual with an open mind and a healthy prostate. And that makes him vulnerable to compassion for a poor defendant who could be locked up for the next twenty years and not getting any."

Still seeking to adjust his neck to his collar, for his collar was not the type to meet anyone halfway, Amos fretted in the heat. He asked a few snoopy questions and subsided.

The jury was sworn in.

There were two women (not counting the female alternate juror) and ten men. One of the women was the grandmother, the other a faded widow. The men were of middle age with the exception of a young shoe salesman and the retired minister. Now that it was done, Mark covertly eyed the jury as doubtfully as Amos was doing. Misgivings assailed Mark even as he sent them a smile as loving as a benediction. As Amos was doing. Outwardly rejoicing, inwardly quaking (as Amos was doing), Mark found himself exchanging a long and eloquent appraisal with Amos. Not breaking his hold on Mark's gaze, Amos slid his hand along the counsel table until it encountered his gold mechanical pencil with the ring loop set in its top. The hand brought the pencil to Amos' mouth, and delicately, pensively, still taking Mark's measure, Amos nibbed the gold ring with his front teeth. This served to recall to Mark that Amos had always reminded him faintly of a rodent with his teeth leaning backward toward his palate. Mark's mind stated in the positive tone of an expert witness, say, an orthodontist: Teeth like that, Amos, can't have a very good bite. Ah well, his mind went on blithely, Amos' bark is nothing to write home about either. He realized gradually that he was grinning at Amos, and by way of riposte Amos dealt him a supercilious sniff, then ducked his head to show Mark the neat traffic line bisecting the tarred-top surface of his crown.

Judge Fickett was informing all, with many a chirp, that

it was Friday, and wishing all a good week end. This done she slid from her massive chair, cast a suspicious eye at the staff of the flag, managed to trip over it, somehow negotiated the steps leading to the bench, and bolted like a bird after a grub for chambers.

As the deputy came for The Feeb, he stretched forth a proprietary hand to lay on The Feeb, and found instead he was clutching the solid meat of Archibald Forbes. "Keep your shirt on" Forbes said to the deputy in the voice of one expecting to be obeyed. To Mark he snapped, "Are you daffy? Kicking the only sensible dame in the whole outfit off the jury! Why, she could have—"

"Not only could have, but would have," Mark assured him. "She all but fashioned nooses out of the windowshade cords, waiting her chance to get into the box."

"And the prissy Bible-whacker. What's the big idea of not—"

"I want you to do something this week end," Mark put in, unruffled. "You're to think about that jury. I'll brief you on every one of them. And—"

"*Brief* me? You sound like some goddam English solicitor or whatever they are."

"And you're to find something to like about each and every person who will be sitting in that box. You understand me? *Like* them. Put your will to it and do it."

Forbes weighed this advice, then acquiesced. "Yeah. I get it. A showman is always at his best when he likes the audience. They can feel it, too. I'm going to love them like I love my jazz."

The deputy took it into his head to be jocular. "Come on, Feeb, you can't jazz a girl; don't give me that."

A flicker of an eyelid and The Feeb was back whimpering, "Well, I can dream, can't I?"

Then the reporters and photographers were upon them. The Feeb simpered sorrowfully while his custodian thrust out his lower jaw and edged closer so that each picture would be graced with his image.

Mark went to lean against the rail of the bar, looking on,

as was Mr. Pentlove. "He handled that 'jazz' taunt well," Mr. Pentlove observed quietly.

"Yes. Evidently he's making himself popular with the boys upstairs."

"Upstairs?"

"What we call the jail, of course."

Mr. Pentlove looked down his nose. "Well, really, D'Andor. You could hardly expect *me* to be familiar with a thing like *that*."

The photographers were working around toward Mark, the reporters now hard at preserving for all time The Feeb's lisping tale of the nice lady who threw him a flower for his lapel.

"What are your plans?" Mr. Pentlove asked of Mark.

"Well, soon as I get my likeness took, I'm going home and get blotto. Unless you wish a conference?"

Mr. Pentlove must have been feeling dyspeptic; his manner was decidedly acidulous. "D'Andor, I feel it only fair to warn you that I don't tolerate drunkenness in someone under my hire."

"That makes me no never-minds," Mark said affably, and waited politely to learn if Mr. Pentlove wished to deliver further home truths.

Instead, Mr. Pentlove was studying Mark intently. "Why is it," he said, "that you deliberately talk like a hick sometimes?"

And with that deliberation of which Mr. Pentlove had accused him, Mark retorted, "Wall naow, Pentlove, I'm only funnin'."

Mr. Pentlove's sole reply was a slow cryptic smile.

CHAPTER NINETEEN

Having been opposed by T. Amos Slake before, though mainly in preliminary hearings, Mark took no little interest in his development as a trial lawyer. For all his sartorial decorum, Amos had a bent for the dynamic. Being political-minded, Amos hated to lose, though he was training himself to accept defeat gracefully. As well he might, Mark reflected, for the loss meant only that the accused was set free. After a trouncing he could sleep of nights; whereas when Mark was bested he had "hoosegow widows" camping on his doorstep, weeping to know who would support the children now that Papa was ungainfully employed in the penitentiary jute-mill. Still, Mark had never lost a client to the rope, and was therefore on a par with Amos, who had not yet been fortunate enough to deliver a neck to the noose. These considerations among others were at the front of Mark's mind—and Amos' too, Mark had no doubt.

It was not to be wondered at, then, that on Monday morning Mark could himself have given Amos' opening address to the jury, had Amos suddenly been called elsewhere. Mark had arrived in the courtroom feeling durable, if not fit, on his breakfast of raw egg, coffee, Irish, and a few stray gumdrops he had forgotten to put out for the skunks. Amos was quietly resplendent in a fresh Herbert Hoover collar, a spanking-new suit in a shade of tender blue made of some material that Mark thought of as being "crinkle-crêpe"—it had another name when tailored, but Mark could not bring it to mind—and a glow on his cheeks that could probably in part be attributed to his starched neckwear. Also, Amos had the cool of the morning to aid him in his presentation. He fairly crackled with energy, and Mark thought: I knew it, I knew it, Amos has decided to be electrifying. Next to the unprepossessingly frayed Mark, Archibald Forbes displayed the dewy toilette of an adorable infant, only the shabby posy in his lapel striking a note not quite in keeping with his Johnson's-baby-preparation aura.

Judge Fickett, having completed her treacherous journey from chambers to bench, invited Mr. Slake to proceed. At once several of the jurors, notably the retired gentleman of the cloth, uncapped pens and held them poised over their notepads. Amos walked to the jury box and ringingly declared, "Your Honor!"

Her Honor was watching the bailiff adjusting a window-shade.

Amos made a half-turn and cried out passionately to Mark, "My learned opponent!"

Mark was frowning over a hangnail.

Amos whipped about to the jury. "And ladies and gentle-men!" Amos then looked each and every juror in the eye. (Oh God, thought Mark, Amos is going to be thyroidal. He really ought to see a doctor about having those glands of his toned down a notch). "I am going to tell you the tragic but true story," Amos said, "of the life and death of a beautiful young woman known professionally as Muffin Naismith."

That's a large order, Amos, Mark thought.

"Yes, a young woman in the prime of her beauty, who was seized by a lustful *monster*—" Amos swung round to point at the Feeb, who looked back like a little fat boy trying very very very hard not to cry. Somewhat unnerved by The Feeb's mimetic ability, Amos returned to the jury. He did not again make the mistake of inviting them to observe The Feeb. "A monster," Amos repeated, "of such brutal tastes and overpow-ering strength that he could force rape, indescribable indigni-ties, and death upon a helpless woman. O, ladies and gentle-men," Amos begged, "do not be deceived. O, ladies and gentlemen, let us be clear on this point right now. Archibald Forbes is on trial for a vicious, malicious, and heinous murder. Archibald Forbes! Not some shadow flickering across a silver screen. Not the figment of someone's imagination. Not a harmless comedian. But Archibald Forbes, behind whose actor's face—O, yes, he is an actor, as I'm sure we shall all see—if he *dares* to take the stand in his own——"

Her Honor looked down to Mark in question. Mark smiled with his eyes only: Let it go, Your Honor. Judge Fickett shrugged.

". . . behind that actor's mask a heart so malignant . . ."

The Feeb neither flinched nor blinked. He kept his bewildered gaze steadily on Amos, his countenance as ample a seat as woe ever sat.

". . . will prove to you, so that you will see it as with your very own eyes, the shocking pattern of events, link by gruesome link, that led down the bloody path culminating in murder," Amos promised with relish.

Amos, Mark thought, let us hope you have used up your ration of metaphors for the day.

At each bend of Amos' oratory the jury stared at Forbes, picturing in their minds as best they were able and as Amos had bade them that mass of despondent flab leaping down a hallway after his intended victim, and after locking himself in with her, attacking her person with his own—well—his own vile person. And then, when her screams had brought others to pound on that locked door, Forbes, the beastly assailant, committed yet a more horrible——

Yes, yes, the jury seemed to be thinking, spit it out. Did *what*? For the very expanse of the Feeb's anatomy seemed to preclude any one such insignificant portion of it being construed as an instrument of death—a murder weapon.

". . . ice!" Amos shrilled. "In his depraved lust he——"

A thought spoke itself in Mark's mind: *No ice, no dice.* It had a familiar ring, yet he could not quite place it.

Amos finished in a low thrilling voice, warning the jury to steel itself to withstand the shock of the forthcoming testimony. The grandmother juror set her jaw; Mark surmised she was more than ready—avid even—for all the muck Amos could hurl at her, and more. Easeful on the surface, Mark's nerves suddenly seemed to corrode. A juror with a taste for lip-smacking details usually liked to top off the meal with a large helping of retribution. *Vengeance is mine, saith the Lord;* but Grandma might feel there was still plenty to go around.

Fallen silent, Amos again looked each and every juror in the eye. When he sat down, he seemed satisfied that he was but a hop and a skip from a verdict of murder in the first degree.

Some ass or other in the spectator's section began to applaud, and while disciplinary measures were being taken, Mark said to Forbes, "You can stop posing for the jury for a while. They'll be more interested in the witnesses. I don't want you tensing up visibly, so grab every opportunity you can to let up. When the heat's on again, you'll know it."

"Yeah," Forbes said in a fretful whisper, "but what about that *ice*?"

"That," Mark said, "has been my question all along. Well? What about it?"

"But he can't get somebody to say—"

"Stick around," Mark said, "and you'll find out he can. And will. Now shut up, Forbes. From here on in, unless I speak to you first, don't speak to me. If you want to say something, write it down on your pad. I mustn't be distracted, no matter what."

The disturbance attended to, Mark rose to announce he wished to reserve his opening statement until the prosecution had concluded its case. It was a tactic of his, affording him the opportunity to learn the vulnerable points of the prosecution's case, the better to attack them. He could make of flexibility a weapon. Judge Fickett instructed Mr. Slake to produce his first witness.

Amos promptly put his witness from the coroner's office on the stand, and asked of that witness his name.

Mark got to his feet casually and requested permission to approach the bench. "Oh, fer the love of—" Amos muttered, but galloped along at Mark's side when permission was granted.

Mark asked in a low voice that the prosecution's witnesses be removed from the courtroom. In a harsh whisper Amos protested, "Your Honor, this is *the* most improper re—"

"If you do not lower your voice, Mr. Slake," Her Honor rasped loudly enough to be heard by Chester Dander, who was already preparing to shoo Snowdom out, "I shall have to remove to chambers. Counselor?"

"Several of the witnesses have already made conflicting

statements under oath, and on issues herein involved," Mark said.

"Your Honor, in 14 Cal 2nd—" Amos began.

"In my discretion I think your point is well taken, Mr. D'Andor," Her Honor decided. "I shall therefore—"

"In 14 Cal 2nd—" Amos resumed doggedly.

"Amos," Mark said cheerfully, "I read 14 Cal 2nd not five minutes before entering this courtroom. Did you?"

"You really should, Mr. Slake," Her Honor urged; "you'd find it most instructive. You just cited an authority that upholds my decision on this issue. You will designate those witnesses to be removed, Mr. D'Andor."

Amos was whipped and he knew it. "Thank you, Your Honor," he said in a loud pleased voice. He stepped back smartly to his counsel table, shoulders square, as if he had just triumphed in some obscure but telling technical point.

Standing up to let Dr. Snowdom out into the aisle, Chester Dander grinned in derision at Mark, who was sauntering back to his own place. Amos knew a thing or two himself about snatching a victory from the jaws of defeat. As for Rookie Castle, he wouldn't have missed this little byplay for the world. Mark was rueful, thinking: They'll rag me raw over this.

And so they did, for Her Honor declared a recess for the witnesses to be removed, and Mark scampered for the Men's, flask of Irish sloshing in his breast pocket, only to encounter Chester washing his hands and Rookie leaning against the wall. "Oh, *thank* you, Your Honor!" Rookie catcalled. And when Chester looked about him with dripping hands, and Mark wadded up a towel and threw it at Chester with all his might, Chester caroled, "Oh, thank *you,* Your—"

"I happen to be defending a man charged with murder," Mark raged childishly. "Why you boys should think that so hilarious—"

Amos entered. He looked at Rookie not at all, his manner stating that where Rookie stood was only empty air.

"Any of you gentlemen for a drink?" Mark said, holding out the flask to Rookie.

"I think I'll be getting back," Rookie decided.

He and Chester went out, not speaking.

"Amos," Mark said to his back, "was it really necessary to cut Rookie dead like that?"

Amos said reasonably, "I don't have to cut him dead. He did it for himself years ago. I'm sorry for him, but I simply can't afford to be seen on a friendly basis with—well—a deadhead."

"So far he has not contaminated me," Mark said mildly.

Amos turned around and examined himself with tender loving care in the mirror. He ducked his head to make certain that his part was straight as the path of an arrow. Then he stretched his neck the better to accommodate his unyielding collar. "Going to hit a hundred in that courtroom this afternoon," he said. "Wonder if they'll ever install that new air-conditioning in courthouses?"

Mark said slowly, "Amos, what if I were to tell you that I have every reason to expect that I shall be placed on the bench in the very near future."

Amos laughed lightheartedly. *"Place* is right, Mark. You'd break your drunken neck trying it under your own steam."

While Amos looked on, Mark drank deeply from his flask.

"You . . . pettifogger," Amos said with insulting pity.

Mark bowed. "Oh, thank you, Your Honor!"

Amos stalked out.

The witness from the coroner's office resumed the stand. He established the death of Muffin Naismith. That fact and one other. Though the immediate cause of death had been septicemia, there was evidence of physical abuse. The body was bruised on arms and thighs, and aside from clear indications that an abortion had been effected through dilatation and curettage, there was also revealed a tear or lesion in the vaginal wall.

"Could this tear—this lesion—have been made by a rapist?" Amos asked.

Mark shut his eyes. If Amos had a particular talent, it was for making of himself a pain in the neck. Opening his eyes, he said quietly, "Objection."

"I should think so," Judge Fickett said.

"I will rephrase the question," Amos conceded in a prickly voice.

"Do," Judge Fickett advised him.

Amos hid his discomfiture under a scowl of strict attention to his papers, which somehow he conveyed to the jury were of the greatest moment, whereas those of Mark's were mere scraps and jottings. "Could this lesion," he asked the witness, "have been made during the commission of rape?"

"Yes," the witness said accommodatingly. "We see this sort of lesion all the time in cases of—"

"Let me proceed to the next question," Amos said, an instant before Mark could break into the continuity of the testimony again. "Would you describe this lesion more accurately, please."

"Well, it was like a rip in the tissue. In the wall of the organ. That is, it was jagged."

"You do not believe, then, that it was caused by a surgical instrument?"

"Amos," Mark put in mildly, "will you please cut it out." Raising his voice he said, "Objection. Leading the witness."

"Sustained."

Amos was as pleasant as a sunny morn. "Let me ask you this, then. From the appearance of the lesion, would you say it had been caused by a surgical instrument?"

"No," the witness said, "I wouldn't."

Amos thought nothing of standing around for moments at a time; in his mind, it would appear, he was demonstrating for the jury a pregnant pause. Several of the jurors made notes; the rest felt obliged to, but couldn't think for the life of them what to write down. Satisfied he had slammed the door on the possibility of Snowdom's having bungled the abortion, Amos plunged on, "Were there other marks of violence discernible on the body, as well as the bruises?"

"This lesion, like I said. And there was considerable swelling of the genital area."

"One more question. Could the lesion of which you spoke have been caused by ice?"

You may speak of ice till the heavens fall, Mark thought,

but I defy you, Amos, to produce it. On the other hand, I wouldn't be the least surprised if you tried.

"Ice?" the witness was saying, as it seemed every person even remotely connected with Muffin Naismith was destined to say sooner or later. "Oh, *ice!*" the witness said.

"Yes. Could the lesion have been caused by a piece or pieces of ice inserted into the birth canal of Miss Naismith?"

"Amos," Mark said, "have you ever thought of putting a ring through his nose? You can lead 'em anywhere that way," he ended in a soft confidential voice not heard by the jury seated to Amos' right.

"Tut," Judge Fickett said to Mark sternly. "Have you an objection, Counselor?"

"Yes," Mark said, and at the exact moment the witness also was saying, "Yes." Then, courteously, Mark changed his mind. "I withdraw my objection, Your Honor." The witness' reply had been lost in the byplay.

The vaguest of unfounded suspicions seized Amos. What with D'Andor's nagging interruptions, undignified asides, and sagging quips, could it be that D'Andor was attempting to mar the mood he, Amos, hoped to establish in his presentation of his case?

If there was one thing T. Amos Slake insisted upon (he was known for his luminous expositions of the subject), it was that he be able to establish at the very outset of a trial the "tone" of the proceedings. His preparations were devoted almost as much to mood as to content. Yet, invariably, when D'Andor ambled into a case, Amos had the helpless feeling of one trying to slaughter May flies with a cannon. It struck Amos that it was equally bootless to train a cannon on D'Andor —say, one of the canons of legal ethics. For *State v. Forbes* Amos had settled upon a swiftly paced melodrama, but with his first witness D'Andor was already backstage manipulating the lighting, or down front playing prompter and feeding the wrong lines.

Her Honor was speaking and Amos pulled his straggling thoughts into line. "I am pleased, Mr. D'Andor," Her Honor was saying, "that you have withdrawn your objection. The Court does not, of course, wish to limit your right to object in any way, but moderation on your part—and that of Mr. Slake too, to be sure—will expedite this trial to the benefit of all."

"I shall exercise the greatest discretion, Your Honor," Mark said smoothly. "It is my earnest desire also to bring this case to a rapid conclusion. My client has many business commitments awaiting him, and the sooner he is able to return to his profession—"

"Your Honor!" Amos wailed. "Counsel is speechifying! If counsel is to be permitted to indulge in long monologues, then I——" But Amos did not pursue that sentence further as it raced ahead of him into the no man's land of contempt.

"Yes?" Judge Fickett asked airily.

"May I continue with my examination of this witness?" Amos murmured.

"Pray do," Her Honor said, and flopped back behind her Codes.

In a loud unhappy voice Amos said, "So that the jury may have the benefit of your answer, I will repeat the question. Could a piece or pieces of ice have been responsible for inflicting the lesion you discovered in the birth canal of the deceased?"

"Yes, I think it possible," the witness said.

Amos looked soulfully at the jury. Then, abruptly, he was done with the witness. Taking up his gold mechanical pencil, he held it poised over his legal pad, signifying that Mark might now cross-examine.

Mark assumed an air of one confused and lost among the technicalities of medical lore. It was a firm rule of his never to ask a witness to explain difficult points in language the jury could understand. Always and ever he asked the witness to enlighten *him*, simple fellow that he was. He began, "Let me see if I understand your testimony correctly. A lesion is a rip or tear?"

"Not necessarily. It could be both. Or something different, too."

"Oh." Mark frowned in thought. "Give me an example of the something different."

"Why— Any sort of an injury could loosely be classified

as a lesion. Then it might not mean a wound at all." The witness unconsciously slowed his speech as if addressing a lackwit. "It could mean a local morbid condition."

"A local morbid condition? Does that mean a local *dead* condition?"

Patronizing the ignoramus, the witness said, "Again you're confusing generalities with specifics. By *morbid* I mean as applied to the particular tissue only. Such as a localized burn. The entire skin isn't dead, only the burned area."

To all appearances, Mark was having great difficulty sorting all this out. "Then will you tell me if the lesion you discovered on the vaginal wall of the deceased could have been what they call a toxic lesion?"

The witness tautened almost imperceptibly. "If you mean by that, that it was connected with or the result of the septic condition of the deceased, then I would answer no."

"Tell me what you said in words I can understand, please," Mark requested winningly.

"Certainly. The lesion we're talking about was not the result of a septicemic condition. It occurred before the infection. Though it could easily have contributed to, or even been the cause of, the infection."

Mark had blundered, and it was cold comfort to have Rookie unobtrusively slip a note under his hand: *Remember what Buckner sayeth, "More cross-examinations are suicidal than homicidal." Here endeth the lesson. Amen.*

"But you would not say that the lesion could possibly have been the sole cause of the septic condition, would you?"

The witness, realizing that if he had gotten Mark out on a limb, he too was clinging as well to that slender support, refused to advance another step. "No, I would not swear that the lesion could have been the sole cause."

"Nor can you be certain that it contributed in any way to the infection, is not that so?"

"No, I never said it did."

"Let me see if I'm clear on this now. You don't know that that lesion had anything to do with the death of Miss Naismith?"

"No, I don't."

"You don't really know what caused it, do you?"

"I am satisfied in my mind that a surgical instrument didn't," the witness affirmed affably.

"Well, then, could a garden tool have caused the lesion?"

"Could . . . a . . . *what*?"

"A garden tool," Mark repeated, himself as affable as the witness.

"What? I don't under—"

"Am I not speaking loudly enough for you to hear me?" Mark asked, coming around the counsel table, as he had been desiring to all along. Now he need not ask his questions with Amos firmly planted between him and the jury, at his counsel table.

"I can hear you all right, but . . . "

"Let me repeat the question," Mark said in a voice louder than he had employed thus far. The jurors held notebooks in readiness. "Could the lesion have been inflicted with a garden tool?"

"Well, of course not!"

"Oh? What is a garden tool?"

"What is a garden tool!"

"Yes, what is a garden tool?"

Amos belatedly came to the rescue of his witness. "I object to this line of questioning as being irrelevant, incompetent, and immaterial."

Judge Fickett perused Mark as she might a book of parlor tricks. "Mr. D'Andor?"

"Another question or two, Your Honor, will demonstrate that I am developing a relevant line of testimony."

"In a case such as this," Her Honor said, "I will grant reasonable latitude in cross-examination. However, if you do not develop the line shortly I shall entertain another objection from Mr. Slake."

"Thank you." Mark returned to the witness. "Can you tell me what a garden tool is?"

"Look, I'm a medical expert, I object to this—"

Judge Fickett reared past the volumes of Codes pressed together on her bench by bookends in the shape of the California bear. "You will answer the question," she said to the witness. "What is a—"

"Something you garden with!" the witness snapped.

Satisfied, Her Honor sank back in her chair.

"Would you place it beyond the realm of possibility, then, that a garden tool could have inflicted the lesion?"

"Don't you put words in my mouth!" the beleaguered witness shouted. "I won't place it beyond the realm of possibility. Only probability!"

Amos was on his feet, and to him Mark said temperately, "Don't waste your breath, I aim to go on with this."

To Amos' own visible amazement, he accepted Mark's advice and sat down. He did, to be sure, then cast a wry smile to the jury, inviting them to share his distaste for Mark's monkeyshines.

Mark said to the witness, "In answer to one of Mr. Slake's questions you said that the deceased had had a surgical abortion performed on her, did you not?"

"I did."

"But you placed it beyond the realm of probability that the lesion we are speaking of could have been inflicted by a surgical instrument?"

"I did."

"What is a surgical instrument?"

The witness sighed. "A surgical instrument is something you perform surgery with. And before you ask me again, I'll tell you that a garden tool is a—"

"Thank you, but I hadn't intended asking you again. Will you tell me, instead, what is the shape of a piece of ice?"

"Why don't you ask me how far is up?"

"I'm coming to that. Will you tell me what is the shape of a piece of ice?"

"A piece of ice is shaped the way that particular piece of ice happens to be shaped."

"Wouldn't that apply to a garden tool as well?"

"That it's shaped the way that particular tool is shaped? Well, certainly!"

"And a surgical instrument?"

"*And* a surgical instrument."

"I will try to reconstruct your thinking as you performed your autopsy on Muffin Naismith, and then I will ask you if my reconstruction is accurate or not. You discovered the lesion. And you said to yourself that it was beyond the realm of probability that the lesion had been caused by a surgical instrument. Is that correct?"

"I did and do think it beyond the realm of probability."

"Then you concluded that it was beyond the realm of probability that it was inflicted by a garden tool. Correct?"

"No it is not. That lesion's being caused by a garden tool never entered my head!"

"Yet, on discovering that lesion you did say to yourself, 'Ah, here's a lesion that was probably inflicted by a piece, or pieces of ice!' Isn't that so?"

"That is utter nonsense."

"It is your privilege, Sir, to regard your earlier testimony in any light you choose. I have no further questions." Then, as was the custom from which he never deviated, Mark said to the witness, "I thank you."

"Oh, that's all right," the witness said huffily.

Amos, bent on repairing his mood as much as rehabilitating his witness, had a question on redirect examination. "When you were performing the autopsy on the deceased and discovered the lesion, did you form any positive opinion as to what might have caused it?"

"No, not positive."

"Did you eliminate any possibilities?"

"As I said, I did not think it was due to a surgical instrument."

"And that possibilty was suggested to your mind and then eliminated because there was evidence before you that the deceased had undergone surgery?"

"Well, dilatation and curettage comes under the broad heading of surgery, yes."

"And this procedure is performed with surgical instruments, is it not, and not with garden tools?" Amos sneered.

But one of those tricks of fate that turn tragedies into travesties overtook poor Amos Slake. The witness said bluntly, "From the looks of the uterine wall, I wouldn't be too sure in this instance."

Mark would not have been in the least scornful of Amos had he buried his head in his arms and wept. Mark thought:

Well, that last turned a few cats loose in the alley, and they'll multiply without my help. In a drab voice Amos said, "No further questions."

Judge Fickett decided it was time for lunch. All rose to watch her toddle down the two steps without incident.

CHAPTER TWENTY

Had Amos Slake been a drinking man, he might have succumbed to temptation at lunch, drowning his disappointment in lieu of his first witness. As it was, Mark D'Andor at his own lunch enjoyed a nip or so, lacing his coffee from his flask. An invitation to Mr. Pentlove to join him in a drink was received with a disdainful wave of a hand and a dour warning, "Alcohol can warp your judgment, you know."

"I should know—I'm defending The Feeb, aren't I?" Mark extended the flask to Rookie, who primly refused.

In the presence of the affluence and influence that was Mr. Pentlove, Rookie was uppity, still smarting from the slight Amos Slake had dealt him and unconsciously inviting another. He looked past Mr. Pentlove to the paneled wall of their private booth, then examined with undivided attention the floating dome over their heads, its ocean-blue tile giving the exact effect wanted—that of being in some underwater grotto never reached by a direct ray of the sun.

Mr. Pentlove seemed intent on making a nag of himself, like a temperance lecturer. "I meant that alcohol can drive one permanently insane. It happened to someone of my own acquaintance."

As the waiter pushed open the swinging doors of their booth and began to set out the chowder, the oysters, and lastly the bowl of puffy oyster crackers, Mark said in the cozy tone of a gossip, "Why, Pentlove, you don't mean to sit there and tell me that some big movie producer is a wetbrain."

"Tell me one who isn't," Rookie said.

"Don't be pugnacious," Mark told him. "Or go take a poke at Amos, if it'll make you feel better."

"As a matter of fact," Mr. Pentlove said, "he was a bootlegger."

"Manny Amen!"

"Why, yes."

"Rookie," Mark said, suddenly inspired, "find out what Manny's visiting hours are, will you? See if I can possibly come talk to him some night after court. The sooner the better. There's an off-chance he might have heard of or from Muffin before her death."

"He will be a far better example than anything I can say," Mr. Pentlove pronounced, still on the topic of the evils of liquor.

Mark poured more Irish into his coffee. "And to think, poor Amos is eating Swiss on rye in his office and sucking a NeHi through a straw."

"Is he teetotal?" Mr. Pentlove inquired with great approval.

"A teetotalitarian," Mark assured him. "Amos doesn't drink, and he doesn't want anyone else to."

Dispensing with levity, Mr. Pentlove said, "I was seriously asking myself for a time this morning if you knew what you were doing."

"You mean the garden-tool gambit?" Rookie put in, ever the chessplayer.

"I do. I thought for a time there the whole case was going to crash about my ears in a shambles." Mr. Pentlove studied the bowl of round crackers, each like its mates, and carefully, daintily selected the one of his choice.

"Oh, the witness was just being a touch too facile for my taste," Mark said negligently. "He was too insistent that a surgical instrument—any surgical instrument—could not have caused that lesion. So I brought up a garden implement to introduce a touch of the absurd. And also to confuse the witness with probabilities and possibilities, when all he wanted to talk of was absolutes."

"Ummm. I liked your old style better," Mr. Pentlove decided. "Although I must say our Mr. Slake did badly in asking those final questions of his. A stroke of pure luck, that."

Mr. Pentlove bent to select another oyster cracker, then arrested his hand. "Or was it, D'Andor?"

"I was as dumbfounded as Amos," Mark said. "When our coroner's boy said he wasn't prepared to swear for sure whether Snowdom had used surgical instruments or garden tools, he really knocked the spots off me."

Mr. Pentlove laughed with no conviction and suddenly devoted himself to his oysters. A neat mouthful disposed of, he said again, "I liked your old style better. You seemed more incisive when sober. Watching a tipsy man on a tightrope is very bad for my liver."

"Then you and your liver had better go to a movie this afternoon," Mark said. "Amos won't put on Snowdom yet, you can bank on that. And Mrs. Adele Tobino is this moment undoubtedly swapping tidbits of information with Miss Pritchard. So unless Amos puts Pritchard on, which I doubt. . . . No, my guess is Tobino. She'll be a hellcat, all right."

Mr. Pentlove efficiently dipped and washed an oyster in its sauce, reminding Mark of his 'coons dunking cookies in their dish pan of water before devouring. "I'm sure Mrs. Tobino understands her position as regards the Industry," he murmured confidently.

"She may have," Mark agreed. "But that was last week. Rookie has discovered that Mrs. Tobino has left the bed and board of Mr. Tobino. Isn't that how she put it to you when you talked to her, Rookie?"

"I think she felt crowded out," Rookie supplied. "Amos' subpoena seems to have shown her a way to get back at the— ah—Racket, is that what you call it? Oh, excuse me, *Industry*."

To his dismay Mr. Pentlove saw that he had finished off his oysters. "Should I order more?" he debated. But he made his decision at once. Looking at Rookie, Mr. Pentlove said flatly, "I believe I have had all I intend to take."

"Mrs. Tobino," Rookie said, "is going to swear that she saw The Feeb all but ram a glacier up Naismith."

"Rookie," Mark put in indulgently, "will you kindly go poke Amos in the nose as I suggested, and leave old Pentlove here alone!"

Mr. Pentlove drew himself up, only to lose his presence

of mind entirely as he heard Rookie say, "Mark, will you kindly quit lapping up the hooch, and eat your chowder. You've got a dandy afternoon ahead of you, and you're making old Pentlove here nervous. In fact, you're making me ner—"

"Mr. Pentlove," Mr. Pentlove said automatically. His face was once more as composed and factory-fresh as if he had unpacked it that morning.

"You're making old *Mr.* Pentlove here nervous," Rookie said.

Mark was dutifully eating his chowder.

"I do not—understand—attorneys at all," Mr. Pentlove concluded, as if voicing only the caboose on a long train of thought.

"I daresay I don't either," Rookie concurred. "But then . . . I don't happen to be one. You'd better eat your chowder too, Mr. Pentlove."

Like a man at the zoo not wishing to disturb an animal while feeding, Mr. Pentlove addressed himself to Rookie, the keeper. "Does D'Andor know how that young woman died?"

"Not even I know that," Rookie said. "Shall we go ask The Feeb together?"

"I would imagine Mr. Slake will do that for us."

Mark laid down his spoon. "Over my dead body," he said.

Pushing his way through the movie fans and the scandal-mongers and the garden variety of cannibals come to feast on the devil's brew Amos was cooking up for himself, Mark saw none other than the intrepid Deputy District Attorney himself talking to a garish beauty. She was wearing a hat with a long chartreuse plume that curled down one cheek and nuzzled under her chin so that only the tip of her nose was visible in profile, but her carriage alone made the prideful statement that her features did not shame the rest of her zestful body. As for Amos, he had taken precious time away from his Swiss on rye and NeHi to shave and had punished his throat with a fresh collar. Recovered from this morning's jolt, the face Amos presented to Mark was placid. "Amos," Mark said, "I do fear you are right. It is going to reach a hundred in that courtroom this afternoon. In short, I aim to make it hot for your witnesses." To Amos' brassy companion Mark said, "Pep, where have you been keeping yourself?"

"Within hearing distance of the phone, Counselor. How's tricks?"

"I must inform you," Amos put in, blissful that he had stolen a march on Mark, "that Miss Baines is one of my witnesses."

"Ah?"

"Ah," Pep confirmed.

Amos had the temerity to twinkle.

Grinning, Mark warned her, "Pep, I'll cross-examine the drawers off you, and you know it."

"You always come up with a new approach, don't you, Bagel," Pep drawled.

"Now really, Mark," Amos protested. "We can get too— uh—lax as respects our respective—er—roles in court by—"

"Why don't you start all over," Mark told him, "and figure out what it is you really want to say." He returned to Pep. "How's about our getting together soon. We'll have a nice long talk."

"Just you and me?" Pep cooed.

"Well . . . with maybe a few close friends. Make it an even dozen, not including ourselves. You know, I like that hat!"

Pep preened. "Empress Youjeenie. Chick, huh?"

"Eugénie," Mark corrected her. "And it's the cat's spats. By the bye, where can I reach you these days?"

"Oh no, you don't!" Amos burst out. "Miss Baines, you are not to inform Mr. D'Andor of your whereabouts."

"Come, come, Amos, face a few harsh facts. You keep a pretty girl like Miss Baines out of circulation and you can make her a back number overnight."

"Have you been drinking?" Amos demanded, adding, "Again?"

Pep fondled her plume. "Answer the cute man, Bagel."

"Why state the obvious?"

"That's the very question I put to Mr. Slake!" Pep chattered.

Mark's affable grin did not alter. "Pep, you're picking up legal lingo pretty fast."

Pep smiled coyly. "Well, beings I'm an actress, I'm used to learning lines. But Mr. Slake seems to think I'm an awfully quick study." She beamed at Amos. "Mr. Slake said I learned twice as fast as any other of his—"

Amos snatched at Pep's arm. "Miss Baines, I'll have to ask you to go to the witness room now."

"Yeah, Pep," Mark said. *"Right* now."

"See yuh soon," was all Pep managed as a farewell, though whether it was for laughing at the irate Amos or the rapidity of her journey through the crowd Mark was not prepared to say.

Himself again breasting the mob, pulling Mr. Pentlove in tow with Rookie bringing up the rear, Mark called out to a sheriff who extended him an arm like a lifeline. Once safely inside the courtroom, Mr. Pentlove took his seat and dusted off a bit of his talcum powder as he might have dots of sweat. "Shattering," he muttered in complaint of the mob's naughty conduct.

The Feeb was ushered in, and Mark noted with approval that he too had shaved again, so that his infantile rolls of fat glistened as if with innocence. Mark said to him urgently, "Listen close, now. At the Eden that week end, was there a girl named Pep Baines present?"

Forbes doubted this but could not swear to it.

"You damn well better be able to swear to it," Mark said. "This Pep Baines is a big redhead, a real hot momma. Now *think!*"

"No," Forbes said. "Sligh knows bettern to bring me something like that. He knows I won't accept any bimbo isn't petite. How old is she about?"

"Twenty-eightish."

Forbes was quite without hesitation. "Naismith was worn-out jazz enough for one week end, thank you."

"How about at any of the other bungalows? Think, man. Did you so much as glimpse a big redhead?"

"Ask Tobino, he did plenty of peeping around the Eden. I think he thought he was in the penny arcade."

"I shall ask him."

Forbes was amused. "You on edge about something? You shouldn't be."

"Really? Why?"

"I've seen and I've been as funny as hell in my time," Forbes said with artistic fervor, "but I never was so close splittin' my gut as this morning. When that doc said that Snowdom could of scraped Naismith down with a trowel for all he knew. I like to died."

"You may yet."

"I'm bound to," Forbes agreed, unconcerned. Looking past Mark, his large eyes followed the progress of Mrs. Tobino into the courtroom. Mark found himself inspecting those great eyes from the side; he could not ever recall having observed the human gaze in profile, watching the orb slide about with the ease of liquid in its socket and the iris deepen in color as the unknowable thoughts locked in the skull drifted by like dark shapes, submerged. Unaware he was going to ask, Mark said softly, "Forbes, what did you do to Naismith?"

The eyes actually sank into the surrounding folds of fat, the lids easing down for protection. The Feeb squinted out in silent jeering past the white lashes imbedded in tissue no firmer than mucus. "Ask her," The Feeb giggled, wheeling his head to indicate Mrs. Tobino as Amos ushered her into the bar. "Ask her what shape a piece of ice is."

Mr. Pentlove, having hung his comely face bare inches from attorney and client to hear their conference, sighed.

The jury came in bearing palm fans as well as notepads now, and looking pleased as paddy about it. In short order Her Honor tripped up to the bench and court was in session.

The Feeb raised his grotesque hand and, with the hushed air of a child seeing a butterfly alight, touched the shaggy paper rose in his lapel.

No sooner had the last juror begun to ply his palm fan than Mrs. Tobino was taking the oath, her left hand smoothing the back of her skirt while the right was as stiff and gloved as that of a traffic cop. She was as Mark had remembered her, chillingly Eastern, the dark hairs bristling at the neckline of her shingle bob somehow endowing her with the ability to scowl fore and aft. If her golf shoes and crisp frock had seemed out of place in the Eden breakfast patio, she had outstripped herself by coming to court costumed in black crêpe, hat, gloves, and a garrote of pearls. She strongly reminded Mark of an extra taking a short cut through one set stage on her way to another.

Amos was touchingly pleased with his soignée witness. It would be unthinkable for her to make sport of the Deputy District Attorney as that Miss Baines had, and in front of the defense attorney at that. With the bulldog drive of one who sees himself as future gubernatorial timber, Amos elicited from Adele Tobino her name, address (no longer the Eden but a downtown hotel, The Obispo—owned by Mr. Pentlove), and occupation. Her voice was low, cultivated, bearing no trace of the brusqueness Mark had met during their talk at the Eden. The grandmother juror leaned forward the better to hear Mrs. Tobino, listening with an alarming intensity. And even during the introductory questions Mrs. Tobino looked down on The Feeb with the implacable expression of a witness who has put his head together with that of the prosecution and worked out something very snappy in the way of damaging evidence.

All deference, Amos was working his way toward the heart of her testimony. "We go back to the afternoon of, that is, Sunday afternoon, October the. . . . Bungalow Nine. . . . Will the record please show that the witness has pointed out the defendant, Archibald Forbes. . . . The defendant and three other people. . . ."

Mrs. Tobino was saying, "No, I don't see the other man in the courtroom. The other man who was in Bungalow Ten with Mr. Forbes." Then, her demeanor free of any nasty-nice reluctance, she and Amos got down to the meat of the matter. "One of the girls was called Flirt," Mrs. Tobino said. "She introduced herself to me when she came to our bungalow to borrow some ice."

"Borrow some ice," Amos repeated.

"Yes."

"When was this?"

"Oh, I should say around ten A.M. Sunday morning."

"And did you lend Miss Flirt some ice?"

"My husband took some over in a napkin."

"Your husband took some over to Bungalow Ten in a napkin?"

"Yes."

"And then?"

"Then my husband came back. I saw him leave Bungalow Ten without the ice."

"Without the ice."

"Yes."

"Then what, if anything, happened?"

"I heard screaming. A woman screaming. Although it was more like—howling."

"Like howling."

"Yes."

"And you—"

"I tried to ignore it. I recognized the voice as being that of the woman who had kept me awake half the night. With her hysterical laughter. But this time her voice sounded as if she were in pain."

"In pain."

"Yes."

Mark, who had so far held his pose of lackadaisical mental wanderings, suddenly caught the eye of Her Honor. The moment to make his request had matured. He rose and said with circumspection, "Excuse me, Mr. Slake, but I must intervene. Would Your Honor ask that the last five questions and responses be read aloud by the stenographer?"

"Certainly," Judge Fickett said.

"What?" Amos yapped. "Your Honor, to interrupt my witness—On what basis does my learned colleague—" But he had wasted an invaluable two seconds in permitting himself a sneer at Mark, voluble as a catcall, and was brought up short by Judge Ficket's piping reprimand. "Mr. Slake, you will be quiet. Mr. Stenographer, you will read the last five questions and answers aloud, please."

Amos slapped his behind hard on his chair and began scribbling furiously on his legal pad, sending up to Her Honor many dark looks foreboding appeals, motions for mistrial, and other dire consequences.

In a dry rasp Mr. Stenographer read each question, each answer, and (with no slightest change of intonation) read as well Amos' repetition of every answer.

Her Honor reared up over her Codes. "Well, Mr. D'Andor?"

"If the Court please, I ask that Mr. Slake be admonished," Mark said silkily. "I ask that he cease his pointing up the testimony by repeating it after the witness. I'm certain the jury are able to digest the material the first time."

"I shall now admonish both you gentlemen," Her Honor said. "You, Mr. Slake, for needless repetition, and you, Mr. D'Andor, for compounding what was a needless waste of time. You will continue, Mr. Slake."

Amos rose heavily while Mark sank gracefully to his seat. To anger Amos was to rattle him, and Mark, admonished though he be, rested content.

"Uhhh . . ." Amos said, and cleared his throat. "When you . . . No. At the time you. . . ."

"I heard the woman, Muffin Naismith, cry out in terrible pain," Mrs. Tobino said.

Her Honor popped up over her Codes but said nothing.

Mark raised his brows and looked to the jury as if asking: *What was that question again? Did you hear any question?*

"Yes," Amos said, startled. Clearly, Mrs. Tobino was keeping her head when all about her a fair number were losing theirs. "You heard Muffin Naismith cry out in terrible— That is, what if anything did you do next?"

"I went over to Bungalow Ten to see if help was needed. The front door was open and I walked right in. There was a hallway off the front room, and a door at the end of it. The girl who said her name was Flirt and another girl were banging on the door."

"Do you know the name of that other girl?"

"No."

"Would you be able to identify her if you saw her?"

"I would."

Sunk in his spurious languor, Mark mused. Tobino surely would not perjure herself to the extent of placing Pep on the scene had Pep not been there. So intent was he on the threat

Pep presented that his shoulders drooped as if he were half-asleep. The grandmother juror found herself somewhat distracted by the remarkable attitude of Mr. D'Andor, and her hand, hesitant in the motion of waving her fan, spoke to Mark of her inattention to Mrs. Tobino.

Mrs. Tobino was explaining, "I noticed that the other girl was redheaded. Or, I should say, what they call strawberry blonde."

"You saw the two girls pounding on the door. What did you do?"

"Well, since the girls obviously couldn't get in the door, I decided to walk around to the side of the bungalow. I had happened to notice, quite by accident I assure you, that there is one spot from where you can see into Bungalow Ten from the outside. I mean, you can see into the bedroom. So I went out to this spot and I—" Mrs. Tobino made a valiant try at staring the jury down, dropped her eyes, and finally fixed them miserably on Amos. "Well, I looked into the bedroom of Bungalow Ten. You see, that's where all the howling was coming from. Of a woman in pain."

"Tell the jury what you saw."

Safely past the humiliation of having to admit to her proclivities to peep into bedrooms, Mrs. Tobino was able to hold up her head again. "I . . . saw . . . Muffin Naismith on the bed. She was writhing and making those awful sounds. And *he*—" she wheeled on Forbes with the flourish of a Roman orator "—that man there, Archibald Forbes, was on the bed too. But they weren't—at that moment, at least—weren't—ummm——"

"Ask be stricken," Mark murmured, as if the interruption were irksome but necessary. "The words 'at that moment, at least.' "

His motion was granted.

Mrs. Tobino, like any witness cut off at the height of her story, glowered and resumed without prompting. "Muffin Naismith was fighting Forbes off, and he was holding her down. And as I watched, he reached out with one hand and took some ice out of a glass on the bedstand. Then he shoved the ice into Miss Naismith."

Shoved, Mark's mind repeated after her, much as Amos had been doing earlier.

"In what part of Miss Naismith's body?"

"He thrust the ice up into her vagina. She screamed again."

"Aside from the screaming of Miss Naismith, was anything said?"

"Yes. Forbes was saying to Miss Naismith, 'You bastard.' And then he said, 'Here's how I take care of a—.'" Mrs. Tobino's courage had failed her, yet her pleading look was directed not to Amos but to the jury. "I can't," she said helplessly to the grandmother and the retired minister. "I can't bring myself to say the word."

Amos was tender as a lover. "Tell the jury, Mrs. Tobino, what sort of word it was."

Nothing loath, Mrs. Tobino said with rich throaty diction, "It is the filthiest word in the English language designating a woman, or her . . . private parts . . . or both."

"Thank you," Amos said quietly, blushing to his ears. After a suitable sepulchral pause, as if Judge Fickett had suddenly announced there would be a minute's silent meditation, Amos raised his head. "And what then, if anything, did you do?"

Dammit, Mark thought, they make a nifty combination. They pulled that off beautifully between them.

"Well, I stood there, outside the window, and watched Forbes drop the ice back in the glass. And his victim tried to—"

"Ask strike word 'victim,'" Mark interposed.

Mrs. Tobino shouted at Mark, "And *Miss Naismith* tried to get away from him. Then Forbes began pulling the sheets out from under her and stuffing them in the closet. She was staggering to her feet. I didn't look any more after that. I . . . simply . . . couldn't."

"Did you see the condition of the sheets?"

"Yes. They were bloody."

"What did you do next?"

"As I say, I left the window. And went into my own bungalow. Then shortly after that I saw the two girls walking

Miss Naismith back and forth in the pool. That was the last I saw of any of them. After they took her dripping from the pool."

"Did you hear Miss Naismith saying anything?"

"No. She was sobbing, but I couldn't distinguish any words. As they took her out of the pool I thought I saw blood running down her legs. She was dripping wet, as I say, so I couldn't be sure."

In a ripe voice Amos said to Mark, "Cross-examine."

Mark contemplated Mrs. Tobino listlessly. She stiffened, longing for battle, aching for it; there was a dark element of sexual torment in Mark's protracted withholding from the clash; knowing though not understanding it, he held Mrs. Tobino in trembling thrall. "Thank you," he said to Amos. "One moment, please," he begged nicely of Mrs. Tobino, and bent to his notes.

He weighed a notation: *W T △ trst/shuvd i on D ∴ no Q on X-exam*. In his kindergarten shorthand he used the Greek delta to indicate the defendant, and *D* for direct examination. *W* was witness, and *T* stood for testified. His little pyramid of dots said to him *Therefore*. He translated: Witness testified that defendant thrust and shoved ice, therefore don't question this point on cross-examination, thus allowing the witness to heighten effect.

Too, there was the issue of the key in the door. Mrs. Tobino had been silent on the point. By the time Mrs. Tobino had taken her post at the window, had Forbes already gotten the key and placed it in the lock (thus nearly putting out the eye of Miss Flirt Smith at the keyhole)? Mark had no choice but to observe the old rule that if he did not know the answer to a question, he would be foolish to let a witness enlighten him in cross-examination. He looked up at Mrs. Tobino casually. She drew in her breath, set her jaw, and returned his regard unblinkingly.

"No questions," Mark said.

Adele Tobino sagged, jaw slack. The shoe clerk in the jury box snickered, then covered his youthful gaffe by pretending to cough. Judge Fickett propped herself up to determine if the choking juror were in need of assistance. Evidently assured that he was not, she bent her gaze on Mrs. Tobino.

"You may step down," Judge Fickett said in a tone which asked if the witness intended spending the afternoon gawping at Mark.

Mrs. Tobino stood up, smoothed the back of her skirt with a hasty motion which betrayed her fear that it had stuck to her bottom, and thus alerted Mark to the fact that she had been sweating more excessively than the heat of the day could account for. Wearing a look of vague insult and disappointment, she stepped down.

"Oh, just a moment, Mrs. Tobino," Mark said. "There is one thing I should like to be made clear on. If you please."

Mrs. Tobino sauntered back up to the stand, openly displaying her disdain for Mark's woolgathering conduct.

The witness seated again, Mark asked, "I will ask you if you recall a conversation you and I had in the patio of the Eden. It took place on Saturday the—"

"I recall it," Mrs. Tobino interrupted him bluntly.

"And you will agree that that was the only conversation we two have had?"

"The one and only," Mrs. Tobino said, snippy.

"During that conversation you discussed what you had seen when looking into the bedroom window of Bungalow Ten, correct?"

"Correct."

"And at that time you told me that you saw Archibald Forbes apply ice to the person of Muffin Naismith?"

"That's what I saw. I saw him shove—"

"Excuse me, that was not my question. I asked you if during that conversation you did not use the word *apply*?"

"I may have."

"You *may* have? Don't you remember insisting that you saw Forbes only applying the ice?"

"Well, I don't know what you mean by 'insisting.'"

"I'll refresh you. I asked you if Forbes had inserted the ice into the body of Miss Naismith, and you refused to say the word *insert*. Is that not—" Mark broke off to say just loudly enough for the jury to hear, "Mrs. Tobino, don't look to Mr. Slake. Look at me. I am asking you a question. Now you refused to say 'insert,' didn't you?"

"Really, I don't recall refusing or not refusing—"

"Mrs. Tobino, we were not alone in the Eden patio at that time. There were other people there. Within earshot. I will ask you again: Did you not say *apply*?"

"Very well, I did."

"Of course you did," Mark said with kindly approval. "And didn't you tell me also that Forbes was applying that ice to Miss Naismith to calm her?"

"Well, I may have thought at first that that is what—"

"Excuse me, but you are not answering my question. Didn't you tell me that you saw Forbes attempting to calm a hysterical woman with ice?"

"If I did say that—"

"Please do not preface your answer with 'if.' Did you or did you not say that?"

"What if I did? I wasn't under oath when I—"

Mark interrupted firmly but gently as ever. "And, during that same conversation, did not you deny seeing Forbes making any use whatsoever of ice?"

"What do you mean, *deny*?"

"I am asking you if you did not tell me later in that conversation that you saw no ice in that bedroom at all?"

"I'm telling you here and now I saw ice!"

"I did not ask you that. I asked to tell me what you said during our discussion. Mrs. Tobino, did you not say to me, and I quote you, 'No ice, and no dice'?"

Mark moved from the side of the counsel table to stand between Mrs. Tobino and Amos. Immediately she sought to give the impression that she had been looking past Mr. Slake and not at him. Not deviating from his courteous ways, Mark repeated, "You did say that to me, didn't you? *No ice, and no dice.*"

"Well, I don't see what any of that has to do with—"

"Will you answer my question?"

"If you'd just stop trying to—"

And again Mark interrupted, alert to the heartening sound of Amos tapping his gold mechanical pencil nervously. "I asked you if you did not say to me 'No ice, and no dice'?"

"Since you're so sure I did, then have it your—"

Again Mark cut in. "Mrs. Tobino, what I will have is an answer from you."

Amos shouted "You got it!" but was tardy in the saying of it. Overriding Amos, the hot and harried Mrs. Tobino snarled at Mark, "And you'll get an answer just as soon as you shut your own mouth long enough for me to get a word in edgewise!"

Mark inclined his head, then extended a pleasantly spoken invitation to Mrs. Tobino, "Would you care to repeat that remark, and in the exact same tone of voice, Mrs. Tobino?"

Her hand flew to the garrote of pearls at her neck. "I said—" She tossed her head. "Oh, never mind. I'm not up here to teach a boor how to— Forget it." She blinked rapidly many times. She firmed her mouth.

"Are you ready to go on, Mrs. Tobino?" Mark asked, all concern.

"Yes," she said tightly.

Though he had her in a swivet, he had not succeeded in breaking her. Mark asked, "Then you did say, 'No ice, no—' "

"All right, I did!" Mrs. Tobino allowed herself the luxury of a hard smile of triumph at having interrupted Mark for a change. Quickly reminding herself that one skirmish does not constitute a battle, she hastened to place her admission in a better light. "Only at the time I said that, I had. . . . I had my reasons."

"Did you. And what were they?"

"For one, you had led me to believe—"

"You are under oath, Mrs. Tobino."

She gritted her teeth and spoke with enraged exactitude. "I *thought* at the time that Miss Naismith had died because of an illegal operation. And I *thought* that you'd come skulking around to get me to say things that would save the hide of some criminal abortionist. It never occurred to me that an attorney, a man who has *sworn* to uphold the law, would dare or dream of daring to come round and act the way you were. Trying to get me to say things— After all, Mr. D'Andor, you did come pussyfooting around and sneaking, and pretending to be a policeman!"

"Are you saying I had some sort of a uniform on?"

Mrs. Tobino snorted. "Naturally I'm not saying any such thing! Do you take me for a fool?"

If there was one tactic of which Mark was inordinately fond, it was what he thought of as being the "Carson pause." Here was a golden opportunity, and he enjoyed it to the fullest, standing at ease before Mrs. Tobino, smiling at her quizzically while her last remark rang—or, rather, tolled—in her ears like a knell. Moments passed; eons lapsed for Mrs. Tobino. A pulsebeat before anticlimax set in, Mark resumed in a level voice, "I did not tell you or indicate to you in any way that I was a policeman, did I, Mrs. Tobino?"

"No," she said sullenly.

"It was you who jumped to the conclusion that I was acting in behalf of an illegal practitioner, an abortionist, wasn't it?"

"Have it your way."

"And laboring under that impression, you told me you saw no ice whatsoever in that bedroom, didn't you?"

"All right."

"Is your answer yes?"

"Yes!"

"So that when you said to me, 'No ice, and no dice,' what you meant was that you would swear in a court of law that you saw no ice in the hands of Archibald Forbes, no ice within the vicinity of the person of Muffin Naismith, and no ice anywhere in that bedroom, isn't that what you meant?"

"It doesn't matter what I meant then. I'm here to tell you now, though, that I did see him shove—"

"You say that now."

"Yes!"

"What would you have said under oath, Mrs. Tobino, if I had proved to be the attorney for a quack, an abortionist? Well? Which version would you have graced us with then?"

Mrs. Tobino squeezed her mouth with her hand, twisting to look past Mark to Amos. Mark stepped each time to block her view, and if he was not quite nimble; if, once, he swayed, no one seemed to remark it for staring at Mrs. Tobino fighting for control and actually wringing out her lips with her hand.

At last Mrs. Tobino half-rose from her seat, turned to the bench and cried out, "Am I expected to answer an . . . insulting . . . cheap. . . ." She fell back onto her chair.

From over the Codes floated the Judge's voice. "In this particular instance only, Madam, you are at liberty to answer or remain silent. As you will."

Mark walked to the side of his counsel table, affording Mrs. Tobino full access to what support or comfort Amos might see fit to give her. "Will you answer my question, Mrs. Tobino?"

"You've got me so confused," Mrs. Tobino said in hot accusation, "that I couldn't tell you what day it is, much less. . . ."

"No further questions," Mark said, tagging on his invariable courtesy, "and thank you."

"Redirect!" Amos said blithely, as if some minor slip of the tongue on the witness' part must be put to rights. Once again he led Mrs. Tobino through her earlier testimony, but gave it up as a bad job when he noted that the jury, one by one, had taken to fanning themselves and watching Mr. D'Andor as he leaned back in his chair and leisurely read through some lengthy document or other.

Mrs. Tobino was permitted to stand down and parade her finery and fiery nose through the bar and past the spectators, then to depart the courtroom forever. The opposing attorneys, Mark with fountain pen in hand, Amos gnawing at his gold pencil, exchanged fleeting wry glances. Mark was not at all certain he had successfully impeached Mrs. Tobino, and Amos hadn't the remotest idea if he had been successful in rehabilitating Mrs. Tobino after Mark had so successfuly impeached her.

Rookie Castle had slipped from the courtroom as soon as Amos had begun his redirect, and now the clerk motioned to Mark that there was a phone call for him. Coincident with this came Her Honor's decision that, owing to the oppressive heat of the late afternoon, court would adjourn.

The reporters, torn between Mrs. Tobino, now en route to her car parked on Spring Street, and The Feeb, ran in and out babbling; one such, rendered helpless by indecision and the heat, fell into the seat vacated by Rookie and next Mr. Pentlove's. "God," said the sweating member of the press, "how in the hell can we print the stuff that woman said this afternoon?"

"Why try?" Mr. Pentlove said. "As none of it is true."

Rookie, it would seem, was bringing a gentleman to Mark's office in the happiest expectancy that Mark would give one hundred dollars to this unknown individual. "Good work," Mark said over the clerk's phone. "Meet you there. I gotta go hit old Pentlove for that C-note before he leaves the courtroom."

And Mr. Pentlove said, distressed, "One hundred dollars? Oh dear, D'Andor, is this wise?"

"Maybe I can knock him down to ninety-eight-fifty," Mark said.

Mr. Pentlove was all atitter. "I must remember that one for the polo matches on Sunday. We try to top one another with funny experiences. No, seriously, D'Andor, I would be easier in my mind if you had asked for a thousand dollars. A thousand can usually buy you what you want. A hundred so frequently just buys you trouble. Or, at least, that has been my experience."

"One of your funnier ones?" Mark regretted his sharp tone. "Sorry, Pentlove. I've had a—trying afternoon."

"A trying afternoon!" Mr. Pentlove echoed, counting out some bills. "Oh, that is rich! A lawyer says he has had a— Ninety-five, one hundred. I must remember that for the polo matches on Sun— Oh. Well. See you in the morning, D'An. . . ."

A blunt-jawed man sat at twilight in Mark's office, looking thirstily at Mark's tin of Irish, then suspiciously refusing to partake when Mark offered him a drink. "Thanks, but I'll just keep muh wits about me," the blunt-jawed one said. "You go ahead, though," he added shrewdly, hoping to be able to bargain with a drunk.

"Oh, may I?" Mark said. "Now, then. Tell me, how is Manny Amen?"

"Ask his doctor; I'm only his attendant. He looks like a seal flopping down the ward, if you want to know."

"And his mind?"

The attendant of Manny Amen parted his lips to show Mark what Mark curiously thought of as being two complete drawers of assorted teeth. "What mind?" the grinning attendant sneered. "He's like a little kid." After a moment's thought he added, "But we get along. He's easy to handle." A clenched fist demonstrated for Mark what happened to those patients not so easy to handle.

Wishing to get down to business, Mark said, "Evidently not all of his old friends have forgotten Manny."

"One has," the attendant said with a guffaw. "Yeah, she's took up gardening."

Mark waited to see where this might lead.

"Yeah," the attendant said. "She's gone to pushing up lilies!"

"I'm a busy man," Mark said, wincing inwardly at the weird connecting of gardening and garden tools with Muffin Naismith, who in her life cared for no growing thing but her ambition.

"I'm a poor one," the attendant pointed out slyly.

"You can leave this room fifty dollars richer."

"Or one-fifty."

"Seventy-five."

"One-twenty-five."

Mark got out Mr. Pentlove's money. "Ten. Twenty, Thirty, and five makes. . . . Fifty. One hundred. Take it or leave it."

"I take." The attendant held out a picture post card and grabbed for the money at the same time. Still clinging to the card with his left hand, he rested the palm of his right on the bills and with agile fingers flipped them as one would turn pages, counting. "It's all here," he said in warm congratulation to Mark, and released the card. The money pocketed, the right hand was now presented to Mark. "Shake?"

"Only on my bad days," Mark said, but thrust out his own hand to be clasped. The guffawing attendant was finally done with Mark's hand. "Only on my bad. . . . Say, that's a howl. Mr. Lawyer, you're a real card."

Now alone, the real card turned on his desk lamp and studied the picture post card which had cost Mr. Pentlove one hundred dollars. On the front was depicted Mr. Sid Grauman's Chinese Cinema Temple, upon which Mark could look by merely turning his head to the window at his back. The message side of the card would have Manny know:

> *Wish you were here! Mrs. F. and Sal and Thelma and I all went last night. We talk about you a lot. I am in a little trouble but it will be all right soon. T-Bone is working in the same picture with me, and we talk sometimes even if he is just an extra. He's always after me for dates and stuff. Isn't that a scream?!!!*
>
> *Muffin*

When Mark arrived at the abode of T-Bone Tredwell, he found it dark. Mark returned to his roadster and sat nursing his Irish. The hot Santana wind swept down the canyons making whoopee under a black-iron sky filled with steel stars. Of a sudden Mark was hideously clammy and disastrously close to being sick. Yet he was resolute in his determination to wait out the homecoming of T-Bone. A few parking spaces in front of the roadster loomed the bulk of the sorrowful Packard propped up on its blocks. T-Bone had taken the back seat for his sofa, but Mark discovered that the front was comparatively intact. And there, protected from the wind, he huddled, rationing himself on sips of Irish. He fell asleep, and when he awakened dawn had come to the Gulch, but it had not brought Mr. T-Bone Tredwell with it.

CHAPTER TWENTY-ONE

Arriving in the courtroom haggard, and laggard ("My God," Rookie said. "You look like hell. You're holding up the works. Where you been all night?"), Mark sank into his place at the counsel table. "Rookie, find Tredwell. Ask him if he knows anybody called Sal, Thelma, or Mrs. F. Find out where any or all of them live."

As Rookie hastened out, Mr. Pentlove asked suavely, "Do you want me to put Savant on those people?"

"If you please, Pentlove," Mark said, and pinched himself cruelly on the bridge of his nose. "Headache," he explained with a grimace.

"Did you get my hundred dollars' worth?"

"Well, we'll see," Mark temporized as The Feeb was being ushered in.

T. Amos Slake had himself an immaculately uniformed, ponderously solemn deputy sheriff sitting on his right hand, while on his left trembled the housemaid from the Eden. As The Feeb passed the maid he greeted her in an offhand, friendly manner. Her sole response was to lower her head and giggle mournfully. None of the brash camaraderie she had shown Mark was in evidence.

No sooner was the jury in and Her Honor safely on her bench than Amos nudged the maid to her feet. She took the oath in a harsh whisper and then sat on the stand, looking down at Amos with black eyes the size of sink-stoppers. He quickly established her name, occupation, duties at the Eden, and her knowledge of the condition of Bungalow Ten after Forbes and his companions had vacated it.

"What was the condition of the bed?"

"Well, it was all rumpled. And there was just the spread. The sheets weren't on it."

"But you found the sheets, didn't you?"

"Well. I found *some* sheets."

"Come now, Miss, you found the sheets from that bed, didn't you?" Amos could not quite prevent a flutter of his lids when Mark stirred, conscious as he was of blatantly leading his witness.

Mark, for his part, had other concerns than Amos' presentation of his witness. The girl was frightened out of all keeping with the customary stage fright and nervousness of the average witness. She knew some fact of great importance, and Mark's clammy chill of the night returned.

"Yes, sir," the maid was saying, "I guess I did find the sheets. They were stuffed in the closet."

"And what was the condition of the sheets?"

"W-what, sir?"

"What was the con— Let me put it this way, what did they look like?"

"Oh."

"Well?" Amos prompted.

Mark conceived the absurd notion that the maid was in such an inward state of tumult that she could barely hold her attention on Mr. Slake and his questions. "Well, what?" she quavered.

The courtroom was beginning to grow hot, and the temperature, or Amos' collar, or the numb stupidity of his witness brought roses of anger to the Deputy District Attorney's cheeks. "What did they look like?"

"The sheets?"

In concert with the spectators, and for the first time, The Feeb laughed. Absently Mark rapped The Feeb's knuckles with his pen. Behind her Codes on the bench, Judge Fickett was bouncing about searching for her gavel or a substitute therefor.

When order was restored, Amos tended to become a touch snappish. Still the black sink-stopper eyes clung to his face as the maid sought to concentrate. At last Judge Fickett reared up to ask the witness, "Is your hearing all right? Can you hear Mr. Slake's questions?"

The maid popped to her feet. "Oh, I can hear fine, sir!" she assured Judge Fickett. "Ma'am. I mean, Your Honorium."

Judge Fickett called a recess.

Mark did not so much as go to the Men's for a drink. The Feeb was taken out to answer nature, and Mr. Pentlove took the opportunity to call Ted Savant. Amos spent the recess lecturing his witness severely. Mark watched Amos at his dressing-down until he found himself oddly locked in a stare with Chester Dander. Mark started, and Chester deliberately raised a newspaper in front of his face and kept it there.

The trial resumed. Mark could not reconcile the bumbling, mumbling, quavering girl on the stand with the breezy creature who had said to him, "Hoo hoo, this is my windfall week. Hoo hoo!"

Amos asked and received permission to question his witness at close range. "Now then, Miss, about the sheets. What did they look like?"

"You mean . . . bloody."

"Of course I—! Well, were they?"

"Bloody?"

"Yes!"

"Oh. One was a whole lot bloody and the other not so much."

"And what, if anything, did you do with them?"

"Well, I thought that Mr. Forbes had had another nosebleed, so—"

"I didn't ask you that!"

The black sink-stoppers rolled toward The Feeb and instantly back to Amos. "No, sir, I guess you didn't."

Amos persevered. At last he managed to establish:

Q: Where was the blood on the sheets? At one end? Or where?

A: Kind of towards one end, sort of. Not so much the middle.

Q: Both sheets?

A: The one was real bloody. And the other had some, kind of along the hem.

Amos closed his eyes and stuck his forefinger down his collar. "Your witness," he said to Mark with vast relief.

The maid gazed at Mark from a face gray with guilt. Still he could not divine what on earth ailed the girl. As Amos had, he came up to the witness stand to question her. "You're not afraid of me, are you?" he asked gently.

"J-just a little nervous."

"Everybody is. Take your time to answer. I'm not going to ask you anything difficult."

"No sir."

"Now tell me, when you came to clean the bedroom of Bungalow Ten, was there a bedstand in there?"

"No, sir."

"Are you sure?"

"I guess I am."

"Why do you guess you are? Have you a reason?"

"Why, yes sir. The bedstand was being refinished. The one was usually in Number Ten was being—uh—refinished. And I just. . . ."

Incredibly, the witness had obviously forgotten what it was she was going to say. "And you just what?" Mark prodded delicately.

"I didn't know Mr. Forbes would be at the Eden, so I didn't put another bedstand in."

"That's all I want to ask you, Miss," Mark said. "And thank you."

"You mean I can go now?"

Mark smiled. "I'm afraid you'll have to ask that of Mr. Slake."

"No redirect," Amos said, as belligerently as if he feared Mark was going to argue the point.

The maid scuttled down from the stand, and it was Mark who held the swinging gate of the bar for her, to facilitate her in her headlong flight from the courtroom.

It was time for lunch. Before The Feeb was led out, he said to Mark, " What in hell was eating *her*?"

"I don't know."

"And why in hell didn't you make something of the fact she knows I get lotsa nosebleeds!"

"If you will remember, Forbes, she blurted that out. And

frankly I was afraid to risk her blurtings on other interesting—and possibly related—topics."

Forbes said coldly, "You're not making sense."

"Let me be the judge of that. However, since we are unburdening ourselves of critical remarks, allow me to say that if ever you laugh at another witness, I will walk out of this courtroom and I will not come back."

From behind them Mr. Pentlove said placatingly, "D'Andor, the girl was deliberately playing the fool. She was throwing sand in Mr. Slake's eyes."

"No. She was throwing sand in mine," Mark said. "Go to lunch, Pentlove. I've got some thinking to do."

The spectators babbled and rattled their paper bags, and the odor of chicken wings and sour peanut-butter sandwiches gathered like a miasma, greasy to the nostrils but invisible in the sunlight.

In due time T. Amos Slake re-entered the courtroom, his toilette and collar both fresh, his frayed temper of the morning refurbished. Not to be outdone, Archibald Forbes emerged from the bullpen as thoroughly scrubbed as a chastened schoolboy and downcast as usual, as was proper for one unjustly accused of an unspeakable crime. The jury plodded in moments after; palm fans were caught up from the seats and held at the ready. Amos stretched his neck this way and that until his deputy-sheriff companion of the morning strode through the bar, and Mark sagged in his chair, feeling peckish and peaked and altogether unfit for the ordeal of monotonous peace-officer testimony.

The afternoon session began with the sheriff's mounting the stand. The sheriff, maintaining an unrelenting military glare, opened his notebook and consulted it before answering each and every question with the exception of that requesting his name and occupation. His testimony was repetitious, routine, and acted as a soporific on the jury. The sheriff and his partner had gone round to the Eden to question the guests and the staff. They had taken turns peeping into the bedroom window of Bungalow Ten, and together had scrutinized some stains on the mattress therein.

"Subsequently," the witness said, "I caused the mattress to

be removed from the premises. I then returned to the substation with my partner and——"

But this was going at a gait a deal too fast for Amos, and so they rehashed the testimony all over again. Up through recess and past it Amos hammered on the insignificant, with many an arch glance at the jury, as if to say: Pay attention now, this is subtle stuff. He was stretching his devil's brew as a thrifty housewife does a stew, with gristly (or grisly) trimmings and lukewarm leftovers from the sworn story of Adele Tobino. When the incredible finally happened—a number of spectators rose to depart the heat and boredom with much rattling of paper bags and groans and snappish entreaties to be pardoned for treading on one another's toes—when that came to pass, Amos permitted the sheriff, himself still as crisp as a stalk of celery, to draw his testimony to a close. "And subsequent to that," the witness said, "I then returned with my partner to the substation where I made out my preliminary report and coincident with that also made notations of my findings while they were fresh in my mind contingent to my being called upon to refresh my recollection from the recorded memory made in connection——"

"Do you wish to cross-examine, Mr. D'Andor?" Amos said abruptly.

An indolent Mark indicated he would, rising to the occasion with understandable reluctance, and asking, "When you examined the mattress was the stain of which you spoke on the surface upmost?"

The witness sat bolt upright and shot Mark a look of stern gratitude; here was an attorney who was not merely conversant but fluent, nay masterly, in his command of gibberish. "It was necessary for me," the witness rapped out, "to turn the mattress face-down whereupon I did discover the stain."

"Did you examine the bedstand, if such there was, in the bedroom of Bungalow Ten?"

"I did not as such there was not."

"You stated that you questioned Mrs. Adele Tobino during the course of a second visit to the Eden. Did you talk to anyone else at that time?"

As the witness sat in silent stiff disapproval, Mark

rephrased his question to suit the sheriff's delicate ear for jargon. "With whom, if anybody, did you converse concerning this matter now under consideration during the course of your second inspection tour of the premises known as the Eden?"

"I made routine inquiries of the occupant of Bungalow Eleven."

"And who, if anybody, was the occupant?"

"Nobody, inasmuch as he was in Santa Monica that week end."

The hapless young shoe clerk in the second row of the jury box fell into yet another coughing spell.

"And did you make inquiries of the occupants of Bungalows One through Eight?"

"I did."

"Will you name them, *seriatim*?"

"*Seriatim*," the witness repeated with relish, and raised his notebook into firing position. "As you requested, they are, *seriatim*: Bungalow One, vacant; Bungalow Two, Mr. John Jones and Mrs. Jones, of Kansas City, Kansas; Bungalow Three, Mr. and Mrs. Frank Smith; Bungalow Four, Mr. and Mrs. George Brown, also Miss Jones, Mrs. Brown's sister, and Mr. James Brown, Mr. George Brown's brother, place of origin unknown; Bungalow Five, Miss Belle Thwait; Bung—"

"Miss Belle Thwait? How did a name like that get in there?"

"That was not one of my inquiries."

Mark looked lovingly on the witness, thinking: I have uncovered Pep, if the fates are with me. "Can you describe Miss Thwait?"

"I judged her to be a woman of fifty, height no taller than five feet two inches, weight around one hundred and forty-five, color of hair: blondined, that is to say of an artificial shade of yellow, Caucasian, wanted for—" The witness broke off, licked his thumb with great irritation, and flipped back a page in his notebook. "I was reading the wrong page. To resume, Bungalow Five, Mr. and Mrs. Harry Miller; Bungalow—"

"Of all of these people of whom you made inquiries, was

any of them a young woman of the approximate age of twenty-eight, color of hair red, height, five feet seven—".

"I must object," Amos interposed. "This fishing expedition on the part of Mr. D'Andor is a flagrant violation of any rule of evidence I could care to mention."

"Not really," the witness said.

"What was that?" Amos prompted furiously.

The witness frowned at his "recorded memory," turning back and forth among the pages. "I would say not really hair red, age approximately twenty-eight, though the occupant of Bungalow Seven answers to the description of sex female, height five feet six, color of hair brown, and was indisposed from two o'clock A.M. Saturday night until four o'clock P.M. on the Sunday following—"

"Oh, let it go," Amos said drearily.

Her honor was not so inclined. "Mr. D'Andor, you will refrain from wandering all over the back lot during your examination, and keep within the limits of the direct."

"Thank you, Your Honor," Mark said, while the jury snickered breathily in appreciation of Her Honor's quaint use of Hollywood terminology and Mr. Pentlove sighed audibly in pain. "I think there will be no more questions," Mark said to the witness, "and thank you."

Flushed with the triumph of her wit, Judge Fickett decided to call it a day. The spectators stampeded for the comfort rooms, and The Feeb, finding himself surrounded by reporters, was launched on some obscure branch of Hollywood apologetics, during the course of which he uttered the words *kiddies* and *faithful fans* a revolting number of times, and ended up assuring one and all that though he was being made to suffer, his art would not; on the contrary it would be heightened, much to the benefit of the kiddies who needed laughter in their little lives, etc. And Amos crooked a patronizing finger at Mark, who in friendly fashion wandered over to hear what Amos might have in the way of an apologia.

"And just what," Amos wanted to know, "do you think you gained by that last inane cross-examination of yours?"

"Why, for one thing, I learned that unless the Jones and Smith families are having a convention in town, you're suffering from a dearth of witnesses. Consider if you will, noble Amos, *I* could have been bedded down in the Eden that week end and you'd be none the wiser. When the law showed up, those guests must have scattered like buckshot, the floozies in one direction and the errant husbands making tracks for the old hearthstone. And you haven't managed to flush them out, have you?"

"I've been as successful as you've been flushing out Miss Baines. Let me tell you something, Mark; you're too cocky about this case. All this lolling in your chair and smelling like a whole bathtub full of gin." Amos snorted inelegantly and lashed the buckles on his brief case shut. "If you'd used your head and come to me with a halfway decent attitude, I'd have been willing to work a generous little manslaughter deal out for you."

"The very jim-dandiest of manslaughter raps, I'm sure." Mark laid his hand on Amos' brief case to detain him a moment. "That you would most generously grant me. But what if a manslaughter verdict is all you can wrest from me, hmmm? Won't that make you look rather small in the eyes of the public? A pint-sized would-be giant-killer who can't swing a jury into line worth a—"

Amos cut in tightly, "The one who's going to swing is Forbes. I want a verdict of murder in the first degree and I'm going to get it."

"You're talking through your hat," Mark assured him earnestly.

"Am I? Oh, am I? I'm just talking twaddle, am I?"

"Well, now that you mention it—"

"What you don't seem to realize," Amos began by way of a parting shot, "is that after you lose this case you'll have about as much of a career left as that cur of a Rookie Castle. I deeply and genuinely pity you, Mark," and with that Amos galloped away exactly as if Mark had slyly put a burr under his saddle.

Once The Feeb had been safely led back into the bullpen, the courtroom emptied in no time. Besides Mark there were only Mr. Pentlove elegantly smoking a cigarillo and Chester Dander seated in the far shadowy end of the last of the

spectators' rows. By way of an absent dismissal of Mr. Pentlove, Mark said, "You can reach me later at home. In case
Savant has come up with any pertinent information." Mr.
Pentlove did not so much as raise a plucked brow at Mark's
strangely distant attitude. Yet as he strolled toward the doors
he gave Chester Dander his undivided attention and, having
reached the doors, looked back to see Mark standing as he
had been, also studying Chester. Mr. Pentlove made no
attempt to conceal his curiosity, but with a shrug went on out.

Mark then walked to the last of the spectators' rows, and
said on a rising note, "Well, Chester?" Receiving no answer,
he joined his colleague, his exhbition of sprightliness at best
feeble. "Have you some good news for me? Such as deciding to
spirit Snowdom out of town after all?"

Chester smiled wanly but did not speak.

"I suppose you told him of the bouquet the coroner's
assistant threw him gratuituously?"

"I did," Chester said. "It riled Snowdom somewhat."

"It didn't exactly deepen the dimples in Amos' cheeks
either."

Chester's smile began to look as if it might live after all.
"I enjoyed your examination of that tin soldier of a sheriff."

"Why, thank you."

"And I thought your 'Carson pause' was most effective
when you let Mrs. Tobino have it."

"Chester, you'll be turning my head," Mark said with
pleasure. "Hey, who told you about my 'Carson pause'?"

"Who else? Rookie, of course. Said he wisened you to
the trick."

"That ingrate! That thief!"

Chester laughed. "Thumbnail description. Only Rookie
neglected to tell me to what the pause refers to."

Crankily Mark said, "That's because I wouldn't tell him.
He's turned over half the books in the Law Library looking
for it. What he doesn't know is that Carson's an English
barrister. That thief! Of all the crust! To say that he—"

"I cross my heart and hope to die if I tell Rookie,"
Chester broke in. "Tell me."

"Well, all right," Mark said, still grumpy. "J'ever read the

Oscar Wilde trials? The point at issue was whether Wilde was a sodomist or not. It seems that he had a craving for the company of young boys. And Carson was cross-examining Wilde. Brilliant! Both of them. Then Carson got on the matter of the young boys. He asked Wilde if he had ever kissed a certain one of them. And Wilde said in his best pansyfied voice, 'Oh, dear me, no! Kiss that boy? But he is so dreadfully ugly!' And Carson said nuttin'. He held his pause until Wilde could no longer maintain his pose. Carson just let Wilde's remark lay and lay and lay, until they practically had to haul it out of the courtroom before it could stink up the place. That's all there is to it. When a witness says something damaging, just let it sink in and in and in. Now you know." Mark took out his flask, offered it to Chester, who primly refused, then took a drink himself. "Now, what can I do for you, Chester?"

Grave as a headstone, Chester said, "Lay off Snowdom. I know that's asking a lot—you could boot me out of here for it—but I'm still asking. He's got a daughter in college back East. She's . . . passing too, naturally. The rub is, she doesn't know she is."

"Would it be such a disgrace to find out?" Mark asked with genuine mental acquisitiveness. "Would it be such a terrible blow to her?"

Chester laughed rudely. "Mark, no white person can ever come close to knowing how it feels to be a Negro."

"But you're more than half-white yourself. How does it feel to be white?"

"I'll never know," Chester rejoined. "Ask Snowdom, he can tell you. It works on the all-or-nothing principle, you see. But I do know this, Snowdom would rather cut his daughter's throat than let her go through some of the things my wife or my mother went through."

"But, dammit, Chester! I've got to discredit Snowdom's testimony somehow. What am I to do? Send my client to the scaffold so some snob of a flapper from Vassar can . . ." Mark calmed himself and said simply, "Look to your motives, Chester. Are you by any chance taking a vicarious enjoyment from Snowdom's deception?"

With scrupulous care, Chester said, "I think that would be a fair statement."

"God, Chester! Your honesty— You make it difficult for me. But you are still asking me to sacrifice my client for yours."

Chester nodded. "If I'm making it difficult for you, you're making my position untenable."

Mark said bluntly, "Tell him to vanish. To get lost."

"And leave Amos up the creek without a paddle? T. Amos wouldn't be likely to forget a thing like that. The moment Snowdom crept back into town Amos would charge him with everything but violating Peaches Browning. And then too, Mark, without Snowdom The Feeb will get away with murder. That thought—offends me."

"You're kidding. You give a damn?"

Flushing a delicate tint of heliotrope, Chester murmured, "Much as I'll hate to see Amos dragging your body behind his chariot, I want you to lose this case."

"I see. It's a matter of 'I've got a rope, who's got a tree'?"

"We are talking at crosspurposes," Chester said.

"Are we? First you ask me to risk my client's neck so yours can go on living in his precious little fantasy world. And next you tell me that you want to see my client convicted anyway. How very good of you, Chester, all things considered."

"Then consider this: Forbes manhandled and ripped at a helpless woman until she died. Snowdom is convinced that the perversities The Feeb practiced on Naismith induced her to abort. And he knew she was pregnant, but that didn't deter him one iota! After all, he's a big shot, he's a whole bag of berries in Hollywood, and she was nobody, she didn't count. What does it matter if he leaves a string of bodies strewn all the way from the Eden to your doorstep? It matters only that you get him turned loose in time for the next apocalyptic frolic. Why, I want to see him swing in the name of common humanity, if for no other reason! We—we Negroes—we——"

"Chester, has the heat gotten you?"

But Chester was only warming to his subject. "We Negroes have fought like sons of bitches to prevent our women from getting treated like female dogs; why can't you? She was your woman, wasn't she, Mark? Wasn't Muffin Naismith your woman? You answer me!"

"It would take me more hours than we have left before court convenes tomorrow to do that. Is there anything else, though, you would like me to tell you?"

In a strange, faraway voice, Chester said, "No, I'll just tell you something instead. I don't want to keep you any longer than I have to away from your lord and master, away from that hairless reptile of a Pentlove."

Mark broke down into painful, helpless laughter. "I'm sorry, Chester, but your description of Pentlove's reptilian poise—"

"But if I could prove what I strongly suspect," Chester went on, "I'd be banging on Amos' door this minute. As it is, I'm going to sell Snowdom down the river instead, and only you know how apt that expression is. Amos must have Snowdom's testimony and since I can't prove—"

"Prove what!"

"What would, among other things, ruin you. Your client is guilty, you know."

Mark drank from his flask while Chester watched with pitiless self-control. "And just how, Chester, did you arrive at that conclusion?"

"Logic. Mark, listen to me, if you lose this case, you're through. Get out of it. Collapse. Get admitted to a hospital. It's going to happen sooner or later, anyway. Don't subject yourself to such an—ignoble—defeat before you have a physical breakdown."

"Chester, are you saying that you are in possession of facts—"

"No, don't ask me anything more. I must protect my informant. He is ignorant but well-meaning. And he has no idea of the import or importance of what he told me. Besides that, he told it to me in confidence."

"And, pray, who is this mysterious individual?"

"My brother-in-law."

"The Reverend Parker Kingdom? He told you?"

"Yes. Only he has just half the facts, and I have the other. I was wondering how long it would take him to put two and two together, but at that point he went off into one of his idiotic trances. The detestable ass. He thinks he's clairvoyant or some such superstitious nonsense."

"Well, is he?"

Chester said angrily, "In some instances, yes. Much as I hate to admit it. He can take an object—say, someone's possession—and tell you amazing things about its owner. He misses a lot of the time, but when he's right it's frightening."

"I'm sure it is. And you think the Reverend Kingdom is correct in his—surmises—this time? What does he say about The Feeb?"

"The Feeb," Chester said, "did not enter into it one way or the other." He got up, climbed past the mystified Mark, and walked out to the aisle. Placing one hand on the door, he took stock of Mark. "They say that when whiskey gets a certain hold on a man, he can no longer be blamed for what he does."

Mark took exception. "I may be a drunk, but I demand that I be held accountable for my actions! Don't you wag your head in pity at me, Chester."

"It's my head; I'll wag it any way I like. You know, I once thought, I honestly thought, you had the makings of a great man. A real trial master. A Darrow or an Earl Rogers. Like your pet 'Carson pause,' there would have been a—oh— 'D'Andor dilemma.' Such as the one Mrs. Tobino found herself in. That was good, Mark, but I doubt if that alone will justify building any monuments."

"So be it, Chester. I am contented with my lot."

"Coming from you, that is not a frame of mind, that's an epitaph." Chester pushed open the door and left Mark alone, sitting in the last row of the deserted courtroom. He thought: I hope to God there's a bottle of hooch waiting for me at my door. For I fully intend to get me dead to the world tonight. That, or I'll find myself at the feet of the Reverend Parker Kingdom next, begging him for visions and revelations, joining Chester in his anguished resentment of the cruel powerful white world, and ending at the foot of the scaffold shouting indecencies up at The Feeb.

CHAPTER TWENTY-TWO

Mark's bootlegger, that exemplary citizen, had, true to his word, left a package by Mark's door, with an accompanying note wishing Counsel D'Andor "the luck of the Irish" in his defense of The Feeb. And in the kitchen the cupboard door had swung open in welcome, as was its custom whenever Mark drove the roadster in overhead. Armed with liquor, glass, his transcripts of the testimony of the trial to date, and a plate loaded with food for himself and his wild animals, Mark sought the comparative coolness of his bedroom. He sat at the window, his feet on the cellarette, and tossed gumdrops to the skunks, urging them "Eat up, me hearties." The sound of his own voice seemed unreal in the thick silence of the night. Not a leaf stirred, and the heat was catastrophic. "Earthquake weather," the old-timers called it, but the scattered hill-dwellers feared far more the "dry thunder." On such nights storms boiled up, the scalded rain evaporated before it could reach the earth, and the lightning set fire to the brush which needed the flying cinders and the heated updrafts to spread its seeds. But tonight there was no dry thunder, only a faint crack from the eucalyptus tree like the knuckles of an oldster creaking as he dozed.

All over the city people were longing aloud for rain; or crowding each other at the soda fountains; or lying in bed, side by side, too miserably sticky to dream of making love; or quarreling.

To the evident pain of Chester Dander, he and his wife Dorothy were one of the quarreling pairs. The dining table, the hub of their family life, had been cleared of dishes, white tablecloth removed (Dorothy was content to use an oilcloth on the kitchen table, but in the dining room she insisted on linen and napery), and the children sent to their schoolbooks. Under the light with its great round milk-glass shade, hung the correct thirty-seven inches above the center of the table, the couple faced one another, Chester with arms crossed and Dorothy leaning toward him, ticking off her points with an indignation that would have done credit to T. Amos Slake.

"Has the heat got you?" she demanded. "Do you hate Parker so much you'd try to mix him up in this Feeb scandal?"

"That's exactly what Mark said to me this afternoon," Chester retorted, irked. "Asking me if the heat had—"

"Mark, Mark, Mark! Who is he? Sylvia or somebody? Can't we get a new refrain around here? I'm sick of hearing about that drunken bum. Why, if George Willis or Horace Bosworth came within a nautical mile of acting like Mark D'Andor, you wouldn't spit on them. And you know it."

"Mark is a friend of mine," Chester said huffily.

"And my brother isn't!"

"You are hardly on the most cordial of terms with my mother!" Chester countered.

"If she'd stop trying to fill my kids' heads with the same hot air she filled yours—"

"My mother will not be discussed in that tone of voice. Nor have I any intention of wrangling with you over her."

"Well, I have! She wasn't in this house five minutes before she started in on the kids about 'Yew have the blood of French kings in your veins.'" Dorothy's mimicry was too accomplished for her own good. Even as Chester bent on her the immobile visage of an affronted aristocrat she plunged on recklessly, "And what does that make me? My kids are French princes. Am I a field hand?"

"That's an absurd thing for a former schoolteacher to say."

"No more absurd than the insinuations the Contessa, or the Marquise, or whoever she thinks she is, says to my children."

In his disdain, Chester looked as if he were spitting grape seeds rather than speaking. "My mother has never made any such fool claim about our forbears. She merely said that Grandmother was of the direct line of D'Andors——"

"That is so . . . so insanely . . . fanciful that I cannot—— Your mother is a servant. And her mother, and her mother's mother. All of them slaving for white trash and sticking their noses in the air, telling themselves they're really queens in disguise. Bearing children out of wedlock, and proud of it, so they could keep their royal names. Your mother is only Miss Dander, just as I'm only Mrs. Dander, so where does she get off?"

"My mother does not work for trash, I'll have you—"

"Oh, no? Their pictures are in the papers constantly."

"On the society page."

"Oh, my! Well, I guess there are standards and standards," Dorothy conceded loftily. "*My* mother always taught me that a lady's name appeared in the papers three times in her life. When she was born, when she married, and when she—"

"That's as outdated as the tin lizzie."

"Do tell? But I guess you're right. These days respectable people get in the papers once when they defend vile murderers, and once when they pass out cold in court dead drunk, and once—"

"No one ever has troubles and worries but you, Dorothy. When a good man hits the bottle, all you can think of is that he belongs in the gutter."

"Excuse me, I forgot. He's some kind of a French king too, isn't he? He must be if he's a real dyed-in-the-wool D'Andor. That does make a difference, doesn't it? He can come to court drunk and defend a man you secretly think is guilty, and that's fine. A respectable man, a decent man like Amos Slake you sneer at."

"I consider Amos a very able attorney," Chester said loftily. "But he is also rude and unfeeling. The other day he displayed a disgusting lack of breeding."

"No! He lacks breeding, *tsk!*" Dorothy leaned back, hands on her hips. "Do you mean to tell me Amos Slake isn't entitled to wear a coronet embroidered on his underwear?"

"I think I'd better go to the office this evening," Chester decided. "I have things to do."

"Such as trying to implicate my brother in a disgraceful—"

"Dorothy," Chester said with enraging patience, "no one is at all interested in Parker's vaporizings. Mark did not take me seriously in the least, and I wouldn't be paying Parker the slightest attention but for his saying something that struck me as being so outlandish that I wondered if there hadn't to be a grain of truth in it. But I would as soon present Parker's mumbo-jumbo maunderings to Amos Slake as I would those of a witchdoctor."

"Thank you. You say the nicest things about the brother who gave up his own education to help me get mine. And yet when I so much as hint that your sainted mother isn't the Queen of England, and your father the Nabob of —"

"You knew very well who my father was," Chester said with quiet pride.

"I do? All I know is some cock-and-bull story your mother cooked up about a drunken judge climbing into her bed."

"He was a judge. He was a guest from the East, and a friend of the people my mother still works for. And, yes, he was drunk."

"I'll tell you one thing he wasn't," Dorothy said recklessly. "He wasn't a gentleman," and putting her head in her arms she began to cry.

"Baby!" Chester protested, coming round the table to her, "don't do that, Baby. Look, I honestly believe the heat has got us both."

Dorothy sobbed out a series of incoherent self-accusations. Chester patted her and rested his cheek on the top of her head. "Now cease and desist the breast-beatings, Baby," he said, and was rewarded by a moist giggle. "My mother is an obdurate and proud old woman, but I promise you, she's humiliated you for the last time."

". . . wonderful woman . . . shamed of myself . . ." was all he could distinguish from Dorothy's gulpings. He sat next to her, arms around her, seeking a way to comfort her, saying inadequately, "Hush, Baby. We all say things we'd like to cut our tongues out for." He held her and was mute, unable to confide in her even to this day of a regret of his own, as worn and threadbare with use as the carpeting on the floor of the D'Andor law offices.

During the first year of Chester's practice of law he maintained an office little larger than a hall closet. And to him had come one day a poor black wretch, just out of the South, with too many children and not enough marbles. The client shuffled and whined and fawned; he was a walking defamation of his whole race. He was going to be evicted from the two-room flat he was living in, he and his wife and their seven children—and his sister and her four children. They had no place to go, and the white owner of the building had finally sent the sheriff to warn them.

Hearing this, Chester knew that the sheriff's office had been used, as was a frequent thing among lawyers, to serve a process. In clipped tones Chester asked for and received the complaint so served, and was also treated with the sight of a filthy shirt in which the paper had been concealed, along with an unmistakable hint of unwashed person. "You've got too many people living with you in that one flat," Chester said, reading over the complaint.

"Whose side you on?" the client whined.

While debating how best to tell this wretch he hadn't a legal leg to stand on, Chester's eye fell on the name of the attorney who had drawn up the complaint. Explaining to his client that time was the only thing he, Chester, could gain for him, Chester's gaze remained on the pleading, noting the Hollywood address and phone number of D'Andor, the firebrand and a new staple in the literary diet of the tabloid readers. Then Chester picked up the phone.

When he got his number, he said, "This is Chester Dander, I'm an attorney. May I speak to Mr. D'Andor?"

"Hello?" Mark came on easily.

"Mr. D'Andor, I'm Chester Dander—" Chester found himself uttering a nervous little laugh at the similarity of the names.

"Of course," Mark said. "What can I do for you?"

Chester stated his client's problem. He concluded, "So if my client could be granted a little time to find new quarters— You see, I realize that in the event of litigation the outcome is—ah—preordained. So if you could extend the courtesy of——"

"Be glad to," Mark said. "I'm sure my client will agree to anything reasonable. How much time would you like before filing an answer? Which, of course, we both hope won't be necessary."

"Would thirty days be satisfactory?" Chester ventured.

"Make it sixty," Mark said, with no indication that he felt himself admirably generous. "I can keep my client quiet that long. Or I can always distract him with certain other things I'm handling for him."

Is he being so *princely,* Chester wondered fleetingly, because he's assuming the white man's burden? Momentarily demoralized, Chester took refuge in formality. "That is most considerate of you, Mr. D'Andor. I'll have the stipulation to that effect, in tonight's mail. It ought to be on your desk in the morning."

There was a brief silence, lasting no longer than it would take to glance at one's watch. Then Mark said with no change of intonation, "As you wish." He had no more to say.

An unease almost amounting to dread seized Chester, as if he were about to become aware of the seepage of secret internal bleeding. He thanked Mark, he could not remember how or in what words, and hung up.

The black wretch of a client, at once a stupid and cunning fellow, dared the faintest of grins at the spectacle of Chester flushing fiercely just from talking fancy with a white man. "You have thirty days to get out of that flat," Chester yelled at him. "You understand that? *Thirty* days. To get yourself and your wife and sister and that passel of pickaninnies out of there!"

The client snarled, "You talkin' pretty big foh a——"

"Thirty days," Chester shouted. "I'll get the Reverend Parker Kingdom to help you. You don't owe me any money, just get yourself going." It came to him he was hollering and gesturing as if he were speaking to a foreigner. "Thirty days," Chester repeated, faltered, and had to look down at the complaint, pretending to read it.

"Sure, Boss," the client said, grinning openly now. He shuffled to the door, looked back once to impress on his memory the ridiculous figure Chester cut acting so uppity, and was gone.

Chester was a stranger to himself, a stranger who was dangerously close to tears. What had he done that was not common practice? Attorneys frequently, usually, most of the time, always reduced most—no, all—stipulations to writing.

Attorneys, yes. Gentlemen, never.

Nigger, nigger, nigger, Chester thought, but in his mind he spoke not to himself but to a woman, now dust, who had lain with a D'Andor over seventy-five years before, and then had returned, pregnant, to the slave quarters where she belonged.

Not too many weeks later, Chester saw Mark D'Andor in the corridors of the courthouse and went up to introduce himself.

"Nice to know you," Mark said, shaking Chester's hand. "I'm just on my way to grab a cup of coffee. What say you join me?"

There was no mention made of the fact that the stipulation somehow never did reach Mark's desk.

Now, years later, Chester found the charity in him to forgive himself, and, smiling, he shushed his weeping wife. "Hush, Baby, hush. I'm sorry for anything I've said about Parker. And don't worry about his reputation getting sullied. After all, it was I who put my own construction on what he told me. He has absolutely no way of knowing what implications, if any, could be attached to it."

"There you go talking like a lawyer," Dorothy said, and gave him a salty kiss.

"Why, I very much doubt if the Reverend Parker Kingdom knows that that trial is going on. He's got his own fish to fry," Chester said stoutly.

The Reverend Parker Kingdom was just getting his griddle hot. A happenstance, a certain succumbing to temptation on the part of one of his sheep, a little cleaning maid, had focused his attention on the Forbes murder trial. He had raced to Civic Center to get the proper permission to erect a tent on a vacant lot on Central Avenue, and he had whipped himself up a splendid Revival that was playing to capacity congregations every night.

The Biblical connotation of the Eden suited the Reverend Kingdom down to the last bound buttonhole, and the Sodom and Gomorrah overtones of that which allegedly took place at the Eden scandalized him and lit his tongue with fire. Tonight, in the oppressive heat, he knew that his Master was ready for him to spread a conflagration in the hearts of sinners.

Eschewing a pulpit or even a lectern, the Reverend Kingdom stood on the edge of the platform, drawn up to his mighty height, with a battered Bible in his left hand.

". . . and God looks down on his fair land, and He sees not good folk and happy little children, but abominations!"

"Amen!"

". . . and Gooood is not napping! He knows, He knows! He sees his children in a land of milk and honey where the sun shines all the day and cannot light up the dark places in our hearts. He looks down and sees whoredoms and scarlet women, yes! and vileness everywhere, on foot and riding around in purple automobiles. And He sees death, and the tablets of Moses ground to powder under the feet of the wicked."

"*Amen!*"

"And He sees all, but He looks in vain for one prayer!" The Reverend Kingdom took a step to the side and, placing his hand to his brow as if shading it, looked everywhere about the tent. "No, nobodies' doin' any praying at all out there," he said to the left of the tent. "Nary a one here!" he accused the right. Suddenly the Reverend Kingdom looked down at his feet. "But behold, says God! What is this we got here?" Taking his hand from his brow, he went on, "Why, it's one of those big round metal lids we got in the street. The lid that opens to the sewer. The Los Angeles Water Department put it there. And what does it say? Why, lookee here, there's the letters plain as day—El Aye Double-you Dee. LAWD! That's what it says—*Lawd*!"

"Lawd, lawd!" the congregation moaned.

"That's our prayer, a single cry on a sewer lid, hiding the filth and abominations underneath, but looking straight up at heaven and crying out, 'Lawd, Lawd!'

"And I had me a terrible dream last night, I did. I dreamed my gentle Lawd, my sweet Jesus came down to see how we were all doing here in this land of milk and honey. But we was all too busy to give Him the time oh day." Unconsciously the Reverend Kingdom was slipping into the speech patterns of revival oratory. "Yas, we was all too busy. Too busy with dancin' our Charleston, and our women was all painted and powdered and smokin' *cigarettes*—"

"Lawd!"

"—and our children was all at the movies watching women with next to no clothes on kissin' and huggin' and drinkin' booze! And our young people was puttin' down they Bibles to read in the papers of fornications and murders, and lawyers who'd defend Satan himself for money, but wouldn't stand up for our sweet Jesus Hisself 'fore Pilot—lessen' you paid 'em thirty pieces of silver to do it!"

"Amen!"

"And everywhere my sweet Redeemer wandered bout in my dream, He couldn't get nobody to talk to Him bout nothin but bathtub gin—"

"Amen!" confirmed a most prosperous-looking man in a check suit, with a gargantuan gold ring on his pinkie finger.

"—and how to *steal from they employers*—" the Reverend Kingdom said with peculiar emphasis "—and the young girls too busy decoratin' they bodies to please they candy-men; and East and West and North and South our sweet Lawd walked His feet to blisters and blood, but He found no one, no one to say Him a prayer. Not even The Feeb!

"And Jesus wept.

"And He returneth to heaven, whence He come, and His countenance was it long! And God the Father said to Him, said, 'Gentle Jesus, my divine Son, how are my children in they land of the fatted calf and the sunshine?' And Jesus said, 'Father, smite them! Rise in Thy wrath and smite them hip and thigh. Drive they automobiles into the sea, and make the earth to move and quake. Father, visit Thy children with pestilence; and as Ye rent the veil of the temple, rip they silver screen from top to bottom! For it is they holy of holies, and they worship at it. Smite them, Fath—"

The platform under the Reverend Kingdom quivered momentarily as a mild earthquake rippled underfoot. He raised his hands on high, his face transfigured, beautiful. "LAWD!" he chanted above the shrillings of the congregation. And when the earth again was still, the Reverend Parker Kingdom said into the fearful hush, "And our sweet Jesus said to His Father, 'Burn their city. Crisp their bodies like cracklin's. Send Angels with flamin' swords to wipe them out and guard the gates. For never has I seen such a scandal in Eden'!"

CHAPTER TWENTY-THREE

The mild earth tremor wakened Mark from a doze. The house heaved irritably, creaking its joints, and ended by tossing a roof tile onto the patio, barely missing the opossum and causing a skunk great distress. "Oh for the love of—" Mark said, hastening to close the window. "The hottest night of the year," he complained to the skunk, "and you have to do *this*." He returned to his transcripts, sat in untold misery for a time, decided, What the hell, it can't be any worse outside than it is in here, and opened the window.

He had waited in vain all evening for information from either Rookie or Ted Savant as to the last abode of Muffin Naismith. On a sudden impulse he went upstairs to phone a certain ancient gentleman, but the old party was either abed or would not be bothered. Mark doubted that it mattered.

He had made the acquaintance of the ancient gentleman several years after Manny Amen had undertaken to pave Muffin Naismith's road to glory. During those years Mark had asked of himself in idle moments how Muffin might be faring, but of her or from her he heard not a word, and gradually he had drifted out of the habit of sending Manny his retainer fee. Once, driving past the cottage court where Muffin had first lived, Mark had seen a blonde child playing in the doorway, and so took it that Muffin had moved—and with sincere good will hoped that it was up in the world. She was being groomed, he supposed, by one of the studio schools for the promising, such as that of Paramount. Another time, while sitting in his stocking feet at the shoe-repair shop, he thought he spied a jubilant Muffin smiling down at him from a glossy new photo adorning the wall, among the fly-specked faded images of Eleanor Boardman and Eileen Pringle and that pale pie tin of a face with the bee-stung mouth that proclaimed that Mary Minter lurked somewhere behind the long golden curls and the pious smirk. Seated in his little cubicle with the low door modestly hiding the fact of his stockinged feet, he craned his neck at the glossy photo. But when he was shod again he made a closer inspection and learned that the newcomer jazz-baby was some girl named Stern. Or was it Bow?

At any rate it was not Muffin and he again forgot her. His life at the time was either serene or brackish, depending on how one looked at it. He had his hoods and his bookies and his divorce cases to occupy him, and he had a gem of a bootlegger who had somehow gotten into the habit of depositing a girl at Mark's door along with his other supplies of an inclement week end.

On a rainy Saturday afternoon Mark had come home to find a rather bedraggled blonde in a yellow slicker perched on the lid of his garbage can in the garage, smoking furiously. She complained in a steady monotone all the while he let her into the house, and only when she was warm before the fire with a drink in her hand did she look on Mark with anything but open disfavor. When he asked her her name she said, "Colette?" as if asking if he found that acceptable. When his phone rang only seconds short of the penultimate inopportune moment, he was inclined to ignore it. But at Colette's insistence he did not, for it might be the bootlegger, and as he had promised to do her a little service, he might be calling about it.

Instead it was Muffin, sounding as soggy as the day outside and declaring she needed Mark at once. She gave him an address so remote from the lights of Hollywood that he questioned her accuracy. Brushing his objections aside, she gave him instructions as to how to reach his destination, telling him finally "I'll leave the elevator door unlocked so you can come on up. I'll be waiting for you at the top; I don't want the Lotus Singer in on this."

Mark returned to his hearth and said, "I'm not sure I heard one word of what I just heard. Have you ever run into anybody called a—uh—Lotus Singer?"

The blonde could not believe her ears, though for a different reason. "Are you nuts? He's only the greatest poet in the whole world, that's all. He's real old now, I guess, but when I was a kid my mother never missed him at a chautauqua. She took me, and I never heard anything so beautiful in all my life, that's all. Him reading his poems. I mean it was real beautiful, that's all."

"I'm afraid I'm going to have to take you back down to the Boulevard." He slipped a bill under her garter. "I've enjoyed your company, but I'm sorry to say that I've been called away. Maybe some other time soon?"

"But you didn't—" Colette began. "I mean, *did* you?" She looked at him with fresh interest. Here was yet another of the male breed to be analyzed, understood, and catalogued for handy reference.

"I regret to say that I did not."

Colette reluctantly put on her dress. "Well, that's all," she marveled. "I mean, that's *all!*"

He deposited Colette at the Hollywood Hotel and continued driving west through a rain as tender as wine. Though it was only the second week in December, he saw several Christmas trees displayed in the large arched front windows of the Spanish houses lining the Boulevard, and he was vaguely disapproving of such premature, such precipitant rejoicing. Soon he was passing only the walls of estates, or vacant lots with weeds flourishing richly in the rains. He began to climb up a winding canyon and shortly was the only car on the pocked road. At the proper turn-off he had to contend with a muddy lane with only a scattering of gravel to give his wheels purchase. A final turn and his roadster brought up before a square cement elevator which thrust itself up the side of the sheer canyon wall. His view from below gave him glimpses of battlements and turrets and narrow blank windows of stained glass, all unlighted and with the insubstantiality of the mist. Getting out of the auto, he discerned that the oaken door of the elevator was ajar and, entering, found himself in a birdcage of lacy metal with a velvet seat upon which lay a book bound in fine leather and stamped in gold. On the operator's panel there was but one button, which he pressed. The door thudded shut, and the birdcage began a leisurely ascent. Mark sat on the velvet seat and watched as a stained-glass lancet window afforded him a view of poisonously green brush past which he slowly crept until another lancet window presented him with dirt-red ivy with swollen magenta veins. He then glanced through the book, as its presence strongly suggested that not to pleasure himself with its contents would be boorish in the extreme. He was holding a volume of *Songs of The Lotus Singer,* one of which began:

> Pan, be my companion,
> Teach me the ways of Spring.
> Meet me in some sylvan glade,
> And you two maidens bring.

Well, that's fair enough, Mark thought. The elevator rose, soft as a sigh, past a yellow window that gave him his first view of Hollywood, far below, as a sulphurous enchanted city, loosely annexed to Hell. The elevator came to rest. Another oak door opened into a weird wild garden of all shapes and species of succulents. To his immediate right was a blockhouse, seeming all but impregnable since it apparently had no means of ingress. A cloister connected the blockhouse with the castle proper, and under the arches stood Muffin, her head and shoulders protected only by a scarf of gray chiffon. She was looking out at the garden, or rather at its fountain, in the center of which was a dreary stone Cupid. At the sound of Mark's steps she stiffened but did not turn to him. He had to say her name twice before, with a darting motion, she looked at him. "I didn't really think you'd come," she said, and the banked fires of hysteria flared up briefly in her eyes.

"Nonsense. I'm here, aren't I?" He was talking too heartily, like a lawyer trying to explain to his client why they had taken a shellacking in court. "Are we going to talk here?"

"Yes," Muffin said, listless.

"Now, what's this all about?"

For answer Muffin stepped out onto a gravel path and began to walk slowly toward the fountain. At her side Mark struggled with the temptation to bluster merrily on the one hand and take flight on the other. "Look, Muffin, if you don't have sense enough to come in out of the rain, I do."

"I never did," Muffin said in a soft little cheep of self-pity.

"Tell me, why am I here?"

"You tell me why I'm here," she said bitterly.

The old compassion, the uncontrollable impulse to offer her solace, was taking possession of him. "Don't fight me, Muffin, just talk to me."

"All right, I live here! And I work here. The Lotus Singer calls me his secretary. Secretary! That's a laugh." She resumed walking, this time around the fountain itself. The great bowl was filled with less than an inch of rainwater, and the Cupid, Mark noted, had lost a foot and was suffering from a severe skull facture.

"What are your duties, then, Muffin?"

"You guess. He's eighty if he's a day. He just happens to think he's Passion's Plaything or somebody."

"Would you like to pack your clothes? We can leave right now. I'll take you to the Hotel Christie and see to it that you have enough to live on until you can get back on your———"

As if she hadn't heard him, Muffin said, "He's not—wicked, or anything. And he has lots of money." She jerked her head in the direction of the castle looming behind them in the mist. "Lots of it. But he's crazy about me. That's the trouble. I met him about a year ago. I was having some trouble with my eyes, and he said I should come stay with him and not bother my pretty head about a single thing."

"He sounds like a very kind Lotus Singer," Mark commented.

Muffin slowly raised her eyes to his, then switched her gaze back and forth in the scanning motion so popular with the lovelies of the silver screen. Still raking his face with that soulful ogle, she spat out, "Icks. An old man like that . . . *Icks!*"

"Oh. Well, I suppose such a viewpoint on your part would have considerable bearing on the matter. You did say—icks?"

"I'll give up my career for you!" Muffin vowed. "I promise. I won't let it interfere any more with our love. It isn't fair to you. I see that now."

"Muffin—"

"You will forgive me? Oh, I know I was cruel to you, but the bright lights beckoned, and oodles and oodles of studios were after me, and I—"

"Muffin—"

"But someday when we are old and gray, we will both—"

"Muffin!"

"—laugh at how important it all seemed. And I promise, Mark Daddy, I'll never set foot in front of a camera again. Except for our wedding photos, of course." She was picking up animation like a train gathering speed. "I 'magine the columns might be a teensy bit interested in the fact that Muffin Naismith is giving up her career for love! I doubt if we can keep it quiet, our wedding, I mean, because—"

"Shall I take you to a hotel or anyplace you might care to go to, or not? Muffin, you sent for me as casually as you would a sample of Princess Pat Powder. But the resemblance ends there. I do not belong to you. I am at your service, yes, but I do not be—"

She struck him on the mouth. "Then crawl back where you came from. G'wan, beat it!"

Taking her at her word, he started off in that casual leavetaking of his before she called him back. She was smiling stiff as stone. "Tell me something, Daddy. You can tell Muffin. What did you do to that stuck-up wife of yours to make her take a flying leap off the Pasadena bridge?" She watched him avidly, at the same time beginning to cry fiercely, defiantly, triumphantly.

Mark looked at the broken Cupid. "Buddy," he said in a spasm of pain, "you're cracked." He left Muffin by the fountain, picking a gravel walk that would lead him to the elevator tower. He was subject to no emotion whatsoever. There had been only one wild pang for his dead Constance before his very heart, it seemed, had fallen silent. During his stroll toward the elevator several of the succulents, bearing angry spikes long and sharp as darning needles, held his eye. He examined them with interest, then moved on. He was stretching forth his hand to open the elevator door when a window in the upper part of the blockhouse was thrown open. A spidery old gent beckoned Mark. "You, down there! You D'Andor?"

"Yes."

"Then come up here!"

The window slammed down and Mark was looking up at a pane that reflected the silver sky. The wall of the blockhouse presented a smooth face to him. Mark found no means of entrance under the cloister, and peering around the opposite wall he saw only a sheer drop with his roadster parked at the bottom. Coming round to the front again, a sound that brought to mind dungeons festooned with chains warned him to leap to one side. A drop-gate set in the face of the blockhouse crashed to the gravel walk. Mark entered and climbed a short flight of iron stairs. At the top, before a cozy gas grate, sat the ancient one.

"Your drop-gate," Mark said, "reminds me of a line from one of my favorite poems: 'The drawbridge dropped with a surly clang.' " He shook hands with his host, noting the overflowing bookcases, and tables and chairs piled high with more books and writing materials.

"My private preserve," the old man said, sweeping a heap of manuscripts from a chair seat to the floor. "Sit down, sit down. So you like James Russell Lowell, eh? Who else do you like? Eh? Have I introduced myself? I'm the Lotus Singer, as you indubitably know. You are familiar with my work? Eh? There is no corner in this world that remains in ignorance of me. Which of my poems is your favorite?"

"Why, ah . . ." Mark relied on sheer inspiration, ". . . one of the—uh—*Songs,* I believe it is. About Pan." He felt like a perfect damn fool.

"Yes, my *Songs.* An enduring piece of work, there. Translated into thirty-two languages. Camel drivers in the endless caravans bearing gold and silks and spices to minareted cities recite my *Songs* to the vast desert night. I personally think they stink. Don't waste your time on them. Take my advice and stick with my *Bagatelles;* I do. I'll give you a copy when you leave. You will be leaving alone, I take it?

"Miss Naismith decided she would not leave as of this time," Mark said tactfully.

The Lotus Singer took a turn for the crafty. His skin, Mark discovered, looked of the same chiffon as Muffin's scarf, but his eyes were as lively and bright as firelight. "She's my pretty fool, Muffin is. I've told her that I'll leave her a tidy sum in my will if she'll stay 'til that day I become clay. Have you a pencil on you? Write that about day and clay down for me, will you? And pour us some brandy."

Mark was kept hopping to comply with his host's requests.

"Come to think of it," the Lotus Singer said, "there is something you can do for me." (Mark could not recall making any such offer.) "I'll give you the name of my attorney, and instruct him to let you read my will at your leisure. If you don't think I'm being generous enough to Muffin, kindly report your opinion to me."

"Oh, I'm sure you're being more than gener—"

"Do you know my *Sonnets to the Choctaw*? Lovely things, wouldn't you say? How do you like the brandy, eh? You don't get a bouquet like that every day of your life. So you're Mark D'Andor. The things I read about you in the papers are atrocious, though I suppose true. You were a lover of Muffin's once, weren't you? Were you ever able to get her off the subject of her movie mania? What could be at the bottom of her obsession?"

"For one thing," Mark said, hardly believing he was being allowed to speak, "she thinks movies are real. And that she isn't."

"Of course she isn't. You have put your finger on it, D'Andor. She thinks she is someone who hasn't gotten her chance to exist. An admirer of my enchanting poetry gave Muffin to me, incidentally," the old man said matter-of-factly. "On the fiftieth aniversary of the publication of my *Songs*. Poor child, she was in despair over her movie career. It was like having someone make you the present of a kitten, only to reach home with it and find it sickly. Runny eyes and all that sort of thing."

"Muffin was sickly?"

"I just told you. Runny eyes. Had to keep them bandaged for two weeks. Some inflammation or other. I read to her constantly. Poetry." The Lotus Singer chuckled. "She hated me because I wouldn't read *Photoplay* to her."

"I did that once," Mark said. "I don't mean about *Photo-*

play. I once read poetry to a sick friend. The same poem over and over and over."

"A few do bear repeating. I have my bootlegger deliver Muffin's movie magazines along with his order."

"Mine leaves me girls," Mark said.

"Did you love Muffin, eh, D'Andor?"

"No, Mr. Singer."

"Simply call me Lotus Singer. I am unique unto myself and need no other appellations. So, you did not love her?"

"No, I couldn't. I had a wife who didn't love me, but I could think of no one else."

The Lotus Singer said bluntly, "Pour yourself more brandy, D'Andor, and we will talk of other things than your wife. We will talk of Muffin. Your affair with her, then, was rather as I had imagined it to be. You were stuck with her, whereas I am stuck on her."

Mark said lightly, "She is almost appallingly pretty, isn't she."

"And loves to bedeck herself. I literally weigh her down with trinkets. I am a lavish old lech, I say it in all honesty. Yet these last few days I have seen the desire to flee me coming on insidiously and rapidly. From the outset, you understand, it was agreed between us that as long as she remained with me there would be no running down to Hollywood to get in the movies."

"Muffin had agreed to that?"

"Yes. Then something she read in one of her fool movie magazines set her off. She asked me for money without a qualm. Asked me, in short, to support her until she got back into the movies. She also wanted my Lancia, which I have taught her to drive. I sensibly refused. And bided my time. She has become accustomed to the security a doting old man can give her, you see. I knew she was casting about in her mind for some other man who would serve as a base of operations. One she could bind to her legally. The man who gave her to me, it must be understood, made her the choice of me or the streets— as she put it. She has no aptitude for working for her own living, as I'm sure you can attest to, D'Andor. Hence, when I happened to see you talking to her from that window over there, I thought to myself that the bridegroom had arrived. But you are not Lochinvar, after all, are you? Only Sir Launfal, eh?, beating the bushes for the Holy Grail."

"I would hardly compare myself to—"

"I would never have taken you for a James Russell Lowell fancier, never in a million years. Tell me more about yourself, D'Andor, you interest me. Were you in the World War?"

"I was unable to attend," Mark said.

"That so? Turn on the lamp there, will you? Too busy, I suppose?"

"No," Mark said, fiddling with the lamp switch. "I enlisted in the Canadian Army, before we got into it. And then I caught influenza. That was in the earlier epidemic, not the globetrotting one that came in 'Eighteen, I think it was. The whole camp came down with it, but a group of American boys who were billeted together were the chief victims. Many of us died. I emerged somewhat the worse for wear, myself," Mark said wryly. "I was shipped home, with the advice to sit that war out."

"Yes," the Lotus Singer said, peering at Mark in the lamplight, "you do have the look of a consumptive about you. It suits you. I suppose the women give you no end of annoyance, as they are notorious, the dears, for falling head over bustle for consumptive—"

"I assure you," Mark put in modestly, "I am not the least con–"

"Do you always interrupt like that? I learned at my mother's knee, D'Andor, never to do such a thing. Rude. Pour us more brandy, will you. Now, tell me, what shall I do about my Muffin? Eh?"

"Why, Mr.—uh—why, Lotus Singer, I think——"

"Oh, I could try it, but it would never work. No, I think I'll just go on the way I am. Pampering her. I'm buying her a little sports model for Christmas. I hope she doesn't get in it and drive away. She's capable of it. Were Muffin a man she'd be a thoroughgoing heel. Do you think she has it in her to love anyone—other than herself? Hand me that book over there, that's it, my *Sonnets*. There's one in there that might apply to Muffin. I have to read my works, you know. I toss them off—

genius never strives—and then they slip my mind. Here it is. No, that's not the one. Hmmm. Excellent!" The old man read, turned a page, and read on. "Delightful!" he said, marking time in the air as if to music. "Sprung rhythm. Oh, and this one! The ladies swooned when I—— Ah, yes! And so very lilting!"

"I must go," Mark murmured, rising.

"Take your *Songs* with you," the Lotus Singer said without looking up.

"I thought I was to have the *Bagatelles,* especially since they are your favorites."

"Capital!" the Lotus Singer cried, but whether he referred to Mark's preference or the lines he was reading Mark could not determine. "You will find the volume is already autographed. Oh, this is exquisite! You must come to dine with us one night soon, D'Andor. Now that you've refused Muffin your hand in marriage, she'll probably take it into her head that she fancies you—purely out of pique. Reach me my pipe, it's on the table. Do you know, these sonnets could be worse, far worse. I'm so glad you asked me to read them to you. Fetch the lamp a mite to the left. My, what a captivating line! No wonder I made a fortune. Next time Muffin calls, get in touch with me before you do anything, won't you? And slam the elevator door shut after you. Make sure it's secure."

"I will leave everything as I found it, Lotus Singer," Mark assured the old man.

The old man uttered a gusty sigh of pure rapture and turned a page.

Just as Mark turned to close the elevator door behind him, he saw a wisp of gray chiffon beyond the blockhouse. Muffin had been eavesdropping, he had no doubt, and even as he looked she came into full view. Her face gleamed in the mist, but she did not speak and he could not read her expression.

He never saw her alive again.

CHAPTER TWENTY-FOUR

Mark wakened to a bed cluttered with transcripts, an empty tin of Irish, and a fine morning. The sun was like a soft stain on his patio, as if, long ago, someone had carelessly spilt a kettle of molten light over the stones, and years of subsequent wear had worn it down into every crevice and crack, polishing it smooth. Even before dressing he made certain his flask was filled, and, next, shaving, noted dispassionately how rapidly drink was aging him.

While his coffee perked, he called Rookie. With the clear morning voice of a butler Rookie had little to report. Despite diligent efforts he had not found Pep Baines, and said himself to be of the dark suspicion that Amos had her safely stashed away in the pokey. He had, however, done better with the trio mentioned in Muffin's card to Manny Amen. T-Bone Tredwell was fairly certain that the Mrs. F. was the widow of a second unit director named Foley, and Rookie now had only to find where she lived. "Keep on it," Mark said.

He drank his coffee, made some toast in the oven that tasted very like buttered emery boards, and went forth into the world to see what the day would bring.

Seymour Pentlove was enjoying the morning at the side entrance of the Hall of Justice. He looked at Mark's hollow face critically but made no comment, girding himself instead to run the gauntlet of the line outside the courtroom. And that ordeal was nearly over when a woman, second in line, reached past him to snatch at the arm of Mark D'Andor. Chico, Mark's capper of old, had urgent legal business with him, but first she must complete her transaction of selling her place in line to a panting tourist scandalmonger from Cleveland.

"You go on in," Mark said to Mr. Pentlove, "I have to wait and take this lady in with me." To Chico he said, "Long time no see," and held the door for her when she was ready. Like a gentleman taking a lady in to dinner, Mark escorted Chico to the first row, then went through the bar to deposit his brief case on the counsel table. Turning around in his chair, he caught Mr. Pentlove bending a look of instinctual dislike at Chico.

Jerking her head at Mr. Pentlove, Chico said, "Mr. High-and-Mighty here safe?"

"You can speak freely, Chico."

"I ran into your Mr. Castle. He's been turning the town upside down for a Pep Baines, but he's afraid they've got her in the cooler."

"So am I."

"That's what I thought," Chico said in a businesslike voice. "So for twenty-five I'll go put a brick right smack through the windshield of Mr. Amos Slake's automobile."

"Give the lady twenty-five dollars, Pentlove," Mark said.

"I will not! I'll have no part of such a piece of senseless vandalism. Besides, I've only a ten and two fifties on me."

"Now that I think of it, Counsel," Chico said, "it really is a fifty-buck job."

"Give the lady a fifty," Mark ordered Mr. Pentlove casually.

"Are you trying to get us jailed?" Mr. Pentlove demanded.

"Only one of us," Mark said over Chico's hearty laughter.

Mr. Pentlove and his money were soon parted, and Chico was on her way with dispatch, brushing past a rosy and all-unawares T. Amos as he entered the bar. Behind him walked Dr. Snowdom, erect and stern. Amos saw to the comfort of his witness, made a to-do of sorting some papers, and at last deigned to notice a grinning Mark.

"Good morning," Amos said.

"Top of the same to you. Will the good Doctor want a blindfold, do you think? Or will he face the firing squad fearlessly?"

"If you have any Sen-Sen on you, use it," Amos retorted smartly. "I'll be inebriated otherwise, just sitting near you."

Mark took it in all good grace, opened his mouth to voice some bantering remark or other, and was distracted by the arrival of Chester Dander. Chester nodded briefly to T. Amos, took no notice of Mark at all, and sat beside Snowdom to whisper to him. Snowdom listened, looking straight ahead, his teeth clenched so tightly that mounds of muscle stood out on his face. Once only his pewter gaze touched Mark lightly, then snapped to another direction. Mark thought: Odd that of all things those pale eyes are the giveaway.

With a roar the crowd was admitted to the courtroom, Chico's customer borne forward and deposited in the first spectator's row. He waved jauntily to Mark quite as if they were old friends, and then, catching sight of The Feeb being brought into the bullpen, screamed a greeting combined with heartfelt words of encouragement, "Hotdog howdy, Feeb! You get on in here and tell 'em. I stutter!"

'Twere better for you if you did, Mark thought.

"Bailiff," Amos was shouting, "can't you—"

The tourist gentleman was now applauding The Feeb, turning hands and body through a half-circle to follow Forbes as he was led to his place by Mark.

"—stop this demonstration?" Amos was still begging.

Archibald Forbes did it for him, simply by rising to face his rioting adulators and stretching forth his hand. He patted the air as if to say how he ached to touch and comfort each one of them. The other hand curled tenderly around the paper rose in his lapel. As one person, the women spectators sighed "Awwwwww!" and fell silent.

Forbes sat down.

"Superb!" Mr. Pentlove murmured.

The jury was brought in, Judge Fickett appeared, was seen disappearing behind her Codes, and court was in session.

"Call Doctor Snowdom," Amos said in a perfectly smashing fashion, all dynamic gubernatorial timber in his crêpe-de-chine suit (*Seersucker*, Mark thought, *that's* what that unpressed-looking material is).

Dr. Snowdom was sworn and induced to announce his

name, address, occupation, education, and that he was duly
licensed to practice medicine in the State of California.

"You are a licensed physician and *surgeon*?" Amos
brought out carefully.

"I am." Snowdom looked not to the jury, not at Mark,
nor to Chester among the spectators, riveting his eyes solely on
the splendid figure of T. Amos Slake. He was launched on his
story, reciting with surgical precision the cut-and-dried events
culminating in the death of Muffin Naismith. After a recess,
during which Mark had recourse to his flask and found himself
in receipt of a large number of packets of Sen-Sen furnished
by a dryly waggish Mr. Pentlove, Amos took Snowdom
through his entire testimony again.

"Miss Naismith was brought in by two women," Snowdom repeated. "They told me their names were Miss Smith
and Miss—"

"Objection. Hearsay," Mark put in, having decided that
if Amos wanted to waste time, he, Mark, would cordially put
himself out to help him.

"Well, really," Amos protested briskly. "The testimony
was not offered for content, or the truth of same, but merely
that the two women did give themselves names."

"And you keep up this repetitious nonsense," Mark said
so softly that only Amos could hear him, "and I'll give you a
pain in the neck.

"Overruled," Judge Fickett chirped.

Mark inclined his head respectfully.

Amos smiled at the jury. "Now, what—ah—medical
history did these two women, this Miss Smith and Miss Jo—"

"The *soi-disant* Miss Smith and Miss Jones," Mark
reminded him politely.

"The *who*?" Amos demanded ringingly. "Counselor, are
you objecting or just what?"

"Let it pass," Mark said.

Amos searched Mark's friendly face and did not care
for what he saw. "Oh, this is going to be harassment-and-
silly-interruptions morning, is it?"

"Gentlemen!" Judge Fickett said in her best mother-hen
manner.

Amos forced his attention back to his witness. "Will you tell the jury, in terms they can understand, what your examination of Miss Naismith showed, and what you did. If anything."

"My examination showed that she was in danger of imminent abortion. There was excessive bleeding, and she complained of colicky pains. Also the cervix was patulous."

"The cervix was . . .?"

"Patulous. It was open." In his rigidity, even the expression lines on Snowdom's face were eradicated. He called to mind a glove stretched over a hand a size too large. "After my first examination I administered fifteen milligrams of morphine subcutaneously."

"You mean you gave her a shot to ease her pain?"

Mark's voice more or less ambled into the cozy conversation between Amos and his witness. "Mr. Slake, let the witness say why he gave the shot. Don't testify for him."

"Oh, for a flyswatter," Amos said directly to Mark, and immediately asked of Snowdown, "What did you do next?"

"I packed the vagina, hoping to decrease the bleeding. I then had her placed in a private room with my head nurse, Miss Pritchard, in attendance. Then, as the bleeding increased to an alarming degree, I prepared to force the expulsion of the ovum. My second examination revealed that the cervix was not only patulous but effaced. I was convinced that abortion was inevitable, that the fetus was dead and already detached, or partially so, because the trophoblast had since ceased functioning."

"Will you tell the jury what all that means?"

"I'm interested too," Mark said clearly, and won a wide smile, his first, from the entire jury.

"It means that there was no saving the fetus—the unborn, unformed child. And that an abortion, or expulsion of the fetus was already in progress."

"Now, then, Doctor, when you made these examinations, did you see any—uh—" Amos could not but glance quickly at Mark, expectant that however he phrased his question Mark would object, or—worse—interject one of his negligent instructions telling Amos how to conduct his case. "Did you notice any other condition? Other than the imminent abortion, I mean?"

"I observed a small rupture in the wall of the vagina."

"Could this rupture have been associated with the imminent abortion?"

"It could have."

"And how is that?"

"During pregnancy, any injury—even coitus—may bring on abortion."

"Coitus? Tell the jury what—"

"That means the act of sexual intercourse."

"And if that act of sexual intercourse were violent, or forceable?"

"It might readily bring on abortion."

"How about the introduction of foreign objects into the birth canal?"

"I would not advise it during pregnancy," Snowdom said in all seriousness. "Except," he hastened to add, "where a physician is conducting a routine examination as to the course of the pregnancy."

"Yes, but suppose a foreign object such as ice or pieces—"

"No foundation," Mark said lazily.

"Sustained," came in a chirp from Her Honor.

"Could the penis of a male human have produced such a rupture?" Amos shouted, wheeling to glare at Forbes.

"Yes."

Forbes' unflagging melancholy composure was intact. He was less The Feeb this morning than a well-bred child required to erase from the washroom walls words he himself had not written there.

Mark did not bother to look up at Amos, serenely continuing taking notes decorated with deltas and X's and initials.

"What then did you do?"

"I emptied the uterus of its contents. That is, with an instrument known as a dilator I expanded the cervix and uterus. Then with a curette I scraped the walls of the uterus and removed the fetus and secundines."

"Again in plain language, Doctor?"

"I removed the fetus and other products of pregnancy. I then administered two tenths of a milligram of ergonovine."

"Is that the customary procedure and medication in such a case?"

"Yes."

"Now, Doctor, I want to be absolutely clear on this. The deceased was aborting at the time she was brought into your care?"

"Yes."

"Would it have been possible for you to have preserved the unborn child by any method?"

"No. Moreover, I had to act as I did in the attempt to save the life of the patient herself. Otherwise she would have bled to death."

"And of what did she die?"

"Septicemia. Blood poisoning."

"Is there any treatment for blood poisoning?"

"Only supportive measures. That means bed rest, and good nutrition. Sedatives and analgesics, of course, to make the patient more comfortable. It's up to the patient, really. Whether she can fight off the bacteriemia. The deceased could not. She succumbed."

"The doctor is helpless?"

"Unfortunately, yes."

"One last question. If I were to tell you that— No, strike that. Could whatever it was that caused the rupture in the vaginal wall also have been responsible for the imminent abortion?"

"Oh, yes. I would say that I firmly believe it was responsible."

"Thank! You!" Head on high, Amos bellowed to Mark, "Your witness! Crossss-eggsamine?"

"If you're sure you won't mind," Mark drawled diffidently.

"This court," Her Honor decided, "is adjourned until one-thirty this afternoon."

Dammit, Mark thought, now Snowdom has an hour and a half to go over his testimony with Amos and chink up the weak spots. Be that as it may, that last statement of his was so damaging that I'll have to ruin him to remedy it.

At lunch in their private booth, Mr. Pentlove dallied with his turtle soup and cast a lacklustre eye on his lobster. Mark laced his soup with liquor and bemoaned his fate. "If I'd known they were going to have turtle soup I'd have filled my flask with sherry."

"Where is that bumptious crook of a Castle?" Mr. Pentlove asked.

"Rookie? Tracking down a lady named Mrs. Foley."

"Oh, yes. So is Savant." Mr. Pentlove toyed with the silver. "Slake made quite a showing this morning, D'Andor. What do you think?"

"Yes, he did himself proud. The only thing he neglected to establish was that Snowdom did not contribute to the death, or bring it on, by his own poor surgical technique or carelessness. But then, Amos is hoping I'll do that for him by hammering on that very point during my cross-examination. He's taking a gamble, but the odds are all in his favor. For all our boning up on medical books, we lawyers are no match for doctors. Amos knows that the deeper I become entangled in the thick undergrowth of medical terminology, the closer I'll come to proving his case for him. I could easily get so snarled up that I'd end by proving to the jury's satisfaction that The Feeb killed Naismith by inoculating her with smallpox."

"You exaggerate," Mr. Pentlove said with little conviction.

"Some."

"What are you going to do?"

"Why, I'm going to smash his life. I'm going to impugn his integrity, blacken his reputation, and attempt to impeach him in a completely illegal, unethical, and unspeakable way."

"Happy to hear it," Mr. Pentlove said. His appetite suddenly returned and he ate heartily.

Returning to the courtroom, Mark asked himself again the question that was one of the imponderables of a trial lawyer's life. How do the spectators manage to sit from morn until dusk in the precious seats, sans the severest necessities of life? Food they came supplied with, but the stomach's loudest screams can never drown out the steady, ominous demands of the bladder. I must ask Amos if he knows the answer, Mark promised himself.

As if summoned by Mark's thought, Amos came strutting in. The expression *full of beans* might have been coined, to the glory of the English language, simply to describe Mr. Slake. Behind him, brittle as a walking stick, came Snowdom.

Mark said to Amos, "And did we enjoy our NeHi?"

"Why a soak like you is permitted to practice," Amos said without rancor, "is beyond me. You're bringing on your own ruination, you know." He took his place.

"Better," Mark said, with an eye to Snowdom, "than having someone do it for you."

When Snowdom had resumed the stand, Mark rose slumberously and regarded his victim with a pleasant impersonal smile. Snowdom's pewter gaze was unwavering. Do your damnedest, his face said, but you'll not get me to cringe before a drunken wreck.

Mark set himself to take the doctor at his unspoken challenge. "Now, sir, did I understand you to say you graduated from Howard University?"

Amos was on his feet. "Your Honor, the time to question the qualifications of this witness would have been in *voir dire* before the direct. Mr. D'Andor—"

From over the bench drifted, "Mr. Slake, I do not understand your heated objections. Counsel is only asking what was covered in the direct. Continue, Mr. D'Andor."

"Will you answer me please, Doctor?" Mark said.

"All right, I did graduate from Howard University!"

Amos sat down as if felled by a blow, while the jury obviously wondered what had Mr. Slake so fussed, the witness so defiant, and the usually sweet-dispositioned Mr. D'Andor as determined and deadly as a cobra.

The time for the kill was at hand. Mark had only to ask: And is that not an educational institution for Negroes, Doctor?

"And is that—" Mark began, met Snowdom's eyes bright with pain, and thought: The hell with it, I'm not an executioner. "Is Howard University an accredited school?"

"It is."

"Was it a part of your training to learn how to perform abortions?"

Snowdom looked as if he had not heard Mark aright.

"Well, Doctor?"

Snowdom's lids dropped over the pewter eyes. "We were —we devoted an hour's lecture to the techniques."

"Isn't it in the fourth year of medical schooling that students are introduced into the surgical theatre?"

"Yes."

"And during your fourth year did you assist in the performance of an abortion?"

"No."

"Did you witness the performance of one?"

"No."

"And when you graduated from medical school, did you not tell us that you served an internship at an accredited hospital?"

"I did."

"And did you at any time during your internship assist at or perform an abortion?"

"No."

"Nor so much as witness one?"

"No. I— In a way."

"In what way?"

"A woman was brought in who had undergone illegal surgery. The abortion was incomplete, there was copious bleeding, and it was necessary to remove the secundines."

"In language we can all understand, please, doctor."

"Well, the retained products of conception had to be expelled."

"You mean like debris?"

"I suppose you could put it that way."

"And if these—ah—secundines, this debris, was not removed, what then? Would there be danger of infection?"

"Oh yes." In his relief Snowdom was growing careless.

"Would you say the danger of infection could be as high as one hundred per cent?"

"Very nearly."

"Would you say that if this debris were not completely

removed from the uterus of the woman that it would be a miracle if she didn't get an infection?"

Snowdom laughed. "If that's what you could call it. Actually, miracles—are rather out of my line, Mr. D'Andor."

"To be sure. But the infection which would undoubtedly follow an incomplete removal of this debris, would it be septicemia?"

"Why—yes."

"That ought to do it," Mark said pleasantly. "Thank you, Doctor." He sat down.

Amos blinked and swallowed exactly as if his Adam's apple were stuck in his craw. He was presented with several possible courses of action. He could make Snowdom appear to be the most proficient, the niftiest little abortionist this side of San Quentin Penitentiary. Or he could, as a desperate measure, lead the jury to think Muffin Naismith was beyond repair before Snowdom so much as touched her with an instrument, which would necessitate proving the unprovable —that the infection had set in at some time prior to the surgery, and, moreover, could still be attributable to felonious acts on the part of Forbes. Or he could dwell lovingly on the battered condition of Muffin Naismith when first she was brought in for Snowdom's ministrations. This Amos did. But the heart of his witness was not in it. Mark thought of him as a man riddled with relief. When the afternoon lacked a few minutes of being four-thirty, Amos asked his last question. "Doctor, your conscience is completely clear on the subject of Miss Naismith's death, is it not?"

A bemused Dr. Snowdom muttered, "Oh, yes, yes."

"I was positive of it!" Amos informed the jury ringingly.

It would seem that the jury took something less than an all-engrossing interest in the convictions of T. Amos Slake. And Mark, who was at this point too sober to be riled, merely mentioned that Amos be directed to save his oratory for his closing statement. Her Honor nodded, then adjourned.

His client again in custody, Mark repaired to a pay phone in the lobby. Rookie's phone rang and rang, unattended. Mark emerged from the booth to discover Mr. Pentlove, Chester, Dr. Snowdom, and Chico rather milling about one another in a pocket-size mob.

Dr. Snowdom pressed forward to pin Mark against the booth. "Sir, you are," he said to Mark in a throbbing voice, "a man of honor and good will. Mr. Dander told me that you would not violate a confidence, and Mr. Dander was right."

"Oh, Chester's usually right as rain," Mark said, a touch embarrassed.

Chester put in jovially, "A really top-notch cross-examination, Mark! You all but hacked Snowdom to pieces."

"Oh, thank you," Mark said feebly, beset with the horrifying suspicion that Snowdom might at any moment burst into tears or vent some other expression of gratitude and relief.

"Does any of this make sense?" Mr. Pentlove wished to know of the phone booth. "When I want to hire someone of honor and good will I invariably find me a Salvation Army lass. D'Andor, will you be so good as to tell me what this is——" But he was not allowed to finish, for Chester and Snowdom were industriously shaking hands all around and mouthing glad farewells.

Chico now took her turn. "Well, Counsel, if Mr. Slake has a girl who comes a country mile of being Miss Baines in the cooler, then I quit the legal business. Just the same old sluts and winos. Oh, and a poor little thing who tried to kill her husband. Her father owns a grocery business, so there's a fat fee there. Want her?"

"Not with this case on my hands," Mark said. "Thanks anyway, Chico."

Chico nodded. "I'll probably send her to Grossman. He's a square-shooter." A slight impatience on Mark's part put Chico back on the subject to hand. "And I don't think Baines is in Boyle or Lincoln either. I asked the batch that come upstairs this afternoon, and they said nobody answering to that description around. Same for the Hollywood bunch."

"Nice try just the same, Chico," Mark said, depressed and needing a drink.

"And do you know what?" Chico exploded to a startled Mr. Pentlove, striking him in the chest with a powerful swarthy swat. "The judge fined me fifty dollars! For malicious mischief. Can you tie that?"

Righting himself, and without comment other than a

sigh, Mr. Pentlove took out his remaining fifty-dollar bill and handed it to Chico.

"So thanks," Chico said. Thumping Mark on the back, she cried, "Well, off to see if Grossman wants the little Ay Dee Double-you."

"And what is that?" Mr. Pentlove asked.

"Assault with a deadly weapon; what did you think?" Chico replied, and was off.

Mr. Pentlove was pensive. Finally he roused. "Did that loud-mouthed peculiar woman really put a brick through Mr. Slake's windshield?"

"I've no idea," Mark said.

"Then just what did that peculiar woman do to earn my hundred dollars?"

"She found out something for me."

"Ah? And what was that?"

"Nothing," Mark said. "Dammit, exactly nothing."

"D'Andor, I do not wish to detain you further from your bottle, but would you tell me one more thing?"

"If I am able."

"Does Amos Slake think he can convict The Feeb?"

"No. Especially if I can think of a way of keeping Forbes off the witness stand."

"But the law doesn't say he has to testify in his defense, does it?"

"No, the law does not. But I've got to find a way for him to avail himself of silence and still not appear to be afraid of taking the stand. You must understand that my best chance of winning is through destroying Slake's witnesses. Slake knows he can't convict The Feeb. He's waiting for my defense, to see if I'll do it for him."

Mr. Pentlove said calmly, "See that you don't," and he too was on his way, and Mark's private little mob was thus dispersed.

Mark thought: Easier said than done, dear Pentlove, with Amos hiding witnesses, hoping to take me by surprise.

CHAPTER TWENTY-FIVE

And so that question, perhaps as vital as the breath of life to The Feeb, still went unanswered. Driving westward, thinking of the coolness of the hills and a tepid tub, and grumbling to himself that the least Snowdom could have done would have been to offer to buy him a drink, Mark sank a sounding into his memories of the near and late past of Pep Baines. He resolved to call 'Melia or, failing to be put through to that sacred ear, present himself at her door and force his way into her sacred presence. Nor was Mark above threatening the good lady to tell Seymour Pentlove certain facts that would make delicious Sunday polo chatter for weeks to come. For 'Melia and Fritzie had been important figures in Pep's past.

Of 'Melia's existence he had been aware for some years, because of Pep, but of late the lady, having grown old and seclusive, was mentioned in the press (reverently) only when she appeared at the Bowl with a few select guests, or sponsored a ball to collect funds to be donated to Unwed Mothers or other societal miscreants.

Of 'Melia, though, little or nothing had been said the night, several years earlier, that Mark presented himself at the apartment in which Fritzie had established Pep and her infant son. Just a block from the Boulevard, the brick-faced building with its leaded panes in the windows had that stolid air of being in good taste. It defied the years to cheapen it as they would the French chateau on the left and the Tudor inn to its right. Pep's mailbox showed her to be on the sixth floor, the choice location. There was no seventh.

The elevator door opened to show a foyer complete with

a vase of sand for cigarette butts, a lone gilt chair, and a moderne umbrella stand with a copper basin for the collection of moisture. Two doors faced each other at opposite ends of the foyer, and Mark, searching in vain for a bell on Pep's, finally thundered with the knocker. Within he could hear a phonograph playing "Yes, Sir, She's My Baby." Pep was singing along with it, changing the gender of the baby, and there were occasional screams of near-unutterable bliss from an unseen infant.

Tiring of the music, Mark tried the door, found it unlocked, and entered. Pep, in lounging pajamas, was squatting on the floor dandling quite the largest baby Mark had ever seen. When the record was at an end, Mark said, "Hey, lady, betcha a drink you can't give me the full name of Rudolph Valentino."

"Bagel!" Pep shrieked.

"That was not one of his names, lady. You owe me a drink."

Yelping happily, Pep left the baby on the floor and came to divest Mark of his hat, kiss him gustily, and manhandle him generally in her hospitable efforts to make him comfortable. Shoving him onto a couch, she prattled, "Take a load off your feet, sweetie, while I put the monster to bed. Then I'll be right back."

"And bring a drink with you, for the love of Allah, effendi," Mark said. He grinned to see her catch up the enormous baby with its orange hair and sling it on her hip. She strode from the room and he was left to himself. Himself and himself, repeated over and over in mirrors everywhere about the room. Having only the vaguest notion of what the back of his head looked like, he was now fascinated with this proffered view of himself. The rims of his ears bore slight depressions somewhat as if, like automobile tires, they had gone flat.

"Yes, Bagel, you're beautiful as ever," Pep assured him, coming in with a seltzer bottle, glasses, and two dimity cocktail napkins embroidered with pink elephants. Plumping herself next him she said, "You look tired. How've you been?"

"Oh, I keep occupied. I have my divorces and my bookies and my hoods, and they comfort me. And lately I've had a run of what my secretary knowingly calls 'lood vagues.' "

"Say, that's a new one on me. Is it fun?"

"Lewd vagrancy? Its devotees seem to find it a real picnic. And hold the seltzer," Mark tacked on hastily. "Three fingers, please. Any ice?"

"This whiskey one doesn't drink with ice, Fritzie tells me."

"I stand corrected."

They clinked glasses and in the mirrors any number of Marks and Peps saluted their populous selves. "And how's the world treating you, Pep?"

"Scrumptious. Too scrumptious. I'm settling down and putting on weight."

"You're not pregnant again?" he inquired chattily.

"God, no. Fritzie shot his wad."

"Quite a wad," Mark approved. "That kid's not a year old, is he?"

"Eight months."

"He's the biggest kid in Christendom."

"*Oiy veh!*" Pep chortled. "Wait'll I tell Fritzie that." She mused into her drink. "But I am happy, Mark. Mebbe too happy. It takes the starch out of you, did you know that? Take the other day. I suddenly realized that I was using my shot glass for an egg cup."

"Over the hill at twenty-four," Mark sympathized. "Pep, you are taken care of, aren't you? Fritizie's not a fourflusher, is he?"

"God, no. Mr. Fuddy-Duddy drew up more trusts for Junior than you can shake a stick at. I got one too. Only thing—I can't get married. Mr. Fuddy-Duddy had me sign a paper I wouldn't. Fritzie was afraid my husband would go loco over the kid."

"Understandable," Mark said. "Only what I think he had in mind was that no husband of yours should stand in *loco parentis* to Junior. That is, have the boy growing up to look on your husband as his father."

Pep tossed off her drink and bet Mark a kiss he couldn't give the second-to-last name of Valentino. He lost and paid his debt with the luxurious moan of a weary man sinking into bed. Pep drew back and eyed him in concern. "Hey, aren't the girls in this town treating you right?"

"They share a common failing; they're not you."

"Huh. Where's Dolly Dimple these days? I mean Muffin."

"Last I heard she was getting groomed for stardom," Mark said with a clear conscience. "The well-known Manny Amen has taken her in hand."

"Oh, uh-huh. Isn't that swell," Pep murmured, politely trying to conceal that she was dubious of Muffin's silver-screen potentialities. "Anyway," Pep said brightly, "she wasn't for you. I always thought of her as being too bitchy for the long haul, if you don't mind my saying so. I'll be in the movies myself in about a year or two. Fritzie and 'Melia don't want the baby to have a full-time nursemaid before then, and I wouldn't hear of it anyway." She began kissing him with enthusiasm. "Gee, I'm glad you dropped in, Mark. I was lonely."

"Me too."

Pep held his head on her full bosom. "Mark, you getting over your wife a little?"

"It— She . . . Let us say I've become accustomed to missing her."

"Bagel," Pep said tenderly, "let us go into the bedroom and me haul your lonesome ashes for you." She begun undoing his vest.

The great orange-haired baby slumbered in its blue bassinet undisturbed. Mark fell by Pep's side to complain joyously, "God, you're a strenuous strumpet!"

"I got all this excess energy," Pep admitted modestly.

In her bedroom there were also mirrors everywhere, except for the expected pictures of teddy bears, clowns, and a Little Bo Peep in bas-relief with a real organdy skirt and a real-ribbon bow tied on her crook. "This place doesn't make sense," Mark decided.

Pep took umbrage. "Fritzie had the best decorator in town fix my apartment. In case you don't know, mirrors are ultra this year."

"I do think your Bo Peep is the last word," Mark conceded. He rose to an elbow, pondering. "D'you think I should get one for my office?"

"Goof!" Pep yipped. "Oh, why don't you come round more often?"

"Dunno. Then I could fall in love with you."

Pep stretched. "You know, I've wondered about that. Why haven't you?"

"Guess I never got around to it."

"Like we never got around to going to a real bang-up funeral. Remember?"

"The minute you hear of anything big doing in that line, you come to my office, or house, any hour of the day or night. Promise?" Mark ordered sternly.

"Promise," Pep said. "I'll be the weeping lady with the red nose."

She was that and more when, some months later, she appeared in Mark's octagon office. Pep's hair was in disarray, her nose on fire with anguish, and there was a ladder up the front of one silk stocking. For an instant Mark seriously thought she had been hit by an automobile. He put her in a chair, put a drink down her, and asked anxiously, "Pep, dear, is anything broken?"

"My heart!" Pep bawled without hesitation. "She wants my baby. 'Melia wants to adopt my baby."

"Tell 'Melia to shinny up a tree," Mark said. "And blow your nose."

Pep continued to sob at a steady pace.

After a time Mark said uneasily, "Is there an alternative, Pep? Is there? What is it?"

"Fritzie will get the court to declare me an unfit mother. He said I was a d-dissolute woman. Like one of your vaguely lewds, I guess he meant. And then he'd ask the court to give him custody of Junior."

"The son of a bitch, he can't———"

Pep laid her cheek against Mark's thigh, clutching his coattails. "He's got pictures of me. H-hundreds of them. That's why all those mirrors. So's the cameras always had something to shoot. One camera was in B–Bo Peep," Pep howled, then paused in her weeping out of sheer awe at the enormity of it. "All kinds of pictures. Fritzie's even got one of me using my eyecup."

"What?"

"My eyecup. It's this little blue glass thingamajig that you put eyewash in—"

"Pep, dear, we can go into that more fully some other time."

"—and then you clamp it over your eye," Pep plodded on, resuming crying her heart out, "and then you blink into it!"

"Thank you. That's a very useful piece of information. Good God, did you say Bo Peep?"

Pep nodded her head, staining his trousers with tears, and wailed afresh.

"He has pictures of you in the bedroom with men?" Mark attempted to lift Pep's chin but she resisted, rolling her head on his thigh. "And the boy? Where is he?"

"In his c-crib. Sometimes . . . standing up," Pep wept.

"Who— I mean, how many men?"

Pep ran a forefinger over each cheekbone to wipe away the mascara streaks. "Five. Not—including you."

"Pep, dearest, when the boy was old enough to look on, you should have put him in another room!"

"Oh, thanks *ever* so for the advice," Pep snarled morosely.

"How about Fritzie's support of you and Junior? I suppose he gave you checks?"

Pep admitted it. "With little bitty teeny words in the left corner. They said, 'For the support of my son,' and then Junior's name."

"And what is Junior's name? Fritzie Baines?"

"Hell, no," Pep gulped. "Fritzie and 'Melia saw to that. Even on the birth certificate. Same as his old man's, what else?"

"But surely you pointed out to Fritzie and 'Melia that if they try to drag you into court, Junior will learn about it when he grows up. That he'll find out they tried to have his mother branded as a lewd and—"

"That's the first thing I thought of," Pep sobbed. Her voice rose to a yell, "And do you know what 'Melia, that pious 'Melia, said to me? She said, 'That's your funeral.'"

"Oh, Pep!" Mark said softly and kissed the top of her head. He called out for his secretary to come take care of Pep; he would be gone for a short while.

Mark drove to the Beverly Hills office of Fritzie's fuddy-duddy attorney in fourteen minutes. Invited to cool his heels in that august gentelman's outer office after announcing his name, Mark strode instead into the holy of holies, slamming the door behind him.

Mr. Fuddy-Duddy looked up in mild reproof from a single sheet of paper which lay on his otherwise barren expanse of desk. "Ah, D'Andor, I believe it is?"

Mark walked to the desk and laid his knuckles on it so that he had the pose of a gorilla. "It is beyond my powers of comprehension," he began shakily, "how any attorney could stoop—"

"There repose in a safe-deposit box," the dignified attorney cut in, "affidavits and photographs which will strongly support the contention that Miss Baines is, and was, engaged in the gainful occupation of prostitution."

"With whom—Fritzie?"

"The affidavits are those of men commonly called 'Johns.' Or so I am told. The term means—"

"I know what it means. And I suffer from no misapprehension that Fritzie couldn't find any number of would-be actors who would be only too willing to perjure themselves. To prove how talented they are by vilifying Miss Baines."

"So you see!" the fuddy-duddy attorney said blandly, spreading his hands, his amour-propre secure. "There is nothing to be gained by litigation, D'Andor. Besides, we must consider the child. The adoptive parents will give the little tyke all the advantages, the love, the education, a fitting place in society, that the heart of a mother could wish for her child. And as the boy will at last be under the roof of his true father, acknowledged heir not only of a fortune but of a name honored throughout the Industry and banking circles in New York—"

"Balls," Mark said, interrupting the graceful peroration. "What's your proposition?"

"Miss Baines will want for nothing as long as she lives. Preferably she will take up residence in some other—"

"Miss Baines' signature on the adoption papers will cost

your client one hundred thousand dollars. Along with a ten-year contract with the studio for two-fifty a week—to start. And Miss Baines will not leave town unless she so chooses. She will be permitted to see the boy at reasonable and regular intervals."

"I think we can come to a meeting of the minds on all but the visitation right. On that point I beg you to reconsider. Miss Baines herself would suffer the most."

"Let's get back to the money," Mark said.

The dignified attorney lifted his upper lip. "Your client is quite the 'gimme' girl, if I may say so."

"You may not. And that crack will cost your client another ten grand."

Mark's colleague did not think so. "I have been authorized to go as high as fifty thousand dollars."

"A wad sufficient to choke a horse," Mark admitted. "But I am certain that Fritzie would have no difficulty whatsoever in shoving it—"

"Seventy-five," the dignified attorney said in haste, lest Mark's observations soil his ears.

"Keep braying," Mark said.

His colleague did not pretend to misunderstand. "You impress me as taking this matter rather personally, Mr. D'Andor."

"I am indeed. I like Miss Baines. If she's ever done a cruel or selfish thing, then it's a closely guarded secret from me."

"The photo of you with Miss Baines," the attorney said in a confidential purr, "is scarcely recognizable. It was only after I was informed as to who the—ah—subjects were that I discerned that it was you. I do hope, though, that that little remark of mine will not cost my client another ten thousand?"

"Of course not," Mark said reasonably. "Laymen have no concern with the respect we brothers of the bar automatically grant one another." He scanned every lineament of the face opposite him. The man had a fine-turned head and a careful way with his facial expressions, totally eschewing grimaces or other unappealing revelations of emotion. "And you think the photo of myself and Miss Baines is the source of my anger?" Mark said. "Why Sir, when I meet up with folk like Fritzie and 'Melia and you, I feel like asking to be scratched from the human race. One hundred thousand dollars and the ten-year contract, if you please. Are we agreed?"

"My hand on it," Mark's colleague said, rising and extending that elegant and immaculate object.

Mark thrust his hands into his pockets. "I will expect all necessary papers and money on my desk in the morning." It was the first time in his life that Mark had ever treated scum like scum, and he was most uncomfortable in the doing of it. "Good day," he said brusquely and stalked out.

As soon as Pep saw Mark stepping out of the elevator she said in a ragged voice, "Well, it's the handwriting on the wall, huh, Bagel?" Her manner was considerably calmed, though her eyes threatened another cloudburst of tears at any moment.

"You'll be a comparatively rich woman," Mark said. "And you'll have a fat and unbreakable movie contract."

"Oh, hot dog for our side," Pep said in despair.

"It's not the pictures alone, Pep. Fritzie has half the bit players in town lined up to swear that you're a prostitute. So you've got just one out. Marry me. And I'll adopt the boy. Or try."

Pep hurled herself at Mark. "You wonderful kind adorable precious angel!"

"I'm glad you finally perceive my true worth. We still have time to get the license today if you shake a leg, Pep."

Pep went back to her chair, her forced smile the most moving exhibition of bravery he had ever beheld. "It won't work. And it isn't as if 'Melia doesn't simply worship Junior. She's got storks in her chimney over him. And if you tried to adopt my kid, Fritzie would smear you from hell to breakfast."

"Oh, I don't know," Mark said airily. "I'm not without friends in this town. Seymour Pentlove—"

"Seymour Pentlove," Pep took up, smiling and smiling, "wouldn't let you hold his horse for him. Unless the cops were to scoop up his million-dollar baby, his sweet Feeb. And besides. . . ." Like the lovely phenomenon of sunshine glinting on rain, tears began running into Pep's smile. "Besides, Mark, Fritzie would never give up. And I refuse to take advantage of your—kindness—the way that awful Muffin did. And . . . and you drink, Mark, darling. They could use that against us, I know. We're licked, amigo."

"Pep, we can try!"

She shook her head. "Just tell me one thing," she said, making a painful attempt of speaking in a light conversational tone.

"Yes?"

"You know the handwriting on the wall? What was it anyway?"

"Why—It's from the Bible. And it's *Mene, mene, tekel, upharsin.*"

"Is that a fact?" Pep marveled, tears showering on her fiercely sunny smile. "And here I thought it was Aimee Semple McPherson."

The recollection was no help in trying to decipher where Amos Slake might be hiding Pep now. Driving up the winding roads to his house, Mark thought: Too bad neither Pep nor I was invited to Fritzie's funeral. It was reported to be the poshest event of the season. Invitation or no, he had tried to reach Pep in her new apartment. Time and again he had come to bang on her door. He could not rid himself of the disquieting suspicion that she was huddled within, staring endlessly at the newspaper pictures of the bereaved 'Melia and her little son.

Coming round the last curve, Mark saw Pep leaning against his door exactly as if she were a delivery from his bootlegger.

Unlocking the door for her, Mark said, "Don't tell me Amos let you out to play!"

"Naw. I sneaked out. What'll we play?"

"Hell, I'm afraid."

Preceding him down the stair, Pep said, "That listens like fun." The curling plume on her Empress Eugènie hat (a lavender one this time, to match her dress) clashed with her hair and was, because of this discord, somehow completely dashing.

"Are you paying off an election bet, by any chance?" Mark asked mildly. "Wherever do you find those noisy hats? I always like your lids."

She grinned over her shoulder at him, then went without hesitation to the left and into the darkened living room. She paused long enough to write *Dust me* on the table bearing the ugly art-nouveau lamp, then continued to the windows— where she yanked the curtains open, hung on their black spears, and stood looking out to the hills covered with dry brush tinged with the same lavender as her plume. Not turning, she said, "I could make good use of a drink, Bagel."

He hastened to the kitchen cupboard, obligingly open, seized glasses, liquor, and (thoughtful host) dumped the last of some stale pretzels (he had decided his 'coons needed salt) into a bowl.

He rejoined Pep, now seated on the couch looking about her critically.

"I've torn this town apart looking for you," Mark said. "Where've you been?"

"Obispo Hotel. For a while I had that pill, Adele Tobino, for a roommate. Like living with a drillmaster, you know? She all but blew a whistle for me to brush my teeth. Am I glad her testimony is over. How'd she do?"

"So so. We had the customary dogfight." Mark hit himself on the forehead with his fist. "The Obispo! God, wait 'till Pentlove learns T. Amos is using that for his cooler. But tell me, Pep, how did you manage to escape the boys in blue?"

"The cops? Easy. The maid snuck me out. We kind of struck up a friendship 'cause we both like you."

Mark was at once wrapped in his practiced lethargy. "She must be a lovely girl. A regular tiger for good taste in men. Do I know her?"

Pep looked at him blankly. "Sweetie! She was a witness."

"Oh yeah," Mark said lazily. "I thought she worked at the Eden."

"She did. But it seems that the Obispo management made her such a handsome offer to come work for them she couldn't refuse."

"I imagine not," Mark murmured. He rubbed his hands

together. "Well! I'm neglecting my duties. Have a pretzel." He began to pour their drinks.

"Make mine light," Pep said. "I don't want to have to face T. Amos polluted when I get back. Mark, you're letting this nice dump go to rack and ruin."

"How do you know? You've never been here before. G'wan eat those pretzels, like I told you. And drink your drink. And give us a kiss. And spill your guts; that's what you came for, isn't it?"

Pep leaned against him in a manner almost marital and, easing off her pumps, propped up her feet. "Now then," she said in a comfy voice, "tell me what you've been up to these days. Any interesting lawsuits or such like that?"

"Naw. Whachew been doin'?"

She rattled the ice in her glass reflectively. It was all Mark could do, sensitive as he was to that particular sound, not to snap at her. "Well, you know how it is," Pep said idly. "Waiting my turn in court, I've got in lots of reading. And, oh, guess what? I got a movie that's going to be premeered next Tuesday."

"You don't say!"

"I've got three whole lines in this one. Would you care for a private preview?"

"I'm agog."

Pep thrust out her chest and chin, placing her arms akimbo. "Oh yeah?" She waited for his reaction. "That was my first line," she said in a tone of command.

Mark bestirred himself. "Oh. Excuse me!" He applauded wildly.

"That's my second line, too," Pep said modestly. "But I say it so different you'd never know it for the same one."

"I'm sure not."

"Here's my third. 'I was coming from the parking lot when I heard some woman crying out in pain and pleading with someone to stop.' "

"Oh, that is a good line, isn't it."

"I'll say!"

"Under oath?"

Pep took a sip of her drink and then began making designs in the sweat on her glass. Mark held himself in abeyance, sensing that she was undecided just how much she wanted to reveal. Reaching her decision, Pep said softly, "And then a man said 'your bastard.' I know everybody else thinks he was calling *her* one. But I'm an expert on the subject of bastards, you know. He was saying *your* all right, all rightie." Again she fell silent, while Mark tried to recollect ever having heard Pep sound sardonic before now. When she resumed speaking she pitched her voice to a light high note, as if they were conducting a cocktail flirtation. "Funny, you know? Us, I mean. The way we met. And all."

"Yes. Looking back I wonder that there wasn't a fanfare at the very least." He thought himself feebly humorous.

"I guess there never is. People who are going to be important to each other never know it. A guy meets a girl he's going to marry, or kill, or something, and he says, 'How do you do.' I mean really, Mark, I'm serious. Like f'rinstance some dame says, 'I hadda date last night with some jerky bit player with a name as long as a snake.' "

"Ending in Valentino? I'm beginning to catch your drift, though."

"Or you take—— Well, like somebody says, 'Mr. De Mille, have you met God?' And they just shake hands and don't think another thing about it."

"That's a very salutary and uplifting thought, Pep."

Again she fell to tracing designs on her glass. Mark dared not so much as offer to freshen her drink or pour himself another, which he very much wanted. At last Pep was ready to unburden herself; he knew it a pulse-stroke before she looked him squarely in the eye. "Mark, you are a stinker! You make me want to vomit!"

"Very well, I'm a cad, and you feel nauseated. What's next on the agenda?"

"Don't you know what The Feeb did to poor little Betty Boop? Is there a girl in town under sixty who doesn't know that he goes after a woman with the first thing that comes to hand? Except the thing he should?"

"Have you ever been with him?"

Pep moved her shoulders as if she were chilly. "God, no! I don't want a bottle or whatever he happens to pick on—"

"Now, Pep, I have the affidavit of a man who was there, who swears there were no bottles in that bed—"

"*Affadavuts!*" Pep shrilled. "Don't talk to me of affadavuts! I got my belly fulla them with Fritzie. God, you slept with little ol' cupcake, Mark; how can you ever sleep again, doing what you're doing? I never saw her more'n six times in my whole life, and I wanted to throttle her when I did, but I'm still sorry for her. And as for you! Why, she sat right over there and—"

"What!"

Pep pointed to one of Constance's needlepoint chairs. "She sat right there, and I was where I am now. And we talked. She had a key made to this house. Didn't you know?"

"Of course not."

"Well, she did. What happened was. . . . It was this way," Pep said in the meditative voice of reminiscence. "I saw her once walking up the Boulevard around dusk. Early this year, I think it was. I was just getting into my car. There was something about her. . . . She was looking up at the lights of your office. And you were standing at the window looking out, only I guess you couldn't see us. Then all of sudden she hopped a taxi. And for some nutsy reason—women always know when another is about to pull a fast one—I gunned the motor and followed her. I parked around the curve, and then I came up to her while she was opening the door. I asked in this joky voice when she'd taken up housebreaking. And so we went in together."

"But what in the hell was Muffin—"

Pep smiled. "Women are peculiar beasts. When they've got a man they don't think he's such a much. But let him get away and she decides she's madly in love with him. That was our Muffin to a *t*. It seems," Pep said, being most delicate for Pep, "that she had asked you to marry her, and you wouldn't. So she'd come up here and take a drink from your bottle, or go lie on your bed. And cry, I guess. You honestly didn't know someone had been in your house, Papa Bear?" Pep blurted out of sheer incredulity.

Mark could only shake his head.

"Well, that time I followed her up, she sat in that chair over there—"

"Stop pointing to that chair!" Mark burst out.

Pep shrugged. "Anyway, she did. And we had us a cozy girl-talk, and she blubbered a bit. I fed her a couple of stiff shots of your Irish and drove her home. She was living from hand to mouth in some fleabag hotel. She'd sold a car she had and was living off the proceeds. I tried to get her a job at the studio, but, hell, they're laying off people. Between radio on the one hand and the Depression on the other, movies are finding it slim pickings. So I slipped her a sawbuck or two and let it go. Then she hit the skids, and she hit 'em fast. All a guy had to do was ask. Only thing—" Again Mark was confronted with the oddity of a sardonic Pep. "Only thing, she was kind of cracked. And when a dame who's half-cracked gets half-crocked—she gets notions. And that's it, Mark." Pep put her glass on the floor. "Any other long-range peeks into the past I can give you? I may not have had a front seat watching everything she did, but like they say, there's immediate seating in the balcony, and the view is just as good from there."

"Who got her pregnant?" Mark asked flatly.

"Are you sitting down?"

"What?"

Pep explained, "That's what the cops are supposed to say when they call you to tell you your husband's been run over—Are you sitting down?"

"Let me have it, Pep."

"Like I say, she was half-cracked. Every guy she slept with she'd call him Mark. And not the way I call every guy—" Pep's head was high, her gaze straight on "—I sleep with Bagel. So, I guess as far as she was concerned, you knocked her up, my friend."

When Mark said nothing, Pep added, "She died believing that, you know." And when Mark still did not speak, Pep said, "Boy and howdy, if I was wearing that look on my face, I'd break down and cry for a week." She took a gold compact from her purse and adjusted her plume to curl just so under her chin. She stood up and slipped into her pumps, and then pushed at Mark's foot with her toe as if she were tentatively poking at something repulsive to see if it were alive. "The one thing I haven't told T. Amos Slake, or anybody in the world, I'm going to tell you now. You can ask me about it under oath next time we meet. If you like. When I was walking past the back of the bungalow from the Eden parking lot I heard Muffin yell out your name. She yelled, 'No, no. It's Mark's.' That's when The Feeb was hurting her, shoving ice up her like Adele Tobino says and telling Muffin he'd fix her bastard for her. That's when she said it was yours." She stepped over Mark.

He caught her arm. "Pep, swear to me, swear to me that you *know* he put ice in her."

"I can't. I only know what I heard. I didn't see anything. Can you swear you didn't put that baby in her?"

"Yes, I can."

"Unhand me," Pep said grandly, then rubbed her wrist. "You know this business of introductions? I mean, how they simply don't cover the situation? I wonder how someone would have introduced us, if they'd known what we do now? Would they say, 'Miss Baines, meet the biggest drunken wreck in a town that mass produces them'?"

"That would do in a pinch."

Pep bent and kissed Mark on the temple. "Oh, Mark, sweetie, if you knew how I hate the high and mighty people of Hollywood! I'd do almost anything to pull just one of them back down in the gutter where they belong."

"Even if the only way you can get back at one of them is through me?"

Pep's laugh was ugly. "That's rich, isn't it? I have to hurt the best friend a girl could want, just to see to it that their pet swine gets what's coming to him. I hate 'em for what they did to me, but I'm beginning to hate 'em even more for what they've done to you. At least I'm fighting. But you, Mark, you've long since gone down for the count." She straightened and filled his glass to the very brim with Irish. Then she departed.

Mark sat on until it was dark and time to twist on the blue bulb. After that, lugging his drink around the room and swaying, he sobbed soggily to himself, "Show me the way to go home, I'm tired . . . I'm tired . . . I'm tired . . ."

CHAPTER TWENTY-SIX

"My name is Miss Pep Baines," Pep said somberly to T. Amos, in answer to his question. "I reside at the Grandeur Manor in Hollywood, and I'm an actress." She looked at Amos as if awaiting instructions from her director. Since her entrance into the courtroom she had not once turned her face in Mark's direction.

Amos led her to an accounting of her whereabouts on that Sunday in early October when Muffin Naismith first began her prolonged dying. "I was parking my car in the Eden," Pep said, and stroked her dancing plume to quiet it. "I decided to walk past the back bungalows and around the pool, rather than walk all around the block on the street. That's what I usually do when I'm meeting someone at the Eden for lunch or something."

"And did you pass the bungalows?"

"Yes. I walked between Ten and Eleven."

"What, if anything, did you hear or observe?"

"The kitchen door to Ten was open, and the back window to the bedroom was open about an inch or two. As I passed it, I heard a woman's voice inside. She was crying in a strange way and—"

"Objection," Mark said. "The witness is drawing a conclusion."

"I most certainly am not," Pep said, but to Amos.

Her Honor reared over the Codes. "Miss, when either attorney raises an objection, you are not to continue talking."

"Excuse me," Pep said with great dignity. "Only it so happens, Your Honor, that I know how Muffin Naismith usually sounded when she cried. And this wasn't her ordinary crying by a long shot."

Judge Fickett subjected Pep to a long scrutiny which Pep withstood with remarkable poise. "Hmmm," Her Honor said. "Mr. D'Andor, I will withhold my ruling on this point. Mr. Slake, you will develop this line of testimony."

Amos did so with alacrity. "Miss Baines, you were acquainted with Muffin Naismith?"

"Yes."

"Had you ever heard her cry, prior to the day of which we are speaking?"

"Several times. The last time she bawled her head off." Pep's eyes dwelt only on the eager visage of Amos, though her plume bobbed nervously.

"I wish to digress from this line of questioning for one moment," Amos said. "Miss Baines, were you subpoenaed to come to this court and testify?"

"No."

"How is it that you are here?"

"When I heard that Muffin Naismith was dead, I came to your office. I asked to testify." Now, for the first time, Pep turned her head and looked at Mark levelly.

"To continue, Miss Baines. Did you recognize the voice of the woman in Bungalow Ten as being that of Muffin Naismith?"

"Not—at— Not right away. The way she was crying was so gawdawful it sounded almost like a dog in pain."

"Did you hear any words?"

"Yes, I heard Muffin say, 'No, no.' Only it was like she was begging. And then I heard a man's voice."

"Could you distinguish—"

"Oh, sure. He said, 'Take care of your bastard.' He wasn't saying 'you bastard,' he was saying *your*—"

"What, if anything, did you do?"

"Heartless wench that I am," Pep announced, "I minded my own business."

Judge Fickett brushed her Codes aside impatiently to have a better view of this Miss Baines. The young shoe salesman on the jury set up his helpless giggling, while the retired minister appeared to approve of Pep's candor, and the grandmother juror found her disapproving attention to Pep's dress and hat diverted.

"Oh, I am sure nobody in this courtroom thinks you heartless, Miss Baines," Amos said fondly.

Mark got to his feet. "Mr. Slake is testifying again. Your Honor, I request that each and every person in this courtroom be sworn, so he or she may give his own opinion as to Miss Baines' heart, or lack of it."

Pep made the sad mistake of hooting at the very idea. Mark listened with evident enjoyment as Her Honor reprimanded Pep, reminding her that she was in a court of law, not on a sound stage. "As for you, Mr. D'Andor," Judge Fickett concluded, "there will be no more levity."

So there! Pep's grin said before she again bent on Amos her former somber gaze. But Judge Fickett was not done with Pep. "Miss, did these sounds and voices coming from the bungalow alarm you?"

"Well, Your Honor, it didn't sound like the woman was very happy about what was going on. Having ice—well, you know—having that done to her with ice."

"And how do you know that, Miss?"

Pep's earlobes, or the one not hidden by her plume, turned a shade less deep than fuchsia. "Actually, Ma'am, I did take one peek. I saw a man's back. And he was brandishing a piece of ice." Pep swallowed. "Only how was I to know he was *killing* her?"

Mark murmured, "Your Honor, I must submit that the witness' responses to your questions are rather—wide in scope."

"So they are," Her Honor agreed. "I will have that last statement stricken. Mr. Slake?"

Amos, who had been lovingly brooding on the jury with many a meaningful *moue* during the Court's examination of Pep, now sprang into vibrant action. "Miss Baines, did you recognize the man you saw in that bedroom?"

"Who else is that fat but The Feeb?" Pep asked reasonably.

"But did you?"

"I'd already recognized his voice, you see."

"Ah. And what next, if anything, did you see?"

"I saw my date."

"You saw . . .?"

"My date. My luncheon date. He was sitting in one of those deck chairs they have on boats on the other side of the pool, awaiting me. So I went on and joined him."

"Yes. And what next, if anything—concerning Miss Naismith, I mean—did you see?"

"Later on I looked out of the main dining room of the Eden and I saw three women in the shallow end of the pool. One of them was Muffin Naismith. The other girls were propping her up and walking her back and forth in the water. She was kind of sobbing. And that's the last I saw of anybody."

"Could you describe the two women?"

"Oh, sure. One was a blonde with those clocks tattooed on her ankles. And the other was a girl of about twenty-one with mousy hair—"

"*Mousy?*" Amos bleated.

"Yes, mousy, only it was dyed pink. She was trying to go Jean Harlow one better, by having her hair stripped platinum and then dyed——"

"Thank you, Miss Baines," Amos put in—rather jarred, it would seem, by his (or anyone's) inability to control the garrulous Miss Baines. "Cross-examine," he said to Mark.

"You bet I will," Mark murmured to Pep. He requested of Her Honor that he be allowed to approach the witness, as her hat obstructed his view; the request granted, he ambled around the counsel table. Watching him, Pep's expression softened; he was rumpled and so hung over that he actually appeared to be ill. "Miss Baines, you said that you were acquainted with Muffin Naismith?"

"Yes."

"You were friends?"

"Noooo. I just saw her around."

"You knew her well enough to know how she sounded crying?"

"You didn't have to know Muffin very well to know that," Pep said.

"Indeed? She cried a lot, then?"

Pep said bluntly, "Most girls in this town have reason to."

"And why is that?"

"Men," Pep spat.

"Men? Ah. You feel that men are unfair to women, Miss Baines?"

"On the whole," Pep said judiciously, "I find them preferable to crocodiles."

"Then you felt a—let us say—sistership or sympathy for Muffin Naismith?"

"I felt sorry as hell for her. Oops!"

"An understandable slip, Miss Baines. So when you heard that Miss Naismith was dead, you ran to Mr. Slake to see what you could do to punish some man for it?"

"Not *some* man. The Feeb!"

"Exactly. And that is why you were willing to swear you saw Archibald Forbes in that bedroom?"

"I saw his back, yes."

"Did you see the woman?"

"No, The Feeb's back was in my way."

"Like your bias, Miss Baines?"

"I don't know what you're talking about," Pep said loftily.

"Then your ignorance is total, because you don't know what you're talking about either."

Her Honor said, *"Counselor!"*

Mark's head was beginning to ache loudly. "When you were listening at the window of Bungalow Ten did you hear any names mentioned?"

"Yes," Pep said. She clutched her plume.

"What name or names?"

"I heard Miss Naismith say the name *Mark*."

"Did you hear her say *Feeb*?"

"No."

"Or Archibald?"

"Now, who's going to call a man Archibald when he's killing you with a shard of—"

"You answer my question, Miss Baines!"

"No," Pep said, jut-jawed.

"No, what?"

"No, *Sir!*" she yelled.

Even Amos could not quite suppress his snickers. Only Mark, dogged and in pain, did not appreciate Miss Baines' ready fund of wit. "I meant, Miss Baines, did your negative answer indicate that you did not hear the name Archibald?"

"I didn't hear that name, no," Pep said, all in all mighty pleased with her performance so far.

"Miss Baines, how did you know one of the women in the pool had tattooed ankles?"

"Had tat. . . . Well, you notice things like that."

"Under water?"

"Well, to tell you the truth—"

Her Honor said, "That would be the wisest course for you to take, Miss."

"Not to mention the sheer novelty of it," Mark said.

Her Honor snapped, "Mr. D'Andor, that way lies contempt."

Mark pulled himself together and said quietly, "Your Honor, I must confess to being utterly contemptuous of this witness."

"I fine you fifty dollars, Mr. D'Andor."

"Thank you, Your Honor. A bargain, if I may say so."

"You may not. Five days in jail at the conclusion of this case."

"Thank you, Your Honor." Mark returned to Pep. She was frightened and out of her depth; if Mark were willing to go to such lengths, she, Pep, wanted no part of it. "I put it to you, Miss Baines," Mark said gently, "that you are lying. The only reason you know one of those girls supporting Muffin Naismith in that pool had decorated ankles is because you were informed of that fact, is that not so?"

"Well, yes, but—"

"By whom?"

"Mrs. Tobino may have mentioned—"

"Tell the truth, Miss Baines!"

"Mrs. Tobino told me about the ankles."

"And the ice?"

Pep cried passionately, "Do you have to see a thing to know it?"

"It helps. When one is under oath, Miss Baines."

"I'll swear to this, then," Pep said through clenched teeth, "The Feeb hurt her and I know it!"

"You know no such thing."

Pep grabbed the arms of the witness chair and yelled, "Well, I did hear her howling in that bedroom. *Howling at the top of her voice!*"

"And what, Miss Baines, do you think you're doing? Is someone killing you?" Mark stepped back. "That will be all. And thank you."

Amos came within an inch of going up to the stand to help Miss Baines down in her spike-heeled sandals. But a quick glance to the jury, which did not escape Mark's notice, decided him against it. The grandmotherly juror detested Pep on general principles. Mark himself offered Pep his hand. She tossed her plume and mulishly refused, waving Mark away. He went back to his seat.

Pep's heels were loud as she advanced toward the gate in the bar. Passing Mark, her lips barely moved, but he thought she whispered, "Ta ta, Bagel. See you in hell one of these days."

It was Saturday, the hour approaching noon. Mark was near fainting, and Amos, noting this, rose to urge Her Honor not to adjourn until Monday.

Judge Fickett inspected Mark and adjourned, instructing that Mark come to her chambers. Amos trotted in right along with Mark. Her Honor said to Mark without preamble, "Mr. D'Andor, I gave you five days in jail this morning not so much because of your conduct, which was contumacious in the extreme, but because of your condition. I expect you to be sober when next you enter my courtroom."

"I shall try, Your Honor."

"Why, to tell you the truth," Her Honor said, unconsciously borrowing Pep's phraseology, "you look like you've been drunk for a week."

"I would say a bit longer than that, Madam," Mark said.

"I warn you, Mr. D'Andor, if you collapse before the jury I will entertain a motion from Mr. Slake for a mistrial. I will have no tugging at the jury's heartstrings."

Mark smiled faintly. "I doubt, Your Honor, that Mr. Slake would neglect to tell the jury of the cause of my collapse.

When he was done, none of them would be moved to send me flowers."

"Precisely," Amos said.

Mark laughed. "Amos, you would not believe in what high esteem I hold you. You fight right out in the open."

"Where else?" Amos wondered.

Judge Fickett nodded briskly. "Fair enough, gentlemen. Have a nice week end."

Mr. Pentlove was waiting in the empty courtroom to buttonhole Mark as soon as he emerged from chambers. "Well? Well? What did she say?"

"Judge Fickett wanted to wish me and Mr. Slake a nice week end."

Mark stumbled out of the courtroom and went home to bed.

CHAPTER TWENTY-SEVEN

Mark lay on his bed in a swelter, thinking; I'm actually swooning, and I thought only maidens did that. He dozed through the worst of the heat, and when the phone wakened him, his pillow was as damp as if Muffin Naismith had newly wept onto it. Weaving up the stairs he felt weak but refreshed, as if he had passed through a crisis. While the phone yelled at him he held his head under the faucet, then at last went dripping to answer it.

"Well, of all things, he's there!" a woman's voice said, speaking to someone else.

"Hello!" Mark said.

"Naturally," the woman said to Mark now, "we didn't expect you to be in your office and court at the same time. But you ought to speak to your secretary, Mr. D'Andor. She hasn't once answered your phone all week!"

"I'm not at my office."

"You— Oh, for. . . . We found this number, you see, among Muffin's effects, and we just naturally took it for your office. I am a goose!"

"Not knowing who you are, I will not contest the point, but—*Muffin*? You said Muffin's—"

"Her effects. Such as they are. The poor little thing had only the clothes on her back and not much else. I think the thing she hated the most was having to wear mended silk stockings. But they are ugly, you have to admit. Makes a woman's legs look *corded*. Oh, she did have a few mementos—"

"Mementos," Mark repeated solemnly, "yes. Who is this, please?"

"Didn't I say? I am a goose! This is Clara Foley. I just

took the off chance that you would be in your office. Only you aren't, are you?"

"The important thing is where are you? May I see you right away?"

Mrs. Foley said that would be dandy.

The Widow Foley lived in a house as narrow as a needle and neat as a pin, reminding Mark of Muffin's own obsession for cleanliness. The Widow herself was something else again, sporting a ramshackle façade composed of the standard half-dollar circles of rouge, a dated Nita Naldi comb riding dyed black hair, a mouth rouged with so unsteady a pinkie that the edges appeared scalloped, and stubby eyelashes so slathered with mascara that they were lumpy and gnarled like her aged fingers. Behind Mrs. Foley two more women hovered, their heavily powdered faces lending them the impersonal blankness of parchment lampshades.

Mark introduced himself, thinking: My God, it's a whorehouse!

"You certainly got here fast," Mrs. Foley observed.

"I live just up the hill."

"Come in, come in." Mrs. Foley's companions drifted, one to each side of her, like aides-de-camp. At close range, Mark was forced to revise his opinion of the character of the house, for one lady was attempting in vain to hide facial scars with her powder and the other to hide a most pathetic and quivering timidity. Chronologically, Mrs. Foley and the timid one were years past first youth; the scarred one appeared never to have been young at all, seeming ageless in the way a brawny, well-preserved athlete does.

Mark was at once engulfed, like a visitor come to a lonely outpost. He found himself seated in a parlor so small and so decidedly elegant that it reminded him of some other room or enclosure. In the dusk he sat with Mrs. Foley crowding him on a velvet settee and opposite him, across a high round table wearing a Spanish shawl, sat the powdered ones. A cut-glass decanter was produced and four wee tumblers were ranged around it. "You'll have a light libation?" Mrs. Foley asked pouring, and distributed the drinks.

The three ladies tossed off the liquor at once, the timid

one shuddering a bit. Mark discovered he was drinking what he took to be straight gin. "And yet," he said conversationally, to cover his unease at being stared at so intensely, "I'd almost swear it's Irish. I mean, this is gin, isn't it?"

"Well, it's *our* gin," said Scarface, whose name Mark had not caught. "I like to touch it up with a smidgin of oil of cedar. It's made from pencil shavings, you know."

"Oh, I didn't know."

"And when you want to make Irish you add both oil of cedar and creosote."

"Sal, dear," Mrs. Foley said, "I do think you put a touch too much isinglass in." As if to confirm this suspicion, she poured straight shots all around a second time.

Along with the ladies, Mark sipped reflectively.

"Shoot!" Sal said. "There might—mind you, I said *might* —be a grain too much pulverized chalk. What do you think, Mr. D'Andor?"

"Oh, I. . . . I'm not sure," he said to the earnest, scarred face.

"The bathtub," Mrs. Foley said cozily, "has one weensy spot where the iron is showing through."

"You don't say," Mark said.

Mrs. Foley nodded impressively. "And when it turns the gin black—and it will do that, you know, do it every time; why if I've told Sal once, I've told her a hundred times—the only way to clarify it is with skimmed milk. Do let me pour you another drop, Mr. D'Andor."

"Why, thank you," Mark said, with more courage than he knew he possessed. "About Muffin, you say she—"

"Her pitiful little belongings," Mrs. Foley said ritualistically. "Somehow I just didn't think she'd want to have the police pawing through them."

"No, I'm sure she wouldn't. Oddly enough, Mrs. Foley, I've been trying desperately to find you." He paused, expectant that one of the trio would divulge what they wished him to know about Muffin.

"I'll never forget," sneered Sal to Mrs. Foley, "the time you tried to clarify it with roche alum." She hooted in coarse laughter, then explained to Mark, "We all went around looking like sourpusses for weeks. The alum. *Euph!*" She sucked in her scarred cheeks by way of illustration.

"Was Muffin living here up to the—uh—time of her death?" Mark put in rather loudly.

"That's right," Sal said flatly.

Mrs. Foley frowned, her position as captain of the team and therefore spokesman put in jeopardy by Sal's ready answers. "Muffin," Mrs. Foley said severely to Sal, "went from this door to her death."

The timid woman nodded tenderly.

"There isn't much we can tell you about her, Mr. D'Andor," Mrs. Foley went on. "Poor Muffin was only with us for a month or so. She was down on her uppers you know. Thelma—" here Mrs. Foley nodded at the timid one "—got her some extra bits now and again. Thelma's in publicity," Mrs. Foley said condescendingly. "Thelma never acted herself, of course. She's always been clerical."

Mark realized he too was nodding inanely at the shrinking Thelma. "Oh," he uttered, feeling the fool.

"As I say," Mrs. Foley took up, "Muffin had only a few extra bits. All Westerns, of course. Outdoor shooting, you know." Mrs. Foley laid a casual hand on Mark's knee. "I know this may sound like a terrible thing to say, but Muffin really died when her career was nipped in the bud. She never got to know the thrill of being a star." After a suitably funereal hiatus, Mrs. Foley said, squeezing Mark's knee, "I guess that's why we girls all treated her like a little sister. Isn't that so, Sal?"

"Sure," Sal said brusquely. Mark noticed suddenly that Sal was holding the ever-silent Thelma's limp hand. "And Muffin couldn't help but be impressed by us."

"We've had our glory," Mrs. Foley commented with rich sorrow. "I know what it is to have crowds at your feet. No one can ever take that away from you."

"No, never," Mark agreed. "But about Muffin—you said her career was nipped in the bud?"

"Klieg eyes," Mrs. Foley said, and stroked Mark's knee. "Klieg——?"

"—eyes," Mrs. Foley confirmed. "From the arc lights.

Terrible, I can assure you. My doctor had me once lie flat for ten days with damp cloths on my eyes."

"I hated the damn things," Sal said explosively. "Always gave me a headache."

"Muffin's case was worse. And it came on her just when she was in the Paramount school—or was it Zucksmith—and—"

"Zucksmith," Sal said.

"Anyway, where they train the future stars. Manny Amen, bless his heart, was her agent. In those days, Mr. D'Andor, agents were rare. In my day nonexistent. In my day, of course, it took seven pictures to build a star. C. B. always said that to me, 'Clara, it takes—' "

"And now one flicker and slam-bam, you're a star," Sal grunted. "Muffin could of made it in three, or I miss my guess. Klieg eyes. God! She told us hers bled. She wouldn't give up, though. Then the doc told her she get in front of the arcs again and she could buy herself a white cane. That did it."

"What a terrible disappointment for Muffin," Mark said. He shifted slightly on the settee, Mrs. Foley having to dig her fingers into his knee to maintain possession of it. The remarkable resemblance of the parlor to something other than a room struck him again. On the wall behind Sal and Thelma he noticed a gilt cornucopia spilling artificial roses. A turn of his head revealed the mate of the cornucopia forever arrested in the act of dropping wax flowers onto his crown. At once he knew that the oddly small high-ceilinged parlor reminded him of the stately electric automobile owned by two maiden ladies in his home town. He had ridden in it to a funeral, the first and last derby he had ever owned slapped down on his brow. The memory refreshed, Mark had to look to one of the tall windows to assure himself that he and the ladies were not indeed moving slowly down the street.

"Heartbreaking," Mrs. Foley said, returning him to the present. "And to think, when she got her Klieg eyes, First National was just about to try out their new incandescent light. Another few years and everybody had them. But Muffin had missed out. And once that happens you never get back; six new ones are all ready to take your place."

"Yes," Mark said. "Tell me, do any of you ladies happen to know a T-Bone Tredwell?"

"Shoot!" Sal said. "Known him for years. One of the best stunt men around until he broke his neck."

"Oh, but that's not why—" Mrs. Foley began.

"He broke his neck!" Sal said positively.

Mrs. Foley smiled with great sweetness, her hand pinching Mark's leg painfully. "Sal, dear, his neck wasn't what made him give up stunting. It was his legs did that. In fact, we used to call him Shinbone——"

"And I'm telling you—"

"Sal, dear," Mrs. Foley said tenderly, "after all, it was my picture." She turned to Mark with shopworn coyness. "I was the star. And T-Bone was to go off this cliff on a motorcycle, you see. They had a parachute rigged up for him, but he was supposed to keep falling as long as possible so they could get a real good shot of it. Only he kept on falling and falling. He couldn't get the parachute open, and when he finally did it only half-opened."

"At least it got him off the cycle," Sal said.

Mrs. Foley patted Mark. "He landed on his feet." She sighed like a Santana wind. "With both of his broken shinbones sticking straight out of his boots. I ran up to him and fainted dead away, I was that highstrung. How about a teensy bit more libation, Mr. D'Andor?" Before Mark could refuse she had filled his wee tumbler. "You know the way T-Bone is always rubbing his boots?"

"Why—yes!" Mark said.

"He got that habit in his sleep. He was always rubbing at his legs because he was dreaming he was pushing his shinbones back inside his boots." Mrs. Foley demonstrated on Mark several times to make certain he fully understood. "You can see why stunt men don't last more than about five years."

"Stunt women," Sal said, "can go for ten."

Mrs. Foley sniffed. "Sal, dear, women don't do the really dangerous things—"

Sal butted in menacingly, "And I was called Suicide Sal for doing the minuet, huh, Clara? Is that why they called me

Suicide Sal? Or was it maybe because I jumped from the wing of an airplane to a horse?"

"They were both going at the same rate of speed," Mrs. Foley said in a disparaging aside to Mark.

Sal tossed off her gin and sulked.

Mark said diplomatically, "Still and all, it doesn't sound like something I'd care to do."

"And what about the balloon, huh, what about *that*?" Sal cried.

Seeing that Suicide Sal was deeply wounded, Mrs. Foley leaned over to refill her tumbler for her. "Yes, dear, that was quite an experience."

"It was supposed to be a comedy scene," Sal said bitterly. "Me and another guy was in the basket of the balloon. He was after my honor, y'understand, and we were wrestling. Then I got outside the basket on this rope ladder, and he was to hang on a rope and keep snatching at me. Only he let go. He. . . ." She drank off her gin. In the last of the evening's light the scars on her face stood out clearly. "He tried to fly," she said bluntly.

Mark started. "What?"

"He tried to fly. When he was falling to his death. He waved his arms and tried to fly."

"They don't make the good movies they used to," Mrs. Foley said, "and that's a fact. In these talkies they got now everybody just stands about and blabs and blabs."

In a matter-of-fact voice Sal said, "Anyway, the next day the goddam balloon blew up." She fingered her scars.

"It *was* still on the ground," Mrs. Foley said deprecatingly, and turned on the lamp, reaching across Mark to do it and availing herself of the opportunity more or less to clasp him to her bosom at the same time. "No, they don't make good movies any more."

"Except The Feeb," Thelma said, speaking for the first time.

Mrs. Foley reared back. "Well, well! Garbo talks!"

Thelma shrank against Sal and nibbled at the rim of her little glass.

Alerted by the name of The Feeb, Mark held his peace.

"Well, Thelma is right!" Sal said protectively.

"Did I say she was not?" Mrs. Foley challenged. "Am I not able to recognize the true syntax of the camera with my own eyes?" To Mark she said, "You really should talk The Feeb into making more silents, Mr. D'Andor. Someone like The Feeb, who understands the syntax of the camera, doesn't need sound. You take D. W. Griff—"

"I was in *Intolerance*," Sal said. "You couldn't count the number of broken heads and legs and—"

"And D. W. had ambulances all ready and waiting. My husband was another one who always did that. When you stunt people are hurt, it's often because of your own faulty preparation."

"I suppose the time I got stuck on the telltales was my fault?" Suicide Sal shrilled, her voice reaching for a high tenor note.

Joining in the spirit of general madness, Mark said, "Telltales?"

Sal gulped off her gin and wiped her mouth with the back of her hand. "Those strap things that hang outside a train tunnel. The heroine—I was stunting for the star—was on top of this moving train, and when it came to this tunnel, I grabbed the telltales and the train went on into the tunnel."

"That was a very poor picture," Mrs. Foley put in with a parenthetical sniff.

Sal grimly maintained her grasp on the conversation. "Only the train didn't back out of the tunnel the way it was supposed to. So there I was, hanging about thirty-odd feet above the track, waiting for the train."

Mrs. Foley took it into her head to lift her voice in song. "Waiting at the altar," she sang, "you left meee in the lurch. Waiting at the aaaalll-tar, waiting at the chur-urch."

Thelma freed her hand to pat out applause while Sal glowered. "So there I was," Sal shouted, "hanging. The cameraman up on top the tunnel was trying to reach down for me, but he couldn't. So about that time I knew I might as well let go and get my legs broken and get it over with. And just as I did—I heard the train coming back."

"My God," Mark breathed.

"I hit the cinders seconds before that train came highballing out of that tunnel like a bat out of hell. I snapped an ankle, and just as I was scrambling out of the way of that train, do you know what I saw?"

"Angels?" Mrs. Foley wanted to know.

"I saw," Sal yelled, "that goddam cameraman up on top the tunnel cranking away at his camera for all he was worth—how 'bout that!" The recounting of this near-miss left Sal panting with rage. Next her, in the shadows, Thelma made a soft sound of commiseration.

"It was a *very* poor picture," Mrs. Foley repeated. She tapped Mark on the knee. "Why didn't you say your glass was empty, Mr. D'Andor? Very naughty man. But then, that's up to the hostess, isn't it? I am a goose."

"No, no," Mark murmured, thinking: Someday, dear Mrs. Foley, someone is going to give you a Carson pause lasting at least a full half-hour when you announce that you are a goose. Aloud he said, "About Muffin. Did she have any men friends other than T-Bone?"

Mrs. Foley pursed her mouth and silently consulted with Sal. "Welll. . . . I, personally, am not the prying type. And Muffin was pretty close-mouthed."

Sal said, "Thelma was the one met her. They were getting ready to kick Muffin out of some hotel for nonpayment. And Clara here just told Thelma to bring the poor little flapper on home with her. Clara said that out of the goodness of her heart."

Mrs. Foley said fiercely, "There is the distinct taste of isinglass in this batch of gin, Sal."

Mark prepared himself for his next question with a slurp of his own libation. "Did she ever say who was the father of—"

"Shoot!" Sal said. "Could of been anybody. I shouldn't be speaking ill of the dead, but that girl had about as much brains as an old model-T has pow. She was the original casting-couch baby. Anybody could give her a line about being the friend of a big producer and she'd—"

"She was desperate," Mrs. Foley put in. "She wasn't as young as she might have been for getting discovered, you know. But she'd read about everybody's getting the new incandescent lights, and she thought she could start her career all over." Mrs. Foley pitched her voice to a lower register. "A—girl—does get desperate, you know, when all the other—girls—seem a wee bit younger than you are. Not," she hastened to say, "that I ever experienced that personally. I retired when I married Mr. Foley."

"About Muffin's being pregnant, though," Mark said. "Was she making any arrangements?"

"Yes," Thelma said wispily, poking her head out of her habitual silence. "I guessed what she was doing. I mean, it was the way she was talking. Real loud."

"As if she were deaf?" Mark asked.

"I'll see you to the door," Thelma said pointedly.

Mrs. Foley squeezed Mark's knee. "When this dreadful thing is all over, Mr. D'Andor, you must come to dinner. And bring the dear Feeb. That he could be accused of such a thing! All you have to do is see one of his pictures—one of the *real* ones, the silents, that is—to know that he's pure as an infant."

Suddenly Mark remembered having seen Mrs. Foley in one of her greatest triumphs. They had shown the picture in a crude little Canadian flicker house outfitted with long wooden benches. Mark and his fellow doughboys watched a handsome middle-aged lady, weighing in at a good one hundred and forty pounds—not including a good ten pounds of black hair braided low on her forehead—clad in what appeared to be the beaded portieres from a sizable drawing room, vamping a justifiably frightened young man some fifteen years her junior. To the boys in the audience she had been as alluring as Mother making breakfast in her wrapper. Mark and his fellows had walked back to camp in the rain. Before the week was out the first 'flu death had occurred. Later, a particular friend of Mark's, a likable youth from his own home state, died as well. "Why, I saw you," Mark burst out to Mrs. Foley, "in *Passion Flower*!"

She bridled, wagging her Nita Naldi comb at him. "Oh, Mr. D'Andor, that was a *very poor* picture!"

He protested that it was not, getting to his feet. Suicide Sal shook his hand manfully, Mrs. Foley patently expected hers to be clasped in both of Mark's; he had a final glimpse of the stately small parlor and the cut-glass decanter, from

which Mrs. Foley was freshening Sal's drink, and found himself in the dark doorway with the shadowy Thelma. The night
was hot and still, but Mark grew chilled to see in the far high
hills an eerie pinpoint of blue fire. Had Muffin stood as he
was now, recognizing (as he was now) the blue bulb in his
solarium?

In her thready voice Thelma said, "At first Mrs. Foley
was going to call the police. But I remembered that Muffin
had told me—in confidence—that . . . you. . . ." She cleared
her throat, "You were in love with her, Mr. D'Andor. That's
why you took to drink." She entreated hurriedly, "I hope
you don't mind my frankness."

"On the contrary, I deeply appreciate it."

"That's how I knew that The Feeb had to be innocent,
or you wouldn't be defending him. Along with what else
I knew."

"Yes," Mark said most carefully.

"The way she was talking so loud," Thelma said. "I
knew it was because her ears were ringing. So I looked in her
dresser drawer when she was out."

A bottle was pressed into Mark's hand. "Quinine,"
Thelma said, "will make your ears ring every time. And a lot
of the time that's about all it'll do. A camphor pack, I told
Muffin, is the only sure safe way. Especially if you take
Beecham's pills too." Thelma seemed on the verge of guilty
tears. "I was going to help her with the camphor pack that
week end. But I guess she changed her mind and went out with
T-Bone instead. She was always giddy, kind of, I don't think
you'll mind my saying that, but I think the quinine made her
worse."

As impersonally as he was able, Mark asked, "Have you
ever had to take quinine yourself?"

"Oh, God!" Thelma said with a thin laugh. "Mr. D'Andor,
I was like Muffin once. I was on the town, too. Then I met Sal
and I went to live with her and Clara. Sal's been more decent
to me than any man ever was. Between you and me and the
gatepost, though, I don't think Muffin was happy with us. She
wasn't ready to give up. She still thought she could get what
she wanted out of men. I know better. These men, all they

want is their fun, and let the chippies fall where they may.
I hope you don't mind——"

"I can't tell you how grateful I am," Mark said honestly,
"that you ladies placed your trust in me."

Thelma grinned shyly and pressed his fingers closed over
the medicine bottle. "Come back and see Clara again," she
said.

"I shall, I shall."

"Anyway, next time," Thelma said comfortingly, "is my
turn to make the gin." She gave him another ghost of a grin
and shut the door softly but firmly in his face.

Mark went to his office and put in a call to Dr. Snowdom,
that gentleman coming on the line with utmost caution. "Yes?"

"This is Mark D'Andor, Doctor. I was wondering if—"

"Oh, Mr. D'Andor! Counselor! Good evening. How are
you?"

"At the moment I'm puzzled about something. I was
hoping you might give me some information of a medical
nature."

"Of course, of course," Dr. Snowdom said cordially.
"Certainly!"

The warmth of Dr. Snowdom's tone had Mark grinning.
"Well, it's this. What physical effect would quinine have on a
woman in the early stages of pregnancy?"

"Quinine sulfate would make her ears ring. After high
dosages."

"Would it cause an abortion?"

Dr. Snowdom laughed softly, wryly. "As an abortifacient
quinine sulfate is most unsatisfactory. A woman could hear
bells ringing, and be so affected mentally that she was psychotic, and the fetus still be firmly attached. Very bad on the
kidneys, incidentally."

"Doctor, suppose a strong laxative were taken along with
the—"

Dr. Snowdom interrupted with another wry chuckle.
"You are repeating old wives' tales, Counselor. A fetus that is
firmly *attached* usually must be mechanically *detached*. With
instruments. A fetus is tenacious, and to evacuate the uterus of

its contents requires drastic measures. Any woman with a grain of sense will seek the services of a—ah—competent—shall we say—abortionist, rather than attempt it herself. Either with drugs or the introduction of some instruments or other into the vaginal——"

"What instrument, for example?" Mark said sharply.

"Oh . . . a long crochet hook, for one, comes to mind. Yes, a crochet hook enjoys a certain vogue at the moment. However, the first try with the hook usually discourages the user. Brutally painful, as you can imagine. And in the hands of a clumsy user, all that is accomplished is the inflicting of cuts and rips in the vagina and cervix."

Mark took a deep breath. "You mean a *lesion* could be inflicted?"

"Counselor, there is no end to the number and variety—"

"Dr. Snowdom, could Muffin Naismith have inflicted that lesion on herself?"

Dr. Snowdom was full of regret. "I only wish I could say. But I simply do not know what or who was responsible for it."

"I see. Well, thank you very—"

"I'm sorry I can't be of more help, Counselor."

"On the contrary, Dr. Snowdom, you have given me the insight into this case I needed. An alternate way of handling the defense has just presented itself."

"I wish you every success," Snowdom said solemnly. "As you must know, I wish there were some way I could repay you for your—um—considerate treatment of me when I was on the witness——"

"You can buy me a drink some day," Mark said. "And thanks."

After some hours with his books, Mark set aside his notes for his new legal maneuver. Looking down on the deserted Boulevard, he thought of Muffin and how like her it was to botch an attempt at abortion as she failed at everything else. Poisoning herself with quinine until her ears rang and her senses were addled. And, very likely, digging and tearing at herself with some long pointed object, until the pain dissuaded her. Yet not permitting drug nor pain nor drink nor exhaustion to interfere with her relentless pursuit of her "silver-screen career"—and The Feeb. And even when she became psychotic, she was crazed in a way peculiar only to Muffin Naismith. In that bedroom in the Eden she teased The Feeb one moment and poked him in the nose the next—and Muffin had a wallop on her; Mark could give evidence of that. Then, as the child in her died and the grinding pains came on, Muffin howled out those fantasies that groped along the dimly lit corridors of her mind.

I am picking up the pieces, Mark thought. It came to him how like Muffin this was too, never doubting, even as she was dying, that Mark would come clean up the mess. She had his number. What was it Pep had once said—"Muffin knows you for an easy mark."

He felt that his task was nearly done. There was the improbable chance that he might learn who had gotten Muffin Naismith pregnant (Mark recalled the irony of T-Bone Tredwell accusing him, and he, Mark, instantly conferring the honor on T-Bone), but it was not one of the pieces that had concerned even Muffin.

Looking down at the darkened marquee of the gaudy movie house Muffin had once loved so, Mark thought of a title suitable for emblazoning there: *Who Fathered the Child of Muffin Naismith?* (A new talkie, with a cast of thousands).

CHAPTER TWENTY-EIGHT

On Monday morning it would have taken a practiced eye to say which of the two men, Amos or The Feeb, had spent his week end languishing in the hoosegow. If the rosy cheeks of Amos spoke of a merry Sunday on the miniature-golf course, The Feeb's pearly baby fat glowed, as if he had been tenderly bathed and oiled and sat to gurgle happily in his playpen under a shade tree. In contrast, Mr. D'Andor looked as if an appreciable amount of his stuffing had leaked out, much like the last limp cigarette in a tin of flat fifties.

Head held high above his Herbert Hoover collar (he could not have done otherwise, had he so wished), T. Amos called for Miss Pritchard to take the stand. In the lampshade hat which she evidently thought suitable for courtroom wear, Miss Pritchard came forth, her demeanor that of a plain woman with a mission. Entering the bar, she did what Mark fully expected of her. Miss Pritchard came to a halt and riveted her eyes on The Feeb. Swiftly, but with his deceptive air of laziness, Mark intervened, "Did you want to say something to me, Madam?"

"I'll say plenty to you before I'm done," Miss Pritchard promised, and flounced into the witness chair.

Once sworn, no juror could doubt but that the witness intended her testimony to be devastating. Her mouth was so minced one might conclude she was drawing in her breath through an invisible straw. Adroitly Amos began drawing from her detail on detail of the suffering and death of Muffin Naismith. Miss Pritchard had staying power, and Amos had trained her well, prolonging her testimony so that it became an ordeal, so that the jury began to appreciate the inexhaustible time one had to suffer from a Sunday to the Friday following, if one spent those hours trying to die and get it over with.

Recess came and went, lunch arrived, and Miss Pritchard was still on Wednesday and its fever charts and antiseptic lavages and oxygen inhalations and bathings and hot broth and analgesic medications, until it seemed that the patient might not live through to Thursday out of sheer inability to escape the indefatigable Miss Pritchard and snatch a wink of sleep.

Then, the jury gone, and the spectators swilling from thermos bottles and swapping a chicken wing for a hard-boiled egg, Mr. Pentlove found himself confronted with another sort of egg, and very hard-boiled about it too. To his plaintive request that they see what the fishhouse had to offer that day, Mark said for Mr. Pentlove's ears alone, "Go to the Obispo, why don't you? Go offer that maid from the Eden another bribe. Frighten her speechless this time. And see what you can do about terrorizing Slake's other witnesses. Get us both thrown in jail. Now you listen to me carefully, Pentlove. I am the attorney on this case, not you. And if a witness knows something damaging about my client, I *must* be informed of it. Now what does that maid know?"

Mr. Pentlove received this with a strange tranquility. "Need she know anything?"

"Why is she working at the Obispo?"

"Oh, that. To persuade her to keep her mouth shut, on the off chance she did know something. An ounce of prevention—that sort of thing. And then, some people will imagine all kinds of things that didn't happen. To get in the limelight. So I make it worth their while to remain obscure. Are we lunching or not?"

"Go 'way," Mark said. Raising his voice slightly, he requested Rookie kindly to get Mr. Pentlove out of there. Mr. Pentlove left with Rookie straightway, though he was far from meek. And Mark returned to yet more notes, compiled the previous day when he had been paying the implacable penance exacted for drinking Suicide Sal's gin.

Miss Pritchard returned to the stand refreshed, while Amos and The Feeb had continued their contest of the noon-hour toilette. Mark sat crumpled, drawing deltas on his legal pad. As the heat of the afternoon intensified and the jury plied palm fans but clung to every juicy medical item set forth, Amos speeded up the tempo.

"Towards the end of her life was the deceased lucid?"

"Oh yes," Miss Pritchard said. "Perfectly. She was in her right mind, you may be sure."

"It is important that the jury be sure, too, Miss Pritchard," Amos rang out.

Miss Pritchard faced the jury pugnaciously. "She was in her right mind!"

"Was she aware of her impending death?"

"Oh, yes, the poor little thing knew she was dying. She even asked me how long did I think she had left. How many hours is what she wanted to know."

"What was your answer?"

"Since that was late Friday afternoon, I had to tell her that she wouldn't last through the night in my opinion."

"What did the deceased reply to that?"

"She said she knew too that she was dying. And then she begged me to see that she was avenged."

"In those words? Tell us her exact words, please."

"She said," Miss Pritchard began portentously to the jury, "that—" she whipped about to point at Forbes, "that 'He hurt me. That fat son of a bitch hurt me. He hurt me bad down there.' And she pointed to the lower part of her body." Miss Pritchard fell back in the witness chair, her head tilted back to prevent her hat obscuring her face from the jury. "And then she said," Miss Pritchard went on, mouthing each word passionately, " 'Don't let him get away with it.' "

"Thank you," Amos said. "Cross-examine?"

"And what she meant," Miss Pritchard continued on, rising above these little interruptions on the part of Mr. Slake, "was that The Feeb be punished to the fullest letter of the law for—"

Judge Fickett loomed up from behind her Codes to see Mark on his feet and listening to Miss Pritchard with great attention.

"—what he did to her!" Miss Pritchard finished.

"And what did she say it was?" Mark asked, easing in the question quietly.

"Why—that he'd hurt her somehow."

"Who?"

"Who! Well, who do you think?"

"No, Miss Pritchard, tell me who the deceased said had hurt her?"

Miss Pritchard was inspired to point at Forbes again. "That man, of course!"

"But she did not name him?"

"Does that matter?"

"It matters to the man who is on trial for his life, Miss Pritchard. Tell the jury, did she name him?"

"Not exactly."

"Did the deceased tell you that she had been hurt with ice?"

"Not in so many words, no, but—"

"The deceased did not name the person who had hurt her, and she did not say how he had hurt her?"

"When you're dying, you don't have time to dot *i*'s and cross—"

"But when the deceased was dying, she was lying down?"

"Lying do— Heavenly days, you don't think she was up on her feet!"

"And lying down, the deceased indicated the part of her body where she had been hurt? She pointed?"

"Oh, it wasn't exactly pointing."

"What was it exactly?"

"She waved her hand."

"And she said, 'He hurt me'?"

"She most certainly said that!"

"But she didn't most certainly say 'Down there,' did she?"

"Oh, I knew right off where she meant."

"Let us be clear on this, please. The deceased said, 'He hurt me. Don't let the son of a bitch get away with it.' Isn't that what she said?"

"I'm telling you, that's exactly what she said!"

"And she didn't point, and she didn't say 'Down there.' "

"Under the circumstances it was hardly necessary," Miss

Pritchard said tartly. "Besides, she was too busy begging me to find you, Mr. D'Andor, as you perfectly well know."

"I do not know. Will you state, please, what the deceased said in connection with me?"

"Why, she had me call you at your office and home over and over. Only I couldn't reach you, you know that. She said to tell you to come pick up the pieces, and those were her exact words!"

Every palm fan in the jury box came to rest.

"So, for all you know, the deceased could have been speaking of me when she said, 'He hurt me, don't let the son of a bitch get away with it'?"

"You know more about that than I do, I'm sure, Mr. D'Andor," Miss Pritchard said, making a vicious swipe at her hat to right it.

"I was not there to hear what was said. Did the deceased mention that I am an attorney?"

"Naturally she did. She wanted to be sure I called Mr. D'Andor, the lawyer. She was very anxious for you to come render her some service."

"The service being to come pick up the pieces?"

"That's what she said."

"She wanted an attorney to 'come pick up the pieces'?" Mark said again. "That was the service she wanted of a lawyer?"

"Can't you understand! She was dying! She was raging with fever and terrible, terrible pain!"

"And she was out of her head, too, wasn't she?"

Miss Pritchard cocked her own head in a peculiar manner, bending on Mark a look compounded of suspicion, violent dislike, and mockery. "She must have been to send for you, Mr. D'Andor!"

Mark received this with containment. "During the week the deceased was under your care you thought she was married, did you not?"

"I don't see what that has to do with it, but yes."

"You called the deceased by some other name than her own?"

"I called her Mrs. Tredwell."

"Did the deceased correct you when you called her that?"

"No."

"I submit, Miss Pritchard, that Muffin Naismith was in a confused mental state when you first saw her, and grew steadily worse with each succeeding day."

"She did have her bad moments, yes."

"At the end they were very bad, were they not?"

"No, no, she became lucid."

"Then you held—you were able to hold intelligent conversations with her?"

"We talked, yes."

"But when she was asking for me you say she was not lucid?"

"Maybe not at the moment."

"When she was lucid did she tell you she was not Mrs. Tredwell?"

"She——— Maybe her having been pregnant, she thought it was nicer-sounding to let people think she was married."

"And maybe she thought it was nicer-sounding to let people think someone had done her a hurt, rather than let them know she had attempted to abort herself. Was that the case?"

"You're just guessing!" Miss Pritchard shouted.

"I am asking! Now, you answer me! You know for a fact, don't you, that Muffin Naismith rammed a crochet hook or some other object up inside her body in order to abort—"

Amos did not want Miss Pritchard to answer that, he wanted the question stricken and the jury told to disregard it, he wanted Judge Fickett to know that he, Amos, had been patience itself during Mr. D'Andor's untoward and unseemly cross-examination and WOULD THE WITNESS PLEASE STOP TALKING!

Throughout the fulminations of Mr. Slake, Mark held the attention of the jury by looking at them in fixed imploration. Silently he beseeched them: Forget all else, but remember my last question. Admit the possibility—just the barest possibility—that Naismith brought on her own death!

". . . a mind as evil as yours would make such a suggestion," Miss Pritchard was shouting, and fell silent in order to draw breath.

"I withdraw the question," Mark said. He asked in a friendly tone, "Miss Pritchard, I'll need your help on the medical terminology, but do you know what is that condition known as the Devil's Pinch?"

"His *what*?"

"It's a condition wherein a person bruises easily, where a person is extremely susceptible to bruising. What is the medical term for that condition?"

"Oh, you mean capillary fragility?" Miss Pritchard said with a superior smile.

"If that is the condition I have just described, then yes. Did not Muffin Naismith suffer from cap—capil—"

"Capillary fragility," Miss Pritchard said, her smile broadening at the stumble-tongued Mark. "Yes, she did. Cap–pil–lary fra–gil–ity."

Mark nodded seriously. "Thank you." The jury had now heard the words a sufficient number of times to satisfy Mark. "And you were unable to avoid bruising the deceased yourself, is that not so?"

"When someone is dying of septicemia she doesn't pay much mind to a few bruises. And don't you go inferring that I used her for a punching bag, just because I couldn't help—"

"I'm doing no such thing, Miss Pritchard. Let us hope the jury won't either."

With a yowl of anguish, Amos rose to nag Judge Fickett once again on the subject of Mark's questions, conduct, and bullying of the witness.

Judge Fickett said, "Mr. Slake, my hearing is normal. Mr. D'Andor, you will cease making speeches and start asking questions."

"If the Court please, I have no more questions," Mark said. And to Miss Pritchard he added, "That will be all. Thank you."

Amos had a single remaining witness, an extraordinarily pretty girl who took the oath, the stand, and then the gum from her mouth, with the sidewise glance to Her Honor of a good child minding its manners, and carefully wrapped the wad in the silver paper in which it had been packaged. This bright pellet she dropped into her purse and snapped it shut with a loud click.

After giving her name and address, she announced her occupation brightly, "I'm in the profession of being a party girl."

"And what is that?" floated down from the bench.

"It's kind of like being a prostitute," the witness said cheerily, and fluffed out her strawberry-blonde bob.

"In what respects?" Judge Fickett asked.

"Yes, ma'am," the witness said.

A baffled Judge Fickett let it go, a look in Mark's direction saying that he might go into it more fully if he wished.

Guided by Amos, the young witness told her version of the week end at the Eden. Forbes wrote on Mark's pad: *She wasn't there.* Mark nodded, aware of the fact. The strawberry blonde chattered along of The Feeb's ardent pursuit of Miss Naismith, ending with the deceased's attempt to elude him by going into the bedroom. "She said she wanted to take this nap," the witness said.

"Now, after Miss Naismith entered the bedroom, what happened?"

"Well, Mr. Forbes ran down the hall and into the bedroom after her. He said he was going to rape her, that's what. And he locked the door. And then all these awful screams came out and we all ran and pounded at the door. Only he wouldn't open it. And then she really started screaming and begging him not to do that with the ice." The young lady came to a halt, wrinkled the flawless skin of her forehead, and pondered. "Oh yeah, I like to forgot. Miss Naismith had took this drink into the bedroom with her. With ice in it."

This point established, the witness went on to say that she had tried to calm the deceased by walking her in the pool, and after that had helped escort her to Snowdom's little hospital.

Amos was quickly done with his direct examination, and turned the witness over to Mark in an offhand manner.

Mark asked, "Miss, do you know what the penalty for perjury is?"

She shook her head in wonderment, then again wrinkled her smooth forehead in thought, as if she had committed the Penal Code to heart but could not for the life of her remember the pertinent section.

"If an innocent person is put to death because a witness has lied," Mark told her conversationally, "that liar too can be tried. And if convicted put to death too. By hanging."

He watched her, his manner kindly but expectant. A half-minute went by. "Yes?" Mark said. The word brought on the tears. Mark allowed her to cry for another moment or so, then said, "That will be all. Thank you, Miss."

Amos stood up, sat down, stood up, and sat down. He jerked his head at the bailiff to help the witness from the stand. This done, Amos addressed the court, "The People rest."

"Mr. D'Andor?" Judge Fickett said.

Mark rose. One thought only flitted across his mind: God, I need a drink. "Your Honor, I respectfully request that the Court now advise the jury to acquit the defendant."

Amos dropped his gold mechanical pencil.

Judge Fickett said, "I will take the request under consideration. We will recess until nine-fifteen. Mr. Slake, and you, Mr. D'Andor, may present arguments at that time."

"What does this request of yours mean, anyway?" asked The Feeb, asked Mr. Pentlove, asked Suicide Sal, asked that soul of honesty Miss Flirt Smith, asked the newsmen. To all, Mark replied in whole or in part, "It means that I contend that Mr. Slake has not presented evidence sufficient to sustain a conviction."

"Yes," Mr. Pentlove said, "but what if that lady judge refuses your motion?"

"Why, then I shall present my defense. Such pillars of society as a pimp, a prostitute, a mannish stunt woman and her light o' love, and a movie cowboy who keeps rubbing his boots to ascertain that his shinbones are inside his legs where they belong—these among others will parade to the stand in defense of The Feeb. Lastly, Forbes himself would just about have to testify in his own behalf."

"He's a consummate actor, don't forget that, D'Andor."

"And by the time Amos is done cross-examining him about his frisky sexual activities with Flirt Smith, for example, his name will be consummate mud. Acquitted, he would still be done for. He could go home and hang up his shield."

"Your logic is sound," said Mr. Pentlove, sounding like a pedant. He reverted then to one of his favorite nautical figures. "Yes, The Feeb would sink from sight, with all hands lost."

"There is also this to consider," Mark went on. "Amos intends to present his real case through my witnesses. He means to rattle them, to get them in such a snarl of facts and fabrications that the jury wouldn't know the truth if it plunked its backside right in the middle of the box with them. Now leave me be, Pentlove. I've got work to do."

That night any number of people reached any number of stages of intoxication. The scandalmongers called lawyers, strangers to them, boldly to ask if Mr. D'Andor's request meant that The Feeb wouldn't be telling his side of the story. Chester and Rookie were up till all hours arguing the merits and finer legal points of Mark's move. Mr. Pentlove minced to bed hiccupping genteelly. Miss Pritchard sought surcease in a cherry tonic (twenty per cent alcoholic content, and as easy to come by as Spanish doubloons); and Dr. Snowdom wrote a dozen letters to his daughter, trying to inform her of certain facts about herself, and mailing none of them, owing to his destroying the first seven or so while the later ones were illegible. Suicide Sal talked deep into the night of her exploits, not caring overly that her two companions had long since fallen asleep over their gin. And Pep Baines broke down in the middle of a game of miniature golf, sat smack in the center of a Lilliputian water trap to weep into the dinky shallow sea of her loss of the best friend a g-g-girl ever had. And even The Feeb, supplied with several clandestine bottles of Mexican beer by his kind keepers, grew mildly tipsy and enacted the plight of a Sultan who had just bought himself a hot fourteen-year-old virgin and—"Get this, now," The Feeb begged, "Bought her and then somehow mislaid her. Get it? Mis*laid*——" Not a mile from The Feeb, the Reverend Parker Kingdom grew drunk on his own oratory, while a certain sticky-fingered maid-servant, late of the Eden, drew forward, moaning, to be saved.

Of them all only Mark D'Andor, the most celebrated soak the legal circle had rejoiced in in years—he remained sober. Working on his transcripts, his points and authorities in support of his request, and his address to the jury, he suddenly did a strange thing. He went down into the very bowels of the house, into the attic under the bedrooms, where hundreds of sowbugs lay curled in death on the cement floor (they were always there, he never knew why, unless they had earmarked his house as some sort of ceremonial dying ground, as elephants are said to do certain places), and at last, from under some old copies of Constance's *Vanity Fair*, he brought to light a worn booklet, hardly larger than a small pamphlet. Inside the cover, fragile now as cigarette paper, was inscribed: *Mark D'Andor, June 1914*. Taking it up to his bedroom, he propped his feet on the cellarette amid his legal scribblings, and read it straight through. Then he flipped the pages back to savor again some of those passages which appealed to him above all others. "We bargain," he read, "for the graves we lie in; At the devil's booth are all things sold. . . ." In times past he had applied these lines to Muffin Naismith, disconsolate because the devil was fresh out of the only wares she wanted to buy. Now, he saw, they could apply equally to him.

Putting the booklet aside, he took up his work, looking in occasional surprise at the untouched tin of Irish as if it had spoken aloud demanding attention. He was refraining through no effort of will of which he was conscious. It did seem to him, however, that his mind was less nimble when sober, like the shy tonguetied guest at a party who needs a drink or two to liven him up.

His work done, he left the booklet, "The Vision of Sir Launfal," on the cellarette among his papers, and fell half-dressed across the bed. To see, as in a waking dream and for an instant only, Muffin in armor—and a comely young knight she made with her spindle-thin figure and dark bangs—riding out in the dawn in search of the Holy Grail.

CHAPTER TWENTY-NINE

On the stroke of nine-ten in the morning, The Feeb, looking a bit the worse for wear, was led from the bullpen to his seat. On the heels of this event T. Amos Slake entered, very full of himself; Mark knew Amos was going to do considerable saber-rattling before the day drew to a close. Pausing to speak to Mark, Amos said, "Counselor, I am going to present such irrefutable arguments to the jury that they're going to reach a murder in the first."

Mark rejoined, "Amos, I do like that tie you're wearing. Such éclat I never saw."

"Oh, droll, droll," Amos said, unconsciously fingering his tie. "You must be taking funny-man lessons from your client." He leaned down to inspect Mark's face. "Are you sober by any chance?"

"Yes," Mark said, then begged, "but do you really think it is becoming?" When Amos pursed his mouth as if he thought Mark to be toying with him, Mark said reassuringly, "Really, it was only an oversight on my part. I'll get drunk during recess. Okay?"

"You just portion out the ruin of your career any way you like," Amos said.

He whirled away and took his seat, only to spring up as if Mark had cleverly thought to place a tack on it, for Judge Fickett was entering.

That lady disappeared behind her Codes, whence her pert voice issued: "Mr. Slake, do you wish to present an argument to the jury?"

"I do wish!" Amos imparted, though more to Mark than to Her Honor. He went to stand before the jury. He then

regarded them, every one, singly, with such a melancholy
brooding stare that Forbes fidgeted beside Mark. "Ladies and
gentlemen," Amos said, as if on the verge of inconsolable
weeping. "We are now presented by Mr. D'Andor with one of
those legal tactics at which he is so adept. You may be asked
by the Court to acquit—"

"And you may not be," said the voice behind the Codes.
"Go on, Mr. Slake."

Unruffled, Amos made a slight bow to the bench. "Ladies
and gentlemen, I may say this, then, with all the conviction at
my command. Mr. D'Andor does not wish to present a defense
to the heinous charges brought and by me proved against
Archibald Forbes. This man—to use the term loosely—this
heartless user of female flesh, is the real beast that lurks behind
the funny mask we know as—The Feeb. What would we have
said, as we sat in the audiences with our innocent children at
our sides, laughing so innocently at The Feeb up there on the
screen, had we known the truth about him? That our innocent
little ones were looking at a creature with so malignant and
abandoned a heart? Oh, would we not have taken them by their
trusting little hands and hastened them from the theaters——"

Mark did so wish he was not required to listen to this sort
of thing—on an empty hollow leg at that. He predicted that
Amos would not depart from the subject of innocent little
children for at least another fifteen minutes.

But fourteen minutes later Amos was done with the
subject.

On the second leg of his journey into the hearts of the
jury, Amos had a short-lived flirtation with facts. He was the
art-lover type of orator, the lawyer who entreats the jury to
"Picture in your minds, if you will, the poor woman all
unknowingly setting foot on the path that led to her untimely
and dreadful death. Picture The Feeb, overbearing, lascivi-
ous—" Some time later Amos was imploring the jury to
"Picture that scene in the bedroom. . . . The indignities . . .
bloody ice. . . ."

Amos could meander on passionately for hours without
end. "Calling her foul names, blaspheming her sacred motherhood, and destroying that little glow of life which nestled in

her, that precious flame of unborn human flesh, laughing in his depravity, and then leaving her broken body behind him as casually as a plate of dog scraps." Amos' voice sank to its deepest gubernatorial timbre: "Do you wonder, ladies and gentlemen, that The Feeb does not want—dares not—speak himself of these things?"

Amos then took himself from one end of the jury box to the other, saying not a word. Of a sudden he brandished his gold mechanical pencil. "Is this not a court of law? Is this not the last best citadel of truth? Are you not twelve good citizens, tried and true? Of what is The Feeb afraid?

"Why, I will tell you what causes those rolls of fat to tremble, what—"

The jury looked at The Feeb. He raised one steady hand to touch the paper flower at his lapel. But two enormous tears were captured in the creases under his eyes. He cried without a sound, without a motion. The palm fans, one after the other, came to rest. The sight was awesome, that monumental body absolutely still—the poor moronic Feeb weeping silently, knowing not what to do nor where to turn, not comprehending even the nature of the crimes of which he was so hotly being accused.

Blithely Amos ranted along until, turning, he himself caught this greatest of performances of the immortal Feeb. Amos began pacing; Amos rapped his gold mechanical pencil; Amos did all he could to distract the jury, but his efforts served only as irritants. Amos was nothing if not game. "All right," he yelled, "let us admire his facile tears! That's a cracking good act he has there. What a pity no movie cameras are turning. Ah, but picture this weeping blob as he was in that bedroom, satisfying his filthy wants. Picture his writhing victim——"

Into Mark's mind came a most unwelcome recollection. *Feature me,* Muffin always liked to say, *Can't you just feature me . . . .*

"Let me at that Feeb," Amos rhapsodized, "and I'll wring some genuine tears from him! He'll weep in earnest before I'm done with my questions." Amos turned his back to the jury and said to The Feeb, "Get up on that stand, cry-baby. If you dare!" And with that Amos was done. He sat down and stuck

GARET ROGERS • 355 •

his long forefinger down his Herbert Hoover collar, much like someone sticking a finger down the throat to induce vomiting.

"Mr. D'Andor?" said Judge Fickett.

Mark came to the jury box, serenely confident of the non-alcoholic scent of his breath. Then, unaware that he was doing it, he ran his hand along the rail, polishing the wood with his palm. He, no less than Amos, stood in silence for several moments, engaging the eyes of each juror. This ordeal, the most terrifying a trial lawyer faces, cost Mark as much in self-control as any of his colleagues. He began his address, "Ladies and gentlemen, a woman is dead. She is dead because she committed a crime. It is a crime in this state, and in this nation, to possess or consume alcoholic beverages. Muffin Naismith consumed such beverages, as we have been told, for a period of some fourteen to sixteen hours, without stopping. But she violated a greater law than that, she violated an inflexible law of nature. A woman who is going to be a mother cannot drink unremittingly for sixteen hours, cannot dance all night, cannot subject her body to such gruelling activities—or, if she does these things, then she cannot hope that Nature will not punish her severely. In this case Muffin Naismith was brought to trial in the court of Nature and found guilty. And Nature punished her without mercy.

"Then, while she lay dying, the poor woman cast about in her pain and delirium to place the blame on someone else. Just as in this courtroom we have heard wild accusations and spiteful attempts to lay the death at the door of Archibald Forbes. Now then, let us examine Mr. Slake's case for a moment. He accuses Forbes of murder. And what weapon does he place in the hand of the accused, pray?

"A chunk of bloody ice." Mark shrugged and polished the jury-box rail. "Ice. A handy weapon indeed for our Mr. Slake to fix on. Could he be expected to bring this 'weapon' into the courtroom, all tagged and ready to be entered as Exhibit A? Of course not. Was he able to wave it under your noses, thundering at you to feast your eyes on it? I saw only a gold pencil in the hands of Mr. Slake."

Mark cocked his head thoughtfully. "Come to think of it, that gold pencil, or one like it, would have served just as well for our imaginary weapon. Or any object which is capable of being inserted into the birth canal of a woman, with the intent of—shall we say—doing an injury to a human life. Ah . . . but which human life? That of Muffin Naismith? Or the unborn infant in her womb? We are caught up in riddles, it would seem. A woman dies as the result of an infection. We are told she underwent surgical abortion. We are told a dying woman accuses a man of having hurt her. But the one thing, the important thing the dying woman did not tell us was how and with what she had been hurt. Is it reasonable to believe that she would take the secret of the weapon to the grave with her?

"But Mr. Slake is nothing if not resourceful. Severely handicapped by the lack of a weapon, he attempts to turn this lack into an advantage. Think of it! He did not have to produce a fingerprint expert to tell you that the hand of Archibald Forbes was clasped about our imaginary weapon. He was not required to produce medical experts to say that our imaginary weapon, and that weapon alone, was responsible for the lesion discovered in the birth canal of the dead woman. Nor was I given the opportunity of seeing it with my own eyes.

"Nor were you." Mark repeated it slowly: "Nor were you."

He paused an instant while several of the jurors shifted themselves about in their chairs. "Well now, as the dead woman neglected to speak of this mysterious piece of ice, we did hear of it, with our own ears, from the witness Mrs. Tobino. But are we to believe Mrs. Tobino when she had two entirely inconsistent versions of what she saw in that bedroom? Shall we toss a coin? Heads up, we credit one version and Forbes goes to the gallows; or tails, and he is set free?

"Thus, if we cannot, if we dare not give credence to Mrs. Tobino, to whom may we? Are we to believe that Dr. Snowdom did everything any doctor could do to save the life of Muffin Naismith? Even though his handiwork suggested to another medical man that he had had to make shift with garden tools instead of surgical instruments? Are we really to accept as truth that ice in the hands of Archibald Forbes caused that lesion, rather than an instrument in the hands of Dr. Snowdom? I . . ." Mark stretched out his hands, palms up. "I find myself in the position of asking question on question. I cannot speak to you in fiery positive statements, because everywhere I turn I find myself faced with new mysteries and mounting doubts. I can only ask you yet another question. Are we to believe Miss Pritchard's lurid notions of what happened in that bedroom, when she herself was not at the Eden? And when *were* those sheets bloodied by Muffin Naismith? Before she was dragged into the swimming pool? Would anyone in this world drag a hemorrhaging woman into a pool to calm her? Is that plausible? Surely they were bloodied after Muffin Naismith was out of the pool and in a state of collapse, lying on the bed where her frightened companions had placed her. And speaking of those companions—who can place credence in the testimony of the last witness? That pathetic little 'party girl' who wept like a naughty child when I told her of the punishment for perjury.

"Everywhere we turn, questions, questions! And Mr. Slake has not provided us with a single answer. Who then are we to believe? What facts have been established? We know one thing only. We know that Muffin Naismith is dead. We know that she died of an infection. We know that the infection was the result of an abortion. We know that the onset of the abortion climaxed a night of drunken revelry and fatigue. Did someone, then, kill Muffin Naismith? I say yes. Muffin Naismith violated Nature's most sacred law.

"And Nature executed Muffin Naismith for it."

Mark moved from the jury and took his place at the defense table. Mr. Pentlove had written him a note: *"Delightful!"*

Judge Fickett looked at Amos Slake for a long moment. Then she bent her attention on the jury. She instructed them, telling them in substance that they were now to retire in order to deliberate; that they might find the defendant guilty of the felony-murder of Muffin Naismith—murder in the first degree —if they so chose; that they might find him guilty of murder in the second degree; that they might find him guilty of manslaughter.

As for herself, Judge Fickett said, "I advise you to return with a verdict of acquittal. You are under no obligation to heed my advice. Yet I do so advise acquittal."

The judge and the jury departed. The deputy sheriff came

to place his ever-possessive hand on the person of The Feeb. When The Feeb rose, he turned to face the spectators, his bearing that of sorrowing martyrdom. At once a dramatic hush fell over the courtroom. Then The Feeb said the most daring, the most outrageous thing Mark was ever to hear in his life:

"Remember, folks, Gethsemane was a garden too." Blessing his deputy with a look of forgiveness, The Feeb allowed himself to be led into the bullpen.

For at least one full minute no one so much as rattled a paper bag. After that the odor of fried chicken began to drift sluggishly on the air.

The spectators settled down to arguing the merits of Amos' case. Bets were made. Amos gathered up his brief case and sauntered out.

Mr. Pentlove leaned forward to gain Mark's ear. "Now what, D'Andor?"

"I shall sit here quietly losing weight."

"I myself," said Mr. Pentlove, "have been meaning to trim down my waistline a notch." He consulted his watch. "How long do you think the jury will take?"

"The usual."

"And how long is that?"

"Forever," Mark said. He clasped his hands together on the counsel table to control the shaking. His palms were slippery. He closed his eyes and sat in the noisy courtroom, going over the case in his mind meticulously, point by point.

After a time Mr. Pentlove said fretfully, "Can't we go out for lunch?"

"You may go anywhere you like."

Mr. Pentlove took a turn for the positively humane. "I'll buy you a drink, D'Andor."

"Thoughtful of you, but no thank you, Pentlove."

Mr. Pentlove sank back in his seat.

Mark's entire body was damp, and the rising heat of the room seemed only further to chill his flesh. Every now and again a spectator came up to the bar to ask him a question or try for a bit of badinage. Mark did not turn his head. In his mind each witness, in his proper turn, mounted the stand.

Mark saw himself, drunk and emaciated, pitting his sodden brain against their clear minds. Yet sobriety served him no better, for he sat drenched in his own sweat, and his joints were beginning to ache.

Toward midafternoon Mr. Pentlove rose without a word and left the courtroom. When he returned, Mark was exactly as he had been, now going over and over his verbal clash of arms with Miss Pritchard. He felt Mr. Pentlove's breath on his neck.

"I wouldn't have your job for all the wealth in the world," said Mr. Pentlove. "That pietistic crack of The Feeb's is actually beginning to make sense."

At nine minutes after four that afternoon the jury returned, the grandmotherly juror smiling at The Feeb coyly. Seeing that smile, Mark's vision blurred momentarily, and he thought: Oh God, oh God, I've pulled it off!

The jury had voted not guilty.

The jury was dismissed, Judge Fickett departed, and The Feeb again burst into tears. One dropped on Mark's hand, and Mark wiped it away as instinctively as if it had been spittle. In another moment Mark and The Feeb were at the center of rioting well-wishers, scandalmongers, and reporters.

The grandmotherly juror was lecturing her own coterie of reporters on the evils of the demon rum and the unpleasant events following on the heels of its use, including miscarriages, automobile wrecks, sudden death, and culminating in taking up the vile habit of cigarette smoking.

The retired minister was explaining in the spirit of brotherly love to a stunned T. Amos Slake that it was never within his, the retired minister's, province to judge his fellow man. Only God had that right. "I said that," the retired minister told Amos, "before I was accepted as a juror. Don't you remember, Mr. Slake?"

Mark began to struggle past The Feeb's fans, catching a glimpse of Mr. Pentlove, who sat in his accustomed seat, as collected as if he were at ease in his taproom. Seeing that Mark was leaving, Mr. Pentlove rose to follow. A bailiff cleared the way for Mark to reach the corridor, and there more reporters and spectators and Mr. Pentlove all sought to capture him.

Mark's need of a drink was racing through his thin frame like panic. "Get away from me, all of you!" he shouted, as in terror.

The crowd fell back. Mr. D'Andor, in truth, was not a pretty sight. Someone said, "He sick?" Someone else said, "Naw, just drunk." Mr. Pentlove moved aside to let Mark pass. Mr. Pentlove was smiling; he always enjoyed a bit of irony.

In Mark's car in the car lot sat Chester Dander and the serving maid, late of the Eden. At Mark's approach Chester got out, dragging the maid after him, holding her arm in a tight grip. At a grunt from Chester she took from her purse a crystal object, long and dangerous as a dagger. She held it dangling from a string threaded through a loop. "I kept the chain I bought for it," the maid said, "because I paid for that with my own money. But the Reverend Kingdom says I can't be saved until I return this to its rightful owner." She sighed as Mark, uncomprehending, accepted the glittering thing. "The prettiest lavaliere I ever saw," the maid said, "and the sure-enough biggest. You'd think it was a diamond, except it's so big. It reminded me," she went on wistfully, "of a beautiful diamond cut from ice. When I wore it with my blue——" But Chester with a single look ended that train of thought. The maid said, "One of the ladies at the Eden left it. Mr. Feeb will probably know which one."

"She found it," Chester said flatly, "in a glass. Under the bed. Bungalow Ten." He tugged at the maid's arm. "You've done your duty; let's go." Pulling the maid after him, Chester said over his shoulder to Mark, "Sweet dreams, Mark."

In the canyon below the fortress of the Lotus Singer, dusk was tinting the world blue. All was quiet, the elevator door locked, and the only sign of life a lizard on a rock doing the ritualistic push-ups of his kind when disturbed. A short search and Mark found a button to press in the elevator wall. He pressed again and again, hearing nothing, suspecting the wiring had long since fallen into decay. He would have turned away had not a window high above him been flung up. Leaning out, the Lotus Singer appeared to be barking at Mark with inordinate excitement, until Mark saw the head of a great dog beneath his master's elbow. "I'll open the door," the Lotus Singer was calling down thinly, "I'll open. . . ."

There was a click and Mark was able to enter the elevator. He sat as he had once before on the velvet seat, and as the birdcage elevator began to rise past its varicolored lancet windows, Mark felt his face turn from a sullen gray to ghastly purple and finally to sulfur yellow as the sun, coming past the rim of the canyon, streamed through the highest lancet window like a spotlight. The elevator came to rest and Mark stepped out to be greeted by the chattering Lotus Singer and a number of merry mastiffs. "This way," the old man said excitedly, and began tottering along one of the paths that led through his cactus garden. The cracked Cupid still surmounted a dry fountain, and the cloister hurled back the noise of the dogs. In the dry heat the cacti flourished, spikes as large as épées edging toward the path, hoping one day to impale a passer-by. "Don't use the guardhouse much any more," the Lotus Singer said, dancing in his joy at having a visitor. Coming to the doors of the castle proper, he flung them open and waved Mark in.

Mark came to a halt, looking about him in awe. He was in a great hall hung with tapestries, a baronial shield over the fireplace casting a blinding reflection from the sun coming in through a window fully twelve feet over Mark's head. In the middle of the hall was an enormous table littered with books, papers, candelabra, an astrolabe, empty wine bottles, and opened tins of caviar over which flies crawled rapturously.

"I'm more or less pigging it these days," the Lotus Singer said, in a tone that also said: Don't you believe a word of it. "Well, well, now, sit down Mr. Lowell Poetry Lover—you see, I never forget, have an astounding memory, in fact—and I'll get some wine and refreshments for the weary traveler."

"No, please," Mark protested. "I can stay only a moment. I came to ask—"

"Have a bottle right here under the table," the Lotus Singer said, producing a Methuselah of wine. "Here, open this thing for me, D'Andor," he ordered imperiously. "Later we'll have a look at the stars."

Struggling with the cork and thinking that his thumbs were in need of practice when it came to Methuselahs, Mark said, "What? Look at the—"

"The stars, the stars! Down, Sir," the Lotus Singer said, to either Mark or one of the dogs. "My scope is on the battlement."

With a waterfall rush the wine gushed from the bottle, and the Lotus Singer thrust two silver goblets to catch it. "Hah, look at that, D'Andor! Yes, yes, stars. Do you remember the charming story about the monk who first discovered how to make champagne? When he tasted it, he cried out, 'Come quickly, I'm drinking stars!' Beautiful story. And how is the trial coming? Are you going to get that beast off?"

"I just have, Mr.———"

"I am certain that I told you once before to call me Lotus Singer," the old man said with a touch of testiness. "I am world-famous as the Poet Laureate of Hollywood. Among other singular honors and titles too numerous to mention. So you got the beast off, eh? Quaff your wine, man, quaff! Have some caviar. Did he kill her? I said *down,* and I don't want to have to say it again! Your health, D'Andor. I see you are looking at me curiously. As well you might. I am engaged in the writing of a masterpiece."

"I tried to reach you earlier this week, one night," Mark put in hurriedly.

"Of course you couldn't reach me. I was on the battlement. Yes, a masterpiece. A novel. I am calling it *For God's Sake.*"

As the Lotus Singer was peering at Mark expectantly, Mark said "Oh."

"Hah! Don't go looking for the title in your precious Lowell, for it's not there. Shakespeare, D'Andor, Shakespeare!"

"I'm afraid I don't quite place it."

"From Number Two Richard. 'For God's sake, let us sit upon the ground and tell sad stories of the death of kings.' It's about the Tower of Babel. That is, my masterpiece is. Do you know what it really was? Don't answer, for you do not. It was an observatory. What else? The Aztecs, or Toltecs, are said to have undertaken the same enterprise some centuries later. With the same results. Yes, the Pyramid of Cholula, built by Xelhua, also ended as a babblement. God and the gods, you know, didn't want mankind sticking their noses into celestial secrets, hence the punishment of babbling tongues. The research I've done and have to do would stagger you, D'Andor. I'm deep in the Building Codes of Hammurabi at the moment. A sturdier code, I am prompted to remark, than our Penal Code, which allowed that beast, that animal—"

"Lotus Singer," Mark said, "did you give her this?" He swung the lavaliere on its string.

The Lotus Singer put down his goblet and touched the crystal with one delicate forefinger. "What a tawdry bauble."

"I thought it might have been the kind of—unusual—jewelry you would give to—"

"No, no. Entirely too bulky, too gross, for a slender little girl like Muffin."

At last, Mark thought, one of us has spoken her name.

Picking up his goblet and looking over it at Mark with a leer, the Lotus Singer said, "That, I take it, is the disputed piece of ice? The newspapers made much of ice, or the lack of it, in the murder room. So he killed her with that, eh? Well? Did he?"

His eyes held by the fire glancing from the crystal, Mark said, "I can't say. If she was wearing it around her neck, it would seem unlikely." Breaking the spell of the lavaliere, Mark pushed back his chair. "Thank you, Lotus Singer. I'd better be on my way."

"Must you go? In a short time Venus will be up. Did you know that that planet has phases like the moon? Oh, yes. Tonight I'll show you a half-Venus. The night will be choked with stars. I can teach you a few rudiments of astronomy before it is time for us to repair to the battlement. Now, as you surely know, the solar system———"

"I sincerely regret to say that I must go, Lotus Singer." Mark got up, treading on a few paws.

The unhappy old man marched Mark out to the elevator, urging Mark all the while to return soon—the next night, or the night after at the latest. And, standing by the elevator, the Lotus Singer patted Mark's shoulder. "She wasn't the failure she died thinking she was, Counselor."

"I wish I could believe that, sir. For her sake."

"Ah, but The Feeb is ruined. She has destroyed him."
As the sun dropped suddenly and left the succulent garden
in twilight, the Lotus Singer said softly, "Occultation."

"What was that, Lotus Singer?"

"An astronomical term. It describes what happens when
a mere planet passes between us and a star. The minuscule
planet obscures a body of an almost infinitely greater magni-
tude. In this case, Muffin and The Feeb. A dead little drab has
eclipsed a mighty star."

"Let us hope so," Mark said, and stepped into the
birdcage.

It was fully dark when Mark entered Clara Foley's tidy
little parlor. In the glow of the lamp he held out the lavaliere.

"Shoot!" said Suicide Sal. "That's no jewelry. That's
Muffin's swizzle stick. I've seen her stir drinks with it myself.
I wondered where it had gone."

"Do you know where she got it?"

The ladies had no idea.

When Mark entered his own door and pressed the switch
of the chandelier below, he took one step down before he
knew. Then, unhurriedly, he descended, went into the dining
room, came out lugging a baroque chair, mounted the chair,
took the crystal pendant from his pocket and hung it on the
hook which had been naked for so many months. At last the
chandelier was whole again. He took the chair back into the
dining room, placing it precisely at the table. Turning slowly,
he looked out at the chandelier bedecked with its murderous
pendants.

The Feeb must have thought that Olive Jones, the
decamped prostitute, had sold it to Mr. Pentlove along with
Muffin Naismith's worn purse and silver compact with its
broken chain. Here was Mrs. Tobino's shard of ice, which,
having served its makeshift purpose, was replaced in the glass
under the bed. The Feeb, impotent, his nose bloodied, and in
a rage, could take no more of Muffin's tauntings. She must,
for a moment, have thought he was going to snap her showy
swizzle stick in half, pleading, as Pep passed, that it was
Mark's. But The Feeb's sexual didoes and anger dictated sev-

eral uses for the pendant, among them that of taking care of "your bastard."

Still held by the sight of his crystal cataract, Mark asked of himself: Didn't Pep say Muffin came to this house more than once? And—as Pep put it—to raid my liquor or go lie on my bed to weep. One time, however, Muffin raided not only my liquor but my chandelier.

Leaving the lights festively ablaze, Mark got his tin of Irish and drank from it straight. He gasped, shuddered, and again drank deeply. In a matter of minutes he grew unsteady, there was a slippage of his thoughts like unsecured cargo in the hold of a vessel. The phone rang loudly at his side, and he smiled slackly, looking around for the source of the noise. He staggered and his outstretched hand fell on the phone for balance. He lifted the receiver and said into it playfully, *"Yersh?"*

"That you, D'Andor?" T. Amos Slake said sharply.

Mark slid to the floor, put his tin aside for the moment, and clutched the mouthpiece. "Amos," he begged soggily, "if you're going to appeal, tell me tomorrow, huh? I've been sober for two days, and there's a limit to a man's endurance."

"I'm not going to appeal," Amos said. "But I did want to tell you something. I waited until after the trial, but I thought you ought to know. That Pentlove—"

"Mister Pentlove," Mark said with a cackle.

"That Mister Pentlove person came into my office bold as brass and offered me a bribe."

"Oh, gor. When?"

"Day before the trial started."

"Amos, you should have thrown him in the can. Me with him, mebbe."

Amos said irritably, "I knew you had nothing to do with it. And to be perfectly frank, I can't afford to make an enemy of someone with that much power. He can manipulate quite a few political strings. As I say, I knew you had no knowledge of it. You wouldn't pull a trick like that—not even sober."

"Buh whah happened next? If . . . anything?" Mark said in a silly voice.

"Why," Amos said with crackling righteousness, "I kicked him out on his talcumed ass."

"I gotta hang up," Mark said. "But 'fore I do, Amos, I wontchu know I think you're the gnu's shoes. Absolutely."

Amos cleared his throat. "Why—thank you, Mark. I'll let you . . . I'll let you get back to your drinking now."

Mark sat on by the phone niche, drinking. When it rang again, he climbed his hands up the wall in order to get to his feet. Swaying, he fixed his eyes on the chandelier, with its prodigal pendant hanging so demurely over his head.

"D'Andor," said a voice of quiet authority. "Pentlove here."

We have enacted this before, Mark thought, Pentlove and I. Only last time I was less interested in taking whatever case he had to offer me than in asking myself for the hundredth time who could have pilfered my pendant, and for what mysterious reason.

". . . for your brilliant handling of a most distasteful affair," Mr. Pentlove was prattling.

"Sure," Mark said. "Only don't ask me to fix the occultation. No damn thing I can do about that." As with many a drunk, Mark was foolish on his first few drinks, and then approached sobriety, or a grotesque form thereof, as he imbibed more deeply.

"Occul—?" Mr. Pentlove said. "Some procedural detail, I suppose. Tell me, has Forbes been by yet?"

"No, and he'd better not be, Pentlove. I'll commit infanticide on your Feeb, and I've got just the nifty weapon to do it with."

"Let it pass," Mr. Pentlove said. "However, we must meet soon to plan for your future. I think you'll recall a promise I made to you, and I intend to keep that promise."

"You mean put me on a bench?"

"Isn't that what we agreed upon?"

But Mark hadn't a pinch of patience left for this dainty mogul. "Listen, Pentlove, I have about as much right to be on a bench as a three-time loser. Chico would make better juridical material. Dammit, I have some vestigial respect for the law, even though it may not be apparent to the naked eye."

"I'm sure you do," Mr. Pentlove said suavely. "However, I pride myself as being a man of my word. Now, the thing for you to do is take a rest—"

"Oh, I'm sure I shall. Soon as Judge Fickett remembers she gave me five days in the pokey for contempt."

"But that will make a fine start!" Mr. Pentlove said bracingly. "And you dry out a bit then, too. After you come out, you can start to build up physically. The most important thing right now is for you to get sober and stay that way!"

In his most courteous courtroom voice, Mark said, "Fat chance," and hung up.

Carrying his tin of Irish tilted under his arm, so that unwittingly he lost most of its contents, Mark stumbled down a second flight of stairs and out onto the walled patio. He had forgotten to put out food for his animals, and took another drink to give him strength for his journey up to the kitchen. Then the quiet of the night held him; it was unholy, the eucalyptus tree as rigid as an etching against the heat-swollen dark. A planet, Venus he guessed, commanded the night. He tried to mumble the word that meant the glory of a mighty star was obscured by what was a mere speck of dust in comparison. Only moments ago he had said it to Pentlove, and again had it on the doorstep of his recollection when a night-bird directly overhead uttered one sharp cry and took wing.

The cracking sound streaked the length of Mark's perception like lightning, and looking up he had time to think "I've heard these damn trees will let down without warn—" before the branch, thick around as his waist, ended its swishing leafy flight and settled itself about him with final little rustlings like a woman arranging her skirts.

He was down, but he was not in pain, and with that inward chortle of triumph that comes when one has narrowly escaped death, he sought to remove the branch from his chest. It took him a second or two to realize that though his arms were pinned, he could not have moved them in any event. Either his back or his neck, or both, were broken. And he was voiceless as well. Buried as he was, he could see part of the wall, a fine open stretch of sky littered with stars—and, with great effort, he caught a glimmering of the light from the chandelier, so far to his left that it appeared to be winking on, off, on, off, on, off. . . .

He thought: When I sober up this may be rough going.
He fell into a fainting slumber.

CHAPTER THIRTY

When Mark awakened he saw first the arc lights sweeping the sky clean of stars; a pair of them, searching, meeting, and passing. On the Boulevard somewhere the fans were in the bleachers, and the movie stars, the beautiful anointed ones, were displaying their scared selves for the rabble before entering the theater to see Pep's premiere. In his mind's eye he saw Pep step from a limousine, her audacious grin on her lovely mug, strutting her furs and her fine body and her three speaking lines in the picture—"Oh, yeah," and "Oh, yeah," and—— She never did tell me what the third one really was, Mark remembered. He followed her into the theater, drawing on the only premiere he had ever gone to for source material. (By some crotchet on the part of Fate, he had been invited to the premiere of *The King of Kings,* opening in Mr. Grauman's Chinese Cinema Temple. There were fans galore, and a stupendous fountain. And there were speeches. By a quarter to eleven the film had not yet been shown. Mark walked out, later to learn that *The King of Kings* was revealed a few minutes after he had gone.) I never did get to see the thing, he thought, watching the arcs overhead.

I'm not going to think of Constance, he warned himself, because it will mean I am in despair. Then to find himself listening to Constance say, "That tree is the only living thing in Hollywood I like." Though it was getting topheavy she could never bear to have it trimmed. Mark had agreed; it would be a desecration, like chopping off her pale chignon. Now, lying on the patio with a crushed voice box, he said to Constance, "Yes, I did prize you. But when they picked you up from the foot of the bridge you were nothing but a smear, and I didn't prize that smear, but I loved it. Only for a little while, that afternoon, when in my mind I accused you of having the makings of a harlot in you, did I love you less. Ah well, we worked it out sensibly, didn't we, Princess? You took to the bridge and I took to the bottle. But you're damn right I prized you! You were pale and remote and everything that wasn't florid and loud. . . . And one more thing you were, you were irreplaceable. . ."

Again he slumbered.

Now the night was at peace. The arcs of the premiere were dead, and the half-Venus gone. On opening his eyes Mark saw Us, the cat, sitting on the wall washing a paw in the moonlight. She was gaunt, though she had also a rangy grace. Upthrusting her hind leg with the anomalous white foot ("Only five dollars, because of this one itsy flaw. Oh, Mark Daddy, please buy it for Muffin?"), Us began to bathe her behind. He could not recall when he had last seen her, nor heard her war cry defiantly telling the whole world where to get off. Done with her washing, Us raised her head and inspected Mark, pinned under his branch, without recognition or interest. With a shock he discovered that one eye reflected the moonlight as does the marble of deserted ruins. He was certain she was half-blind. Could she hunt with her impaired sight? More important, would she not be killed by some predator stalking her just beyond the periphery of her vision? Yet she sat with sublime indifference to danger on his wall.

Until he had seen Us, he had felt no more real pity for Muffin than could be piled on the tip of a knifeblade. It was the cat Muffin had cast out, the creature who had challenged the Hollywood wildlife and wowed 'em, that brought at last an acid compassion for the measly life and the messy death that was Muffin's lot. And Us, for all her courage and stamina, would end no better; she would go down fighting (maybe Muffin had?), but down she would go.

I am crying, Mark thought, and then felt the wet heat of his tears. His crushed vocal cords could make no sound, but the physical efforts of trying to weep brought the first of the pain to life. This time he knew himself to be fainting rather than falling into a sleep.

There was an incredibly weighty blanket of green on him, the odor of leaky sewage that is peculiar to the eucalyptus tree confirming the nightmare that he was pinned under a branch. As if his act of waking had emboldened dawn, the day came on with a rush. The pain was quite active, quite busy now, racing his body to find places it might have overlooked. He attempted to turn his head, and by squandering his last resource did so. A leaf which later would have shaded his eyes now guarded only a cheekbone. He had a view of part of his bedroom window, and of a pair of stone steps to the right of it, down which a small chewing-gum-colored snake, sporting a narrow collar of orange, was gaily spilling himself.

Mark wanted water. He thought it hilarious that a man with a broken back and a broken neck, and a broken God knew what all, was required to suffer a hangover as well. But when the sun shot past his roof and found his exposed face, he never quite regained the humor of his situation. His closed lids began to prickle, then to burn.

His phone rang and rang and rang.

Then his doorbell startled him with that hollow sound they all use to tell the would-be visitor that nobody is home, dammit to hell, take your fresh finger off my button and leave me *alone*!

Then he heard the carefree "shave and a haircut two-bits" klaxon of The Feeb's sporty roadster.

Then he heard nothing at all but the sound of the sun, roaring like a fire in his head, consuming his retinas. His lids had swollen so that they pressed on his eyes like thumbs. When even the sun grew dim, watery, Mark suspected he might be more than merely losing consciousness again.

An immense vexation seized him. *Now just a moment. Don't tell me this is the old el foldo!*

God taught him to what lengths a Carson pause could be stretched.

From the dining-room window, Chester Dander yelled to his brother-in-law, the Reverend Parker Kingdom. "Jesus Christ, you were right, he's down there!"

"Just like I saw him in my vision," the Reverend Kingdom said, joining Chester at the window.

Witless with shock, Chester confessed, "Oh, God, I always wanted to fill his shoes!"

"Brother, they're empty now."

CHAPTER THIRTY-ONE

Mr. Pentlove arranged for the Eulogistics to take place at a small mortuary just off the Gulch. With his back to the closed coffin, Chester Dander told those few assembled that Mark was a "good man and a kind one. He always expected the best out of everyone he met, and then was too gentle to be disappointed when people couldn't live up to his expectations."

In the third row Mrs. Foley nodded her Nita Naldi comb and patted her nostrils with a handkerchief scented with Nights in Paris perfume (send coupon and twenty-five cents in coin, not stamps, for a generous sample).

Rookie Castle, whose turn it was next, quoted in a rapture of bitterness and self-hatred from the comic operetta *Iolanthe*. "I, my lords, embody the law," he said, and Babe Wilmot unconsciously touched her lumpy jaw and savored the wisdom of this.

The next-to-last and second-highest honor fell to the Lotus Singer, the self-proclaimed Poet Laureate of Hollywood. With his spiderlike agility he danced up in a dusty frock coat not worn since the overwhelmingly successful Chautauqua of '12. "I have written a paean for this sorrowful occasion," he told those fortunate enough to be present. "A mere bagatelle, of course, on such short notice. It is called 'You Can't Expect a Break from God.'" The Lotus Singer then denied this statement sonorously:

> Oh, can we not?
> What then is He there for?
> Did He create us,
> Only to leave us adrift among the wanton
> Stars?

After a suitable pause Suicide Sal clapped with great reverence. The Lotus Singer bowed and took his seat.

It remained only for Mr. Pentlove to have his brief say. Taking his place before the coffin, he said of Mark, "He always meant well." Mr. Pentlove's intonation subtly hinted that he found this trait of Mark's absurd, if not downright offensive.

The Eulogistics were over. Mr. Pentlove stationed himself at the door to shake the hands of those who so wished to avail themselves of this signal honor before departing into the maleficent sunlight of Mark's Heliopolis.

Pep, wearing a smashing black Empress Eugénie hat, said sturdily while crushing Mr. Pentlove's porcelain paw, "Well, we kept our date, me and Bagel did. We made it to the funeral of the biggest guy of 'em all. That's pretty rich, huh?" Soberly she added, "I loved old Rodolpho Alfonzo Raffaeli Pierre Filibert di Mark D'Andor, I really did. Up to a point."

"Oh, indeed, indeed?" Mr. Pentlove murmured with passing moroseness, wondering if this young woman had misplaced her mind.

Behind Pep, Mrs. Foley noted to Suicide Sal and Thelma, "Nobody here at all from the talkie set. Very select. A choice gathering." With the proper sour expression she pressed Mr. Pentlove's hand, passed it along to Suicide Sal, who rid herself of it neatly by letting Thelma do anything she liked with it. These ladies then moved out into the sunlight. "I thought it a very poor excuse for a service," Mrs. Foley said with a sniff. "A *very* poor excuse. They did much better in my time."

"Yes, but our times," said Suicide Sal, "was the real Hollywood heydays."

Finally alone in the mortuary chapel Mr. Pentlove read again the telegram he had received in response to the one he had sent the D'Andor family in a Southern state. The Bar Association had helpfully given him the address of Mark's next of kin, his father and mother. To Mr. Pentlove's telegram informing them of the accidental death of their son, Mark D'Andor, and asking for instructions, Mr. Pentlove received another telegram in reply. It read in full: ARE YOU TRYING TO BE FUNNY. WILL SET LAW ON YOU IF WIRE AGAIN.

It was signed G. D'ANDOR.

CHAPTER THIRTY-TWO

Mr. Pentlove sought unavailingly to prop up his forlorn hope that two million dollars had not gone down the drain.
Exhibitors the nation across were refusing to accept The Feeb's
films. In Connecticut The Feeb was damned from the pulpit.
In Indiana a group of mothers marched on a movie house. In
a Southern state a marquee announcing a Feeb picture was
stoned, the bulbs spelling out his name fragmented.

To that latter state, to the very one-horse burg of the
stoning incident, came Mr. Pentlove, on a cross-country tour
to plead with exhibitors and salvage what he could from the
debacle. He debarked from a train just before nightfall on a
mild Indian summer evening in November. Ascertaining that
the address he was seeking was but a few blocks from the
depot, and finding the clement weather inviting, he decided to
walk. Following the depot-master's directions, he found the
D'Andor house with little trouble.

with wooden lace around the windows and a genuine porch
He went up the walk of a small white-frame bungalow
swing, suspended from the roof by chains, which was still in
motion as Mr. Pentlove mounted the porch steps. Someone had,
moments before, gone inside for a cool drink or another coating
of citronella. The odor of the mosquito lotion hung on the air.
Mr. Pentlove patted his breast pocket, making sure of the safety
of several documents reposing there. One such was a letter
from the State University. Another, a blue paperback booklet.
Mr.Pentlove had barely put his knuckles to the frame of
the screen door when a lamp went on inside and an old man
peered out at Mr. Pentlove's silhouette. "Come in, it's
unhooked," the old man said.

Entering, Mr. Pentlove said with his glassy politesse, "Mr. D'Andor?"

"Yes, yes."

"I'm Seymour Pentlove. I sent you a telegram from Hollywood." As he was saying this, Mr. Pentlove had been engaged in selecting what he felt would be the most comfortable chair in the parlor, and was now an inch from it.

"You'd better sit down and explain yourself," D'Andor said.

"I'm looking for the relatives of a —ah—friend." Seating himself, Mr. Pentlove added slyly, "Name of Mark D'Andor."

The old man slumped back in his worn chair, his thin hands in constant motion, thumbs brushing the other fingers in the "pill-rolling" gesture of the palsied. "You knew my son?" he asked in a faraway voice.

"Why, yes." Suddenly Mr. Pentlove found himself looking at a faded portrait leaning against the lamp. A blond round-cheeked youth in a soldier's uniform smiled inanely back at him.

"My son," the old man said. "And you knew him?"

Stirrings of a vindication long awaited warmed Mr. Pentlove's heart. "I'm sorry, but I fear I've come to the wrong branch of the family. Are there other D'Andors in town?"

"Noooop . . ." D'Andor said thoughtfully. "A bunch of them further South, though, in Louisiana."

"Did your son—his name was Mark, wasn't it—lose his life for his country?" Mr. Pentlove probed delicately. Privately he was settling down for a long gossip, though his manner was that of one preparing for a speedy, if courteous, leavetaking.

"In a way, in a way." The old man fell into a dreamy melancholy. "The First 'Flu Epidemic in 'Sixteen," he said sadly. "My boy couldn't wait to help save the world for Democracy. Ran off to Canada to enlist. Died there of the 'flu. Never got overseas. Never got—anything. Was going to be a lawyer. A bright 'un, he was. Only child." The old man lowered his voice. "Wife's in kitchen, don't want her to hear. He come late to us in life, our Mark did. Wife never did get over the loss."

"Terrible, terrible shock, of course," Mr. Pentlove murmured, pondering his next move. "I have a newspaper picture here. I wonder if you know this man." He handed over a clipping from which all printed matter had been carefully cut away. It was a picture of Mark leaving the courtroom, his cheekbones never looking more as if they had been hacked out with a tin-can opener, his eyes photographing black because of the pupils distended with weariness and drink.

Old D'Andor held the clipping in his trembling hands, then returned it silently, shaking his head, bored with anything not his own concern, not troubling himself to ask the name of the man in the photo.

The blue booklet, "The Vision of Sir Launfal," which Mr. Pentlove had found lying among the transcripts of the Forbes trial, was now produced. Almost holding his breath, Mr. Pentlove extended it. "Would you tell me if you recognize this, Mr. D'Andor?"

The palsied hands did not want to take it; Mr. Pentlove's insisted. The old man cherished the booklet for a long moment as he fondled the cover. Opening it, he read in a voice that threatened tears, " 'Mark D'Andor. June nineteen-fourteen.' My boy's book. Where did you get it?"

"In a secondhand store," Mr. Pentlove said glibly.

"That's gratitude for you!" D'Andor cried. "He asks for it as a present and then turns round and sells it."

"Who?" Mr. Pentlove asked with a catch in his breath.

"Why, the boy who came to see us. The one was with Mark in camp. Said he had got the 'flu too. He stood in this room, right in this room, and told me how he'd read this aloud to my boy when he was dying. Said he wanted it—" old D'Andor's voice broke with bitterness "—as a keepsake."

"Do you remember the name of the friend?"

"Him? Oh . . . Williams. Miller. Something like that. Said he was from the next county over. We never heard from him again. I guess he died in the War," D'Andor said on a hopeful note. "Nice enough feller. Split so high he was hardly worth heading."

"I beg your—— He *what?*"

A chuckle, rusty from disuse, burst from the old man. "Oh, that's just a way of saying he was long-legged. The wife said he had roan-colored eyes. Like a good horse's coat, a nice red-brown. Mark's eyes were real blue. True blue, that was my boy. Died May the twelfth of nineteen-sixteen."

"One other question," Mr. Pentlove ventured. "It may strike you as being a bit odd . . . but was there a public hanging in this town about twenty-five years ago?"

"Noooop. Coupla lynchings, but they don't count," old D'Andor said judiciously. "Say! There was a jim-dandy over in the next county. Last public hanging in the country, so they say. Went over to see it myself. Rode thirty miles. This feller had raped a woman. And you just listen to this, Mister!" Old D'Andor reached out to tap Mr. Pentlove's knee. "The feller's son was there!"

"The hanged man's?" Mr. Pentlove inquired fervently.

"Sure was. The hanged man was some kind of hired hand, and had him this boy. Nobody rightly knew who the mother was. The boy was just a by-blow. The hanged man, though, they say he was part Cherokee." D'Andor laughed. "Guess he got hold of some firewater and went after white meat. Oh, it was a real necktie party, let me tell you!"

"And the hanged man's son?"

"Oh, I heard they just kept him on at the farm where his daddy had worked. But my, you shoulda seen the good-looking piece of pulchritude his daddy raped! Big buxom woman, the kind that look good in those real loud flowery dresses they wore then. Kind of loud-voiced, though, when I think on it. The feller who raped her musta had to fight tooth and nail to get it. I'd say," D'Andor's tone grew judicious again, "I'd say he musta earned it!"

"But where the hanging took place," Mr. Pentlove persisted, "were there any D'Andors there?"

The old man was sure of that. "Like I told you, I'm the only one around. The rest are way down South. Except for some nigger D'Andors. We used to own 'em, you see."

"I won't trouble you further," Mr. Pentlove said. He pointed to the blue booklet. "Would you like to keep that, Mr. D'Andor?"

The old man's eyes glistened with sorrow. "You're mighty kind." He fondled the booklet again. "Nother thing I recollect about that friend of Mark's. He said if there was one thing in this world he wanted to be it was a lawyer, the way Mark was going to. My boy, he'd had three years at the University, but I wonder if the other feller could spell cat. I told him right out that he'd never be able to work his way through college and law school. Take him forever. And he still wouldn't make it. I told him he'd just have to take up some other life, that's all."

"Yes?" Mr. Pentlove said, almost in a hiss.

"Well he looked kind of funny for a minute. And then he said that's just what he'd have to do. Take up another life." The palsied fingers crawled lovingly over the booklet. "To sell my boy's book . . . Well, what can you expect from trash?"

"Trash?" Mr. Pentlove echoed, as if this were sweet to his ears.

"Oh, he put on airs, the feller. You'd have thought he was a gentleman like Mark, to hear him talk. But if he'd come of a decent family, he'd of talked about them more. The wife couldn't get two words out of him on the subject. So who was he? After all, who was he?"

Precisely, Mr. Pentlove thought. Though I think we may safely say he was present at his father's hanging.

"There's nothing sacred to that kind," D'Andor babbled bitterly. "Selling my boy's— The wife, for years she asked God on her knees why He had spared the other and taken Mark. Well, like as not, he got killed in the War."

"I have a train to catch," Mr. Pentlove said, supremely satisfied about something. He debated showing old D'Andor the letter from the University, the contents stating that in August of nineteen-sixteen, the sum of one dollar had been paid into the registrar's office with the request that the transcripts of Mark D'Andor be sent to a law school in Los Angeles. Yet Mark D'Andor had died the preceding May. Mr. Pentlove decided to keep the delicious secret to himself. He rose from his chair. "Thank you very—"

"About the feller you sent the wire about," D'Andor put in hastily. "The one you say happened to have the same name as my son. Wonder what branch of the family he's from?"

Mr. Pentlove was crafty. "I'm not really prepared to say."

"Living and breathing and walking around all these years with my boy's name——" Suddenly the old man brightened. "But your wire said he's dead?"

"He died in a disaster."

"Oh, is that so?" the old man said happily.

"Yes. And other, more important people were killed too."

"My, my!" D'Andor's joy was boundless.

"I, fortunately," Mr. Pentlove said, "was saved."

"You don't say! Well, well, strange are the ways of Providence, aren't they?"

"Not very," Mr. Pentlove disagreed calmly, and walked out into the balmy night.

Leaving the porch for the walk, old man D'Andor's words echoed in Mr. Pentlove's ears. "Oh, he put on airs . . . you'd have thought he was a gentleman . . ." He thought cozily: Ha, Mr. Hanged Man's Son, that will teach you to be hoity-toity with Seymour Pentlove!

At the curb was a gloomy streetlight attracting ghostly hordes of green whispery insects, swarming in soundless frenzy in the Indian-summer night. Mr. Pentlove stopped to observe the phenomenon of the delicate unknown creatures assaulting the dirty globe, beating themselves to death with their own wings. At the base of the light standard the dead were piled up; drained of life they were without any hue at all, resembling as much as anything a silver pile of discarded snips of film.

Mr. Pentlove moved on, light of step. His trip had been eminently successful. What he had seen of the Depression in his journey, the pockets of poverty and terror each small town represented, had told him that the people needed desperately to laugh, and would press a new comedian frantically to their fainting hearts.

He resolved to take another look at the screen test of the cripple with the mirthful drawl and the lovable limp. Or was the time for that sort of thing past? No, people were people. Mr. Pentlove himself never thought in terms of styles or eras or fads. In the uncrushable fabric of his cynicism there could be no such thing as a new wrinkle. Life had taught him that the same monstrosity was always erected on the ruins of the one that had gone before it. Mr. Pentlove began to trot toward the train that would take him back to Hollywood; he felt suddenly such a vast urgency to return that it was almost as if he would not arrive in time to lay the cornerstone of some splendid new world.